Imperial Deserter

Decline and Fall of the Galactic Empire

Book 1

Andrew Moriarty

Andrew Moriarty

ISBN 978-1-956556-09-4
Version 1.05

This is a work of fiction.

Names, characters, businesses, places, events and incidents are either the products of the author's imagination or used in a fictitious manner. Any resemblance to actual persons, living or dead, or actual events is purely coincidental.

Special thanks to my dedicated team of beta readers – Bryan, Scott, Vince, and Alex, and to my editor Samantha Pico.

CHAPTER 1

"You the one they call the 'Duke?'" the prisoner asked.

"Here, they call me prisoner 24571," Dirk said.

"I'm Blake," the man said, putting down his meal tray and sitting next to Dirk.

Dirk looked around the empty prison cafeteria. "Plenty of other places to sit, youngster," he said.

"I like it here," Blake said. He took a tortilla from the top of his stack and used it to sop the nameless stew. "This is a stupid way to eat, using bread as a spoon."

"No utensils for you to stab me with," Dirk said.

"Why would I stab you with all the guards watching?" Blake said.

The clattering pots from the kitchen interrupted Dirk as he started to speak. He waited 'til it ended. "To collect the reward for killing me. That's why you are here. Suss me out. Try to frighten me."

"There's a reward for killing you?"

"Last guy who tried mysteriously fell down a flight of stairs."

"Imagine that." Blake rolled a tortilla around some more stew and shoveled it into his mouth. Dirk watched him for a moment, then resumed eating.

"What are you in for, Duke?" Blake asked.

Dirk ignored him and kept eating.

"Me," Blake said, "I'm in for murder."

Dirk continued to ignore him.

"I didn't do nothing. It was all a big misunderstanding. Guard at a station got in my way. We got in a tussle. Didn't mean to hurt him. I told the judge it wouldn't have if he hadn't jumped onto my knife."

Dirk stopped eating. "You actually used that phrase in court, 'jumped onto my knife.'"

"Sure."

Dirk shook his head. "I keep thinking that nothing stupid people can do will surprise me, but the universe is determined to prove me wrong."

"Think I'm stupid?"

"You're in prison."

"So are you."

"Yes, but at least there is a reason I'm here. For you, there isn't."

"Murder isn't a reason?"

"I am afraid not. Murder isn't an Imperial crime, unless it's an Imperial official. Murder is planetary, and this is an Imperial prison. Only Imperial judges can send people here, and they only do it for the big stuff. Piracy. Rebellion. Insurrection. Spitting on the deck, things like that."

Blake digested this for a moment. "No other murderers here?"

"Just you." Dirk took his final tortilla and swirled up the last of his stew. He pushed it in his mouth, chewed, then swallowed. "Your story doesn't check out. You should have done more research. Listen, kid, you're not here to serve some sentence, you're here to kill me. Somebody sent you, but they didn't give you a good briefing."

"This is no way to make friends," Blake said. "I come over here all friendly like, trying to make my way here, and all you do is abuse me."

"Not true," Dirk said. "You did something stupid

somewhere else, somebody offered you a deal, you were told you'd be sent somewhere else, and all you had to do was stick a knife in some pampered Imperial aristocrat who was in jail, and you'd be free. They've probably told you that the knife will show up in your cell tonight, and all you have to do is shiv me tomorrow at roll call and walk away. No investigation, no blowback. Am I right?"

Blake stopped eating and was quiet.

Dirk continued. "You're welcome to try. The last three didn't do so well. And even if you make it, you'll never get out of here alive. At least one of the guards will shoot you for trying to escape." Dirk looked down at Blake's plate. "You going to eat the rest of that? I'm always hungry." When Blake didn't say anything, Dirk swapped trays and ate the rest of Blake's stew with his fingers.

Blake looked pensive. "What are you really in for, friend Duke?

"Mass murder," Dirk said.

"Mass murder?"

"I killed five, six thousand people," Dirk said. "Totals vary."

"You killed six thousand people?"

Dirk nodded.

Blake's lips moved. "How long did that take? I mean, even if you killed five or ten a day, that would take—"

"I started a war."

"A war?"

"Small war. I'll give you a piece of advice, youngster. If you're going to start a war, make sure you start a big one, kill a lot of people. A million is a good number. I should have killed a million. Then I wouldn't be here."

"You wouldn't be here if you had killed more people?"

"You kill a thousand, and you're a criminal. You kill a million, and you're a statesman. They make statues. Can you see me in bronze somewhere?" Dirk tilted his head and assumed a heroic pose. "That would be me, if I was just a more effective murderer."

Blake laughed. "I don't believe you. Who starts wars?"

"I didn't really start it. I just made it worse. I tried to evacuate some former Imperial Marines who wanted off-planet. The planetary forces didn't want them to leave."

"Why not?"

"They weren't really former Marines. They kind of fought for the losing side. Unofficially. And there was this confederation auxiliary warship there. And an Imperial-registered transport. I kind of got the Imperials to fire at the confeds."

"How did you get the Imperials to fire at the confeds?"

"I might have made it look like they shot me first."

"I didn't hear this on the news."

"That's why you have courts-martial and not civilian trials. You can do them quickly, quietly, and with no reporters."

Blake continued to look at him. "You're not what I expected."

"You have no idea what's going on, kid. You're in way over your head. Best you get out of here somehow. Tell your sponsor you can't get near me or tell them that somebody else tried. But whatever you do, do it soon."

"Why? Something bad going to happen soon?"

"Bad? No. I have a Tai chi class this afternoon, and I don't want that interrupted. You think you could try to kill me before lunch, as a favor? Get it over with."

Lights pulsed, and an alarm gonged. "Lockdown. Lockdown. Lockdown." Everyone in the cafeteria got up and walked back to their cells.

"Dammit," Dirk said as he threw his tray in the bin. "I was looking forward to that class."

***

After about an hour of lockdown, the main lights went out, and Dirk sat in the darkness. The emergency lights were supposed to come on but didn't. Dirk was impressed. This was the most organized attempt yet. He sat on his bed and listened to a clink in the distance and a shuffling of feet. Then a fizzing sound, and the smell of burning plastic. There goes the camera control panel at the end of the hall.

He wasn't surprised when a voice outside the bars of his cell called out, "Prisoner 24571?"

It wasn't Blake.

"Wrong cell, old chap." Dirk got up off the bed. "One level down, two cells past this one. You'll recognize him when you see him. Very handsome fellow. Well-spoken. Snazzy beard. Sharp dresser, too. Tell him I said hello."

"Funny," the voice said. Dirk squinted in the gloom. He didn't recognize the voice, and he couldn't see anything except shadows. He thought he could make out the outline of body armor and what looked like lowlight goggles.

"I'm renowned for my snappy repartee," Dirk said. "But truthfully, I've had that one loaded up for a while."

"Greetings from Lady Crystal," the voice said.

"I don't believe I've had the pleasure of meeting her grace," Dirk said. "And truthfully, I'd be surprised if you had ever met her either."

"I met some of her money, though, and me and her money, we got along famously," the voice said. "She wanted a message passed along."

"Pass away," Dirk said. "If we get this done quickly, I still have hopes of making my Tai chi class."

"She wanted to talk to you about her daughter."

"Her daughter was a fine officer and a credit to the Imperial Navy. I deeply grieved her loss."

"She doesn't think you grieved enough."

"Really?"

"Yeah. She told me to help you with that, the grieving."

"You're a grief counselor?"

"I'm a specialist in making people sorry about things. I'm here to make you sorry." He stepped forward and pushed something through the bars. Dirk made out the shape of a weapon.

"Emperor's balls," Dirk said. "Did you read that in a book somewhere? 'I'm here to make you sorry.' That's the dumbest threat I've ever heard. First, you have no idea how truly, deeply, horribly sorry I am. There is no way that you can make me any sorrier than I am now. I despise myself every waking moment of every waking day, and there is nothing, nothing that will make me feel worse about myself."

Dirk's voice had risen. "This is the fourth—or maybe the fifth—assassination attempt I have had to deal with. And every time, every time, I fight back. And I wonder why I bother to fight back? Bother to even try to defend myself? When I could just let it succeed and end my miserable existence? Do you know why? Well, do you?"

"Um. No," the shadow said, sounding uncertain.

"Because it would be embarrassing. So, so embarrassing. To be killed by you would be embarrassing because you are so incompetent."

"I'm the one with the gun, buddy," the shadow said, thrusting the weapon forward.

Dirk snatched the man's hand holding the gun and pulled it toward him and past his side. A bang and a smell of powder blasted the cell. Chemical weapon, probably an officer's revolver. He turned around and pulled the arm over his shoulder, leveraging himself to bang the arm against the cell's bars. A crack led the man to drop the revolver. Dirk swung the arm sideways as far as he could and was rewarded with a scream. He kept the pressure on the injured arm and leaned toward the shadowy face.

"Only the stupidest, laziest, dumbest Imperial turds let a man get inside their reach when they have a firearm," Dirk said. "Look at me! Look. You can't kill a man locked in a jail cell? I'm actually behind bars. I am a literal fish in a metal barrel, and you still can't kill me, you useless, Imperial vagina."

Dirk gave a mighty heave and shoved the man back into the far wall. It was still dark, but his eyes had adjusted to the light so that he could see him slump down.

Dirk squatted, picked up the revolver, then pointed it at the shadow man. "Officer's revolver. Good choice. Kind of ironic, really, to be killed by a service weapon." He regarded the shadowy form. "This has been going on too long. And I'm just tired, tired of having to deal with all you idiots, tired of having to kill you all, just tired of the sheer bloody incompetence. What's next, schoolgirls in knee-high socks and pigtails trying to stab me to death with hair barrettes?"

Dirk spun the gun once, then tossed it into the hall. It slid to the shadow man. "Here, try again," Dirk said.

The shadow scrabbled for the gun, picked it up, and pointed it toward Dirk. "What's wrong with you?" it asked. "Do you want to die?"

"I just can't handle the incompetence anymore," Dirk said. "It's very tiring, and I don't have a lot of energy these days. Well, try again." He spread his arms out, slapped his chest, then spread them farther. "Try. Again."

The man didn't move.

"What, you can't shoot a man when he's facing you? Or do you only shoot people when they're running away? Here." Dirk jogged around the cell. "I'm running, I'm running. Shoot me in the back. Go ahead. Shoot me."

The man still didn't move.

"Or is it the uniform? Here. I'll take it off." Dirk stopped running and stripped his prisoner's uniform coveralls off until he stood in his underwear. "Come on. I'm naked now, naked and running." Dirk jogged around his cell. "Naked and running away. Is this better? Big threat. Shoot me. Shoot me now. Shoot me in the ass."

Another boom and a smell of gunpowder erupted. Dirk stood there, unscathed. He looked at the shadow man. "You missed me. YOU MISSED ME. From two meters away?"

"I'm no good with my left hand," the man said. "I can't control a gun with it."

"This is worse than getting tortured to death," Dirk said. "What sort of a killer are you if you can't kill a man with a revolver at two meters?"

"I told you, I don't work with my left hand."

"Did you never practice?"

"No."

"Not even once? You didn't even consider, for even a second, that you might hurt your dominant hand and have to shoot offhanded?"

"Didn't think of it."

"The emperor's hairy testicles. You would never make an Imperial Marine. An Imperial Marine would be able to kill me with either hand. Or a foot, or an ear, or anything. With a gun. Without a gun. With their fists. If they couldn't find anything else, they'd, they'd—" Dirk searched for something insulting enough. "If they didn't have a gun, they'd just grab a fire extinguisher and spray me with it and beat me to death with the case. They'd do something. They wouldn't just stand there and whimper, 'My hand hurts—I can't shoot my gun.' Complete and total incompetence."

Dirk shook his head, then looked up. "Do you have any reloads for that gun?"

"Reloads?" the man asked.

"Extra rounds. Do you?"

"Twelve spare."

Dirk leaned forward and put both hands on the bars. "Just start shooting, then. I'll just lean here 'til you hit me. Keep shooting at me 'til I fall down, then reload, and empty the gun into me again. Even an idiot like you is bound to hit me four or five times, and that will be enough."

It was still almost pitch dark in the hallway. Dirk caught the motion of the revolver rising.

"Took you long enough," Dirk said. He straightened.

A terrific boom rang out, and the brightest light Dirk had even seen in his life flared in front of him. He yelled and made an involuntary hop back. It was that bright. A bullet sliced his arm, and a crack ripped next to his ear just before he stumbled onto his bed. The light hurt his eyes, even though he kept them closed. Several more booms burst, then a thwack, a meaty thud, and a series of softer meaty thuds.

"I think you got him," a woman's voice said.

"Just want to be sure," another voice said. Dirk recognized it as the Blake kid from earlier. "Can you move the flare? Without armor, I don't dare get near it."

"Got it," the woman's voice said. A skittering noise scraped the floor, and the light dimmed.

"Sir, can you open your eyes?" Blake said.

Dirk tried, but it hurt. "I can't see a thing. Is that you, Blake?"

"Yes, sir. And some friends. Marine friends. I have your sidearm here, sir. If you reach forward, I'll hand it to you."

"My sidearm?" Dirk said.

"Well, it was buddy's here, but he won't be needing it."

"Don't forget to load it, Blake," the woman's voice said.

"Right." A series of clicking and snapping noises flitted around. "If you'll just hold out your hand, sir," Blake said.

Dirk tried to pry his eyes open. It hurt. He managed to open them to the barest slit. An exceptionally bright light hidden down the corridor illuminated everything.

Blake was standing next to the cell and had pushed a revolver through the bars butt first. Behind him, on the ground, was a man in a Marine uniform wearing loose body armor. He had a dent in his head, and a bloody fire extinguisher was on the ground next to him. Another Marine was kneeling next to the door lock panel, fiddling with the wires. Her face shield was flipped up so Dirk could see it was the woman.

"Blake, what was all that about in the cafeteria? The questions?" Dirk asked.

"Had to make sure we were rescuing the right person. This is Stephens, sir."

"We'll have you out in a jiffy, sir," Stephens said. "Great speech, sir."

"Yes, sir," Blake said. "Great idea about the fire extinguisher. I took you up on that. Flare was my idea, though, since he had night vision on and all."

"Indeed," Dirk said. He took the proffered revolver, then looked down on the would-be assassin. "A well-executed plan. Are you supposed to kill me now, private?"

"Not currently in my orders, sir. If you wish to amend them, I'll give it a go if you want, though, truthfully, sir, I wouldn't fancy my chances. If you can't be killed while you're locked naked inside a cell, probably even harder outside a cell."

Blake looked down at the woman messing with the lock. "That assumes that Stephens, here, ever gets the lock open."

"Want to try bashing it with your fire extinguisher, Blake?" she said. There was a click, and the lock mechanism disengaged. She pushed the door open.

"What happens now?" Dirk said.

"We walk out the front door," Stephens said.

Dirk looked around the cell. "You're breaking me out of jail? Really breaking me out?"

"I know that you're navy and all, sir, and a lot of the navy officers are a bit dim, but please try to keep up. Sir. That's the general idea, and we don't have a lot of time."

"Former navy. I killed thousands of people," Dirk said. "I deserve to die in jail."

"That was the confeds, sir. And you're not officially discharged 'til you serve your sentence, so still an officer."

"Hundreds of Marines under my command died in a needless slaughter. I should be punished."

"After you and your crew flew down to try to rescue them, sir."

"What if I want to stay here?"

"For the Tai chi class, sir?"

"That, and because I'm a worthless, cowardly ass?"

The two Marines looked at each other. "Lots of people worked hard on this rescue, sir. Be kind of ungrateful not to take advantage of it."

"Marine, this is quite tiresome. I don't suppose you could just kill me and be done with it."

"Oh, no, sir, Centurion would speak to me if that happened. She'd be . . . perturbed. You don't want a perturbed centurion on your conscience, do you?"

"I might be able to live with that."

"But all this work, sir. We've already done so much. You don't want to let us down now, do you, sir?"

Dirk pulled a string hanging from around his neck, attached was a silver band with blue stones. He regarded it for a moment, then rubbed it with his finger.

"Not again, no."

"There will be a shuttle out front in five minutes. What size are you, sir?"

"Five minutes? Well done," Dirk said.

"Thank you, sir. Your size?"

"My size?" Dirk looked at his chest. "Men's large, last I checked."

Blake and Stephens looked down at the man on the floor and his bloody, stinking Marine uniform, then back at Dirk.

"Thing is, sir," Blake said, "shuttle is through the administration building. There are cameras and a few people. We can cut the ankle band off you. But, well, see, sir, you can't be wearing a prison jumpsuit when we leave."

Dirk looked at the disgusting mess in front of his cell, sighed, and began to dress.

CHAPTER 2

"The full extent of your plan is to punch a man in the jaw and hope for the best?" Dirk asked as they stepped from the shuttle. He was dressed in a stained Marine jumpsuit over a standard Marine skin suit.

"No, sir, there's way more to it than that," Stephens said. "Take this for after the security desk, sir." She pushed a small package into his hands. As soon as all the Marines exited the shuttle, she led the way across the busy cargo floor to the customs desk and access to the rest of the station.

"What did I miss?" Dirk asked

"There will be some kicking, too," Stephens said. "In the middle, if you please, sir." The group of a dozen Marines coalesced around Dirk, moving as a body to the customs desk. They had left their weapons and armor on the shuttle. They didn't even have a knife between them. They were just a group of friends, going on leave together, checking in at the customs on their way to the bar.

Dirk was pushed, politely but firmly, toward the rear of the loose circle. He turned to Blake, walking next to him.

"That's her plan? Start a fight?"

"She likes to fight," Blake said.

"Why are you going along with this?"

"She used to be our sergeant. She isn't any more."

"Why not?"

"She likes to fight," Blake said. "Take this as well, sir." He handed Dirk a comm unit. "Nothing special, cheapest grade, but you'll look odd without one." He leaned over and pulled Dirk's cap brim down as low as it would go. "Sir, once you're through the gate, we can't help you anymore. This is a system station, not an Imperial facility."

"Got it, private. I'll be fine. I have a plan."

"We expected that, sir."

"I'm going to find a bar and drink 'til I fall down."

"Outstanding." Blake sniffed a bit. "Might want to find a fresher stall at some point, sir. You smell like prison."

"Smell like prison?"

"Blood and armpits, sir."

"How truly good," Dirk said.

"Honor to the Empire, sir," Blake said. He made the Imperial crossed chest salute.

"The Empire," Dirk agreed, making the same salute. The group surged across the loading dock to the customs desk. Stephens was a step ahead. People stood in a line, waiting their turns for one of three customs agents behind low counters. Two were digging through bags. The third had just dismissed a freighter crewman, then gestured the next man in line through.

Stephens pushed past him and walked up to the counter. The man in line objected and tried to grab her shoulder as she went by. The next Marine grabbed his arm and bent it backward, causing the man to yowl.

"You'll have to wait your turn, Marine," the agent said, "and it's one at a time."

"You cheating, Imperial turd," Stephens yelled. "Did you even mean a single thing you said to me?"

"I don't think—"

"And then I catch you with my best friend the very next day."

"What? Wait, you've got me confused with somebody else."

"Confused? I'll give you confused." She leaned forward and thwacked him across the face. His hat flew off, and he staggered back. Stephens hopped over the counter and slapped him again. Then again. He stepped back and tried to grab her arms, but she evaded them and punched him in the face. He staggered, then closed and caught Stephens in a bear hug. She pushed him down.

The other two customs agents did a double take, then

ran around their desks and raced to the struggling pair. Two more Marines stepped forward and tripped them.

An alarm bonged in the background. A door to the left opened, and a group of four uniformed customs officers carrying shock sticks rushed out. The group of Marines pushed toward the customs officers and met them halfway. The customs officers had the initial advantage because of the shock sticks, but they could only shock one person at a time. The Marines swarmed them, the ones in front taking the hits so that the others could get into the fray. Their first act was to disarm the customs agents by knocking the shock sticks away.

Blake had his hand on Dirk's shoulder and pushed him through the crowd and past the struggle. They passed Stephens's original customs victim, who was hors de combat on the floor, as was Stephens, hit by a shock stick. The man they had originally pushed past had a friend, and the two of them were duking it out with two Marines. The remainder of the line had melted back as everybody watched the melee. Several Marines lay on the ground, some shaking a bit as the electric charge dissipated. The others traded punches with customs agents.

Dirk looked back. One of the customs agents had retained her shock stick, and was methodically engaging a Marine at a time, waiting until an opening appeared, then shocking them into submission.

"Give her another couple of minutes, and she'll stun the whole group," Blake said.

Dirk and Blake weaved around the fight, and a dropped shock skittered in front of Dirk. He kneeled to grab it and passed it behind him to Blake. "Help your friends out. I'm on my way."

Blake flicked the shock stick away. "No, sir, that's a deadly weapon. Assault with a deadly weapon on planetary officials—that's a hanging offense. A little fisticuffs, that's just thirty days with bread and water. Path's clear, sir, off you go. Currunt ad bellum." He gestured a crossed breast salute, turned around, and tackled the shock stick-wielding customs agent. She shocked him square in the chest, but his momentum propelled his unconscious body into her, knocking her backward. Dirk pushed his way through the bystanders, who had gathered to watch the fun. Some stood with mouths agape, but at least one group cheered for the Marines. Customs departments anywhere were never popular.

Dirk reached the back of the crowd, then slowed down and strolled deeper into the station. Look casual, he thought.

He turned twice, then upgraded to a brisk walk. He made another turn into an empty corridor that opened to offices. Nobody was around, so he stripped off his Marine coveralls, opened the package, and pulled out a pair of coveralls. They were bright, shining red, and had the logo of a ship repair company prominent on the breast and stitched into the back. A bright red ball cap a size too big for him completed the outfit. Not exactly inconspicuous but nothing like a Marine uniform with its muted grays and blues. Dirk swapped coveralls and rolled up his old hat and Marine outfit. He pulled his new hat down his forehead, shoved the old clothes in the next recycler, then walked confidently from corridor to corridor.

Time to find out if his girlfriends remembered him fondly or felt the same way the rest of the Empire did.

CHAPTER 3

"Aren't you dead?" the waiter asked. "That's what the vids said."

"Officially, yes," Dirk said. "But I was resurrected to come back and enjoy your sister's cooking." He sniffed. "It smells wonderful. What's on the menu today, Teddy, my son?"

"If I know Tasha, probably some cursing, then a face slap, followed by a drink poured over your head," Teddy said. He was short, with blue eyes and straight black hair. He dressed in black pants and a white shirt and carried a tray.

"Anything to follow?"

"Mussels. Steamed in a white wine sauce with herbs, and crisp potato fries, with an excessively minerally white Sancerre from the south continent."

"That all sounds great, except the cursing and hitting. I'll skip that."

"Sorry, sub-commander, it's a prix fixe. No substitutions. You'll have to take the hit." Teddy smiled. Dirk had once broken Teddy's finger when Teddy objected to Dirk kissing Teddy's date. That was before he met Teddy's sister, Tasha, of course.

"Well, I guess I'm stuck then," Dirk said.

"Sister!" The waiter turned toward the kitchen and raised his voice. "Come see who's here." He turned to Dirk. "I'll bring you your order, sub-commander."

"I'm not a sub-commander anymore."

"I know." Teddy's smile widened. "We watched the court martial on the vids. I just like reminding you of it," he said before walking to the kitchen.

Dirk looked around. Tasha and Teddy's Beach Restaurant was, as the name implied, a restaurant on a beach. It was a fake beach but good enough for an orbital station.

A woman wearing a chef's outfit charged out of the kitchen. She was a feminine version of Teddy but looked better. Her blue-eyed, freckled face was just short of Dirk's chin, her straight black hair in a tight ponytail. She stopped dead as she saw Dirk sitting at the bar.

"Hello, pretty girl," Dirk said and gave her his best smile.

She launched herself forward and swung her arms. Dirk reached for her grasping hands but was too slow. He was expecting a girlish slap, but instead, she rammed a full punch right into his jaw. Thrown off, he fell backward, his hands behind him to break his fall.

The woman stepped forward and flung him a swift kick in the ribs, then another before he grabbed her leg.

"Twice is sufficient, Tasha. Three times is excessive," he said. He released her foot, and she stepped back and glared at him.

"That hurt," Dirk said as he struggled to his feet.

"It was supposed to," she said.

She bawled, and Dirk cradled the crying cook. He rocked her and grasped her to his chest. Her strawberry-scented hair wash brought back fond memories. "Good move with the punch. Who taught you that?" he said.

"Brad did."

"Did he teach you to kick people when they were down?"

"When they are down is the best time to kick people. I figured that out myself. I got Brad to show me how to kick without hurting my foot, though."

"Smart man, Brad. I always said he'd be good for you."

She looked up and glared at him. "And you were no good for me."

"I believe we established that in the past."

She sniffed for a moment. "You smell bad."

"Blood and armpits. It's the latest thing."

"I knew you weren't dead."

"Why would I be dead?"

"The news said so. You were just so good at weaseling out of things, we knew you would turn up."

"Well, here I am. I can't stay. They're looking for me. I need help."

"Help? After all you've done to me, you need help?"

"I'm begging you, Tasha. I'm in a fix."

"I don't owe you anything."

"No, you do not," Dirk said. He waited.

Tasha glared at him for a while, then sighed. "Did you really kill all those people?"

"They are dead. I was there when it happened. It's complicated. Does your cousin still work with that export company?

"Timra? Yes."

"Can he do his thing?"

"If I ask him."

"Will you ask him for me?"

"Maybe."

Her brother came out, carrying a platter. "Mussels. Fried potatoes. White wine. And dipping sauce."

"What's this sauce?" Dirk asked.

"It's for the potato fries," Tasha said. "We make it out of tomatoes, vinegar, and sugar. My grandmother's recipe." She plucked one of the fried potatoes, dipped it in the red sauce, then offered it to Dirk. He took a bite, then another.

"Exquisite," he said before shoveling the fries into his mouth.

"How did you get out of jail?" Teddy asked.

"The Marines busted me out and hid me on a shuttle."

"The news said you were dead. Hung yourself."

He stopped shoveling fries, picked a mussel out of the broth, and swallowed it. "You were always wonderful with seafood, Tasha."

"I have lots of practice. The suicide?" she said.

Dirk thought for a moment. "I don't remember committing suicide. What did the news say?"

"That you hung yourself in your cell last night during a riot or something."

"There was a riot. But that was to cover somebody killing me, not me killing myself."

"The news said they found a corpse in your cell," Tasha said.

"They probably did. There was a corpse. They think I'm dead."

"That's the news."

"The emperor's hairy testicles—those Marines are more creative than I imagined. Tasha," Dirk took her hands, "I've got maybe four or five hours before they have to admit they got it wrong and that I escaped." He took a big drink of the wine. "It is very minerally, but that works with the salty mussels."

"You think it's too minerally?" Tasha asked.

"Yes."

Tasha shook her head. "You don't know anything about wine. It's perfect. I'll call my cousin. He can get you on a shuttle with some sort of identification. Get you to the outer rings. You can hop a long-haul freighter there."

"What if I can't find a freighter?"

"Then you can burn in Hades for all I care. We're quits. I don't owe you anything after this."

"Actually, you don't owe me anything right now."

"If I don't owe you anything, why did you come here?"

"Because you are too kind for your own good. You should turn me in."

She looked at him for a moment. "You think I'd turn you in?"

"No, I don't. That's why I'm here."

"Finish your lunch. I'll set things up with my cousin. You'll be on your way outbound in an hour."

"Thanks."

"Goodbye, Dirk."

"Goodbye, Tasha."

She turned.

"Um, Tasha. One more thing."

"What?"

"I don't have any money. I can't pay for lunch."

***

An hour and two glasses of wine later, Dirk spun a locking hatch open and stepped into an office. A sign on the wall said T&T Exports. Shipping and Insurance.

The man behind the counter could have been Tasha's twin. A little taller, a little darker, but mostly the same. Instead of a chef's outfit, he wore a soft skin suit with the company logo on his breast and a checker's scanner on his belt. Lined up on the table in front of him were identical scanners. The counter shone, and cleaning solution wafted about.

"Tasha sent me," Dirk said. "You must be Timra."

Timra stood, and Dirk scanned him from top to bottom from behind the desk. "Well, well. So, you are the infamous Dirk that broke Tasha's heart."

"Broke her heart? That's a bit rough, don't you think? We were just good friends who had fun together."

"She cried for a week after you left her for that red-headed navy girl."

"There was nothing there for her to be worried about. That navy girl was purely a professional relationship. We were appointed to the same station, that's all."

"She said she caught you and navy girl together in the hot tub on the outer ring."

"A man needs to relax after a long day. Hot water is good for that."

"You were both naked."

"Nakedness isn't treated the same way in all cultures. Especially in hot tubs. Somebody has to wash your back."

"Tasha said you were getting something else washed."

"I have no idea what you are talking about," Dirk said.

He sat in a chair in front of the desk.

"It doesn't matter," Timra said. "Tasha says you want off the station?"

"Off this station, out of this system."

Timra sat and brought up a screen. "The vids say you are a mass murderer."

"I dispute some of the details, but they are largely correct. I got a lot of people killed."

Timra typed on his screen and regarded it for a long moment. "Tasha watched the whole trial. She said you were railroaded, that it was all unfair."

"Disagree. As a legal scholar, Tasha makes an excellent cook. The trial was fair. More than fair. Given what happened, I would have voted to convict myself if I had a vote."

A bong from the desk vibrated, and Timra tapped another key. "News flash. Now you are reported possibly alive. And there's a reward. A big reward." Timra named a large sum.

"I'm impressed. I don't think I'm worth that much."

"I agree."

Dirk got up. "Right, well, pleasure meeting you. Call it in for the reward. I'm going back to the restaurant to have some more of those mussels before they catch me. And another glass of wine."

Timra kept reading the screen. "You are assumed to be armed and dangerous. Bounty will be paid alive or dead. Security suggests shooting first and asking questions later."

"Two glasses of wine, then. And something less minerally than that Sancerre."

"Did Teddy tell you that? He doesn't know anything about wine."

"Can't argue with that."

"But he did correctly label you as a duplicitous dirtbag who was taking advantage of his sister."

"Can't argue with that, either."

"I think you're a duplicitous dirtbag, too."

He took a breath.

"And you smell so bad, I'll have to burn that chair when you leave."

Dirk turned to the door. "We're done here. If you're not going to help me, I am going back and having some wine. Security can come and get me and take me back to jail, or just shoot me, or take me back to jail and shoot me, or shoot me and take my corpse back to jail, or any combination of shooting and jail that they want. I'm very, very tired, and I don't have a lot of energy for this escape thing."

Timra crossed his arms. "You really don't want to escape? You're just going to roll over and let them shoot you? That doesn't sound like the Hero of New Madrid."

"The definition of a hero is somebody who gets other people killed. I meet that definition a thousand times over. Several thousand times over. The only reason I'm in your office is that people I respect worked hard to get me here, and I didn't want to let them down. Again."

Timra leaned forward, typing. "Tasha is my best friend in the family. She cried for a week after your trial." He looked up. "You can pilot and navigate, right?"

"That's a stupid question."

Timra continued typing. "Well, I think you're a stupid person. Got just the thing. Tramp freighter. Long range jump. Heart's Desire. We just went through the process to seize her for defaulting on her mortgage. Needs to go out-system as soon as possible. She's registered in Rigel and can only stay for seventy-two hours. She's already been here sixty-six. If we don't get her out soon, customs will take her over for exceeding her permit and impound her. So, it's either move her or abandon her."

"Move her where?"

"We've got an agreement with a shipyard a couple systems over—they give us great rates. All we need is three jumps to get her there. You're the man. I'll send the details to the ship's computer."

"Why not my comm?"

"I don't want any record of you being here or of us talking to you. Far as the records will show, you saw a notice on the station board, went to the ship to apply, and they took you. Nothing to do with us."

"Who's on board?"

"The Medic—Mikelson, something like that."

"Engineer?"

"We hired some newbie from the transient pool—no idea who. They'll be there today."

"Other officers? Crew?"

"It's a tramp freighter. You want an administrative staff? That's what we got today. And even better, from your point of view, it's precleared. They haven't taken or landed any cargo, so they have blanket customs clearance. As long as we don't show any passengers, all you have to do is drop."

Dirk leaned back in his chair, feigning a smile. Timra leaned back, mirroring the grin.

"You hate me, don't you?" Dirk said.

"I hate anybody who hurts Tasha."

"Then, why are you helping me?"

"I told you, Tasha is one of my best friends. And I like Brad. You're trouble, and you're no good for her. Getting a dirtbag like you out of her life is a public service."

"Dirtbag? Again? That's harsh."

"You've got six hours to get on that ship and drop. Take it or leave it."

"Taken. Pleasure doing business with you, Timra."

"Not with you, Durriken Friedel. Get out of my office, and I hope I never see you again."

***

Timra waited 'til Dirk left the office, then pushed his comm. A man's voice answered. "Carlos," Timra said, "theoretically speaking, will our insurance pay out if somebody steals one of our ships from the dock?" He listened carefully, then nodded. "Good to know. What do you know about this reward for this Dirk Friedel guy? The one who used to date Tasha."

This time, the other party spoke a lot longer, and Timra's eyes widened. "Well, we certainly wouldn't want to get on the wrong side of that organization. Again, theoretically speaking, how would we go about contacting them?"

CHAPTER 4

"Here's to finally graduating!" The brunette girl swayed upright and held up her glass of beer. Her friends cheered. "Our last night together. Who's first?" They all clinked glasses in unison and downed their beers. It wasn't their first, not by a long shot.

Gavin examined the group from his spot in the corner. Eight of them, all mid-twenties, about his age. All wore brand-new ship suits over generic skin suits. The logo of the planetary merchant academy was sewn on the shoulders.

He sat alone in the Runabout Bar. The floor was metal, the walls were metal, and the tables and chairs were bolted to the floor, all of which were made of metal. The glasses were plastic. A quick drink of beer explained the choice of materials. Plastic and metal were easy to clean, and the temptation to spit the beer out on the floor or on the table was hard to resist, and many hadn't.

A blonde woman with unbelievably perky breasts sauntered from the left side of the bar and slid into the seat next to him. She smelled like apples, and her blue top was low-cut. She leaned over the table to give him a better view. "Hi, handsome. I'm Suzi. Looking for some company tonight?"

Gavin looked down, then gave her a huge smile. He dropped his right hand below the table as he spoke. "Love to," he said. "Is this going to be expensive?"

Suzi squeezed her shoulders inward to grant him a better view. "It's not what you pay that's important, honey. It's what you get."

Gavin gestured to the small pile of coins next to his drink. "That's all the money I have in the world. What do I get for that?"

Suzi slumped, drooping her shoulders. "Jove's testicles. Why is everybody in here broke tonight?"

Another shout came from the students' table. One of them stood, consulted a screen, and read out a ship's name. "Dropping in two days!" she screamed. All the students yelled, clashing beer glasses again.

"Except for them," Gavin said. "What are they up to?"

"Local tradition," Suzi said. "The merchant academy guarantees every graduate a one-year assignment. To make sure everybody gets a place, they do a lottery thing. Once a week, a pool gets its orders. They come here to open them up."

Another student stood and read the name of another ship. The students cheered and whistled.

"How do you know all this?" Gavin asked.

"Dated a few graduates."

Gavin laughed.

"Well, more than a few."

The first of the students stood and read out her orders. "Heart's Desire, dropping in . . . Emperor's testicles, six hours! Gotta go! Here's to us!" The students stood and clanked their glasses together. Two of them dropped full glasses. Beer spun around the room, fountaining the bar.

"The emperor's anus," Suzi said, wiping beer out of her hair. "What a night. Somebody should sort that group out." She stood and stomped toward the bathroom.

Gavin watched her, then glanced at his right hand, still concealed below the table. It held a six-inch fighting knife. He pivoted it and slid it into a holster concealed in his sleeve. She looked harmless, but who could be sure?

Gavin inhaled, and spilled beer replaced the apple scent. Suzi was almost at the bathroom door when she waved at a group of men and women sitting at a table, then stopped and talked to them. Four men, two women. Four were in uniform. Imperial Marines. The fifth was a merchant from the concourse with whom Gavin had transacted some business earlier.

The sixth was station police.

"Uh oh," Gavin said. He slumped and looked around. That group was between him and the door. He scanned the bar for another exit but didn't see one. A shout made him look toward the obnoxious graduates. Somebody, several somebodies dripping beer, had jumped in to sort them out. The discussion was getting heated, and one of the students stood, drunkenly pointing at the yelling man. The man's punch initiated general mayhem.

The crowd dissolved into two- and three-person fights. Someone whacked the brunette girl, who was speaking earlier, upside her head. She fell back and landed on Gavin. Her attacker turned to deal with one of her classmates, who was trying to beat him to death with an empty plastic beer glass. Gavin wished him the best of luck.

The girl on his lap tried to stand. "Help me up," she slurred. "Gotta help." She staggered to her feet, tripped over the chair, and fell again.

Gavin caught her. She burped, her face turning pale green. He set her down and rolled her to her side just before she puked. "Miss, why don't you just sit here for a while? Relax a bit." He stepped back from the smell.

"Floor cold, feels good," she said, then puked again.

Gavin glanced around. Everyone was watching the fight. He quickly went through her pockets. A credit chip, a commlink, an ID chip, and what looked like a ship pass. He pocketed the credits and the ship pass, scrutinized the ID chip for a moment but then left it there.

He sat and slipped the ship pass in his comm. The Heart's Desire. Tramp freighter. Dropping in six hours. "Perfect," he said and slipped out the bar's entrance, just ahead of the station police's arrival.

***

"Don't often get many of you Jovians out here. What are you doing so far out?" the thin man asked. He slouched with his hands in his pockets and watched Lee load two duffel bags with boxes of medical drugs.

She closed the first one and shoved it forward. The thin man's assistant, a thin, dirty girl, with the name Scruggs on her coveralls, hefted the first one on her shoulder. "Off you go, girl. Take it to the office. They'll sort it out."

Lee shoved the last of the medical equipment into the duffel. "Travel broadens your horizons. That's the lot. Where's my money?"

"You'll get it when we inspect it and test it back at the store," the man said. Not only was he skinny, but at some point, his face had lost a battle with acne. His coveralls said Consolidated Medical Supplies on one side and Singh on the other.

"No, I'll get it now," Lee said. She put her hand on her holster and glared at Singh. "That was the deal. Money now. That's the honorable way of doing things."

"Honorable?" Singh said. "What's honorable about stealing medical supplies?"

"I'm not stealing, I'm just getting my back pay. I haven't been paid in six months. And these are duplicates."

"That meets your definition of honorable, does it?"

"Are you calling me dishonorable?" Lee asked. She unsnapped her holster. "I serve the emperor. His honor is mine. If you are calling my honor in question . . ."

The man held his hands up. "Easy, easy. Just asking. Duplicates or not, better hope that you don't need them out in the dark somewhere." He sniffed the air. "Is that fungus I smell?"

"We're not going anywhere, not with this ship in the shape it is."

Singh shook his head. "I hear you Jovians always tell the truth, so I guess I'll take your word on what's in here. Maybe you can pray about it later."

"Maybe I can. But that's between me and Paterfather Zeus."

"Have a nice chat with him. Tell him I said hi. Here." Singh thrust a credit chip at her. Lee pushed it into her comm pad and glanced at it. It was what they had agreed on. "The Blessings of Zeus upon you," she said.

"Yeah, yeah, good luck, hearty."

"Hearty?"

Singh pointed to the ship's name and registration by the door. "That's the name, isn't it? Heart's Desire."

***

"Off shift already, Grandpa?" the bartender asked.

"Don't call me grandpa, you little rat. Or you'll regret it," Ana said. The bar was dim, with soft lighting and discrete booths. Ana sat in the middle of the brightest part of the bar, where he was clearly visible.

"So sorry, Senior Customs Inspector Anastasios, my pardon. I should be showing you the proper respect due to a senior non-commissioned officer of the Planetary Customs Force."

"Buzz off and give me my drink, you little worm," Ana said. "Or I'll take it up with your boss."

"And what would she do to me, I wonder," the bartender said.

A woman stepped out of an office at the end of the bar. "Shut up, Glen. Give him his drink and then go away."

"Yes, Sophie," Glen said. He stuck his tongue out at Ana, then plopped a shot and a glass of beer onto the bar. Ana sniffed them. One was almost pure alcohol, the other the horrible spacer's beer they brewed on the station. Ana tipped the shot into his beer, then took a long pull.

Hands on her hips, Sophie glared at Ana. "You're late."

"I'm here. What do you want?"

"Nothing. Just sit here and have a few drinks. Look official. I have some business to conduct. In fact, here they are now."

She waved at two figures who had walked in the door.

Both were big men dressed in stained coveralls. The taller of the two had the name Armand blazoned on his breast. He walked toward her. They were carrying a spacer's duffel bag between them, and whatever was in it strained the seams. They hauled the bag toward the bar. The bag clanked as it hit the floor.

Sophie jumped. "Careful. That's delicate equipment," she said.

"Never you mind your pretty little head, missy. If it can survive a vacuum, a little bump won't hurt it." Armand looked up. "That's a customs uniform. What's the customs doing here?"

"Don't worry your pretty little head, mister," Sophie said with a grin. "He's bought and paid for."

"That so," said Armand. He looked at the customs man. "You bought and paid for, Mr. Customs?"

Ana surveyed him but didn't say anything.

"He's bought and paid for by me, isn't that right, Ana?" Sophie said. When Ana didn't say anything, she repeated, "I said, 'Isn't that right, Ana?' You've been paid."

Ana ground his teeth but forced them apart. "I've been paid."

"There you go," Sophie said, smiling. "Leave your friend here with the scanner, and we'll discuss some things in the office." She turned toward her office, and Armand followed.

Ana stared at the other spacer. His name tag read Belanc.

"Good benefits in the customs service, then, Senior Customs Inspector?" Belanc asked.

"Shut up, you Imperial turd," Ana said. He slugged the rest of his beer and gestured to the bartender. Ana knew that he'd get his drink. Glen wouldn't want to cause any sort of ruckus when his boss was conducting business, so Glen scurried to replace the drinks. He and the spacer next to him carefully ignored each other. Ana finished his second set of drinks and gestured for a third. Maybe I shouldn't drink so much on duty

Ana's comm beeped. He glanced down at it. The header said Gullfield. That was a problem. Gullfield shouldn't be contacting Ana directly.

Big riot at the gate. Senior officers on site. Starting an investigation. They know about the money, and the box. Get off station soonest. I'm gone.

Ana closed his eyes. It had finally happened. He'd hoped for longer, but it was not to be. He checked his comm for the next ships out. When he saw the list, he grimaced and tossed his drinks off. He gestured toward the bartender. "Glen, another round." He had enough time for his last drink on the station before heading out to this tramp freighter, the Heart's Desire.

CHAPTER 5

"You sure you want the Heart's Desire?" the cargo loader asked.

"Sorry, what?" Dirk asked, distracted. For practice, he always smiled at any pretty girls he saw, and dozens of them streamed by in the corridors of Bishop High Port. One of the liners must have docked, and the tourists loaded up on supplies before going to the beaches down below. He'd stopped at a busy cargo lock on Bishop High Port and asked a passing cargo gang for directions to the Heart's Desire.

A stunning redhead walked by, and Dirk accompanied his genuine smile with a full bow. When he straightened his back, he turned and watched the redhead. She winked at him over her shoulder before she and her giggling friends rounded the corner to the access stairs.

The man repeated his question, and Dirk checked the notes that Timra had given him.

"Am I not in the correct docking ring, my good man?" Dirk said. "I have instructions."

"Right ring, but, well, who wants that ship?"

"I hear they are looking for a new pilot?" Dirk said.

"Captain, Engineer, Navigator, Nozzle Polisher—I'm sure they are looking for all of them."

"I'm applying for the job of a pilot."

"Really?" the cargo man looked at his buddy.

His buddy shrugged.

"You don't look insane, but what do I know? I'm not a doctor. Ring F, section two-thirty-seven." He pointed to the stairs. "Go up there. Free trades."

"And free trades to you, too, my good man."

Dirk sauntered down the deck toward the stairs. Up two rings and around to section two-thirty-seven was the docking bay.

The display next to this one showed the correct name, the Heart's Desire, but no other information. No destination. No drop time. Dirk walked down the short tube to the air lock and examined the controls. The light was red, indicating a vacuum in the lock. Unusual when a ship was docked at a High Port. He pushed the intercom button and waited and waited and waited. He pushed it again. Nothing. Not even an automated "We'll call you later" message.

Dirk frowned and inspected the air lock controls. Everything seemed in order, so he pushed the button to pressure the lock and gain entry. Fans whirred, the lock flashed green, and hydraulics swung it open. As with all station locks, this one opened in. Escaping air would slam it closed in an emergency. He stepped over the coaming and into the lock and pushed the button. He waited for it to seal shut, then he walked over to the ship's side.

The controls showed green, but again, nothing happened when he hit the intercom. The ship's air lock door had the standard round control valve, but this one had a metal pipe jammed in it. He stared at that for a moment and then a motion caught his eye. A figure stood beyond the glass.

Dirk pushed the intercom button. "Is this the Heart's Desire?" Dirk said.

The intercom lit. "Open the hatch. We can't hear you." The voice was scratchy, and Dirk couldn't even tell the sex of the speaker.

"I'm here for the pilot's position. On the Heart's Desire," Dirk said, louder than last time.

"I can't hear you. Use the pipe."

"Is this the Heart's Desire?" Dirk screamed. His face was turning red from the effort.

"The intercom's broken. It only works one way. You can hear me, but I can't hear you. Use the pipe to open the hatch."

A woman came into view and made a twisting motion with her hands. Dirk realized that he was supposed to use the pipe as a lever. He kneeled, jammed the pipe in the locking wheel, and used the lever to spin the wheel counterclockwise.

"Stand clear," the woman's voice said. "I have to kick it open."

Dirk stepped back as the woman performed swinging acrobatics on the other side. Her feet came into view, striking the door just below the port level. It swung back with a screech, then rammed back to the stops. Dirk jumped back just in time to avoid the swinging hatch. A blast of stinking humid air spewed out, and Dirk tasted sulfur. He gagged, then coughed, leaning against the wall as he gasped for breath.

"Welcome to the Heart's Desire," the woman said.

***

"Medic Two, Lee Michaelson," the tall, skinny woman said. She reached out to shake Dirk's hand. "Are you the new captain?"

"Ah, I don't think so," Dirk said. "I'm here to apply for the pilot's position. My name is Dirk. Can you take me to the captain?" They stood in the vessel's own air lock, hatches above, below, front, and back. It was a universal air lock designed to be used on any sort of station, with a ladder below to drop on a planet. The inside hatch opened to a darkened corridor. Only the emergency lights were lit.

"Nope, Pilot Dirk. Long gone. Captain left as soon as we got here," Lee said.

"He left yesterday?" Dirk said.

"Yesterday? No, he left when we got here, months back. Five, six months now."

"You've been here five months? I thought you were here only three days?"

The woman shrugged. She reminded Dirk of a pole vaulter he had seen on the vids. Taller than him, thin but all muscle. Her hair was long, black, and gathered in a ponytail. She had piercing green eyes, flecked with vivid yellow. If she hadn't been on his crew, he would have wanted to get to know her better.

"Almost six months now. Engineer left three months ago. That's why we have a problem with the air. Life support's kind of on the fritz. Needs repairs."

She stepped inside the ship and gestured Dirk to follow her. Dirk stepped out of the lock and felt a cough coming again, so he hit himself on the chest and forced it out, then looked at the woman. "Why is it so dark?"

"Station cut off power a month ago, Pilot Dirk. Water and environmental, too. Owners stopped paying for them."

"No power? No environmental? And please call me just Dirk, not Pilot Dirk."

"Wouldn't be proper, Pilot Dirk. Made us keep the lock closed, too, keep the atmo between us and the station separate."

"Doesn't the dark bother you?"

The woman stopped and looked at him. "It's not dark."

"But," Dirk looked down, "you're Jovian." He couldn't see his feet in the dim light. Then something clicked.

"The blessing of Paterfather Zeus on you, Pilot Dirk. Is that a problem?" she asked.

"You're not just a Jovian Acolyte, you're a genetic Jovian. You can see in the dark."

"Again, blessing of Paterfather Zeus on you, and again, is that a problem?"

"I hear you can see radio waves," Dirk said.

"I can't actually see them, but sometimes, I get a feeling." She pointed at her yellow-speckled green eyes. "I can see infrared and ultraviolet."

"Not a problem for me," Dirk said. "I was in the scouts for two tours. We get all kinds. Met some Jovians."

"My third cousin was in the scouts. She said they were

good to Jovians." She nodded. "Let me take you to the control room, Pilot Dirk."

They propelled forward. "Ever been on a far trader?" Lee asked.

"No, all my service was in . . . smaller ships," Dirk said. "Could we just have a single 'Pilot Dirk' at the beginning of the conversation and just assume it from then on?"

Lee frowned for a moment. "As you wish. We've got the usual two container rings in the back, just front of engineering, but they're retractable—we can pull a cover over them for landings."

"Right, for landings," Dirk said.

"And there's a regular hab module behind the bridge module, but the next set of two rings are pressurized, so we can carry loose cargo. And there's a big truss assembly after the pressurized hull and another just before engineering, so we can sling oversized cargo.

"A truss, you say? How big?"

"You'll have to ask the engineer. Any engineer. Ours left months ago. When are we dropping?"

"What? I mean, I'm not, I just got here."

"You are the new pilot, so I assume it's up to you. Didn't the employment agency send you something? A cargo run?"

"Well, yes, they talked about it, but I'm not really sure . . . they said they were sending an engineer."

"Are we dropping soon?"

"Well, yes."

"Better be soon. Before they seize the ship," Lee said.

"Indeed," Dirk said. He stopped. A large clank came from the air lock. "Do you hear that noise?"

"I don't hear anything," Lee said. "Jovian, remember?"

Dirk looked at her for a moment. "Higher frequencies. Right. Let's go see."

***

Gavin banged on the hatch. He'd figured out that the

pry bar spun the door open. He was hesitant to hop in, since going through doors without permission often yielded unfortunate results. Plus, the ship reeked of sulfur.

He banged with the pipe again, and two figures appeared inside the lock. Gavin pulled himself up into attention.

"Enough banging. Thank you, my good man. How may I help you?" the shorter one said.

"Would you be the captain?"

"The pilot," Dirk said.

"Gavin Crewjacki, Engineer Two, sir." Gavin saluted, deliberately messing it up. "Pilot Dirk, I've been assigned here by the labor pool. I'm reporting aboard." Gavin extended a chip that said he was an Engineer Two and was reporting aboard.

"Call me Dirk. I'm not officially—"

"He's Pilot Dirk, and good enough for you to report to," the taller woman said.

Dirk took the chip and placed it in his comm before reading it.

The tall woman extended her hand and Gavin shook it. "I'm Lee Michaelson, Medic Two," she said.

Gavin looked into her gold-specked eyes and swallowed. He could drown in those eyes. "Gavin, Engineer Two." He glanced at her necklace. "That's a Praetorian shield."

"Yes," Lee said.

"You're a Praetorian? What are you doing out here?"

Dirk looked up from his reading. "She's our medic."

"That's a Praetorian symbol on her neck," Gavin said. "Only members of the emperor's personal guard can wear it."

Dirk stared at her locket. It was a Praetorian shield. He couldn't make it out in the dark before. He had seen that necklace once before, around a different woman's neck. "Shouldn't you be guarding the emperor?"

"The emperor has graciously given me leave to attend

to some family issues," Lee said. "I return to his service when they are complete."

"What type of issues?" Dirk asked.

"Private issues that have no bearing on my work here, Pilot."

"Of course. My pardon for asking," Dirk said.

"I've never met a real Jovian before," Gavin said. "I didn't expect you to be so . . ."

"Tall?" Lee asked.

"Beautiful," Gavin said.

Lee blinked and blushed.

Dirk looked up from his comm. "Indeed. Let's get you settled, then." He turned, climbed down the central walkway, and passed through the first deck.

"Why is it so dark?" Gavin asked.

"That will be your first task. Second task will be to fix that intercom."

"Of course, sir."

"We don't stand for ceremony much here, as I said. Just call me Dirk."

"Yes, Dirk. I smell sulfur. Lots of sulfur."

"Right. That will be your first task. Environment. Then power, then intercom. Here we go. This will be your quarters," Dirk said.

He slid the door open. Inside, a pile of boxes filled the room from floor to ceiling, almost hiding an acceleration couch, a closet, and a tap. There wasn't room for a person to step inside the door—never mind live in it.

"Sorry, wrong room," Dirk said.

They moved around a sixth of the walkway to another door. Dirk slid the door open to another full room.

Dirk smiled at Gavin. "Wrong again."

"Why are you storing things in staterooms and not in the cargo hold?" Gavin asked.

Dirk ignored him and pulled open a third door. That room was empty. Dirk gestured, and Gavin stepped in and stowed his duffel in the locker.

"That's all I have, sir. When do I get to meet the chief engineer? I'm looking forward to continuing my learning under them," Gavin asked.

"You are a fully trained Engineer Two, then—are you not?" Dirk asked.

"Well, yes, sir—I mean, Dirk. That's what the license says, of course. But, well, truthfully, I wasn't exactly an A-level student, if you know what I mean. I was looking forward to extending my training under a seasoned hand."

"But you did graduate?" Dirk said.

"That's what the license says, sir."

"The license also says that you are six inches shorter than you are. You don't look five feet tall to me," Dirk said. "And you also don't look twenty-one standard years."

Emperor's balls. I forgot to fix all the physical characteristics, Gavin thought. I missed the height. "Is that still on my records?" Gavin said. He faked a laugh. "That was a screw up when I joined in. It's because of this." Gavin whipped his ball cap off, revealing his bald head. "Makes me look shorter than I am. Sign-in clerk misread the scale."

"And the age?" Dirk asked.

"Shaved pate makes me look older than I am. But I like it—I think it gives me a look of gravitas." Gavin shot Dirk a sunny smile. "Like your beard. But enough about me, sir. Tell me more about the ship. Will the other crew be joining us shortly? I hear we're dropping very soon."

"Yes, in just a few hours, perhaps sooner if all the clearances get set up. Did you bring your tools?"

"I have a few personal tools, but I was counting on the senior engineer to help me get that set up."

"Well, perhaps you could go back and see what's in the lockers in the engineering section and—"

A banging and a yell rung out.

"I believe that I'm called to the air lock—one moment, please."

Dirk turned and climbed back to the air lock.

***

Ana glared at the Jovian in front of him, blocking entrance to the rest of the ship. "Will the captain be long? I have lots to do today, and it's best if I'm not kept waiting."

"Pilot Dirk will be along as soon as his duties permit," Lee said.

Ana looked her up and down. "I don't like freaks. They always cause trouble."

"I don't like customs inspectors. They always make trouble where there isn't any," she said, turning as Dirk approached behind her. "Pilot Dirk, this is Senior Customs Inspector, Anastasios."

"Senior Customs Inspector, good morning. Welcome to the Heart's Desire," Dirk said.

"Enough of that," Ana said. He flipped open his comm like he was reading from notes. "You have been randomly selected by the customs department for supplemental testing of our new scanning system. Take this equipment to your cargo hold and tie it down as close to the mid-point of the ship as possible." He gestured at a series of long crates in the back of the air lock. "And these duffels here, those contain my commo gear. Show me to a cabin, please, and have them delivered there. Any questions? No. Good. Get at it. Who is going to show me to my cabin?"

Dirk looked at Lee. Lee looked at Dirk. Dirk faced Ana. "I'm not clear exactly what's going on here."

Ana flicked open his comm unit and looked at it.

"This is the Heart's Desire?"

"Yes," Dirk said.

"You are scheduled to drop within the hour?"

"Well, four or so . . ."

"That's been expedited. You'll drop right now, immediately."

"Immediately?"

"Do you want to lose your customs clearance and stay

here another six months? Get your people moving and get out of here."

"Of course. Immediately, as you say, sir. Uh, Senior Customs Officer, how are you getting back?" Dirk said. "To the station, I mean."

"A customs cutter will pick me up."

"What course would you like?"

"Course? Whatever you want, you morons. Now, somebody show me to my room." Ana stomped into the ship.

"But if they aren't able to intercept our course—"

***

Tapping snagged Dirk's attention. He looked back at the end of the station lock. A man was tapping on the view port. He was nobody Dirk had seen before, but the green and gold colors of his uniform coveralls was that of planetary constabulary.

"On second thought, let's get going. Lee, show our guest to a cabin," Dirk said as he grabbed the duffels and shoved them in her hands. "We'll be dropping right away."

Dirk waited 'til they climbed down the ladder to step into the ship and swung the air lock door closed behind him. He paused and looked at the police behind the door. If he closed the air lock door, they could repressurize inside. He left the ship's outer door open, stepped in, and closed the inner door. He climbed up the short distance to the control room, flopped into a pilot's chair, and flared the screens on. About a minute later, Lee slid in beside him.

"Where are the undocking screens?" Dirk asked.

"Last captain customized them," Lee said. She leaned over and paged him through to the undocking screens. "It will be great to be working with a skilled pilot. You must have done thousands of undockings."

"Not this big—this kind," Dirk said. He dimmed the control lights to see the screens. Old sweat and electronics festered in the room.

"The outer air lock door is still open," Lee said.

"We'll get it later. The magnetic grapple won't disengage."

"It won't engage, either. We don't have one. Last captain sold it. Have to use the chains."

"Where's the chain screen?" Dirk banged his way through displays.

"The remote doesn't work, either. Have to do it manually. You want me to?"

"Go drop the chains, please." Dirk hit the radio. "Engineering, we need power on the thrusters, and bring up the main drive."

After a long pause, Gavin said, "Say, Skipper, Gavin here. This might take me some time. I'm willing to give it the good old college try and all that, but you know, I'm still learning these things. Can you give me a couple of hours to sort things out?"

Dirk punched the intercom button. He released the button and thought about his new engineer. His ID, his manner, his age. He tapped the button on his screen. "That's no problem, Gavin. I'll just hook us back into the dock. There's a squad of station police there who want to talk to us. I don't know what or who they want to talk about. I'll just have a chat with them, shall I?"

"The police?"

"A squad of police. Standing at the air lock."

"What do they want?"

"Shall I ask them?"

"Nope. Thrusters first, then maneuver, Captain?"

"That's the ticket, old chum," Dirk said.

***

Gavin looked at his engineering board. After speaking to Dirk, he had scuttled back to the engineering module. A clank chimed as the lights next to the chains changed from green to red. They were floating free from the station, and all they needed was for Dirk to gently engage the thrusters to pivot the ship, then push them away. Once they were far away, he would engage the main drive, and they would proceed leisurely out-system until they were far enough away to start the jump drive.

Problem was, he had no idea how to do that.

Gavin brought the engineering console up to the main settings. It was overlaid with monitors and gauges for engineering systems. Almost everything was yellow, but nothing was actually red.

"Gavin, anytime now," Dirk said over the speakers.

"Working on it, Skipper," Gavin yelled. He had at least the knowledge to set the comm to external speakers.

"Got to get power up first," Gavin said. He walked over to the second console and set that up to show the fusion plant. He'd actually done this before. He tapped through the correct sequence. A fuel warning flashed, but he dismissed it.

"Captain, you should show an increase in electrical production now," Gavin said.

"Confirm fusion spin up. That's great, old sport, but we need thrusters, please."

Gavin went back to the first board, paged through screens, and found one labeled Startup Sequence. He pushed the Initiate button and felt a gentle hum in the room.

"My main drive just went to standby from off," Dirk said over the speaker.

"There you go, Skipper," Gavin said. "Free trades!"

"Gavin, I can't fire a main drive five meters from a station—we'll fry all sorts of things, and if we don't fry ourselves, the first cutter we meet will shoot us to bits for being dangerous idiots."

"Working on it, Skipper," Gavin said. He paged through a bunch of other settings. Steam blast? Let's try that. He punched the button and heard a whoosh.

"Old sport, while I appreciate your dedication to

hygiene, now is not the time to steam clean the heads. Let's get thrusters up, shall we?" Dirk said.

"Emperor's balls. Who puts a cleaning cycle in the drive menus?" Gavin said. He punched another button, and the hissing steam dissipated. Where was the thruster override? He stabbed at menu page after menu page. Reading each one. There. "Thrusters up now, Skipper," Gavin said and punched the button labeled Thruster Override.

It was only in that last crucial part of a second that Gavin realized that, unlike all the other yellow and green buttons he'd been punching, this one was actually red— bright red. He had a brief thought to wonder what would happen.

A low-pitched hum grew louder and drowned out everything else. A heavy power line above him began to short-circuit. Sparks flew everywhere, and power arced from the line to others surrounding the compartment. A smaller line arced back to the main one, then broke completely off the wall and crackled as it whipped back and forth.

Sparks landed in a bucket of grease, and a low whomp followed over the hum, then flames shot up from the bucket. Smoke filled the engineering compartment, and alarms began to pulse.

Gavin tapped the control sequence to shut down the override, but it wouldn't take his instructions. He tried again, and this time, the screen flickered an Override? Y/N message. After a short pause, the lights blew out in the compartment. Upon a reboot, a fire burned.

Gavin wheezed and coughed, choking on the smoke. He threw himself on the floor and crawled to the forward hatch, where he had left his helmet. He squirmed the entire way and reached to grasp the hatch's handle when a different alarm sounded. The fire suppression system fired off.

The system blasted Gavin backward, away from his

helmet, by a jet of foam. He rolled and whirled out of the way. A sparking wire writhed about and slapped his back, a jolt of electricity stinging him. Painful, but he didn't pass out.

The foam pushed him into a corner, and he crouched there, wheezing and gasping. The foam extinguished the fire little by little, but the toxic atmosphere threatened him. He looked forward. His helmet lay near the forward air lock. The deck was slick with foam, smoke billowed around the compartment, and a single electrical wire flopped just in front of the lock, spitting high voltage electricity.

Gavin closed his mouth and resisted the temptation to take another breath of the acrid air. He looked at his helmet. His vision was starting to tunnel, but he could still see it clearly, five feet away, just below the fire suppression panel.

The live wire just in front of the panel whipped back and forth, sparking each time. It seemed to swing up, then down, then up, on a fairly regular pattern. Gavin watched it for a second. He didn't have any more time. He gathered himself, pushed off from the back bulkhead, then sprinted toward the forward air lock. His feet slipped on the foamy floor, but he managed to keep moving forward and leaped toward his helmet. The live wire slapped him as he went by, the insulated sleeve grazing him, just missing the electric splitting end. He skidded into the forward bulkhead and grabbed his helmet and slid it down over his suit. It locked solidly, and the suit automatically began pumping air from the emergency bottle at his belt.

He sat and gasped the fresh air into his lungs, gathering his thoughts. First, shut off the alarm, next, cut power and turn off the fire suppression, then cycle the air. He crawled up the hatch handle and reached over to tap the Alarm Suppression button. He couldn't see very well, but he had noted the button positions before everything went dark. It didn't give at first. He had to flip up a cover and then push.

Unfortunately, he had misread the buttons. Instead of suppressing the alarm, he vented the compartment.

***

"He doesn't seem like a very experienced engineer, Pilot Dirk," Lee said. "I'm not sure he'll do. Perhaps we need somebody older."

"Lee, we talked about that Pilot Dirk thing. By Zeus, for emperor's sake, or by the shaved head of Zeus, please stop it."

Lee slapped him, hard. "Do not take the name of Paterfather Zeus in vain, less his wrath descends upon us." She looked at her hand in horror. "Oh no."

Dirk looked at her for a moment and lifted his hand to his cheek, rubbing the sting. Then he laughed. "Understood, Medic, no taking Zeus's name in vain. That was rude of me, and I apologize. But you have to stop calling me Pilot Dirk. Just Dirk is fine."

"But—but it's not proper."

"That's how we did it in the scouts. That was the appropriate way."

Lee stared for a moment, then nodded. "If that is the appropriate way, then it is honorable."

"Good, now what were you saying about Gavin?"

"Something is off about him. I'm not sure how thorough his training has been."

A sudden flash of red warning lights lit up the boards. The ship leaped forward, substantial acceleration slamming them into their seats. Then they slowed to a coast.

"Well, I'm not sure how skilled he is, but he's certainly resourceful. He vented engineering, and the plume pushed us away from the station. Another minute at this vector, and we'll be far away enough to bring up maneuvering." Dirk leaned forward and tapped the console. A gong sounded. "Strap in, everybody," he said over the intercom. "Maneuvering in one minute."

Imperial Deserter

CHAPTER 6

"Message coming in from the High Port, Pilot Dirk," Lee said.

"Give me a minute," Dirk said. He fiddled with his board. A noise behind them made them turn around. Gavin had arrived. His suit was smeared with engine room filth, dripping fire suppression foam. Charred material covered his upper leg and part of his back. His helmet was flipped back, and blood flowed from a cut above his eye.

"Engineer Two, are you all right?" Lee asked.

"Good enough, thanks. Skipper, about the thrusters," Gavin said.

"You did a great job, kiddo," Dirk said. "We're on our way."

"I did a great job?" Gavin said.

"Yes, that burp to shoot us away from the station was a great idea. Very resourceful. Glad to see the younger generation hasn't forgot how to think."

"Thank you," Gavin said. He wiped some foam from his face.

"Engineer Two, why are you covered in foam? And were you burned?" Lee asked.

"Just a little malfunction," Gavin said. "A line shorted out. No problem."

"Your face is bleeding. And your eyebrows are burned off," Lee said.

"Nothing—just dropped a wrench," Gavin said.

"On your forehead?" Lee asked.

"Skipper, I . . . uh, I need to shut down the thrusters for a bit while I reboot the computers and check a few things," Gavin said.

"No worries," Dirk said. "We've got the main drive running now. Just a leisurely cruise at one g 'til we're past the jump limit, then a quick jump out of the system. Won't need the thrusters for a while."

"Where are we going, Captain?" Lee asked. "We left in such a hurry that I didn't find out our next port."

"Yeah, Skipper, what's the next port of call?" Gavin said.

"Well, the owners have decided the ship gets some much-needed repairs. So, we're going to Parsifal. It's six parsecs away, but we're jumping two. So, three quick jumps, and we'll be there in less than a month. No shore leave 'til then, I'm afraid. The other two stops will just be a quick in-and-out, just long enough to get fuel and move on."

"Parsifal?" Lee asked. "I've never been there. What's there?"

"Don't know," Dirk said. "But that's where we're going. That's the routing I was given. I have the course here." Dirk took the course chip and put it in the appropriate slot. He could navigate, sort of, but he preferred computer-generated courses.

The boards lit up with a navigation display. All of them examined it. Gavin's eyes opened wide. "Skipper, we don't have the fuel for that."

Dirk looked at him. "You can navigate, Engineer Two?"

"I can read a navigation screen, Skipper. And I can calculate fuel. We have enough for one jump. Just barely."

"Are you sure?" Dirk asked.

"Yes, I saw the warning on the engine screen. We're nearly critical for fuel for even one jump. We're burning through fuel for maneuvering as well. If we burn too much, we might not even make the jump."

Dirk leaned forward and shut off the main drive. The gravity imparted by acceleration disappeared, and the Heart's Desire switched to a ballistic course. He turned to Lee. "Can you confirm that?"

"I'm the medic," Lee said. Dirk said nothing, just raised

an eyebrow. She blinked, then turned to her board. She paged through screens. Dirk watched her over her shoulder and mirrored her choices. Soon, he had an inventory screen up.

"Gods. That's tight. Okay, we have enough to power us for one jump and a little to spare for maneuvering at the far end. Looks like plenty of food and other consumables. You will be glad to know, Engineer Two, that spare parts are a little light but reasonable. So, we should be good for this single jump." Dirk turned toward his screen. "Let me find us a world within a parsec where we can get some supplies."

"Shouldn't we just go back to the station and get more fuel and supplies before we go?" Lee asked.

The console bonged. Lee looked at it. "Captain, that message is for our inspector person."

"I forgot about him. What's it say?"

"It's encrypted. Should I call him?"

"No," Dirk said. "Just wait."

"Wait for what?" a voice said from behind Gavin.

Dirk turned in his seat. "Senior Customs Inspector," he said. "Thank you for joining us. There is an encrypted message for you here. Should I send it to your room?"

Ana glared at Gavin and shoved him aside. "An encrypted message for me? What does it say?"

"How would we know? It's encrypted," Gavin said.

"Shut up, you pup," Ana said. "I know it's encrypted. He just said that." Ana switched to glare at Gavin, then turned to Dirk. "Captain, it's time for me to inspect my equipment. Show me where it's stowed."

Lee looked at Dirk. Gavin looked at Dirk. Dirk looked thoughtful. Ana looked angry. But then, he always did.

"Where is my gear, Captain? I need to see my gear," Ana said.

"Well, you see, Senior Customs Inspector," Dirk said. "In the normal confusion of undocking, sometimes things get missed. And we don't normally load gear through the air lock at the last minute, so this was a kind of non-standard operation. And, well, there, you see, old chap." He smiled at Ana.

"What are you talking about?" Ana asked.

"The captain is saying," Gavin said, "that we didn't . . . well, because it wasn't on the checklists . . ."

"Where is my equipment!" Ana screamed. "Where is it?"

Everybody went silent.

Dirk swallowed. "We left it behind."

Ana went totally pale. "You left it behind."

"In the confusion, we left it in the station air lock," Dirk said.

Ana slumped against the door. "You left all my equipment behind."

"I'm sure it's still there."

"All of it, all the boxes."

"Well, yes, all of them."

Ana slid down the door frame. His breath came in gasps, and he clutched his heart.

"Senior Customs Inspector, are you all right?" Lee asked. She bent toward him.

"Keep your hands off me, freak." Ana snarled. He looked at Dirk. "Two years. Two years in that Empire damned dump, and you left it all behind."

"I'm sure I don't know what you are talking about," Dirk said.

Ana stood and aimed a fist at Dirk's head. Lee slapped his fist with her tiny hand so that it impacted the bulkhead next to the console. Dirk had ducked. Gavin stepped up behind Ana and pushed his arms up behind his back.

Ana struggled for a second but then stopped. "You Imperial turd," Ana said to Dirk.

"No need to be like that, Senior Customs Inspector. We'll figure something out about your cargo."

"It's too late, far too late," Ana said. He suddenly went limp and fell back into Gavin. Gavin struggled to keep him upright but had to release him to keep from falling. Ana reclaimed his arms and looked at Gavin. "That was a nice control hold, but it's vulnerable if your opponent just leans into it. Where did you learn how to do that?"

"Where did you learn how to do what you did?" Gavin said.

Everybody was silent for a moment, then the radio squawked.

"Heart's Desire, Heart's Desire, this is customs control. We have a warrant for the fugitive onboard. Cut your acceleration. Heave to and wait to be boarded by customs personnel."

CHAPTER 7

"Well, the police are chasing somebody here. Which of you is the miscreant, then?" Dirk said. He stretched in his seat to look at Lee beside him at the second console, then turned his gaze on Ana leaning against the door.

Standing behind him, Gavin yelled, "Surrender yourself!"

Everybody's eyes darted from one to the other.

"Might not be us," Gavin said. Every eye turned toward him. "I mean, how do you know it's one of us—could be you that they want, Skipper?"

Every eye shifted back to Dirk.

"I am an honorable gentleman," Dirk said. "That remark does not deserve an answer." He turned to Ana. "Senior Customs Inspector, your behavior is somewhat unusual. This discussion of your packages. Tell me more about them again."

"None of your business," Ana mumbled. He floated along the hatch, trying to slump to the floor.

"Just ask," Lee said.

"What?" Dirk said.

"I'll just call them and confirm who they are looking for," Lee said, "then I'll—I mean we'll—just surrender ourselves. Himself. They can take the miscreant. I like that word. They can take the miscreant."

Dirk looked at Gavin. Gavin shook his head. "Now, no real need to do that," Gavin said. "No need to ask them. It must be the customs inspector here. Not our business. It's customs' business, right, Skipper?"

"Indeed," Dirk said. "I'll just call them up and arrange the transfer. They can take the customs inspector here, and we'll be about the good work."

Ana stirred. He looked up from the floor. "Idiots. You

don't want to mess with the customs. If they come on board, they'll tear this ship apart. First, they'll ID everybody. Full record checks. Retinal Scans, DNA. They won't let anybody go until they know what they are dealing with. Then they'll check for any sort of contraband. You free traders are the scum of the earth. I haven't yet met one of you who isn't as crooked as a tabbo's tusk. Whatever you're hiding on this ship, they'll find."

"What do you mean by ID check?" Lee said.

"If they can't figure out who you are, they'll send you dirtside. There's an Imperial prison right on this planet. Full scanning and record facilities."

Everybody was quiet and looked inward for a moment.

"An Imperial prison?" Lee said.

"In the mountains," Gavin said.

"A total Hades hole," Dirk said. "Out in the middle of a scorching desert. It's hot there. Very hot there. The rocks get hot enough to blister bare feet."

"Nobody escapes from there," Ana said. "Once you go there, you never get out."

A long pause hung in the air. The board pinged again. Another message.

Gavin pulled himself up. "I gotta get something from my room—back in a tick of a tabbo's claw." He stepped over Ana and pulled himself down the hallway. "You figure it out, Skipper, you're the boss," he said over his shoulder.

Ana stood. "I need to see to some of my instruments. My remaining instruments." He dragged himself through the hatch after Gavin and carefully felt his way from handhold to handhold.

Dirk watched them go, then unbuckled himself. "Watch the boards for a minute, Medic Two, and I'll be back in a moment." He spun in the air, braced himself against the console, and pushed down the corridor and toward the habitation level.

Lee stared at the light blinking on the board for a long

moment. "Paterfather Zeus, forgive me," she said and put three fingers to her forehead. She unbuckled, somersaulted over her chair, and dove through the lock and out the hatch on the far side, touching nothing. She caught a grab bar as she dove past the first hab unit and swung inboard. Her momentum carried her up to the ship's lockers. She slid down two handles to the one labeled Arms Locker and slid it open.

***

Dirk stepped out of his stateroom and into the lounge, jamming single rounds into a gun. He had found his revolver right away but finding where he had stashed the ammunition was the problem. Eventually, the frangible rounds he was seeking turned up in the pocket of one of his spare ship coveralls. As he stepped onto the walkway, metal rasped, and something cold touched his neck

"Don't move," Gavin said.

"Gavin, why are you holding a knife at my neck?" Dirk asked.

"The knife is to hold you still while I show you the grenade in my other hand."

"That's not a grenade. That's fake."

"Want me to pop it and see what happens?"

"For the purpose of discussion, then, let's assume it's real. Tell me about the knife. Is it real, too?"

Gavin released the pressure on Dirk's neck and threw the knife across the room. It thudded into the dartboard in the lounge. "That was the first one. I've got another."

"That was a heck of a shot," Dirk said. "Do you ever gamble in bars about that?"

"Made some money that way. Listen, we can't let those customs people catch us."

Ana emerged from his cabin, brandishing a long gun.

"I quite agree. Hello, Senior Customs Inspector," Dirk said.

"Am I interrupting something?" Ana focused on the

knife held at Dirk's throat, then the grenade. "Shouldn't you kiss him first? Not just jump right into the rough stuff? That's a ship fragmentation grenade you have there."

"Is that a machine gun?" Dirk asked.

"Excellent shipboard weapon, grenades. Not a lot of penetration, but that's the point, right? Might not penetrate even a skin suit, but you'll be hurting. And yes, it's technically a submachine gun. Smaller, easier to transport. Doesn't take much skill, either. Just have to know how to pop the top off."

"An Imperial Army machine gun?"

"Yes. Move, and I'll blow your head off."

"And I'll blow your head off if you turn around," Lee said from above, floating in the hatch, her feet hooked around the hatch's handle. She pointed a ship's shotgun down from above.

"Where'd you hide a shotgun?" Gavin asked.

"Ship's locker," Lee said.

Dirk nodded at Ana. "That's a standard Imperial ground forces gun," Dirk said. "Issued to senior non-commissioned officers."

"Four hundred seventeenth division. Donaldson's Devils. Hoorah!" Ana said. "And it's Senior Centurion, not Senior Customs Inspector."

Everyone was quiet for a moment, then they all spoke at once.

"I'd rather not meet those inspectors," Dirk said.

"Keep going. Don't stop for the customs," Ana said.

"There may be a problem with some equipment I sold," Lee said.

"Might be a slight issue with my ID," Gavin said.

Everybody stopped. Dirk looked at Gavin, then Ana. Ana looked at Lee, then Dirk. Lee didn't move her head, but her eyes roamed.

Dirk cleared his throat, and everyone looked toward him. "I'm going to put my gun away." He used two fingers to ease the revolver back into his belt holster. "I have some issues with the Imperials, and I'd rather not stop for a meeting. Gavin?"

"Great idea, Skipper," Gavin said. "There might be some problems with my ID that might complicate things. Let's just ignore that message and move along." He removed his knife from Dirk's neck, then slid it into his arm holster. "Centurion, what do you think?"

Ana brought his gun to port arms, then clicked the safety and slid the gun over his shoulder. "Those customs inspectors are a bunch of thieves and liars. Best not let them on board."

Everybody looked up at Lee. Her eyes switched back and forth, then she pulled the shotgun back. "I had a private business deal that may have gone sour."

"May have?" Dirk asked.

"Well, as soon as they check the contents of their boxes, then yes."

"I see," Dirk said. "So, we're all agreed, we're running away?"

Three heads nodded at him.

Dirk smiled big. "Best crew ever!"

CHAPTER 8

"Tribune, we have a situation in high orbit," the comm tech reported.

"Show me," Devin, Lord Lyon said. He was a very short man with black hair, black eyes, and a dark complexion. Rather than working ship coveralls, he wore a neatly pressed dress uniform. He sat easily at the command console with his hands crossed on his lap, staring at nothing.

A display appeared on the main screen ahead of him.

"Customs are chasing a freighter heading out-system," the comm tech said. "They want our help to intercept. I've got a senior customs official on the line."

Devin frowned. "Why would we help them? We're an Imperial warship, not a customs boat. They can deal with that themselves."

"Yes, sir," the tech said. She turned to her board and spoke into her comm.

Devin looked around his bridge in approval. The Pollux was a crack warship. A full Imperial frigate, with a control room spanning three levels and multiple consoles, spread in a semi-circle around his command couch. The bridge was nearly empty—only communication, helm, environmental, and engineering were manned. Defensive weapons were on auto. There was no need for offensive weapons this far inside the Empire.

The light delay was about six seconds, and the tech was waiting for the incoming message to complete. "Sir, she insists on speaking with the commander. I . . . uh, could say you are asleep and that I'm not willing to wake the captain for such an issue."

A good crew. Imperial ships kept capital time, and this was mid-third shift. Devin would normally be asleep, but he was brooding about the message he had received earlier. The offer to protect him from this trivial task warmed him. But duty was duty.

"Thank you, but no. She'd just insist that you wake somebody else, like the subprefect. I'll take it and put an end to this matter."

A button lit on his console before he said, "This is Tribune Devin, the Lord Lyon, commanding ISS Pollux. What is your concern?" He sat for the twelve seconds of delay, waiting for a response.

"Your arrival is fortuitous, sir. Well, for us, it's not fortuitous for some others. One of our cutters is chasing a ship with a customs violator on board. We need you to turn around and assist in the intercept. Course follows."

The hatch behind him opened, and the subprefect entered.

"Need? Did that ground worm just tell us what to do?" the subprefect said. One of the bridge techs must have warned him that the tribune was in a mood and unobtrusively given information about the situation. A very good crew and well used to working together.

"Indeed, he did. But I shall put an end to that," Devin said. He leaned forward and pressed a button on his screen, ignoring the person. "Customs, this is an Imperial warship, not an inspection scow. We fight enemies of the Empire, and we are not interested in some sordid, local smuggling issue. Customs is a planetary responsibility. We will not be participating in your little out orbit circus, no matter what you say you need. You do your duty, and we will do ours. Cease communications." Devin cut the connection. "Accept no more communications from that source," he ordered the tech. She smiled and typed on her comm. "Understood, sir."

"A bit harsh, sir?" the subprefect said.

"Colonials. They need to be told their place. We are not here for their benefit."

"Why are we here, sir?"

"To kill a friend, Lionel. To kill a friend."

***

"Can they catch us before we jump?" Dirk asked. He was back in the control room, sitting at one of the consoles. Lee was next to him. Gavin had gone to one of the consoles in the second row and was running engineering specs on it.

"No, Pilot. But they can figure out where we're jumping to," Lee said.

"That's stage two. Let's get out of here first," Dirk said.

"Skipper, if we take your route, the next ship behind us will broadcast that we're fleeing customs," Gavin said. "The other system might interdict us."

"Customs is a local thing, not a sector thing."

"Yeah, but some planets cobble together to enforce each other's rules and give advantages to local ships."

"Will they do that?" Dirk said.

"Probably will, especially if there is a lot of trade between them."

"Well, Engineer Two, do you have a better idea?"

"Yeah, Skipper. Let's go somewhere else, load up on fuel. We just need a place with water. We can land, remember? We've got all those streamlining things attached. And if we can get water, we can crack it with the fusion reactor. We've got an emergency cracker."

"We do?" Dirk said.

"Back in engineering. A big one. Big one for this size of ship, anyway."

"Huh," Dirk said. "Okay, now we need a destination with water. Lee?"

Lee had already begun digging. "Here. Within our jump range. Our current fueled range. This one. Doesn't even have a name, just a catalog number: 86-75-309. Water. Mountains. But there's a note about the local weather being extremely hazardous."

"We just want water. We're not going camping," Gavin

said. "Any population?"

"Very limited. Less than a thousand, according to the last survey, which was nearly a hundred years ago. Could be none by now."

"So, we can find a nice isolated place to land without a problem."

"And if we get there and get enough fuel, we don't have to go near your route at all. We can jump directly here," Lee pointed at the star chart, "and bypass all your known routing legs and get where we are supposed to go."

"Close enough for government work," Dirk said. "Won't they notify their customs buddies, regardless?"

"Maybe, but unless it's a hot pursuit, they won't do anything about it," Ana said. He slid up behind everybody and sat at a console.

"Why not?" Dirk asked.

"It's one thing to seize a ship registered to another planet—if you have a communication direct from that planet's government, especially if that request comes from one of their courier boats that just jumped into your system. It's totally another thing if you are operating on second- or third- or fourth-hand information. Who wants to take the risk? Especially since, by treaty, you usually only get a percentage of the haul."

"Percentage of the haul," Lee said. "What do you mean?"

Ana ignored her. Everybody waited, then Gavin cleared his throat. "What do you mean by that?"

"Customs departments work on narrow margins. Selling seized goods is a good source of revenue."

"Credits? Is that why you are such Imperial anuses?" Lee asked.

"Shut up, freak," Ana said.

Gavin glared at Ana. "She's not a freak."

"So, away we go, then," Dirk said.

"Don't go on your vector 'til the last second," Ana said.

"Why? So you can sell us out?" Lee said.

"There's an anti-laser sand caster on this screen. Does it work, freak?" Ana said.

Lee looked quiet for a moment. "I don't know. I didn't know it was there."

"I don't want to meet those customs people any more than you three. I have a plan," Ana said.

**

"Well, is he dead or not?" Devin said. The Pollux was loafing in polar orbit, passing within communication distance of the district prison every ninety-four minutes.

"We believe him to be alive, sir," the prison director said. He was sweating, either because the prison was in the middle of a desert, and it was hot, or more likely because an angry nobleman with nuclear weapons was circling overhead.

"The news media had reported that he had committed suicide. Then they cited a report from your office, saying he was still in custody, authorized by your staff. But now, you say he isn't there."

"He didn't kill himself, sir. That was a false report."

"Why did the media say this?"

"Who knows why those news types say anything, sir?"

The subprefect leaned forward to whisper. "The prison initially confirmed the death, then denied it."

Devin cut the comm for a moment, then put it back on. "What is going on down there, Director? Where is Durriken Friedel? Is he in custody?"

The director swallowed. "He is not."

"Is he dead?"

"He wasn't when he left."

"Left?"

The director mopped his brow. The sweating worsened. "Some of my guards reported that they had found him dead in his cell. He had hung himself."

"And had he?"

"Sir, when additional guards and medics arrived at his

64

cell, they found a person in a guard uniform disabled on the floor, and the prisoner was gone."

"A person in guard uniform? Not an actual guard?"

"No, sir. Someone pretending to be a guard."

"Who?"

The director tried to mop his brow again, but it was a futile effort. He just smeared sweat into his hair. "Tribune, we don't know yet. We can't identify him. The guard—or fake guard, I mean. We're questioning the guard who was supposed to be there. We found her at home drunk. And I have some people in my admin section under lockdown. They confirmed some erroneous reports about the prisoner's death, and their reasons don't stand under scrutiny."

Devin sat back. The director opened his mouth to say something, but a glance from Devin shut him up. Devin thought quietly for a moment. Then he smiled. "Were there any Imperial Marines onsite when this happened?"

"Sir?"

"Check your access logs. See if a party of Marines was in the prison about that time."

The director looked puzzled but muted his comm. He looked off to the side and spoke to somebody else for a few moments. Then he turned back to the screen.

"Tribune, a party of Imperial Marines was here yesterday for unspecified duties. They departed late third shift."

"Of course, they did. Did you count them in and out? You didn't, did you?"

The director looked confused. "Did they have something to do with this?"

"Why don't you ask them."

"Sir, Marines aren't under my authority. Perhaps you could-"

"They are not under my authority, either. And I think, in this case, even if they were, they wouldn't answer. Very well, my liaison will arrive shortly. Give them all your information. Pollux out."

Devin tapped his comm off. "I should have known better." He massaged his forehead with both hands.

"Where is he?" the subprefect asked. "What happened?"

"The Marines got him out. But we'll get nothing from them."

"What about the suicide?"

"One of the families trying to be cute, and it backfired on them. Send somebody down to collect information. Somebody scary. Not you, somebody junior. Let them have fun with it. Threaten beheadings, that type of thing."

"What are you going to do to the director?"

"Nothing. He's an excellent fellow. I checked his record. Hardworking, diligent, loyal to the emperor. His staff will have been suborned. Money probably. If they had tried to stop this, the Marines would have shot their way in and out and then where would we be? We'd have a bunch of dead bureaucrats, killed just for doing their jobs, and we'd have to hang some brave Marines for their loyalty."

"Are you going to call the Marine command?"

"No. When you have people who swear on their lives that they will defend the Empire and kill people that the nobility tells them to kill, you can't get angry with them when one stupid noble tells them to kill the wrong people. It just confuses them."

"What happens next?"

"I wasn't kidding about the director's record. He's smart and hardworking, and with our arrival, very motivated. He'll figure this out and tell our liaison everything. Let him do his job. Just pull his string from time to time. Once we know where Dirk went, we'll know where to go next."

***

"Heart's Desire. Cut your thrust, or you will be fired on," the comm speaker said.

"Can they hit us?" Dirk asked.

"At this distance? Of course, they can," Ana said.

Everybody was in the control room. Dirk at the lower left with the pilot's screens up, Lee at lower right with navigation and the ship's status. Ana was at the upper right with a gunnery screen in front of him. Gavin sat in upper left, with engineering screens up. All of them turned to look at Ana.

"What's the plan, then?" Dirk said.

"Let them get closer so they can get a better shot," Ana said.

"A better shot?" Gavin said. "Why do they need a better shot?"

"Because they are lousy gunners. I've seen them in action. They couldn't hit the proverbial side of a tabbo."

"Tabbos have sides?" Lee asked.

"Shut up, freak, we're working," Ana said.

"Stop telling her to shut up. She's part of this crew," Gavin said.

"We're not a crew, we're just a bunch of people running in the same direction," Ana said. "I should turn you all in for the reward."

Gavin flashed a knife at Ana. "If you try, I'll cut you," he said.

"You can certainly try, punk," Ana said. "I've seen the likes of you off before."

"Nobody is going to cut anybody," Dirk said. "We need to get away from the customs. We all need to get away from the customs. We need an engineer, and this trick of Ana's is to get away." He turned to Ana. "And, Senior Customs Inspector. No, wait, I meant Senior Centurion, would you mind sharing your brilliant idea?"

"Make them think we went somewhere we didn't. How long to the jump limit?" Ana said.

"Ten minutes. Less."

"Can you set up a different jump in that time?"

"Why a different jump?" Dirk asked.

"I can," Lee said. "If you'll take help from a freak."

Ana compressed his lips in a grim line. "Pilot boy, line us up for a jump to Procyon. Set everything up. Charge your jump drives. Let them see it. I'm going to start pumping out some sand. Get ready to jump."

"And we'll just jump out to Procyon with them behind us? So they can call the customs on the far end?" Dirk asked.

"No, you benighted twit," Ana said. "At the last minute, we'll pump out more sand, you'll pivot, change your aspect behind the cloud to point at this 86-75-309 place, and punch the jump button. Can you set that up, freak?"

Lee looked up at the clock and nodded once, typing on her console.

"Won't they see where we really went? I mean, if they stay and scan for it?" Gavin asked.

"Customs work is boring," Ana said. "This chase is the most excitement they've had in a year. The sand will confuse their scans. They'll be too busy planning how they're going to spend their share of the capture bonus to think straight, to check things. They'll jump right behind us, to Procyon, show up there a week later, and wonder where we are. It will be three weeks before they get back here, and by then, we'll be long gone."

"That's actually a great plan," Dirk said. "Well done, Senior Centurion. Gavin?"

"Skipper?"

"Bring the jump drive online. Lee will calculate the jump to 86-75-309." Dirk looked at Lee. She nodded. "I'll set up for the pivot," Dirk said. "Fire when ready, Senior Centurion."

Ana looked at his screen. "Targeting. Stand by. Fire one." The ship shook mildly. "That'll confuse them"

"Nobody move," a voice behind them said. They all turned. A very young woman with pasty blond hair stood there. She had on dirty coveralls with Scruggs on the nametag. She swayed, holding a shotgun in her hands. "This is a hijacking," she said.

The control room went dead silent before Dirk said, "Of course it is."

***

"Good morning, Brigade Commander Santana," Devin said over the comm.

"Tribune. How may I help you?" Santana said. He had neat, black hair, trimmed short. His uniform was pristine, every seam straight.

"I'd like to inquire about some of your men."

"Inquire away."

"What were they doing in the prison a few days ago?"

The brigade commander looked offscreen at somebody. After a muted verbal exchange, he nodded. He returned his attention to the tribune. "It was an internal Marine matter. It was authorized."

"I see. Please give me details."

"No."

"No?" Devin raised his eyebrows.

"No."

"You can't just say 'no' to an Imperial tribune," Devin said.

"I can, and I just did."

"Do you serve the emperor?"

"Absolutely. I do not, however, serve the Navy."

"It's the same thing."

"Not to the Marines," the brigade commander said.

"I'm a tribune."

"And I'm a Marine. I don't work for you."

Devin laughed. "You got a pair of Imperial gonads, don't you? You know I could have you shot?"

"I've made twenty-two combat drops. I was at St. Darts. Nothing, nothing you can say will scare me in the least."

Devin smiled. "You broke a convicted deserter out of

an Imperial prison, and you are harboring him right now."

"I did nothing of the sort."

"How did you get him off-planet?"

"On my honor as a Marine, I have never, ever, helped any fugitive escape off-planet."

"Is he on your base right now?"

"Tribune, you're just wasting your time."

Devin rocked back in his chair. He smiled at his comm. "Well, you have to admit, it was worth a try. Some folks would have caved in."

"Some folks, not some Marines," the brigade commander admitted. But he was smiling now, too.

"I want to speak to your commander," Devin said.

"She's about six, eight jumps away by now, with a task force. You could always go to the sector capital. I'm sure there is somebody there who ranks me."

"That's even farther," Devin said. He shook his head. "Well, thank you for your time."

"Will you be in-system long, Tribune?"

"Until I get this mess sorted out, yes."

"We have a dining in two days. I would be honored if you could attend."

"Even though I threatened to have you killed."

"No offense taken. This is a pretty boring planet. We need the excitement."

***

Scruggs waved the gun toward the group. "This is a hijacking. Take me to Procyon."

Dirk twisted to look back at her. His eyes flickered to her face, then to her shotgun, then back to her face. He smiled. "Not right now, pretty girl. We have things to do. Gavin, how is the jump drive?"

Gavin leaned sideways and focused on the gun, then sat up and smiled. "Coming up, Skipper. Two minutes, and it will be ready for a jump."

"Lee?" Dirk asked.

Lee eyed the gun herself, then switched her attention back to Dirk. "Jump course laid in, Pilot Dirk. I took the liberty of putting vector adjustments on your screen. Click the icon, and the ship will pivot, then the jump drive will fire," Lee said.

"I said this is a hijacking. Take me to Procyon," Scruggs said.

"You're that girl that was with Singh. The box carrier," Lee said. "What are you doing here?"

"Never you mind," Scruggs said. She brandished the shotgun again. "Take me to Procyon."

"Sorry, pretty girl, not today. We're going somewhere else," Dirk said. "We're a bit pressed for time, so if you can just relax for a while, we'll deal with you shortly. Lee, you don't think I could maneuver the ship fast enough to keep this course?"

"It's just an automated sequence, Pilot. Use it or not. But it's all laid out in advance for you," Lee said. She glanced at Scruggs. "How did you get on board? Where have you been hiding?"

"I just waited in the corridor, then I squeezed into one of those rooms and hid behind one of those piles of stolen medical supplies," Scruggs said.

Ana, Dirk, and Gavin turned to look at Lee. She ducked her head, shrugged, then focused back on her screen. Her neck, visible above her skin suit, turned a bright red.

"Very industrious, young lady," Dirk said. "I approve. Ana, clock's running." Something flashed on one of the display screens. "And that's a warning shot."

"A wide warning shot," Ana said. "I've been dumping sand behind us. I've only got three more canisters. Jump soon."

"Why is nobody paying any attention to me? I've got a gun," Scruggs said.

Ana reached over and snapped his right hand on the barrel of the shotgun, reached behind and grasped the stock with his left, and spun the gun forward overhand, breaking it free from Scruggs's grip. He spun it backward and into his own arms and pointed it directly between Scruggs's eyes.

"And it's a very nice gun, too. Boarding shotgun. Well maintained. Somebody's been polishing it, cleaning it regularly. But not you, girl, I don't think," he said. "You don't have much experience with guns, do you?"

Scruggs's eyes were huge. She looked at the barrel pointed between her eyes and shook her head.

"I didn't think so," Ana said. He swung the shotgun back into his hand and pushed it toward her. "Put that back in the ship's locker, in the rack. Make sure you do it correctly. I'll check later. Good weapons should be respected. Respect them, and they will be there for you when you need them." He used his free hand to place Scruggs's left, then right hand on the shotgun, then turned back to his board and slapped a key. "Firing third last sand. There. Ready when you are, Pilot."

"I don't understand why you aren't listening to me. I've got a gun," Scruggs said. She looked around the cabin with wide eyes.

Gavin smiled at her. "It's unloaded, baby girl. That model shows a color band right near the stock when there is a round chambered, so you can tell what type, frangible, solid slug, or whatever. No color means it's empty." Gavin turned back to his screen.

"And you also have the safety on," Lee said. "It's that lever on the side."

Scruggs blinked. "I didn't check that."

"Is this your first hijacking?" Gavin asked.

"Yes."

"Well, don't worry, you'll do better next time," Gavin said. "Jump drive coming online, Skipper."

"A question, young lady," Dirk said. He tapped his screen and frowned. "Is it that you want to go to Procyon specifically, or is it that you just want to get away from

Bishop's world?"

"I don't want to go back to Bishop's world," Scruggs said.

"Good 'cause neither do we," Dirk said. "So, settle down and enjoy the ride."

"Have you ever jumped?" Gavin asked Scruggs.

"Lots."

"What type of ship? A big liner? Where they do it while you're asleep?"

"Yes."

"Better go sit down," Gavin said. "Your first one awake is sometimes rough. It's fun, though. The first time."

Scruggs stared at him for a moment, then smiled. "I'll go buckle up." Her smile got wider. "Adventure awaits." She went back down the corridor.

"That's the spirit," Ana called after her. "Never as good as your first time." He watched her go. "I remember those days. Everything was fresh and exciting, and the galaxy offered endless possibilities. Action. Adventure. Botched hijackings."

The other three crew members turned to look at Ana. "What?" he said. "I was young once, too. Firing second last sand."

A thump rattled the ship.

"Everybody hear that?" They all nodded. "Know what it was?" Ana asked. Everybody shook their head. "The sound of doors closing. Options receding. Time running out. Our personal universes heading to heat death." Ana tapped his screen. "Life running through our hands like sand."

"Thanks for cheering us up, Centurion. Coming up on our jump," Dirk said. "Status everybody. Lee?"

"Course laid in still looks good, Pilot," she said. She gestured to a countdown clock. "At one, we'll spin, and at zero, jump to 86-79-305."

"Ana?" Dirk said.

"I just slaved my last salvo to the freak's clock. It'll fire at two seconds and obscure our pivot."

"Gavin?"

"Drive is online and in the green. Ready as ever."

Dirk watched the clock count down. At two seconds, a slight jar of the sand fired. Then the ship's pivot spun them against their harnesses.

"Jumping," Dirk said.

CHAPTER 9

"First job," Dirk said, "We get the sulfur and the humidity out of the air." He had called a crew meeting while they were in jump space.

Scruggs was leaning against the wall, eating a ration bar, and the rest of them were sitting, eating food trays and drinking basic, the vitamin and sugar enriched water that every poor trading ship served.

"Can do, Skipper," Gavin said. "I need to adjust the cryo system and speed up the blowers. Run it through a couple times, and I can freeze the water out. Sulfur, too. But how much extra power can I use? We'll need to maneuver when we come out the far side. How much fuel do we need for that?"

"Not much," Dirk said. "That system isn't very crowded. Lee's course should drop us right above that planet. 86-75-309. You can have two percent. Will that be enough?"

"Plenty, Skipper, but it will take a couple, three days to get it all out of the air. By the way, these food trays are disgusting."

Lee looked up from her tray. "What's wrong with them?"

"They taste like anus. Couldn't you have got anything better?" Gavin said.

"Engineer sold all the other ones before he left. He left these ones for me to eat. Nobody would buy them, either."

"What are they?"

"Some vegetable mush. 'Red,' 'green,' 'blue,' they're called. Apple, asparagus, and algae. All As."

"A must be for anus," Dirk said. "Don't they bother you?"

"I can't really tell the different trays apart," Lee said.

"This one tastes of salt, and I like some of the vinegar-tasting ones, but all the rest are kind of bland."

"Why does the water taste so funny?" Scruggs said. She was drinking a plastic glass of basic.

"It's not water," Dirk said. "It's called basic. It has sugar, vitamins, some meds, micro-nutrients. It's good for you. Quite a few calories—you can live on it. For a short period of time."

"And it's cheap," Lee said. "It comes in a powder, and the ship owners just mix it with the water, rather than giving you real food."

"And," Dirk said, "best of all, it's what we've got right now. Drink up."

He held up his glass in a toast, and everybody clinked glasses and took a long drink.

"Skipper," Gavin said. "How long is the jump?"

"Seven days?" Dirk guessed. He looked at Lee.

"One hundred fifty hours," she said.

"Six days. Plenty of time to fix the air."

"Double check your numbers so you don't strand us without fuel," Ana said.

Gavin flashed Ana a big smile. "I'm on this ship, too, old man. I want to get where we're going. I'll watch the fuel."

"Good," Dirk said. "The rest of you, we need somebody on watch to monitor life support and engineering for alarms. I've reset the ship clocks. I'll take the first half a shift. Four standard hours, then I assume, Gavin and Lee, you can both watch a board?"

They both nodded.

"Good, then we'll do four hours on, eight off."

"I can watch a board," Ana said. "I might be a little rusty, but I've done it years ago. Let me sit with you, Navy." Ana pointed to Dirk, "for the first shift to bring me up to speed, and I'll take my turn in the rotation. And we need to get this ship cleaned up. It's a mess. We should all do a shift of cleaning. The freak here," he gestured to

Lee, "probably can't smell much, but I can. The heads need to be cleaned, the gym equipment stinks, and I can't taste the tray over the smell of burned food from that microwave. There must be at least a basic hydroponics closet somewhere. We fix that up, and we'll have better air and possibly some real food. Tomatoes, at least. I've never been on a ship that didn't have at least tomatoes to clean the air."

The rest of the crew had stopped eating and stared at him.

"What?" Ana said, looking around.

Gavin said, "That's just such a, such a—"

"Such a reasonable attitude for you to take," Lee said. "Offering to help out."

"Don't think we're going to some Imperial finishing school together," Ana said. "I don't like any of you. But I also don't like the look of this ship. And I'm not happy with our course, either. But the last thing I need is a tired pilot pushing the wrong button or a tired engineer throwing the wrong breaker, and if something breaks and shorts out, and I get a broken arm, I want my med tech to be well rested, too. So, I'll do my bit to make sure you get enough rest. And I've been sick when water plants get contaminated with dirt, and I didn't enjoy it. It's in my own best self-interest."

"Our apologies, my good man," Dirk said. "We thought for a moment you had morphed into a decent human being."

"Don't give me any attitude, Navy. Or you'll be sorry," Ana said.

"Why do you keep calling him navy?" Gavin asked.

"He's some sort of navy officer. Or was. He had a Navy-issued sidearm. He just switched the ship's clocks to Imperial time and set standard watches, all standard navy protocol. He didn't learn his trade in the merchant service. I'll bet the emperor's testicles on that." Ana took another bite of the basic tray in front of him, then looked Dirk square in the eye. "And most of all, he smirks like a navy officer."

Every eye swung to Dirk, and he gave a broad smile.

"There it is, see, the navy smirk," Ana said.

"You said you served in the scouts," Lee said.

"I, um, was seconded to them from my original assignment," Dirk said. "Very hush-hush stuff."

"Or sent there as a punishment," Ana said. "Navy officers who screwed up but were too well connected to be cashiered get sent out as 'liaison' officers. Send them somewhere crappy and far away to keep them out of their superiors' hair. I've seen a few of those, let me tell you. Knowing how cute this one is, he probably slept with some captain's wife, and got sent out to the back of beyond."

There was a long silence. Ana took another bite. Everybody looked at Dirk.

"It was an admiral's wife," Dirk said. "She was quite . . . demanding. We weren't as discrete as we should have been." He dropped the smile. "Will that be a problem, Senior Centurion?"

"You're a senior centurion?" Lee said.

"Yes, freak, you heard that before. Did you forget it?" Ana said.

"Why are you so mean to her?" Gavin asked. "You've only just met her."

"This isn't mean. Sometime, I'll show you mean. But Jovians are freaks. I don't like freaks," Ana said.

"Because they are different? You don't like different?" Gavin asked.

"Different is good," Ana said. "And she's the perfect spacer. Genetically engineered to have better balance, move better in zero gs, and she can handle more acceleration than we can. Breathe worse air and function better in spaceship atmosphere for longer. I don't hate her for any of that. I hate her because she's a Praetorian." Ana pointed at the locket around Lee's neck. "One of the emperor's personal freaks."

Scruggs's eyes widened. "You're a Praetorian? Really? One of the emperor's personal guards?"

"One of the emperor's assassins, more like," Ana said.

"Assassins?" Scruggs said. "The Praetorians are the bravest, most loyal troops the Empire has."

"No, the most cold-hearted killers in the Imperial forces. The emperor's personal death squads. Whenever the emperor wants to massacre his opponents, he sends in his trusty Praetorians. They don't take prisoners. Kill everyone, military, civilians, men, women, children, pets. Burn the planet down. When the Praetorians come in, they kill everybody."

"That's not true," Scruggs said. She looked around. "Is it?"

Gavin looked at Lee. "You hear rumors. Rebellious worlds that are attacked, then interdicted, nobody on or off-planet. Rumors that everybody was killed. The last unit there was a Praetorian guard unit."

"But you don't kill civilians, do you?" Scruggs asked.

Lee looked around. "My family served on an Imperial transport as crew. We shuttled members of the extended Imperial family around."

"Which kind of begs the question," Ana said. "What's a Praetorian freak doing out here all by herself, without her unit? Especially a purebred Jovian one."

"I serve the emperor," Lee said.

"How?"

"You don't need to know."

"For now," Dirk interrupted, "She's our medic and navigator, and let's leave it at that. I believe we decided that everybody's past is past."

Scruggs smiled at Lee. "I tried to join the Marines, but I really hoped that I'd get to become a Praetorian. Are there any non-Jovian Praetorians?"

"Some," Lee admitted. "But you have to swear direct fealty, and you usually have to become a Jovian Acolyte."

"And that's another thing I don't like," Ana said. "Their kooky religion. I'll give them this, though, they're good navigators, and they make good medics, too. But they're the emperor's private killers first and foremost. In a crisis, they're not on your side."

"And should we rely on you in a crisis, Senior Centurion?" Dirk asked.

"I've already done my bit. I know my way around heavy weapons, and I volunteered my help, what I can do on a spaceship." He shrugged. "I'm a ground pounder, and I know it."

"Imperial Army—no. No, not quite right," Dirk said. "A colony army. A big one, though."

"Decata. Twenty-five years. Retired as senior centurion," Ana said.

"Well, if you can't get into the Navy, Marines, Scouts, or anything worth joining, you can always join an army. No wonder you're angry," Gavin said.

"I'll show you angry, punk," Ana said. "There's a gym here. We can go a few rounds anytime you want. Only it will be a few, because I'll have your arms broken and you screaming on the floor in no time."

"I'll have to insist you don't do that," Dirk said. "We need a functioning engineer, not a casualty in the med bay."

"Who put you in charge, Navy?" Ana said.

"He's the pilot,' Lee said.

"He's the Skipper," Gavin said.

"I appointed myself as the most qualified," Dirk said. "Would you like to discuss the appointment, Senior Centurion?"

Ana stared at him for a moment, then shook his head. "Not now. You can drive a ship. I can see that. And that's what we need for now. For now." Ana looked around and scowled. "I'll take this kid here, get her started on cleaning things. We'll do the heads first, and then I'll come sit with you, Navy." Ana stood. "Come with me, kid," he said.

"Or what?" Scruggs said.

"Or I take your worthless butt and toss it out an air lock. You're a stowaway. You've got no rights here."

Scruggs's eyes widened. She looked around the group. "Can he do that?"

"Do you have any skills that are ship-related?" Dirk asked.

"No," Scruggs said.

"It's only fair that you do your share," Dirk said. "And if you can't do anything else, cleaning counts. Go with the centurion here. He'll show you what to do."

"Let's go, kid," Ana said and walked down the corridor.

***

Ten minutes later, Scruggs was staring at the primary head, holding a stiff brush and some cleaning solution.

"You're on shift twelve hours now," Ana said. "First shift and half of second. Every morning, you'll wash the primary and secondary head, the lounge, and then the gym. Then lunch, and in the afternoon, you'll clean every stateroom and all the common areas. Then, for the last four hours, we'll rotate cleaning the med bay, the control room and engineering, and all of the working compartments. That will depend on what's going on. Don't get in the pilot or the engineer's way."

"Every day?" Scruggs said.

"Yes, every day," Ana said.

Scruggs stood and looked at Ana. "I won't do it."

"You won't?" Ana said. "Really?"

"No," Scruggs said. "It's demeaning, and I don't take orders from you. You're not my father."

"Thank the emperor for that," Ana said. "I'd be so embarrassed that a wimpy, whiny, little brat like you was related to me. How old are you, anyway?"

"Nearly twenty-two. Eighteen standard."

"Eighteen standard. As of when?"

"Yesterday."

"You hijacked a ship on your eighteenth birthday?"

"Yes."

"Probably a story there, but I don't care to hear it. You tried to join the Imperial Marines?"

"Yes."

"Why didn't they let you?"

"Too young, they said."

"Well, time will fix that problem. Finish cleaning."

"I won't. And I don't think you'll throw me out of an air lock."

Ana laughed. "You got me there, kid. I won't be doing that."

Scruggs stuck her tongue out again and pushed past him. Fast as lightning, Ana grabbed her by the throat and lifted her. Scruggs was tall for a girl, almost Ana's height, but he hefted her with little effort with one arm and slammed her against the wall. Blue spread across her face, and her arms scrabbled at his fist. Her feet kicked, but Ana just pushed up closer where her flailing legs couldn't touch him.

"Thing is, you're right," he said. "I won't space you, not at first. Spacing is a lot of work, and it annoys some people. In my opinion, you're just a useless brat, a waste of food, air, and resources. Just a mild irritant, really, but I don't like being irritated. So, this is your last warning. Clean this place up. If you don't clean it up, I'll take some tools out of the tool locker and beat you with them. On the back, on the leg. Handles work well. They hurt a lot, and they bruise you really badly. You'll be in pain for days. But they don't break anything. You'll still be able to work. It will just hurt. Really hurt."

Ana dropped her.

Gasping, she looked at him, her neck already bruising.

"Now, after a few days of that, if you still don't work, then I'll throw you out. But I'm a fair man. I'll give you a chance first. Even though I kind of like spacing people. Why, I remember my old century." Ana smiled. "One morning, at formation, I beat three recruits bloody with the flat side of a jack tightener. Then myself and the senior decurion manhandled one particularly useless recruit into the lock. He crapped himself on the way there. I had to clean up before I had breakfast. It was pancakes." He smiled. "The best pancakes I ever had. I like pancakes."

Scruggs lay on the floor and wheezed. She grasped the head to pull herself up but didn't take her eyes off of Ana.

"Now, I'm going to see the pilot. When I come back, which will be very soon, this head better be pristine, and you better have started on the next one. Understand?"

Scruggs nodded. "Yes."

"Yes, what?" Ana said.

"Yes, Senior Centurion," Scruggs said.

"Oh, I'm not in the army anymore," Ana said. "'Yes, sir' is fine. No need to call me senior centurion." He smiled. "Unless you want to." He turned around and walked back to the control room bridge, whistling. Scruggs turned to the wall and scrubbed the fixtures.

CHAPTER 10

"Please don't let him space her. She's just a kid," Lee said, finishing her meal at the lounge table.

"He won't," Dirk said, tossing an empty tray into the recycler. "He's too smart to do that. He knows that, if he throws her out, he'll be right behind her. He can't fight all three of us. He has to sleep sometime."

"Besides," Gavin said. "This Scruggs kid is young and afraid. Senior Centurions have dealt with that for centuries. He'll scare her to death, tough her up a bit, get her working, teach her not to touch things she shouldn't touch, and have her so tired that she won't have time to be afraid."

"And we'll get a clean ship out of it," Dirk said. "He's right about the heads and the air and the water. Contaminated water is no joke."

"For sure, Skipper," Gavin said. "What are we going to do about the centurion?"

"Do?" Dirk said.

"He's obviously the one the customs people were after."

"I think he's the one the customs people are after," Dirk said. "But they don't have jurisdiction outside of their system, and by the time we fuel up and jump again, we'll be four parsecs away, and he can get off the ship and do whatever he wants. It's not our issue."

"Maybe there is a reward for him," Lee said.

"Could be," Dirk said. "Should I just dock at the next Imperial base I see and ask about the reward?"

Everyone at the table was silent.

"Thought so," Dirk said. He turned to Lee. "What should I know about this ship that I don't know?"

"What do you mean?" Lee asked. "I'm just the medic. I don't know anything."

"Well, what work was pending? I was told it had been docked for only three days. My contract was to take it to Parsifal for its annual maintenance. What sort of maintenance?"

"Three days," Lee laughed. "We'd been attached to that Empire-damned station for about six months. We had a maneuver drive failure when we first came in-system and had to be towed in. That was the third time it had failed. The captain walked off when we arrived—said it was just a rusty coffin. The engineer arranged for the maneuver drive to get fixed, but he had to trade all the cargo for it. We got a shiny, new maneuver drive, a big docking and towing bill, and no money to pay it. The owners stopped paying for anything, and we were stuck."

"How did you live?" Gavin asked.

"The engineer sold all the food and engineering supplies that he could, but eventually, got a berth on another freighter. He took his apprentice—not really an apprentice but his nephew—or second cousin or something with him. Another cousin was the cook. The three of them kept things up pretty well when they were here, but after they left, it was just me. I just stayed in my room. I can't fix anything, and I didn't know what else to do. I had food and power. Well, most of the time."

"What do you mean, most of the time?" Dirk said.

"Oh, the power plant shuts down about once a week or two. It seems dependent on the power draw. That's why I kept the lights down and most of the systems shut off. The last engineer showed me some screens to monitor. When it fails, you just have to reset the power plant, shut it down, and restart it."

"Shut down and restart the power plant? The power plant that provides all our air? That power plant?" Dirk asked.

"It only takes about two hours to go through the

sequence. There's plenty of air in the ship to last two hours," Lee said.

"You're Jovian," Dirk said. "You breathe thirty percent less oxygen than we do, and there is only one of you. We need, collectively," Dirk paused to calculate, "eight times the air that you do. We won't survive two hours without air, not all of us."

"Are there spare skin suits?" Gavin asked. "And spare O cylinders?"

"No spare suits," Lee said. "Every spacer has their own. Why would we need spare suits?"

"I don't think the centurion has a spare suit," Gavin said.

"No great loss," Lee said.

"And I'm sure that kid, Scruggs, doesn't have one, either."

"Ohhh," Lee said.

Dirk rubbed his chin. He'd need to shave soon. "Lee, go to engineering with Gavin. Show him those screens that the other engineer told you about. Gavin, find out what's going on with our power and report back. We're committed on this jump now, but I'd rather come out the other side alive."

"Will do, Skipper," Gavin said as he stood. "Let's go, Lee."

Dirk drained his cup. "I'll go watch the board."

***

Dirk paged through the controls on his board, arranging them to his liking. This model was unfamiliar to him, but it was similar to some he'd trained on. Ana slid into the control room behind him and sat at his own console.

"Show me what you want me to monitor, and I'll put it on my screen here," Ana said.

Dirk mirrored Ana's console to his and pointed out different settings to monitor. "Start with oxygen percentage. That's the most important. How's our stowaway?"

"She balked a bit, so I had to strangle her. She should be terrified now. I'll go back in a while, make sure that she keeps cleaning."

"Strangled?"

"It's the most effective way to hurt somebody that doesn't impair their ability to work. And it scares them. What's this red-rimmed alert here?"

"That's carbon monoxide. Should be very, very low. Do you like scaring little girls half your size, Senior Centurion?"

Ana laughed. "Do you remember your first drill sergeant, Navy?"

"I do. Sergeant Rotterdam. I was terrified of him."

"Do you remember him offering to fight any two of you? And beating whatever two idiots offered to fight him?"

"Yes. They were in the infirmary for a week afterward."

"That's because, when you are fighting two people at once, you have to take the first one down hard right away—no time to pull punches. That demonstration always puts at least one of the students in the hospital, usually both. No time to be gentle. But it serves to show the hundred or so new recruits that you are not to be messed with. I don't have that option right now. There's just one of her, so I have nobody else to make an example of. But with just one person, I can be more judicious in my use of violence. What's this yellow one here? Carbon dioxide? That's not as important, right?"

"Carbon dioxide isn't really a problem. You can ignore it unless it flashes red. Strangling her was judicious?"

"She isn't in a hospital. She can work. And now, she's scared to death of me. She believes I'll space her. I'm the bad guy. Anything I tell her to do, she'll jump to it. But she'll glom on to you as the good guy. Anything you want, she'll jump around to help you out. We'll get her coming and going. Give me two months, and she'll be your best crewmember. Drill Sergeant 101."

"Don't space her, whatever happens," Dirk said.

"I'll make my own decision on that."

"No, you won't. I'm in charge of this ship. I make the rules."

Ana twitched a thin-lipped smile. "Are you saying you're in command, then?"

"Not quite. We're not the military, but I'm the pilot. I decide where we go."

"Who gave you the authority?"

Dirk swung his console screen to Ana. "Feel free to input the commands that send this ship somewhere." He pointed at the screen.

"I don't know how to do that," Ana said.

"Right, and I do. So, I decide where we go, which makes me in charge. It's what the lawyers call de facto rather than de jure."

"What if I decide to exert a little de facto persuasion to make you go somewhere particular?"

Dirk tightened his own thin-lipped smile. "You think you can take me, Senior Centurion?" He held his arms near his side. He had no visible weapon, but if he had one hidden, his hands were in reach.

Ana leaned back. His arms shifted in his harness, but his eyes stayed focused on Dirk's. "Yes."

Ventilation fans whirred. Ana leaned forward and turned to his board. "But there is no point to that right now. We need a pilot. When can I get off this ship?"

"You can get off at the next planet if you want, but it's not on any space lanes. No population. Some sort of environmental flag in the database."

"So, I'm staying on for that, then."

"Next one after that might do you, but again, off the space lanes."

"When is the next real port?" Ana asked.

"Parsifal. Four jumps."

"Right, 'til then, I'll go about my business, do my share of the chores, help out with this stowaway, watch a board. I'll be model crew. Truce. Agreed?"

Dirk nodded. "I'll treat you as I treat the rest of the crew."

"Please don't," Ana said. "We're not friends. We're just trying to keep the same ship in one piece 'til we get somewhere that we can both get off."

"Fine. I'll treat you like the scheming opportunist you really are."

"And one other thing, Navy," Ana said.

"Yes?" Dirk said.

"I sleep with a detonator next to my bed. It's linked to a grenade somewhere in the ship. Somewhere you won't find. Somewhere important. That way, I can sleep soundly at night."

"No worries here," Dirk said. "I like people to have a good visit to the arms of Morpheus every night. First class service on this passenger line, I say."

The main lights flickered, then went out. The whirring fans stopped. The consoles darkened, illuminating the emergency lights.

"What level of service is this, then?" Ana asked.

***

"We've never been formally introduced," Gavin said. "I'm Gavin Crewjacki, Engineer Two. Call me Gavin."

He and Lee moved into the engineering space, the burning plastic's smoke floating throughout, water condensing on the bulkheads.

"Medic Two, Lee Michaelson. Please call me Lee, Engineer Two."

Gavin raised his eyes. Lee looked abashed. "Sorry, Jovians are used to formality. Please call me Lee, Gavin."

"You are a formal people. I understand. But we'll be crewmates, so we're kind of like extended family, aren't we?"

"I suppose. Let me look at that cut on your head. And are those burn marks?"

"Yes, sort of. Look, we need to get on this fusion plant thing."

"Medical issues take priority over routine, expedited, and critical maintenance. Only emergency procedures have a higher priority. That's in the ship's manual."

"The ship has a manual?"

"Well, I follow the Jovian standard guide to space operations. Most Jovians do. Let me go get my kit." Lee swept off to her cabin.

Gavin sat at the engineering console and brought up the fusion plant status. Lee arrived with a medical kit and examined him.

"Take off your shirt," she said. "I need to fix up all of these."

Gavin partially disrobed while she fussed over him. She put cream on his burns, swabbed his cuts, and ran a portable scanner over his arms and legs.

"No broken bones, but I'll have to staple this one shut, or it will never heal. Let me give you a topical anesthetic and then I'll work on it. Just take a minute.

"Thank you, Lee," Gavin said. "You're taking great care of me."

Lee leaned over Gavin. Like most Jovians, she wore a curve-hugging skin suit and eschewed coveralls for tool belts and packs. She had to lean over Gavin and brace herself on his shoulder while stapling his cuts.

Gavin smiled at her, and Lee returned the smile. She leaned just a little extra into Gavin for a better brace.

She's really warm. And up close, she smells good, like flowers. She must use special perfume, Gavin thought.

"So, Lee," Gavin said. He coughed. "So, where's home for you?"

"You wouldn't like it," Lee said. "I left there a long time ago. I don't keep in contact."

"That's too bad," Gavin said. Lee stretched more,

causing him to cough again. "Do you—"

The lights went out.

"Emperor's anus," Gavin said.

"That's what happened before," Lee said. "All the lights went out, and the consoles went out, environmental shut down. Two hours 'til we're out of oxygen."

***

After the lights went out, Dirk unbelted from his chair. There was no gravity, so he flipped backward and up, grasped the hatch, and pulled himself hand over hand down the central corridor toward engineering. Ana followed him at a sedate pace.

Scruggs stuck her head out of the secondary head. "What's going on?"

"Nobody told you to stop cleaning," Ana said as he muscled by. "Keep it up. If you need to know, we'll tell you." Scruggs's head snapped back into the head. "Say, Navy, how good is this engineer? You vouch for him?"

"I only met him for the first time a few hours ago. He was assigned to the ship by the owners."

"Only just met you, and already, he pulled a knife on you."

"I could say the same about you, Senior Centurion," Dirk said.

"Fair enough. But he seems a bit young, not too experienced."

"That's the truth," Dirk said. "He may not be the engineer we want, but he's the engineer we've got."

Dirk arrived at the engineering section, swung the hatch to the air lock open, then stepped through. He banged on the inner hatch, and a moment later, it swung open. Lee and Gavin were arguing over a console.

"Status?" Dirk said.

Gavin ignored him for a moment. "Are you sure we have to put everything in shutdown?" Gavin said to Lee.

"That's what the previous engineer said. Shut down

power, life support, computers, the works. Then restart everything. Life support comes back up in the middle."

Gavin turned to Dirk. "Skipper, I want to just try a manual restart of just the power plant, but Lee says that she always did a full system reboot."

"What's the difference?"

"Time. A manual restart takes an hour. A full software reboot takes two."

"Why are there not any emergency systems online? Emergency heat?"

Gavin looked at Lee. She shrugged.

He turned to Dirk. "I have no idea, either, Skipper."

"So, why not take the shortcut?"

"If it doesn't work, and we have to do both, then we're going three hours without air. That's close to the limit on our suits, even if we scavenge some air from the ship."

"What about our jump?" Ana asked.

Dirk waved him off. "Jump drive is self-sustaining. As long as it gets fuel, it will compress space in front of us, and we'll keep moving." He looked at Gavin and Lee. "Do either of you know why it failed?"

Lee and Gavin shook their heads.

"The last engineer didn't know, either, or at least he didn't tell me why," Lee said.

"So, you might go through this restart and then have the problem happen again?" Ana asked.

"You want to jump in here, old man?" Gavin asked. "Think you can fix it."

"Nope," Ana said. "I was just asking a question. Unlike some, I know my limitations, and engineering isn't my skill set. I'll let the professionals do their jobs." Ana smiled. "But if we start running out of air, I'll shoot you first."

"No shooting," Dirk said. "What about the kid? Will she have enough air?"

"If we do the short start, yes."

"You know," Ana said, "to increase our flexibility, we could just—"

"No," Dirk said. "Don't say 'just.' Nobody dies by accident in my crew."

"Your crew? Are we your crew now?" Ana asked.

"Yes," Dirk said.

"I don't want to be your crew," Ana said.

"It doesn't matter what you want. It's about how I feel. I'm the pilot, this is my ship, and nobody is going to die. Gavin, start the short restart. Now. Lee, help him if you can. Ana, go back to your room and call cadence or something. I'm going back to talk to the kid."

"I'll come with you," Ana said, following Dirk out of the engineering section.

Dirk pulled forward along the grab rings but stopped and turned to Ana. "Do you have a suit?"

Ana pulled up his coverall leg to expose the skin suit's cuff.

Dirk recognized the material. "Combat armor?"

"Lightweight and versatile. Ballistic cloth, anti-laser coating, functions as a skin suit with helmet and gloves, which are in my quarters. And thanks for asking about me. I notice neither of those two back there thought to ask."

"They probably wanted you dead," Dirk said. "That's a very expensive model you are wearing there."

"Feel free to pry it off my dead body," Ana said. "But you won't be able to do that because, if you ever become a threat to me personally, I'll be the one shooting first."

"I'm not a threat to you?" Dirk asked.

Ana laughed. "I'm not worried about you at all."

"I'm not dangerous?"

"You are the most dangerous person on this ship. After me, of course, but you're not dangerous to me."

"And why is that?"

"Because you are not stupid, Navy. Mission oriented, yes. I'm not in the way of your mission, and I might even help, so you'll ignore me until you either need me to help or need me dead. And I might be able to help, so you'll put up with as much annoying badinage as I can provide."

"Badinage. You're a puzzle, Senior Centurion."

"I contain multitudes." Ana smiled.

"Would you really shoot the engineer?" Dirk asked. "Toward the end, I mean?"

"Of course."

"Why? We'd all be dead soon enough."

"Yeah, but I don't like him. Shooting him would be very satisfying."

***

Dirk and Ana spoke to Scruggs as they passed. Dirk told her everything was fine. Ana told her to clean the gym. Ana retreated to his room, and Dirk went up and ran scenarios on his board. Environmental wasn't his strong suit, but with some research, he confirmed everything Lee and Gavin had said. Once the environmental system stopped processing the air, things would go bad quickly. The ship was large, but the aired volume was small, and it was in bad shape to start with. Normally, with a ship this size, a small crew could breathe for several days, but the carbon monoxide and other poisons in the air hadn't been properly filtered for a long time. But the biggest problem was heat. It would get cold fast, and they'd probably die of hypothermia before asphyxiation.

He was running a scenario where they'd all cram into a room and insulate it when the lights came back on. His consoles started up. He reached for the grab bars, then realized that the intercom probably worked. He sat and pushed a button.

"Great job back there. That was only, what, twenty minutes?"

"Thanks, Skipper, but we're not done. I'm bringing atmo back up and then heat."

"Keep up the good work," Dirk said.

He mirrored the consoles. Everything looked good. Jump drive? Check. Maneuver? Online.

The lights went out again, and the consoles died.

"Emperor's testicles," Dirk said.

***

By the time Dirk pulled himself back to engineering, Lee and Gavin had already started the full reset.

"Why'd it fail?" Dirk said.

"Don't know, Skipper. We made it as far as the heating systems, and something tripped. We just pushed the button for the full reset."

Ana had stepped through the engineering air lock. "How long?" he said.

"Two hours," Gavin said. "Like Lee said before, make sure your bottles are full and keep them close by. Noxious gasses will start building up shortly."

"What about the kid?" Lee said. "Will she be okay?"

"Unless we can find a way of putting her in some sort of a shielded compartment that we can control the air in, she'll keel over in a few hours."

Ana sniggered, then laughed.

"What?" Dirk said.

"I know a place where we can put her," Ana said.

***

"But I did everything you said, Senior Centurion. I'll go back and clean them again. I'll do better this time, I promise," Scruggs said. "You don't need to space me."

"Scruggs, don't worry too much about this. It's just a temporary thing. We just need you to be here so we can control your airflow," Dirk said.

The three of them stood near the open air lock's door. Scruggs shivered. It could have been the cold or in terror. Dirk tried reasoning with her, but she kept looking at Ana.

"If you had a suit, this wouldn't be a problem," Dirk said. "But we can't keep the whole ship aired up. If you go in there, we can get you some emergency heat and pump in more air as necessary. That way, you'll be able to wait out the whole systems-restart thing."

"Senior Centurion, please don't kill me," Scruggs said.

"Recruit," Ana said, "when I decide to kill you, I won't ask for your acquiescence. I'll just do it. And I won't even need an air lock. This is a maintenance issue and an order from the captain. Follow it."

"Recruit?" Dirk asked.

"She wanted to join the Marines, so I'm treating her as a military recruit."

"She didn't really sign up as crew, Senior Centurion," Dirk said.

"Yes, she did. Stowing away is the same as signing the articles."

Dirk looked at Ana for a moment. "That's kind of true. I never thought of it that way, but legally, it is the same. Does that mean you are under my orders, too?"

"In a manner of speaking." Ana grimaced. "Pilot, will you be needing any of my skills during the current emergency?"

Dirk shook his head. "This is an engineering crisis, and the engineers are on it."

"Very well," Ana said. He stepped through the hatch into the air lock. "Recruit, you're with me. We'll wait out here, out of the way, and let the professionals do their work. Step inside."

Scruggs's mouth dropped, and she looked at Dirk. He looked as surprised as her.

"Now, cadet," Ana said. "The pilot has work to do."

Scruggs skipped over the coaming and helped Ana pull the hatch closed to dog it shut. Ana went and sat against the far wall. Scruggs stared at him for a moment. "Thank you, Senior Centurion."

"Thank you for what?"

"For coming into the air lock with me. I know, with you inside, they won't try to space me."

Ana laughed. "You've got it wrong, cadet. It's entirely opposite."

"I don't understand, Senior Centurion."

"The engineer doesn't like me, and if he needs somebody spaced to save air, he'd probably try it with me first. But he won't try it if you are in here."

"You're afraid of being spaced?"

Ana laughed louder. "I'm not afraid of some junior engineer. I'd break him in half if he tried. But then, we'd have no functioning engineer, and this crisis calls for engineering talent. I'm just removing the option so that he can concentrate on fixing things. Remember that, cadet. In a crisis, everyone should do the job they are best suited for."

Scruggs nodded slowly. "Thank you for explaining, Senior Centurion. What should I do?"

Ana looked around the compartment and pointed. "That tool locker there. It looks dirty. Get shining."

CHAPTER 11

"This doesn't make sense," Gavin said. He tapped another button to continue the full system restart. "Why does a failure in a single system stop the whole system?"

"No idea," Lee said. She tapped her screen. "Fuel pumps are running. Everything is green here."

"Ramping up the fuel," Gavin said, tapping screens. "Watch the power output."

"Still green. Power output is up."

"Next step." Gavin consulted a checklist. "Ramp up the power draw." He tapped a screen.

"This part always works. But it fails later, in the middle, if I do the short setup," Lee said.

"What do you mean by the middle? Always at the same place?"

"Not the exact same place. But in the middle, somewhere."

"But where, exactly?"

Lee shrugged. "Who remembers where, exactly?"

"Any good engineer, that's who."

"I'm not an engineer. Do you remember exactly where it failed last time?"

"No."

"Does that make you a bad engineer, then?"

"Something's not right," he said. He got up and paced the engineering room. "Restarting blindly isn't going to fix the problem. We'll just hit it again."

"The longer we wait, the less air we have, and the colder it gets. If we go below freezing—"

"All the free water in the ship will crystallize and break all manner of things. Why is the whole system shutting down? And why at different times? If it was a subsystem failure, the subsystem should shut down, but the full restart should continue. And why does the whole system crash?"

"Should we ask the Skipper?"

"Does he strike you as being useful in an engineering emergency?"

"Well, not really. But he was in the navy."

"Was being the operative word, he's not anymore, and I'll bet they threw him out. Or he deserted."

"The pilot wouldn't do that," Lee said. She raised her voice. "Imperial officers don't desert."

Gavin smiled at her. "I don't think you've met the same type of Imperial officers I've met. What if there were two problems? It never fails at the same point, correct?"

"Correct. Always about the middle."

"What if there are two things wrong? The actual problem and something about how it reacts to things."

"We need to keep doing the checklist."

"No, we need to fix the problem. Not the same thing."

The lights buzzed out again. Gavin tapped a screen. "Full system shutdown," he said. "And we weren't doing anything at the time. Nothing at all. So, something in the system is reacting to something else."

The engineering hatch opened, and Dirk slipped his head in. "What did you do this time?"

"We don't know," Lee said.

"No, we do know. We did nothing," Gavin said. "Nothing we did caused this."

"Not helping," Dirk said.

"Actually, helping a lot," Gavin said. "Let me check something." He swiped through screens.

"Wouldn't it be better to restart the systems again?" Dirk asked.

"No," Gavin said. He continued typing.

"No?" Dirk said.

Dirk looked at Lee. She shook her head.

"Engineer—"

"Logs say the main engines gave a regular status update just before the system restarted," Gavin said. "Then the system restarted."

"We can restart without the main engines," Dirk said.

"Yes, but that's the only update from the engines in the log for hours. So, it may have caused this failure, but it didn't cause the other ones."

"That's no help at all," Dirk said.

"It's tons of help. If the engines didn't cause the shutdown, then the only other thing that was involved there . . ." Gavin typed some more. "Lee, you said you got a new drive system at the station and something about the software being updated."

Lee nodded. "The new system was months ago. And there was some problem with the software controlling it. They reinstalled an old system so it could talk to it."

Gavin tapped screens rapidly. Dirk looked at Lee. "We need to get this system restarted, so why not just try again?"

Gavin got up and pushed by Dirk. "Move." He ran to the back of the engineering room, pulled off a quick access panel, and stuck his head inside.

Dirk said, "I don't think—"

Gavin's muffled voice yelled out from inside the panel. "Lee, read the model number from that screen on the engineering console. The thruster model number."

Lee stepped over, analyzing the screen.

Gavin pulled his head out. "Wrong model. They picked the wrong model." He ran back to the engineering console, nudged Lee aside, and tapped. "The computer is configured for the wrong engines. I'll bet that, when the engine sends an update, it gets confused. But nothing happens, then. The next failure causes the system to restart. It thinks it's a catastrophic engine failure or something." He tapped the screen. "I'll try a different model. Let's start again."

"You changed it to the correct model?" Dirk asked.

"No, the correct model isn't in the database," Gavin said. "I'm just trying similar ones 'til we find one that works." He smiled at Dirk. "Let's hope I'm a better guesser than they were."

"How many choices do you have?" Lee asked.

"One thousand four hundred and twelve," Gavin said. "Let's get started."

***

The next hour had yielded a series of failures. The first two choices failed at the first step of the restart with various errors. The next three succeeded beyond that point but ultimately failed. Halfway through the sixth try, Gavin had begun coughing and wheezing, and he had to switch onto his suit air for a break. By the tenth try, he was in his suit air more often. By the fifteenth, his breath fogged in his suit, rendering the need to engage his suit heating.

The intercom bonged. Dirk had been standing behind Gavin, watching him work. Dirk answered the call so that it wouldn't distract Gavin.

"Getting mighty cold in here," Ana's voice said.

"Would you like me to come and give you a hug?" Dirk said.

"Not me. The kid could use it, though. What's going on?"

"Software was misconfigured. Engineer's working through it. How's your air?" Dirk asked.

"I've already vented and refilled twice. There's enough in here for two more."

"When that fails, call me, and I'll give the kid my air bottles."

"How noble, Navy. Just what I would have expected. But it's not a problem. Hypothermia will get her before then. Besides, I kept a spare bottle for her."

"You have an extra spare?" Dirk asked.

"I do not. I'll make do with what I have. She can have mine."

101

"Very noble yourself," Dirk said.

"Mission first, troops second," Ana said. "I'm a very, very distant third."

Gavin touched his screen. The atmospheric system whirred to life and pumped freezing air around.

"O system started," Lee said. "All green."

"Starting main heating system," Gavin said. He took a deep breath and wished he hadn't. It made him cough.

"Seeing warnings on the heating system," Lee said. The lights went out again.

Gavin didn't even bother to curse. He just played with his screen. "Changing engine type. Stand by." He began to cycle through a menu, then stopped. "How old is this ship?"

"It's old," Dirk said. He coughed. "And who cares about that?"

"I've been trying newer systems," Gavin said. He toggled through the screens to the last one. "This one is probably the setting that came out of the factory. Trying again."

The screen came up, and they restarted the sequence. "Starting heating systems," Lee said. She looked at her screen. "All red. Heating system failure."

Gavin smiled. "That's it. It failed."

"Yes, we'll have to restart," Lee said. "Wait, it didn't crash. It's actually reporting the error messages."

"Keep going," Gavin said. They sped through the remainder of the checklist. "All systems, except main heating up and running," Lee said. She grabbed Gavin, yelled, and gave him a big hug. Gavin returned it. Lee pulled his head up and kissed him on the cheek, then blushed and stepped back.

The intercom bonged, and Dirk hit the button again. "We're getting fresh air in here," Ana said. "And all the lights are on, but we're still freezing."

Gavin leaned over to the speaker. "Main heating is down, but everything else is up, including the emergency heating. It will warm up slowly. We'll be cold, but we won't die. In the meantime, turn on everything electric with motors or that might generate heat. Drills, water heaters. Go up to the galley and microwave some food. The heat will bleed into the ship."

"That's going to make us warm up?"

"It will keep us from dying," Gavin said.

"Great job, Engineer," Dirk said. "Both of you. Great job."

"Does this mean I don't get my hug?" Ana said.

CHAPTER 12

"That planet doesn't look particularly hospitable," Gavin said. He was strapped in at the console in the control room he had made his own for engineering notations. Dirk was at the pilot's station, and Lee had the navigator's console up. Ana sat in what was now called the weapons console, even though their only weapon was a sand launcher—purely defensive in nature. They had all cast various screens to scrutinize the planet below them. Stark black mountains bisected jagged continents with blinding white deserts reaching out to a blue sea, a sea shifting into a dusty red where the water deepened.

"It's got an atmosphere we can breathe in without respirators, a temperature we can stand without special equipment, and a flat spot next to a freshwater river we can land this beast at," Dirk said. "Perfect time to take a fusion plant apart and figure out why it goes into shutdown and crack some water into fuel."

"It also has twenty-thousand-foot mountains that generate hurricane-force storms, oceans with hundred-foot waves, massive salt pan deserts, the air stinks, and the salt water is acidic enough that, if we tried to use it for fuel, we'd eat away at any metal in the system," Gavin said. "And it's hot. Very hot."

"We're just here for long enough to fuel up and fix up, then we're off on our way to Parsifal," Dirk said. "It will do. Right, Lee, engage the auto-landing."

"Pilot?" Lee looked confused. "Aren't you going to bring us down manually?" Lee asked.

"I usually let the computer do that. That's what computers are for," Dirk said.

"All the pilots I've worked with before always wanted to do as much manually as possible," Lee said. "They'd take every opportunity to do things themselves."

"I'm not all the pilots. I'm me. I don't take unnecessary risks. Let the computer do it."

"We can't," Lee said.

"What?" Dirk said. He stopped typing and turned to Lee.

"We don't have the software. When we got the new drive, we didn't have enough money for the new program. The interface wasn't right—something about the main thrusters I didn't understand. The pilot erased the old program but didn't install a new one. We don't have auto-landing capability."

Dirk's face slackened.

"No auto-landing?" Dirk said.

"None," Lee said.

"I have to land us?"

"Yes."

Dirk stared at his console, then unstrapped himself. "I'll be ready in a moment. Just have to get something," he said. He stood and pulled himself down to the hab module. Scruggs was peeking in from the hall, and he didn't say a word but just rushed past her.

The three crew members in the control room exchanged glances.

"That was . . . odd," Gavin said. "I've never seen a pilot who didn't jump at manual landings."

"Me neither," Lee said.

"Have any of you seen him land in gravity before?" Ana asked.

"Pilot Dirk drove us out of Bishop's world with no problems," Lee said.

"Took us out on a straight course to the jump limit with very little in the way of maneuvering," Ana said.

"Pilot Dirk is a skilled professional," Lee said.

"Says you, freak," Ana said. "I wonder if Navy got kicked out because he was doing the admiral's wife or if he wasn't doing something else, like landing without crashing."

All of them stared at the screens displaying jagged mountains and deep, endless, acidic oceans.

***

Fifteen minutes later, Dirk returned to the control room. He sat and belted himself in. A stench of alcohol wafted from him.

"Right, initiating landing sequence," Dirk said. "Pivoting." He pushed a control, and the ship rotated, ready to spin, setting up for a retro burn to drop altitude.

"Skipper, shouldn't we engage the streamlining?" Gavin asked. "Put the shrouds over the containers, retract the sensors?"

"Of course, of course," Dirk said. "Start now."

Gavin turned to his board. Winches pulled special temperature-resistant shrouds over areas that were not aerodynamic to decrease turbulence on landing. Lights faded from red to yellow to green on his board.

"First set of shrouds in," Gavin said. "Starting the sensors now." Ana tapped him with his elbow. Gavin glared. "What is it?"

Ana indicated Dirk with a twitch of his head, lifted his hands, and shook them. Gavin frowned, then looked at Dirk. He noticed Dirk's arms were shaking as he held them over the controls, and beads of sweat were forming on his forehead.

"We ready yet," Dirk said. His voice was hoarse, and he had to swallow before going on. "Speed it up."

"Just waiting. One of the sensors is stuck."

Dirk sat up straight. "Do we need to abort? I can abort if we need to."

Gavin looked up. "No, Skipper, I can winch it in manually. Just give me a minute." Gavin got up and walked back to the engineering section.

Lee cast a worried glance at Dirk. She had seen the shaking as well.

Ana cleared his throat. "Have you ever landed on a desert world before, Navy?"

"Yes," Dirk said.

"How many times?" Ana asked.

"Many," Dirk said.

"I've heard that the mountain-desert combination can set up huge winds that make the landing extremely difficult," Ana said.

"Yes," Dirk said. He looked at his shaking hands and dropped them into his lap, squeezing them together. Ana noted this and looked over his shoulder. He spoke to Scruggs. "Go strap into the couch in your quarters, recruit. This could get bumpy." He snugged in his own straps.

Scruggs left.

Shortly, Gavin returned. "Board shows green, Skipper. All set for atmospheric landing."

Dirk nodded and lifted his hands to his controls. "Starting retro burn." He pivoted the ship backward and pushed a button, firing the main drive at full power.

And fired.

And continued to fire.

Acceleration shoved them back into their seats. This continued for a minute, much longer than any auto-landing program would have run.

Lee looked at her board. "Pilot, do you see those mountains up there? They'll be difficult to overfly on this course."

"No overflying," Dirk said. "Going through." His hands were now visibly shaking as he held the controls. "Stand by for turbulence." The ship shuddered as the atmosphere bit.

"Skipper," Gavin said, "this ship is not in the greatest shape, we might have a problem if something shakes loose."

Dirk tapped a button, the thrust stopped, and the ship spun a full one hundred eighty degrees to present the bow to the landing. They had already dropped altitude, and the planet filled the display screens. He tapped another button, and the ship began a brutal swing from side to side as they swung through giant S-turns to bleed off speed. The ship shook. "Too late. Committed," he said.

Scruggs squawked something from behind them. Ana tightened his restraints and leaned back. A slight smile crossed his lips.

Lee glared at her board. "Pilot, we're below those mountain tops. We're going to crash. Climb."

"Too dangerous. High," Dirk said. The sweat streamed down his face unheeded, and his hands shook as he tapped the buttons. They spun into another vicious S-turn and wove around a mountain face. Lee's eyes widened. Another peak spun up in front of them.

"Watch out, watch out," she said.

The mountain magnified on the screen. Dirk's hand shook on the controls, but the course didn't budge.

"Pilot, shouldn't you go around?" Lee asked.

Dirk continued staring ahead at the expanding mountain.

"You're not alone here, Navy," Ana said.

Dirk's hand spasmed. "Right," he said. He threw the ship into an S-turn, and they flipped over the first mountain to see another behind it. Dirk threw the ship into another turn, and the mountain top screamed by. They dove into the next valley and raced along, only meters from the rocky ground.

"Skipper, we're going to crash," Gavin yelled. He gripped the arms of his chair.

The ground sped past, and they were out of the valley, zooming over a high cliff with the white desert and a blue river ahead of them. Then continued in almost free fall, plummeting at a high speed toward the river below.

Lee shrieked and closed her eyes. Gavin yelled. Ana sat still, a mysterious smile plastered on his face. Dirk issued one final command, and the ship pivoted up on its stern. The main drive flared once more. Superheated air boomed, penetrating the compartment as the engines fought the gravity. The ship stood on its tail and thrust hard, just off the vertical. The engine noise faded, and the ship tipped forward and slammed into the ground on the landing legs. It bounced once, twice, then was still. Their screens only showed dust for a moment, then the wind revealed the flat spot on which they landed, just a few dozen meters from the river ahead.

"Great landing, Pilot," Ana said. "Well done."

Dirk leaned to one side of his seat and vomited.

***

"Just keep dragging those hoses out and connecting them like the engineer showed you," Ana said. "Use that metal box to keep the free end under water, and when we've got them attached, we'll see if that solar backup pump works. Got it?"

"Yes, Senior Centurion," Scruggs said. She was stripped down to a T-shirt and light pants, sweating heavily. Ana had removed his coveralls, wearing only his custom skin suit. It had minor cooling capabilities, but he was sweating as well.

Ana looked around. Two suns burned a bright red on the horizon. Flat, white, salt-encrusted sand extended in all directions, broken by the occasional cluster of boulders. Some clusters were three times the height of a man. A shallow river of pure blue water, perhaps twenty meters wide, meandered around them. The black mountains, the river's source, were visible in the distance.

"Make sure you drink a container of water every hour while you are here. Why are you barefoot, recruit?"

"I only have my ship slippers, Senior Centurion, and I don't want them ruined with dust. This sand is soft enough that I can go without."

"Suit yourself. Let me know if you have any issues." Ana turned and walked toward the ship. All the hatches were opened. The air reeked of salty, decaying vegetation that he assumed emanated from the algae offshore, a different stink than the ship's much abused air. They vented the entire ship and planned on purging the air system by replacing it with O cracked from the planet's water. But first, they had to figure out what was wrong with the power system. The engineer and the medic replicated the entire manual startup process, examining and recording readings to see at what point the whole system shut down. They had breathable air for now, so they could take their time.

Ana walked back to the engine compartment. "Need any help?" Ana asked.

"Do you know how to tune a compressor?" Gavin asked.

"Nope."

"Then nothing from you."

"Suits me. Scruggs will have the fuel system set up shortly, and we'll start cracking the fuel. It will take forever with the solar system. We'll need some real power."

"You'll get it. After I've done my tests."

"Carry on," Ana said.

Gavin looked up and made a rude gesture with his hands. "Thank you oh so much for your permission, you Imperial turd."

Ana returned the gesture, climbed down the engine lock ladder, and walked away from the ship. Dirk was sitting on one of a cluster of boulders off in the distance. Ana strode out to meet him. It was a good two hundred meters from the ship to the cluster, and Dirk didn't move as Ana approached.

"That was quite a landing, Navy," Ana said. He pulled a flask from his pocket and waved it in front of Dirk's face. "Brandy from Amiens. Have a shot."

Dirk looked at the flask in front of him, then took it and glugged several gulps.

"A combat landing, in fact," Ana said.

"What are you talking about?" Dirk said.

Ana looked around. They were in a cluster of rounded boulders, varying in sizes from palm-sized to ones too big to climb up on. Dirk sat on a mid-sized one, and Ana sat on the other.

"Straight down. Use terrain as cover from anti-ship missiles and no multiple orbits so that they can get a bead on you. Go down fast, go down hard, never fly straight, and drop the troops where they need to be. I've been on dozens of those, even been in the control room a time or two. That was in the top half."

"Top half?"

"Yep. You didn't kill us all."

"Not this time."

Ana leaned over, retrieved the flask, and took a drink. "Did you crash other times?"

Dirk didn't say anything.

Ana leaned over and kicked the salt-encrusted sand. "Well, you didn't crash this time. That's important. Here, relax awhile, finish this and then come back. The crew needs you."

"The crew needs me?" Dirk said. He looked at Ana. "Really? Why?"

"Because they're idiots. They think because you're the pilot, you know what you're doing. That's stupid. I know a fraud when I see one. But they want to be reassured."

"You think I'm a fraud?" Dirk asked.

"More or less," Ana said. "I don't think you are a starship pilot at all. Oh, you can land a shuttle, but it was just pure luck that the ship didn't break into pieces on that landing. And then there was that part where you tried to kill us all."

Dirk turned to him. "You saw that, did you?"

"Yep. You were bound and determined to crash us into that mountain."

"I deserve to be dead."

"Don't we all. Except maybe the kid. Why didn't you kill us?"

Dirk took the flask and took another swig. "Didn't seem fair. To you. Not to me."

"Tell you what, Navy, if you want, I'll kill you later. No charge."

Dirk took another drink. "Thanks. What did you say to the crew?"

"Nothing."

"Nothing?"

"They don't need to know. They think the sun shines out of your Imperial anus. It's the accent, the smirk—all Imperial officers have it. They think that no matter how bad things get, you'll fix it. They're wrong."

Dirk made a 'go on' gesture with his hands.

Ana shrugged. "If believing that makes them work harder, then I'm all for it. But they need to believe it. You can make them believe. Finish this." Ana handed him the flask. "Go back there, Navy, and do the Navy thing."

"What about you?" Dirk asked.

"I'm Army. I'm going to go do army things. Scout the area, establish a perimeter, site weapons." He smiled. "And shoot something."

***

Dirk went back to the ship and briefed everybody. Gavin and Lee had shut down everything. They turned systems on one-by-one, using the process of elimination to pinpoint the root cause. Scruggs had been hauling hoses in the heat for two hours and looked beat. Dirk told her to take a break for a half shift, then took a nap. When he awoke, the ship was uncomfortably hot, and the water systems were shut off. Somebody had filled containers of basic and left them out in the lounge. He took a deep drink and almost gagged. The high temperature warped its taste.

He went back to the engineering section. Gavin and Lee had a panel off, and heavy wires thicker than Dirk's wrist hung out of the compartment.

"Any update?" Dirk asked.

"Some good news, Skipper—sort of. We've figured out the heating problem," Gavin said.

"What is it?"

"The capacitors."

"The capacitors?" Dirk said.

"Yes."

"Right." Dirk waited. Silence. Then he shrugged. "Explain," he said.

Gavin brought up a diagram of the ship's circuits on the engineering console. "The capacitors are like giant circuit breakers that protect the ship's systems from power surges. They get charged to full capacity on startup and bleed power to the systems as needed. If the ship pushed too much power, the capacitors absorb the extra input and let it out slowly."

"So, what's the problem, then?"

"They're old. Their internal matrix is breaking down. At a certain point, the ship systems pull too much power, and the capacitor can't keep up. Instead of providing less power to the systems, they just . . . stop. Don't pass any power. They generate an error message, which crashed the old software. All the systems go down."

"All the capacitors are bad?"

"So far, we've found three bad ones. In exterior lights, heating, and powered landing legs. That's why, when we turned the heating on, it blew everything up."

"What do we do?" Dirk asked.

"Three options. Buy new ones, recondition the old ones, or bypass."

"I don't see the wholesale capacitor emporium store around here, nor a shipyard in easy walking distance," Dirk said. "So, I assume we'll have to bypass."

"Already started, Skipper," Gavin said. "We picked a non-critical system—the cargo hatches—and tested the bypass there. It's working. So, we're going to swap the busted ones out with working ones in critical systems. In the non-critical systems, we'll put in bypass cables."

"How long?" Dirk asked.

"Three to five shifts, depending on how the removal goes. I'll have atmo and environmental working in about two shifts, and after that, we can power up everything else. I can selectively power other systems, so you'll have comm, navigation, and enough power to start cracking the fuel."

"We can launch, then?"

"I'd rather not. Some of the secondary systems will be in pieces, and I'd kind of like to spend a day cracking fuel and O, fill up the tanks, and flush all the water and O systems. It won't take long, and the ship will be in much better shape. Plus, we'll need some sleep ourselves, Medic Two, Michaelson and I."

"We have enough food, and I guess it's best that we do that. Can I help?"

"Are you any good with electronics?" Gavin asked.

"I'm all thumbs. I can carry things or drag things around or something."

"Sorry, Skipper, no work like that. Lee knows enough to read meters and hand me tools, so the two of us can do engineering things."

"This is pretty advanced maintenance for an Engineer Two," Dirk said.

Gavin put a wrench on a bolt and spun it.

"Most junior engineers don't have this level of expertise. Where did you learn all this?"

Gavin tightened the bolt. "I worked at a shipyard when I was a kid."

"Which shipyard?" Dirk asked.

Gavin moved the wrench to a different bolt and tightened it but didn't answer.

"Fine," Dirk said. "You do engineer things, I'll go do pilot things. Where's Ana?"

"Up top."

***

Dirk went to the multi air lock behind the control room. It had five hatches: control room forward, hab module astern, and a side air lock. Two other hatches without air locks opened when the ship grounded. The upper hatch was open, so Dirk climbed up.

Ana was sitting ten feet away, under an awning. Telescoping metal poles supported the awning and its heavy fabric. Guy ropes attached the poles and the fabric roof to tie down points on the ship's hull.

"Yow," Dirk said as touched the hull. The scorching metal stung his hands, and he was forced to roll over his forearms, using his fabric-covered arms to protect his skin. He stood and felt the heat burn through his thin ship boots. He skipped across the superheated metal and stopped under the shade of the awning, sweating already.

"Protecting us against the marauding hordes of vicious aliens, Senior Centurion?" Dirk asked.

"All secure, Navy," Ana said. "No movement of any sort to report in any direction. Thermal sensors show mostly undifferentiated heat to the horizon, except for some rock towers in that direction. Areas near the base show colder."

"So, you have nothing to report except that being in the shade is cooler than being in the sun?" Dirk said. He tried to sit down, but the hard, piping hot hull made it impossible.

"Sit on this," Ana said and scooted to the side. Dirk realized he was sitting on a thick survival blanket that he had unfolded to protect him against the hot metal.

"There is some weather forming up in the mountains," Ana said. White clouds in the distance eclipsed the mountain's jagged peaks. A hot wind blew on their faces.

"Too far away to bother us. Where did you get the tent?"

"Survival locker. All the good stuff, electronics, weapons, has been stolen or sold. Anything that would be useful on a station or in space is gone. But the groundside stuff, tents, rafts, ropes, that sort of thing, is still there."

"No weapons?" Dirk asked.

"Just the shotgun the freak tried to threaten us with. There is an ax."

"In case we need to cut down some firewood?"

"Can also be used to cut a boarder in half, but yes, it's for wood."

"Any ammunition for the shotgun?"

"Surprisingly, a couple hundred rounds. Once the fuel cracking is started, I'm going to take the kid out for a hike and shoot a few dozen rounds to get her used to it."

"Several questions," Dirk said. "First, why wait till the fuel cracking starts? Second, why teach her a shotgun? And third, why do anything with her at all? She's a stowaway."

A bong sounded, and Ana picked up his binoculars. Dirk peered at the brand. He'd bought a pair of those when he was commissioned. They had excellent optics, infrared and ultraviolet filters, laser ranging, remote capacity, and a high price.

"Very expensive toy you have there," Dirk said.

"It's saved my life more than once, Navy," Ana said. He scanned the horizon in a methodical sweep. "For your questions—first, I want fuel as much as everybody, so if there is any possibility of me helping with that, I'll stay to help. Once you've started fueling up, no need for me anymore. Second, the kid is actually shaping pretty well. Don't tell her that, but she'd be in the top third of any batch of recruits that I've ever had. She needs to be stretched a bit. Not as much option for physical work on the ship, but a nice tiring march will do her good."

"And the third?"

"Because she's a stowaway? Most of the kids I had as recruits were running away from something, not to something. Giving them something to work toward is good for them, whatever it is. They learn self-discipline, grit, and it gives them focus. Besides, it's what I do."

"And the shotgun?" Dirk asked.

Ana lowered the binoculars. "I like shooting things. Guns are fun."

CHAPTER 13

"We need another day?" Dirk asked. The crew had gathered around the lounge table. They had power again, and everybody was wolfing down a hot ration tray, the first tray of hot food in three days. Transferring the couplings had taken longer than expected, and the fuel processing system had malfunctioned again.

"Yes, Skipper," Gavin said. "About three shifts. Now that the processing system is working, we just need a while for the pumps to catch up and crack enough H for the drives. I'm already filling the O tanks as well. Another standard day, and we'll have full fuel tanks, full O tanks, as much water as we can carry, and the atmo will be as clean as we can make it. And the ship will have dried out so the humidity will be gone."

"Will it stay that way?" Ana asked.

Gavin glared at him. "The filters are old and need to be replaced. So, no, we'll start to deteriorate almost immediately, but it will take months to get back to where we were."

"Not a problem in the short term, then," Ana said. "So, we just wait for the tanks to fill up. Recruit?" He turned to Scruggs.

"Yes, Senior Centurion," she said.

"You don't have to call him that," Gavin said. "You're not in the army. You're not even in the crew. You don't have to take orders from him."

"But the pilot said that a stowaway automatically agrees to crew discipline, like they signed on with the crew. And the pilot has put the senior centurion in charge of me, so I do have to follow his orders."

"Really?" Gavin asked. He looked around. "Really?"

Lee cleared her throat. "The young miss is correct. Stowaways are subject to crew discipline, the pilot is in charge, and he can assign her to report to anybody he wants."

Gavin looked at Dirk. "And you assigned her to report to him?" He gestured to Ana.

"It seemed the easiest way," Dirk shrugged. "And it's worked out well so far. What work needs to be done to get us space-worthy?" Dirk asked.

"Nothing except wait for the fuel to load up," Gavin said. "Lee was able to finish swapping the capacitors and put in the bypasses after I showed her how. She got it all done while I was working on the fuel system."

"What was wrong with the fuel system?" Dirk asked.

"Just rusted old parts that burst under pressure. It hadn't been used in forever. Three times, when we brought the pressure up, things snapped. Different things each time. I had to machine a few fittings—no big deal. There's actually decent tools in the engineering section. I don't know why they weren't sold."

"Too big to carry," Lee said. "Station would have seized them for debts if they saw us carrying them off. That's what the old engineer said."

"Our gain, then," Gavin said. "Nothing critical to do now, Skipper. Just wait. The pumps are on automatic."

"Good," Dirk said. "Senior Centurion, have you detected any threats to our ship in the immediate area?"

"Nothing has changed since we landed around here. The weather in the mountains is going to be brutal, though. Big storms. I can see lightning all the way from here."

"But that's there, not around here," Dirk said. He swallowed a gulp of basic. "I'm declaring a holiday. Everybody, take a day off. Go sleep. Go hiking. Go play in the sand. Do what you want but be back on the ship by the end of second shift tomorrow, and we'll lift at sunset. And recruit, that includes you. You have the next day off as well. No drills from the senior centurion." Dirk looked at Ana and raised his eyebrows.

Ana nodded.

"Do we have enough water to take showers?" Scruggs asked.

"Water wasn't the problem, humidity was," Gavin said. "Closed environment on the ship. Humidity is bad." He turned to Dirk. "But we're just vented to local air right now, so no problem now, Skipper."

"How long to dry us out after launch?"

"We've got lots of fuel, so I'll just freeze the water out and reheat the air. Only one cycle."

"Good." Dirk looked at Scruggs. "Did anyone assign you a day?"

"A day?" Scruggs said.

"Who's what day?" Dirk asked, looking around.

"I'm odd," Lee said. "So is Gavin. You and Centurion are even."

"You can shower on odd-numbered days, then, Scruggs. There's a crate of perfume in the fresher. Use that on your off days." Dirk stretched. "First, I'm going to take a long nap," Dirk said, "then perhaps a short walk to the river."

"There's an oasis of sorts about a kilometer away," Ana said. "One of those piles of boulders actually has a pool of water at the bottom. The recruit and I found it during our patrol. River water, it tested fresh. And it's cool under the boulders. You could walk there."

"A kilometer?" Dirk said. "That seems far to me. I think I'll walk the twenty meters to the river and relax."

"Skipper, I wouldn't mind going for a hike. That oasis sounds interesting," Gavin said. "I'll just get a pack with some water. Do we have a compass or something?"

"Your comm has an inertial compass. It will work," Dirk said.

"I'll go with the engineer, Pilot," Lee said. "I could use a walk as well."

"Whatever you want," Dirk said. "It's a day off."

"I'm going to the river and going swimming," Scruggs announced.

All four of the others turned and stared at her.

"What?" Scruggs said.

"You can swim? In water?" Lee asked.

***

A half hour later, all four of them stood by the river, watching Scruggs swim across it. The river was maybe twenty or thirty meters wide, and usually not more than a meter deep, but Scruggs was clearly swimming, not walking.

"How does she do that?" Lee asked.

"You flap your arms or something," Gavin said. "You can't swim?"

"Who learns to swim in a space station? That's where I grew up. What about you?"

"Nope. My planet was cold growing up. Lots of water, but it was all ice."

"What planet was that?" Lee asked.

Gavin smiled at her, then turned to Dirk. "We're going to head off shortly, Skipper."

"Go ahead," Dirk said. "She certainly can swim. Enjoying it too. Very attractive girl when she smiles."

"No nudity taboo on Bishop's world, either, it seems," Ana said.

"Really, old man. She's young enough to be your daughter," Gavin said.

"If she didn't lie about her age, and I don't see any reason she would, she's only a few years older than my granddaughter," Ana said. "I mentioned it because, if you're going to be a space Marine or any one of a number of specialties, it's best if you have no hang-ups about being nude in front of your squad mates."

Gavin blinked. "You have a granddaughter?"

"I have three granddaughters and two grandsons—and

no, I'm not going to talk any more about it. Go on your walk, punk." A crackle rattled in the distance. They all turned toward the mountains. Lightning zipped in and out of black clouds, striking the distant peaks. "Big storm. Must have blown in from the ocean on the far side of the continent. I'll stay on watch, Pilot."

"I don't think there's any need," Dirk said. "Why not get some rest?"

"Not much I can do underway, so I can rest, then. Best if I keep an eye on things here," Ana said.

"Suit yourself. I'm going to bed. Wake me up in a shift," Dirk said.

***

Lee and Gavin walked along the river. A subtle slope of desert sand lined the near-empty riverbank. It was soft enough that they both removed their ship slippers and pushed their skin suits up as high as they could. The water was clear, with tiny round rocks on the bottom. The water was blood-warm, and even with their feet submerged with every step, the heat was oppressive. They sweated as they walked. They followed the side of the river next to the ship, using their comm tablets to navigate. They waded in the shallows until they found a place to ford the river and walk the other side, then commenced walking across the desert. A pile of rocks rested a few hundred feet away. Even that short distance had them sweating and panting by the time they had reached it.

"This looks great," Gavin said. "Look, there's a cave of sorts at the bottom." The round rocks had tumbled into strange patterns. At the bottom was a dark hole surrounded by rock walls that shaded it from the suns. Light gleamed inside, so they crawled along on hands and knees.

"This looks like fun," Lee said. She tested the water with a hand, nodded, then stripped her skin suit.

Gavin watched in appreciation. Clearly, Jovians didn't

have a nudity taboo, either. Lee was tall and lithe, her muscles prominent as she bent down to roll off her suit. It took less than a minute before Lee was wading in the water. She stopped with it just at below her knees, then sat down. The water came to her chest, and she splashed in it.

"What are you doing?" Gavin asked.

"I don't know. I've never been in this much water before. This is fun. Are you coming in?"

"Sure," Gavin said. He unbuckled his belt with his comm on it and laid it down, then stripped and piled his clothes onto a rock at the edge of a pool. He edged into the water and sat. "Oh, it's cold," he said.

"It just feels that way," Lee said. "Water's just a better conductor of heat than air."

"Well, it's not cold enough to get hypothermia, so I'm not really worried," Gavin said.

"You can get hypothermia on a planet? I thought you only got it when your suit heater failed outside?"

"Planets can get cold, too," Gavin said. "At least some of the ones I was on."

"Which one was that? You never did answer," Lee said.

"No, I never did," Gavin said. He gave a tight smile. "I don't like talking about it." He waded around in the water a bit. "Have you never been on a planet with free water before?"

"Never," Lee said. "I've spent my time almost totally on stations or ships. Very few planets."

"Why no planets?" Gavin asked.

"I don't like talking about it," Lee said. She smiled at Gavin, then dropped her eyes and splashed water on herself. Gavin turned and walked away, the sand grit pressing against the soles of his feet. He wasn't sweating anymore, and even the rotting algae's odor seemed to have disappeared. A splash accompanied by a wheeze and a yelp behind him snagged his attention. He turned around. Lee had jumped up and was holding her head, gasping. He pushed his way through the water to her side. She shook her head like a dog.

"Lee, what's wrong?" Gavin grabbed her shoulder and turned her toward him.

"I hab vater ub my node," she said.

"Water up your nose? What?"

Lee shook her head again and spat. "I ducked my head under the water and rolled over, then the water went up my nose. I wasn't prepared for that, and I thought I was drowning. After I stood, it all ran out. Pretty scary for a second."

"I thought you were hurt," Gavin said. She stood upright, but he didn't take his arm off her shoulder.

Lee coughed once more and looked him up and down. "Pretty muscular type, aren't you?" She looked even closer. "I thought it was just your head that didn't have hair, but you're pretty smooth everywhere." She ran her hand up and down his arm.

Gavin turned to her and smiled. The yellow flecks in her eyes sparkled. "Very smooth, very muscular."

She smiled at him again and said something.

"What?" Gavin said. "I can't hear you. It's too loud."

"I said—wait, what's too loud?" Lee said.

They both listened. A loud humming rumbled under their feet.

"What's that noise?" Gavin said.

***

Dirk was having a pleasant dream about two sisters he knew in Sirivan Six. They had just sat to a dinner of a local squab boiled in a vegetable broth, with small glasses of a mock-plum brandy on the side. He proposed a toast to their two smiling faces. They giggled and drank, then began to bang their glasses on the table. He poured another shot, and they drank again but continued to bang their glasses. Dirk realized he wasn't hearing their glasses but a knocking on his cabin door, and Scruggs's voice penetrated his dreams. "Wake up, Captain, please wake up.

Please, Captain, wake up."

Dirk rolled over on his bunk. "What? What?"

More rapping rattled the door. "Thank the emperor, Captain. Centurion says to come to the main hatch quickly. Right away."

"I'm coming, I'm coming," Dirk said. "How long have I been asleep?"

"Three hours. Come quickly please, Captain, I'm going to help the centurion." Feet pattered on the deck.

"What in the name of the Imperial nostril is going on?" Dirk asked. He dragged his coveralls on and stomped down the hab module, through the covered cargo bay and over to the loading ramp. He stuck his head out and yelled, "What's so important that—Oh. Emperor's testicles."

The placid, blue meandering river from three hours ago was gone. In its place was a boundless roiling mass of dark-green and white water. It frothed with waves and was at least fifty meters wide. It had moved from being twenty meters away to lapping on the landing struts.

"What happened?" he said to Ana. He and Scruggs were splashing in the water as they dragged the last parts of the fuel processing plant back up the ramp into the cargo hold. The wind blew his hair around, and Dirk realized his voice was lost in the wind. He tried again but yelled this time.

"It started about twenty minutes ago," Ana yelled back. "The wind started to pick up, and the water began to run faster. It turned to that brown-green, then the volume went way, way up, and fast. You can see it rising if you watch." He gestured.

Dirk looked out, and just as Ana said, the water had risen since he last looked.

"I buzzed the others about ten minutes ago but no answer. I left a message for them to get back right away. The recruit here and I shut down the fuel processing and dragged it inside before it got swept away."

"Good work," Dirk said. "Did you get everything?"

"Yes," Ana said. "In fact, there's actually an external port we can use if we need to, on that strut there. I found it while I was poking around but didn't want to mess with the setup. But I think I can set it up to keep working once we seal up."

"Where did all this water come from?" Dirk asked.

"I think it's those storms in the mountains. Big rains up there, rushes down the ravines and onto the flats a few hours later.

"How deep does it get?" Dirk said.

"The Emperor's stinking armpits. I'm not a weatherman," Ana said. "But every rock I've seen in this area has been nicely rounded, rounded like it's been bouncing at the bottom of a river for a long time."

"We'll have to go get them," Dirk said. "I'll fire up the thrusters and bounce us over there."

"Are we going to drown?" Scruggs asked. She dumped a hose on the floor and coughed. She was wet and bedraggled.

"We're a spaceship," Dirk said. "We're airtight. If we can keep air in, we can keep water out," he said. "Even if it piles up on top of us, we'll be fine. We can just sit on the bottom."

"But water's much heavier than air," she said. "Ten meters of water is the same weight as a standard atmosphere. If we're in twenty meters of water, won't we be crushed?"

Ana and Dirk shared a look. "Emperor's hairy testicles," Dirk said. "You two, go strap in. I'm going to get the others on the comm and move us closer to that rock pile they were sunning at."

***

Gavin splashed to the edge of the pool and dragged his clothes on. Lee did the same. They stuffed themselves into their skin suits and pulled their slippers on. A trickle of water washed into the pool from a channel. The trickle turned into a flow, and the dark, turbid water stained the crystal-clear pool.

Gavin and Lee moved toward the cave that they had crawled through, but it was already half full of water, and the level was rising.

"What now?" Gavin said.

"Up here," Lee pointed. The two of them clambered onto the rocks next to the hidden pool and hopped from one to the other until they climbed onto the flat top on one halfway up.

"The empress's vagina," Lee whispered. The suns were still up, and their rays were warm on her bare skin. But a cool wind whistled down from the mountains, and the lazy stream they had waded across was now a raging torrent.

"Where did that come from?" Lee said.

"More important—how do we get across it?" Gavin said.

"I can't swim."

"Even a swimmer would have a problem with that."

Lee's comm pinged. "It's the pilot." She tapped her comm. "Medic Two, Michaelson here, Pilot."

"We talked about the titles, never mind. Are you both okay?" Dirk said.

"We're on the top of a pile of rocks, Pilot. We're safe for a little while," Lee said.

"A very little while," Gavin said. "I can see the waters rising. Can he come and get us out of here?"

Dirk apparently was reading Gavin's mind. "I'm coming to get you. Hang on. I'm just powering up the thrusters. I'll be there in five."

"Thank you, Pilot. We'll wait for your timely arrival," Lee said. She closed the comm.

Gavin looked at her. "'We'll wait for your timely arrival?' Like we're sitting in a restaurant drinking a beer?"

"Politeness is never misplaced."

***

"So, hotshot, how you going to do this?" Ana asked from the weapons console.

"As soon as we lift from here, I'll head over as close as I can and set down," Dirk said.

"And they'll walk on the water to get in?"

"I hadn't figured that part out yet," Dirk admitted.

"Can you hover over them and winch them up?"

"Maybe, but there's wind, and I don't want to blast them with downwash."

Ana shook his head. "Always, always, it's the centurions who have to figure things out." He punched a control on his comm. "Recruit. Meet me at the ship's locker. Roust out that rope and that—what did you call it—water thing?"

"The inflatable raft, Senior Centurion?" Scruggs said.

"That's the one. Meet me there and get started inflating." He closed the comm and turned to Dirk. "New plan, Navy. Get us close, land—"

A shudder of the current pushed the ship a few meters sideways. "'Get us close and hover,' I meant to say. Keep us roughly steady upstream of them, and I'll let out the raft thing at the end of the line. They can climb in, and we'll drag them back in.

"What about the thruster's downwash?" Dirk asked.

"Water will absorb it, mostly. Once they're in the raft, we can work it out."

"Takeoff in one," Dirk said.

***

The waters were still rising, so Lee and Gavin had climbed up one more rock level. There was only one more rock above them.

"Pilot says he's going to hover upstream and launch a raft to us. That's something that floats on water. We get in it, and he'll pull us back."

"Can't he hover over us?"

"The downwash will blast us. He says the raft is the

best option."

"I hope he knows what he's doing," Gavin said.

"Me too," Lee said. She looked up at the sky. "Paterfather Zeus, give me strength."

A big wave crashed into the rocks, and the spray soaked them.

"If the ship doesn't get here soon, we're going to die."

"I can't die. I need to finish medical school."

"You were in medical school? I thought you were only a medic."

"I didn't graduate. I want to get married, and I haven't slept with enough men."

"You haven't what?" Gavin said.

"I need to have ten lovers before I get married."

"Ten? Why ten?"

"Priest told me. I'm on my Rumspringa. I'm experiencing the world."

"Rumspringa? We're going to drown, and you are talking about mixed drinks?"

"The priest said I was not secure enough in my faith. I needed to experience the world to test myself. So, I've been exiled from my clan for at least three years. I have to live with the normals. No help from or contact with Jovians. I have to meet new people. And take lovers. Ten."

"Ten? You need ten lovers? Exactly ten?"

"Yes."

"Why not eleven or twelve?"

"No, that would be too many. I don't want to be thought of as a loose woman."

Gavin laughed, then a boom erupted, and they stood and watched as bright lights of fused hydrogen ions flashed in the distance. A roaring followed, and the Heart's Desire rose and pivoted toward them. Gavin could appreciate the artistry involved in moving a starship across the water. The main engines didn't face down, so they had to use the thrusters, and the thrusters were weak. They were mostly used to spin the ship in space so that the main engine could fire. They were also neither speedy nor responsive, so whenever the wind hit the ship, it swayed, and Dirk had to firewall the thrusters to bring it back on course.

The Heart's Desire swung around, upriver of them—if you could call what looked like a mile-wide lake a river. The ship swung 'til it was broadside to them. The cargo door was already open. Ana and Scruggs worked inside.

An orange-colored plastic box slid down the ramp. The sides appeared to be inflated tubes, and the bottom was flat. A rope trailed behind it, and Ana manipulated the rope as the raft floated down toward them.

The rising water lapped at their feet. Lee was looking very nervous. "Gavin, the water is still coming."

"Up we go. Lee, give me a hand up to the next rocks. I'll get up there then pull you up," Gavin said. He demonstrated by cupping his hands in front of him. Lee nodded and put her hands in front of her. Gavin stepped up to grip the top of the next rock. But Lee had misunderstood, and as soon as she felt Gavin's weight on her hands, she propelled him up and over with a mighty toss.

Gavin soared over the top of the rock and fell over the far side. He reached forward and crashed into the rock with a thud, causing his left arm to go numb. Now is not the time for a broken arm. He slid headfirst over the rock and rolled to one side to grip with his right arm. He stopped his forward slide, but he was still lying with his weight forward, his left arm dangling below him. He scrabbled with his right arm 'til he found purchase on the rough surface of the rock. He pulled himself up until he could roll over and onto his back. He lay there, gasping for air.

"Gavin! Help, Gavin, the water's rising!" Lee shouted from below.

Gavin rolled over toward Lee. He rolled onto his numb arm. He braced his legs and extended his working right arm. Lee grasped his wrist with an iron grip, and Gavin rolled over on his back, pulling with his arm as he did so. Lee used the extra impetus to get her feet under her and crab-walked up onto the top of the rock. She collapsed on top of him.

"I thought you were going to leave me there," she said.

Gavin pushed to draw a breath. "And I thought a girl as skinny as you would weigh a lot less."

***

Dirk was having a hard time controlling the ship and getting the raft over to the others. He could control altitude well enough, so they were in no danger of crashing into the water, but the wind buffeted the ship, and his maneuvers were limited by the thruster's power. The corrections were painfully slow.

He tracked the ship from side to side. But the raft swung wide, the minor motions exaggerated by the pendulum effect of the attached rope.

Plus, he couldn't see anything at all. Cameras covered the cargo ramp, the thrusters, the air lock, and a whole host of other places he could cycle through, but none of them pointed out the loading ramp, down ten degrees and out a hundred meters, where the rock pile was. He was forced to rely on Ana's shouted commands on the comm.

"Left, left. No. Back. Stop. Again. Stop. Back. Left. Dammit, Navy, where did you learn to fly?"

"I'm a starship pilot, not a sea captain. Give better directions."

"The emperor's hairy buttocks. Hold steady for a second. Recruit, pull that in. Wait one, Navy. We're getting set up to drift it down again."

"Can we veer off and pick them off after the storm?"

"Only if we want waterlogged corpses. They're up on top of the highest rock now, and the water's still rising."

"We'll try again. Give me a vector this time, maybe."

"I'll—what? No, that won't work. Recruit, don't. No.

No. Crap," Ana said.

"What's going on," Dirk said.

"That idiot recruit just tied a rope on her and went into the water. She said she'll bring the raft to them."

***

Gavin and Lee watched as Scruggs fought her way across the water. Over her shoulder was a rope that was tied to the raft and the other rope. She made determined progress on to them 'til she was just upstream of the rocks. The current was buffeting her.

"Watch out, Scruggs, watch out for the rocks!" Gavin yelled.

"Over here! Climb in on the side," Lee yelled.

Scruggs held herself a few meters off the rocks, then she pivoted to take the shock of hitting the rocks on her feet and rolled up and over to land between Gavin and Lee. She pulled the giant loop over her head and laid it on the rock.

"Wow, you are one crazy kid," Gavin said.

"Paterfather Zeus must hold you specially in his heart," Lee said.

"Pull the raft over, then we can hop in, and Centurion will winch us in."

Lee and Scruggs grabbed the rope and pulled. Gavin tried to yank it in but mostly succeeded in getting in the way.

"What's wrong with you?" Scruggs yelled.

"Broken arm or a sprain—not sure and not important right now. We need to get out of here."

The water was now flowing all around them, and their rock was a tiny island in a sea of disturbed water. Waves lapped over the entire surface from time to time. The raft approached.

"Dive headfirst over the edge of it as soon as it gets close. Roll over once you are inside," Scruggs instructed. "Don't let it touch the rock, or it might puncture and sink.

Lee, you first."

Lee gave one final heave 'til the raft was just to the side of them, swinging in the current. She pulled on the rope and dove headfirst into the raft. She rolled over and turned.

"You next, Gavin," Scruggs said. "I'll go last."

"No, you go next."

"I can swim, you can't. Go now," Scruggs said.

Gavin grimaced, grabbed the rope with his free hand, pulled himself up, and launched himself forward to roll in.

He almost made it, but he hadn't given himself enough velocity, and a wayward bounce of the raft knocked him back into the water. He fell and lost hold of the lifeline, causing it to float away.

Faster than anybody watching could follow, Scruggs draped the loop at the end of the line over her shoulder, dove into the water, and stroked after Gavin.

Gavin started to sink and splashed the water with his hands. He didn't know how to swim, and he didn't have time to learn. He had only splashed twice when something grappled his chest from under the water and lifted him up and out. Scruggs had dove underneath him, ducked behind him, and had him floating on her hip.

"Stay put. I'm attached to the line. They'll pull us in," she said.

Gavin tried to turn his head, but he couldn't see far enough forward. They drifted for a second, and bobbing waves caused tension. Water sloshed over his face and made him gasp, and he tried to wriggle out of Scruggs's grip. He was facing backward, and he couldn't see where he was going. He tried to squirm.

"Don't move," Scruggs said. "I've got you. I've got you. They're pulling us in. Just another minute."

Gavin bobbed up and down but managed to keep his mouth shut most of the time. He held his breath as water splashed his face as long as possible but then had to take a breath that was mostly water. He thrashed around.

"Stay calm. Just another few feet. Stay calm. We're almost there."

Gavin wheezed and fought harder. He had to get out of the water. A change in the motion came as Scruggs pushed him up higher. Strong arms gripped his shoulders and pulled him backward up the cargo ramp. Ana threw him forward into the cargo hold, and he rolled over and breathed the warm, wonderful air.

He watched as Scruggs scrabbled up the ramp. She climbed to the top of the ramp, leaned against the bulkhead, and wiped the water from her hair.

"That was great fun," she said. "Can we do it again?"

CHAPTER 14

"Did you enjoy your dinner, Tribune?" Brigade Commander Santana asked.

"Excellent food," Devin said. "Those mussels are wonderful. So fresh." He took a sip of the wine. "Are you, by chance, related to Lord Santana of Wort?"

"I'm his cousin," Santana said.

"Beautiful planet, Wort," Devin said. "Do you miss it?"

"I go back on leave every two or three years, catch up on family business. But it's not really for me. I like new places. That's why I joined the Marines. See the galaxy."

Devin scanned Santana's decorations. "I see you've seen quite a bit of the galaxy already. Not the nice parts."

"Well, it hasn't been boring," Santana said. "Those other places haven't been. Here, now, that's boring. Good food, good wine, but nothing going on."

"Is that why your men helped break Durriken Friedel out of prison?" Devin asked.

Santana laughed. "Touché, Tribune. More wine?"

"It's wonderful, but no thank you," Devin said.

"Any progress on catching your supposed deserter?"

"Supposed deserter, I like that. No, you can rest easy. We can't prove how he got out. Your men are in the clear."

"I'm sure that I don't know what you are talking about."

"No matter. Unofficially, somebody swapped a soon-to-be released prisoner for a Marine when they were out on a work detail, and once inside, Dirk swapped IDs with the Marine and walked out as the released prisoner, and the Marine walked out as himself with his squad when they came in for some sort of tactical exercise. The details escaped my staff, but it was as clean a jailbreak as we've ever seen."

"That sounds very resourceful."

"It was. If those people were under my command, I'd give them some sort of commendation."

Santana smiled and shrugged. "That's good advice. I think I'll take it—if I'm ever in a position to need it, of course."

Devin smiled as well. "We're now working through station videos and passenger lists to find him. That's taking more time than we thought. But we'll get him."

"But your trail gets colder every hour," Santana said.

"I'm patient," Devin said. "Very patient."

"What will you do now?"

"After this excellent dinner, I'm going back to my ship, and we're on our way out-system. We have to jump eight parsecs away and watch an election on Ekaterinburg."

"That's a long way to go to watch an election. Couldn't you find one closer?"

"The planetary government at Rhys has been complaining that they haven't seen an Imperial warship in over a year, and they worry about pirates. There's some rumblings of an independence movement as well. We're going to do a goodwill tour. Get into orbit. Suppress pirates. Shoot things."

"A frigate to suppress pirates? That's overkill. Can't they do that themselves?"

"They have a customs force. It's well enough equipped for intra-system work, but the pirates may not be in-system. They claim that some pirate attacks have been from converted jump-capable merchantmen jumping in from adjacent systems, seizing ships, destroying them, then jumping out. They want to build a jump-capable system defense force."

"That's not allowed."

"Definitely not. No planetary navies."

"Unless there is a ruling duke."

"They have no duke. They're a colony. I'm going to

stomp on that ambition, remind a few people that even a single Imperial warship is much more powerful than an entire planetary navy. They should vote accordingly."

"And the pirates?"

"We're going to search the adjacent systems for armed merchant ships. If we find any that might be pirates, we'll blast them to smithereens."

"What if you find armed merchant ships that you're not sure are pirates?"

"We'll blast them, anyway. Can't have the locals getting ideas."

A message light flashed on Devin's comm. "Excuse me a moment, Brigade Commander," Devin said. He tapped an earbud. "Yes. Yes. No, don't do that. Bring him to the ship. How much was it? Bring that, too. I don't know, the local base? How long? Never mind. Send my steward to my bank. I'll pay for it personally. Tell him to pick up the money."

Devin hung up. "Your pardon, Brigade Commander, but duty calls. Thank you for the excellent dinner."

***

Two hours later, Devin returned to his cabin on the Pollux. Blood spattered his robe along with the short steel sword he carried. He laid the sword on his desk. His door bonged.

"Come," he said.

Lionel strode into the room, followed by Devin's steward, Imin. "You've got blood in your hair," Lionel said.

Devin cursed and tried to wipe it out.

"Now you're just smearing it around," Lionel said.

Devin cursed some more, pulled his robes off, and threw them to the floor.

Imin picked them up and examined them. "This blood isn't going to come out, Tribune."

"It doesn't matter," Devin said. "Burn them. Get me

another set."

"Won't find another set of senator robes out here, sir," Imin said. "I'll have to send to the capital."

"Do so."

"Beggin' the tribune's pardon, but did you have to use your formal robes?"

"The formal robes signify my consular Imperium. I can't execute a man in a set of coveralls."

"Again, begging the tribune's pardon, but if you feel the need for more executions, that's exactly what you'll be wearing, with you being short of uniforms and all."

"We could get a bib made up for you, sir," Lionel said. "Big white sheet thing—covers everything. You could wear it to executions and any time you're eating seafood."

"Do you think this is funny?" Devin asked Lionel.

"He told you everything he knew. He didn't need to die."

"I didn't torture him. It was a judicial proceeding. What's that?" He pointed at the briefcase sitting next to the desk.

"Twenty-five thousand credits in gold," Imin said. "As requested. The bank had a heck of a time rousing up that much actual metal."

"Give it to—what was her name?—the cousin."

"The one who called you a heartless Imperial murderer," Lionel said.

"Yes, her."

"Tasha. She owns the seafood restaurant on-station."

"I guess I won't be eating there."

"Given what they'd put in the soup, I don't plan to. Up to you, of course."

"Imin, get an escort and bring her the money. Do the paperwork. Fix it so that she inherits it or her name is on the reward. Something. Whatever you need to do, I'll sign off on it. Just get her the money."

Imin nodded, started toward the desk, then stopped. He picked up the sword and cleaned it on the bloody robe.

After shining it, he extended it, hilt first toward Devin. "Your Gladius, Tribune."

Devin took the proffered sword and scowled. Imin gave the crossed chest salute. "The emperor."

"The emperor," Devin agreed. Imin reached down for the suitcase and marched out. Silence creeped in for a moment.

"Well?" Devin asked.

"Why?"

"Why what?"

"Why him? Why now? Why you?"

"Because he aided a known fugitive, because I think these colonials need to be reminded of the Empire's power, because if I think a man should be killed for the greater good of the Empire, I should be willing to do it myself."

"And because you were angry that the Marines got away with breaking him out, and you couldn't get at them."

Devin looked at the screen. "I know why they did it. The trial was rigged from the start. The Imperial judge couldn't afford to offend Crystal Belt, and she was out for blood."

"If you disagree with the verdict, why are you enforcing it?"

"Because it's the law. Because the Empire is all that stands between these people and chaos, even if they don't appreciate it. They will learn to respect the Empire. If we're not strong here, the confeds will come in. Do you want that? Or worse, what if the confeds don't come in? What if the whole place splinters and ends up like the verge? Remember those verge planets? Do you want Imperial citizens living like that?

"You can't just go around, killing everyone who breaks an Imperial law."

"I'm a tribune with consular authority. I can do almost anything. I can depose a governor. I can declare war."

"Declare war? With only one frigate at your command?"

Devin laughed. "But it would be a glorious war, wouldn't it?"

"And short. Right, what's done is done. What next?"

"We go to Parsifal and wait for that ship to show up."

"Then blast it to pieces?"

"Not right away. We'll talk first."

"Have you forgotten that you have an election to oversee?"

Devin cursed again.

"We have plenty of time," Lionel said. "We know where he's supposed to be going. We'll just send word to watch for him. We can jump out, deal with this election, then make it back to where Dirk is."

"Set it up."

"Why the money?"

"What? He's owed his reward."

"He's dead. He's dead because you killed him. Why give him money?"

"Old earth philosopher. He said that men could overcome the executions of their family if it was done legally, but if you took away their inheritance, they would be driven to despair. I don't want despair."

"You'll settle for fear."

Devin walked over and poured a drink. "I serve the Empire." He took a swig. "Get us out of this system. We need to go get a crooked election over with so that we can go back and kill an innocent man."

CHAPTER 15

"All systems show ready for jump, Skipper," Gavin said over the intercom. He was in the engineering room, checking out the systems directly. "As soon as we're far enough away from the planet's gravity well, that is."

"I've programmed a course request for a least time course to Parsifal, Pilot," Lee said. "With all the variables, it will take some time, but we can break orbit and get started to the jump limit. Zeus willing, we'll be there in three more jumps."

"Good work," Dirk said. "I'm going to put us on course to the jump limit, but we have a few things to discuss." He punched the intercom button. "Prepare for one g to the jump limit. Everybody, please meet me in the lounge," Dirk said. He pressed a gong for the gravity change and broke orbit. Then he unbuckled and proceeded back to the lounge.

After their water fiasco, he had flown the ship up and found a mountain foothill that was high and dry. They had waited a day for the waters to recede, then returned to the river. The next day, they sucked up water and cracked O and H for fuel. Nobody had complained when Ana organized a roster of sentries on the top of the ship, and nobody went farther than ten meters from the ship. Lee wouldn't even step off the ramp onto the sand.

Dirk and Lee arrived in the lounge. Ana and Scruggs were already sitting at the table, looking at the display on Ana's comm. Ana gestured at some notations, and Scruggs took notes.

"Showing her the finer points of infantry assault tactics, Senior Centurion?" Dirk asked.

Ana smiled. "Something to help you out, Navy. I'm

showing her how to use radar, infrared and ultraviolet sensors. Starting a course as a Scan Tech, Level One."

"How did you learn to use starship sensors in an army?" Dirk asked.

"Same ones we use for heavy weapons in the legion. Radar is radar. Infrared is infrared. Just read the manual and follow the tutorials."

"And the centurion is showing me how to use the comm equipment," Scruggs said.

Dirk looked at the schematics. They hadn't had much call to use the ship's comm equipment or sensors since leaving Bishop's world, but Ana had worked on the weapons board on numerous occasions, and he'd displayed the deliberate workings that Dirk associated with well-trained techs.

"Your variety of skills are quite impressive, Senior Centurion," Dirk said.

"I'm handy at all sorts of things," Ana said.

Gavin arrived at that moment. "What's up, Skipper?"

"Lee has the computer crunching a course for Parsifal. But I have a suggestion. We don't actually have to go to Parsifal. In fact, I'd rather that we went somewhere else."

"Why don't you want to go to Parsifal?" Scruggs asked.

"Yeah, Skipper, I thought we were scheduled to get an overhaul there?" Gavin said.

"It is a big port, a big shipyard, and it also has a big Imperial base there as well," Dirk said. "Big base means lots of patrols, lots of questions, lots of checks."

"I don't want to go there," Scruggs said. "Let's go somewhere else."

Everybody exchanged looks.

"If Miss Scruggs doesn't want to go there, I don't, either," Lee said.

"Miss Scruggs?" Dirk said. "When did she become 'Miss?'"

"After she saved me from the raging waters," Lee said.

"Raging?" Dirk asked.

"Yes," Lee said. "That is what I called them when I prayed to Paterfather Zeus, the 'raging waters' and I asked what I should do."

"Your crackpot god talks to you?" Ana said. "Does he tell you to stab people in the eye to let the evil spirits out?"

"Pilot, my religion gives much weight to meditation and self-examination to discover the will of the gods. After my deliverance, I acknowledged a debt to Miss Scruggs, and I asked the Paterfather what I should do. The answer is that I should support her like she was my sister. So, if she doesn't want to go to Parsifal, then neither do I." Lee nodded at Scruggs. She turned to Gavin. "Engineer Two?"

Gavin looked nonplussed. "Well, I don't have anything against Parsifal in particular. It seems like a nice place." He looked at Lee. Her brows furrowed, and she frowned at him.

"I mean," Gavin said, "what I meant to say was, no reason to go there at all. Let's go somewhere else." He smiled at Scruggs, Lee, and at Dirk. "Long as I get paid, of course."

"We can talk about that later," Dirk said.

"I want to go to Parsifal, and that was the deal," Ana said. "No dice on going somewhere else."

"Scruggs doesn't want to go," Dirk said.

"She's a stowaway, and she snuck on board with a shotgun. Why do you care what she thinks?" Ana asked.

"I don't care how she got on board or what gun she had," Gavin said. "Lee's right, we owe her, and if she doesn't want to go there, then we're not going there. Doesn't matter what you want, old man. You haven't done anything for me." He faced Ana.

Ana got up. "If I hadn't been watching you, punk, and standing sentry, you would have been washed away before the ship could get over there. Mad swim or no mad swim. And I was the one on the other end of that rope that dragged you in." He glared at Gavin.

Gavin looked pensive. "Point. But we—Lee and I—

owe her more than we owe you."

Dirk spoke up. "Senior Centurion, I believe you were not particularly enamored of Parsifal in particular. You just wanted a major port, correct?"

Ana nodded. "A big port with regular connections to the space lanes."

"And," Dirk continued, "since it was known that I was supposed to take this ship to Parsifal, going somewhere else would delay any . . . official notice that was following us. I think that you wouldn't mind avoiding official notice as well."

Ana nodded slowly. "What other port are you considering?"

"There are several possibilities, all as large or larger, but with very limited Imperial presence. Tetryn is one, but there are others. Will one of them do?"

"How long?" Ana asked.

"Same time as to Parsifal—three more jumps."

"Fine," Ana said as he sat.

"So, we're all agreed, then. We'll recalculate the course, and off we go." Dirk stood. "Lee, if you could join me in the control room to decide on our next step."

"Hang on," Gavin said. "I'm fine with not Parsifal, but this ship is in bad shape. Nothing particular, but with the exception of the maneuver drive, everything is old. Stuff can break at any time. We really need some time in a yard."

"There's that," Ana said. "And there is the most interesting question of all that hasn't been answered."

"What's that, Senior Centurion?" Scruggs asked.

Ana pointed at Dirk. "Why doesn't he want to go near Imperial bases?"

Everyone turned to Dirk. He smiled and spread out his hands.

***

"Okay, let me summarize," Gavin said. The discussion had gone on for two hours. They had cleared the jump limit twenty minutes ago, but they had not decided on a destination. "First, the centurion gets off at a big port within four jumps. Second, we need to be in at least a small yard sometime in the next two months to get some of my list of things fixed up. Third, nobody is getting thrown off anywhere—we can all stay crew as long as we want. Fourth, we have no money to pay for this yard work—or food for that matter, so we need to get some. Fifth, the pilot doesn't admit to this, but the rest of us agree that he actually stole the ship, and the Imperials might be looking for it. Sixth, that really doesn't bother any of us, including me, because all of us agree we want to stay as far away from Imperial notice, but none of us are really being truthful about the reasons, which really doesn't matter because we all feel the same way. But none of us are actually confessing to any crimes of any sort. Sound right?"

Everybody worked through all the commas, then nodded.

"So, we need to pick a next destination. One that isn't an Imperial base, one that is on the way to a larger port, and one where we can earn some money somehow. There will be multiple answers to the first two. Where can we jump to next to get some money, and how do we do that?"

Dirk pointed to a map on the console. "We're a trader, and we have extended jump capability. We could go to any of these planets and trade there. There are three within a jump or two, and they aren't visited that often. We should be able to pick up goods cheap there."

"What kind of goods? And where do we sell them?" Gavin asked.

"Something produced locally that isn't available on a bigger planet. Some sort of rare luxury item that is going to be exotic on other planets," Dirk said.

"That usually means drugs or something like that," Gavin said.

"No drugs," Lee said. "That is not honorable."

"Dried or preserved foods," Dirk said. "Chefs will pay a lot for special ingredients. And they can usually be bought cheap on farming worlds. We just have to find them, make sure we can eat them. Buy a bunch and parcel them out to high-end restaurants. That can work."

"Really? You can run a starship on that?" Ana asked.

"Sure," Dirk said. "We won't make a fortune, but we can live off it for a while."

"If it's that easy, why doesn't every merchant captain do it?" Ana asked.

"They need more of a sure thing. They also have a mortgage to pay. We don't. Being criminals and all."

"What do we swap for these, then? Buckets of sand?" Ana asked.

"Medical supplies," Scruggs said. "There are two cabins below, completely full of medical supplies. Must be stolen. I figure Medic Two, Michaelson has something to say on that."

Then it was Lee's turn to be everyone's target.

Lee blushed. "The former captain of the ship had locked me out of most of the ship's accounts while he was arguing about the bills, and he left without giving me access. But I did have a line of credit they had set up with a medical supply company for medical needs. Somehow, that was left intact, so I ordered as much as I could before they cut me off. I was going to sell it to make up for my pay. I'll donate it. We just need a way to sell it off."

"I've done a bit of trading in my time, Skipper." Gavin said. "But I don't know anything about food or suchlike. I'll have no idea what to get."

"I've got that covered," Dirk said. "I was actually a chef, in another life. I even went to culinary school."

"Really?" Scruggs asked. "But the food on board is so . . ."

"Bland?" Lee said.

"Horrible," Ana said.

"It's not like I have a kitchen here with ingredients and

equipment," Dirk said. "I'm eating trays like the rest of you because that's what we have. But to business. Lee, how much medical equipment is there?"

"A lot," she said. "Mostly common drugs—nothing specialized or dangerous, but low-level anti-pain burn cream and stomach upset pills. Simple tools like forceps and stethoscopes. Stuff I could buy a supply of without attracting notice."

"We can do this," Dirk declared. "Trade some medical gear, get some stock in-trade, pick up enough money to keep us running for a while."

"But not enough for a major overhaul," Gavin said.

"One thing at a time. Lee, let's find us a poor planet with good food," Dirk said and strode to the control room.

Thirty minutes later, they examined the destination in the control room.

"Rockhaul doesn't sound like an appetizing name," Gavin said.

"It's within jump range. It's on the way to the main trade routes—but not on them. It has a small population, a breathable atmosphere, and an agricultural sector of sorts, at least according to the database," Dirk said. "And Navigator Lee has a course laid in."

"I'm not a navigator, Pilot, I'm the medic," Lee said.

"You're navigating, so that makes you the navigator," Dirk said.

"But it's not proper. You can't call me navigator."

"I'll stop calling you navigator when you stop calling me Pilot. How about that?" Dirk said.

Lee was silent, frowning.

"Everybody okay with this as a destination?" Dirk asked.

Silence ensued for a moment, then Ana spoke. "Recruit, you have to answer first."

"Senior Centurion?" Scruggs asked. She sounded puzzled.

"This is a council of war. We go in reverse order of rank. You're junior, you answer first."

"Oh, sure, fine. Whatever the pilot says, he knows best." She smiled at Dirk. Dirk smiled back and winked. His habit was to charm any pretty girl he met, and he did it without thinking.

Ana gave Dirk a sour look, then turned to Gavin. "Engineer Two?"

"Why am I next?" Gavin asked. "You are saying I'm the second most junior?"

"You were the last to join the crew, except for the recruit."

"What's your job, then?"

"I'm the executive officer."

Gavin snickered. "First, we don't need an executive officer. Second, it would probably be Lee if it was anybody, and third, you don't know anything about ships, so what would you do?"

"The executive officer enforces discipline," Ana said, "which has nothing to do with whether we're on a ship or not. I'm good at enforcing discipline. In fact, I feel the need for some enforcement right now."

"The emperor's anus," Gavin said, making a rude hand gesture, "to your enforcement."

Ana's eyes narrowed, and he twitched. Dirk intervened. "Enough, both of you. There will be no enforcement, and, Gavin, that was uncalled for. I expect a basic level of respect from my crewmates to each other."

"I don't like him, Skipper, and I don't trust him," Gavin said.

"I feel the same way about you, punk," Ana said. "But the pilot's right. We both need to do our jobs 'til we're out of this mess. But after we get somewhere civilized, we can meet privately and sort this out."

"Sounds great to me," Gavin said.

"Me too," Dirk said. "That's a great idea. I'll set it up. Behave yourselves 'til then."

Gavin and Ana looked nonplussed. "Skipper?" Gavin said.

"You two want to fight? I'll set it up. Hand weapons but no firearms. Knives or sticks or swords or rocks. Whatever you want. I'll find you a private place, and I'll make sure that it's fair. Just the two of you, face-to-face, mano a mano, or whatever you want to call it. I'll be the referee, Lee will be the medic, and you can pound each other to your hearts' content. We'll have ourselves a good old-fashioned duel. That's what you both want, right?"

Gavin exchanged glances with Ana. "Okay," he said.

"I'd like nothing better," Ana said.

"Good," Dirk said. "In return for my promise, you will do the following. Nothing will happen between you 'til then. You will be polite to each other, no more 'punk' or 'old man.' You will speak respectfully of each other to the rest of the crew. No sarcasm or belittling, and if I tell you to help the other, or even if it's self-evident that you or the other person needs help, you will do so immediately without complaint, to the best of your abilities. We all need to work together to get through this."

"And if we don't agree to this?" Ana asked.

"If either of you breaks the rules, I will join with his opponent to secure your removal from the crew at the earliest opportunity," Dirk said.

"You need an engineer," Ana said.

"We can manage without one," Dirk said. "I've done so before, and I have some training."

"But we don't need an army geek," Gavin said. "Old man. We can do without you."

Faster than any of them could react, Dirk whipped a revolver out of his coveralls and pointed it at Gavin's eye. "Apologize for calling the centurion old man. I demand politeness."

"Skipper, you can't think—"

Dirk pulled back the hammer on the revolver. "I said it, and I mean it."

Gavin's eyes widened. "Skipper?" He put his hands up. "Don't do anything hasty."

Ana hadn't moved, but his eyes tracked Dirk's. "I do believe you mean it, Navy. That's a surprise."

"Decide now, Engineer," Dirk said. "We have places to go, and I need to know if you are part of the solution, or part of the problem."

"I'm onboard," Gavin said. He turned to Ana. "Senior Centurion, I apologize. I will address you respectfully in the future. I look forward to working with you. Until our arranged meeting."

Dirk's eyes turned to Ana.

"Engineer Two," Ana said, "I welcome your assistance. Until our arranged meeting."

Dirk pocketed his pistol and conspicuously turned his back on Gavin. "Right. Gavin, you okay with our next destination?"

"Yes, Skipper," Gavin said. He looked around the cabin. Lee looked stumped. Scruggs looked scared. Ana looked contemplative.

Dirk turned to look at Lee and raised an eyebrow. "Yes, Pilot," she said. "Course laid in."

"Senior Centurion," Dirk said.

"Outstanding choice of destination. I look forward to our arrival," Ana said.

Dirk smiled to himself, then tapped his console. "Stand by for jump," he said.

***

It was going to be almost two hundred hours in jump, and nobody except Scruggs had any specific duties except that four out of every twelve hours they had to watch the nav board. After her initial splurge, Scruggs could handle all the cleaning as part of her work shift every day, and there was no food except basic and trays, rendering no cooking or cleanup afterward.

Everyone caught up on their sleep and browsed

personal entertainment on their comms. Gavin tinkered in the engine compartment, but the mix of spare parts was wrong. Too many had been sold. He made notes of what he needed. They had a lot to do, but there was little he could do with what he had on hand. Dirk and Lee spent a half shift taking inventory of the medical supplies and putting together some notes for trading, but after that, they had nothing special to occupy their time.

Ana worked out with Scruggs every day for two hours in the morning, mostly physical fitness exercises. He began teaching her basic hand-to-hand combat, legion style. He'd also improvised a gym of sorts in the cargo bay, with pull-up bars and weights, and had also found a heavy two-meter metal pole somewhere. Every day, he moved slowly through a complex series of motions that involved swinging and jamming the pole into the wall. The dead slow movements were mesmerizing but didn't look very martial.

Dirk organized a spacer's traditional Zero-G race. Once a day, they would take thrust off. Everybody gathered and pushed off up and down the central corridor, with different exercises and races. Who could go the farthest down the corridor without touching the sides, who could do the most somersaults before reaching the far end, who could touch specific points on the walls the most often.

Not surprisingly, Lee, as a Jovian, was best at all these contests. She could go the entire length of the ship, then pivot and spring back to the start again without touching a wall once. Gavin and Dirk barely made it halfway before they had to correct.

"She looks very elegant when she does that," Gavin said to Dirk. They were watching Lee perform somersaults as she flew through the corridor.

"Elegant?" Dirk asked.

"Like a bird. Flying. Flying through the air like a pretty bird."

Dirk looked at Gavin and laughed.

Most surprising was that Ana was the next best after Lee. He couldn't beat her in anything, but he was at least twice as good in every exercise as the next person behind him. On day three, he went the complete length of the corridor, spinning the entire way, and reaching the engineering hatch without touching anything.

"That's amazing, Senior Centurion," Scruggs said. "Will you teach me that?"

"You think you can learn it?" Ana asked.

"Yes, Senior Centurion. It's just like dancing, isn't it?"

"You can dance, youngster?" Dirk asked.

"My mother was a professional dancer, an actress," Scruggs said. "She made me take dance lessons."

"It's not exactly the same, but it's close. So, eventually, yes," Ana said. "Other drills first, however."

"Where did you learn how to move in Zero-G like that?" Scruggs asked.

"I had a Jovian instructor in the legion."

Lee was drifting down the ladder from the bridge. "You had a Jovian instructor? I thought you hated Jovians?" she said.

Ana shrugged. "I always want to learn from the best. And nobody can touch you Jovians at Zero-G maneuvers. I figure you learn it in school."

"We start in preschool," Lee said. "All Jovians end up going into space, so it's best to have the basics down at a young age."

"If you are the best, could you teach me?" Scruggs asked.

"We do not normally do such things. It is, well, it relates to our religion," Lee said. "The community doesn't look in favor of sharing our methods with outsiders. I'm sorry."

"Oh, that's okay, then," Scruggs said. She grimaced. "Sorry, I don't mean to intrude on your religion."

"I'm sorry, too. I wish I was allowed to help you," Lee

said.

Ana laughed. "That's an odd thing for you to say. That you won't help her."

"As I explained, Senior Centurion," Lee said, "my religion is particular on such things."

"And yet," Ana said, "this is the girl who saved your life, and your own meditations told you that you should treat her as a sister. I would think you could help your sister with something like this."

Lee cocked her head for a moment. "You are absolutely right, Senior Centurion." She turned to Scruggs. "Miss Scruggs, the centurion has pointed out the error in my ways. Insomuch as you are like a sister to me, I will train you as I would a member of my family. Follow me."

"Wait," Ana said. "It's not that simple. You can't start like that, Scruggs."

Lee and Scruggs looked at Ana. "Senior Centurion, I don't understand," Scruggs said.

"Look how you are dressed, what you are wearing," Ana said.

Scruggs looked down. The workouts with Ana were hard, and she always sweated a lot. Since she was the one who had to do everyone's laundry, she had taken to going barefoot and wearing as little as possible to create less work for herself. She was wearing nothing but a sports bra and brief shorts. "Senior Centurion, this is what you told me to wear for physical fitness training."

"I did. It is. But this is different. This is tactical training. You need equipment. Wait here." Ana racked the pole he was training with, then pulled himself up the central ladder. Lee and Scruggs stared at each other, confused. A moment later, Ana returned with a shotgun over his shoulder and a revolver in a thigh holster.

"These are both unloaded. Come here," Ana said. He helped her attach the holster. "Like, so, tighten here till it's snug but doesn't stop blood flow." Then he handed her the shotgun, and she took it and slung the strap over her shoulder. "Both hands," Ana said. "Grip the stock and barrel, barrel upward. That's it. Good." He waited a beat and nodded as she checked that the shotgun was actually unloaded, then checked the revolver as well. "Well done, recruit. You'll train in Zero-G with these."

"Senior Centurion," Lee said. "I can't train her while she carries those."

"No training without equipment," Ana said. "Train like you'll fight. And when you fight, you'll have a whole lot more than that attached to you. If the freak doesn't like it, she can take it up with her god. Shouldn't you get started, freak?"

Lee's eyes narrowed, then she turned toward Scruggs. "Come up to the control room. We will start there."

***

Three shifts later, Dirk was taking his turn on the gym equipment. It was only different weights and bars attached to the hull, but with a little ingenuity, he could do continuous strength exercises. The maneuver drive was running just enough to give an up and a down. The men had split the equipment between them, Ana early on first shift, then Dirk, and later, Gavin. Ana seemed like an early bird, and Gavin a night owl, so they seldom crossed paths, but Dirk deemed it prudent to make it known that he would be using the gym equipment between the two of them, to minimize the possibility of an accidental encounter.

Ana was finishing up with a final series of pushups as Dirk arrived and set up for his workout.

"Ninety-eight, ninety-nine, one hundred," Ana said. He pushed himself up and took deep breaths. Sweat stained his shirt.

"You stink, Senior Centurion," Dirk said. He set weights on a bar and sat on a bench.

Ana reached into his pocket and pulled a small container out. He extracted a yellow pill and slipped it under his tongue. He clamped his mouth shut and breathed heavily through his nose for a few moments longer, then opened his mouth and drew in a deep lungful of air. "No more than usual—probably the engineer is letting us down on the air systems again."

"They aren't keeping up with the smells. I agree," Dirk said. "But I think he's doing the best he can do with the equipment he has."

"I agree. And I owe you a vote of thanks, Pilot."

"Thanks for what?"

"For finding a way for me to not have to kill the engineer and his girlfriend."

"There are no circumstances where you would 'have' to kill the engineer. Or Lee, as I'm assuming you are referring to."

"Self-defense."

"Self-defense?

"He was doing the chicken dance. Showing himself off in front of her, trying to look tough. Given a few more incidents, and he would have convinced himself the only way to prove his manhood was to take a shot at me, then I would have had to kill him. And his girlfriend. Now it won't happen."

Dirk leaned back on the bench and flexed his arms, pushing the weight to full extension, then back down. "What about the meeting I promised between the two of you? The duel."

"Never going to happen," Ana said. "You're too smart for that. The next few planets, it won't be convenient for us to meet, or you'll have some important task that needs to be done, an errand to be run, or you'll make up something. You won't let any meeting happen. Not anywhere that you might need an engineer." Ana leaned over and flexed, reaching for his toes. He easily touched them, then pushed farther to spread his palms flat on the floor.

"But what if Gavin pushes me, says he wants it to

happen?"

"You won't let him. You'll snap him back," Ana said. "Remind him that he promised that you're the 'Skipper,' as he calls you, and that it's not up to him to set terms, and he'll back down. You won't make me kill him." Ana stretched, walked over and unracked the metal pole he used, and began a series of slow motions where he stretched, pointed, and bent, moving the pole through graceful arcs.

"How sure are you that you can kill him? He's younger, he's fast, he obviously knows how to use those knives he carries, and he doesn't panic in a crisis, like with the water. You sure you can take him?" Dirk asked.

Ana exploded into motion. He swung his pole at ten times the speed from before. It whizzed around his hands, over his shoulder, to the left, to the right. He spun around behind him and smashed the tip of the pole into a protruding metal flange on the hull. Then he stepped back and stopped. Dirk looked closely at the flange. A row of five of them lined the hull, each about a quarter inch in diameter, and the middle one had been bent back ninety degrees. The others were untouched and unmarked.

"I can take him anytime," Ana said.

CHAPTER 16

The Heart's Desire loafed into Rockhaul orbit at an easy one g. Everybody crowded the control room.

"Any calls from the planetary authorities?" Dirk asked.

"I don't think there are any," Lee said. "There are exactly three satellites in orbit. Standard colony equatorial weather-comm package. They track storms, watch for forest fires, repeat local comm from ground stations, and give a very limited GPS system. They're definitely older than any of us. Even older than the centurion."

"Keep it up, freak," Ana said.

"Senior Centurion, we spoke of this," Dirk said. He frowned at Ana.

Ana smiled. "Of course. My apologies, Medic Two, Michaelson. I will address you properly in the future." He nodded at Lee, then Dirk. "And my apologies to you, too, Pilot."

Lee looked suspicious but turned back to her board. "The sailing directions says there is one port on the east side of that big island there, except it's not a port. It's just a flat space next to a river. There is a town there, about eight thousand people."

"Let's not go there," Dirk said. "What's the second or third largest place? Something in the middle of a big farming area, away from the trade routes. Someplace we can sell medical equipment for the most with the least questions."

Lee paged through some screens. "Central Falls, on that river there, on the west coast. It's on the opposite side of the continent from all the other people. According to the sailing directions, it's the head of navigation on that river, handles all the waterborne commerce on the west coast, plus that entire valley. Let me put it up on the board." Lee tapped screens, and the planet's horizon spread across them. There were about five large continents and dozens of rugged mountain-capped islands. Large glaciers covered both poles, and sea ice drifted two-thirds of the way to the equator. Most of the population was on a small island continent straddling the equator and its associated coastal islands. Glaciated mountains bisected the interior of the island from north to south, and short rivers rushed to the sea in all directions. Lee had highlighted a dot mid-way up a river on the west side.

"Plenty of space to land on that floodplain," Dirk said. He strapped himself into his chair and produced a flask of something alcoholic.

"And water," Gavin said. "We can land just upstream of that town. How big is it?"

"About three thousand, according to the directions. The numbers might be suspect, though. The last update to the records was twenty years ago, and there hasn't been a census in over a hundred years, since the mine played out."

"There was a mine?" Dirk asked.

"Palladium, according to the records. Closed a hundred years ago, and the miners left. Couple hundred thousand people had moved into the hinterland to take advantage of the farming, build settlements. Lots of wood- and steam-powered stuff there. Plenty of wood to burn, but no coal or petroleum. Main town has a hydro plant on the river. The others use wood or steam. Population hasn't so much regressed as stayed where they wanted to be."

"Wood-fired stoves, subsistent farming—that's what we want," Dirk said. "Honest yeomen, horny-handed sons of the soil, toiling for their daily bread. That's who we want to see," he said.

"Sounds wretched," Scruggs said.

"It probably is," Dirk agreed. He took a long gulp from his flask, wheezed a breath, and took another. He pulled his straps close and tapped his screen. "Prepare to deorbit," he said.

Everybody rushed to strap in.

***

They landed the Heart's Desire on a flat field within about a mile of the edge of the town of Central Falls, just downstream from its namesake waterfall, where a stream cut through wasteland to the river. The main river here was at least a kilometer wide and meandered between steep banks. Lee had originally wanted to be closer to town, but Ana had insisted on something defensible, with good sight lines. He wanted to be five miles away, in the middle of a cleared field. They compromised on a triangle of land across the river from the main town, with steep banks on two sides and a dense forest several hundred yards away. A trail into town ran by the forest. Close enough that people could come and trade but far enough away where they wouldn't be mobbed.

About a dozen warehouses with wharves lined the riverside below the falls, and fishing boats and other sail-powered transports were tied up at the docks. A paddle-wheeled steamer, wood-fueled by the looks of it, cut through the serene waters from one side to the other. The deck was loaded with wagons pulled by what looked like oxen. About a half dozen water mills were set up on one side of the river, with attached millponds and mill races, all taking advantage of the water drop.

All five of them walked down the ramp and inhaled the air. The air was cold, bracing, and smelled of pine, spruce, and woodsmoke. Dirk made it to the bottom of the ramp before puking this time.

"Pilot, sometime, you'll have to tell me about the landing that caused that," Ana said.

"Actually, I don't have to," Dirk said. "It can remain my secret, old chap. Right. Now we all need to, we need to . . . do something." Dirk looked around. "I don't actually know anything about how to trade."

"First, we'll put Scruggs up there with the binoculars so that she can see what's coming," Ana said. "We'll give her my submachine gun—she has to look threatening. The locals will recognize a weapon, but they won't know the range or how lethal, and the longer we can keep them from getting a good look at it, the better. Second, everybody wears a revolver in a holster. Keep it buttoned. Don't take it out unless you are fearful of your life but let everybody see it. Third, I stand at the bottom of the ramp with a shotgun—a loaded one in case one of these hicks can see the difference. None of the locals go on board unescorted. Nobody is outside by themselves—minimum two at a time. Nobody goes more than ten meters from the ship."

The other four looked at Ana, then at Dirk. Dirk nodded. "That seems like prudent behavior for the start of things, Centurion. We don't know these people, and we don't know how things are done here. We need to feel things out."

"I don't need a revolver, Skipper," Gavin said. "I'm better with my knives."

"Probably the truth," Ana said. "But the point is not to win a fight but to look threatening so they don't try to start a fight. The bigger and tougher we look, the more willing they will be to do business with us and not push us around."

"That's actually very astute, Senior Centurion," Gavin said.

"I've studied violence all my life. The best way to win a fight is to start it on your terms, not theirs. When I want to start something, it will start. Not before. Recruit, come with me," Ana said and traipsed back into the ship.

Gavin, Lee, and Dirk watched him go. "He's actually very good at this," Gavin said. "He sounds like the tough-talking, rock-headed non-com, but he always has a plan."

"Well, I don't think we need to worry about our security with him here," Dirk said. A clang rung out as

Scruggs climbed up the ship's dorsal surface. She was back into her coveralls, the submachine gun slung over her shoulder. "She does look quite imposing, doesn't she?" Dirk said. "Very martial. Working with the centurion has certainly cleaned her up."

"I don't understand that, either," Gavin said. "Why go to all the bother of teaching her? That training isn't him just being a pain in the ass. He's treating her as a recruit for a Marine billet. Weapons, Zero-G combat, and the sensor work as well. And he goes out of his way to do it properly. He's actually way more patient than any centurion I know."

"Know a lot of army centurions, do you, Engineer Two?" Dirk said.

Gavin smiled. "Skipper, you know that I might have had a close contact with more than a few. He is different. I'll be sorry when I kill him."

"Not until I say you can," Dirk said.

"I didn't appreciate you pointing a gun at me, Skipper," Gavin said.

"Just recently, if I recall correctly, you had one of those knives that you hide—not very well—pulled out and ready to stick in me," Dirk said. "I don't recall you asking about my appreciation at the time," Dirk said.

Gavin shrugged. "I needed you to send the ship somewhere."

"And I have a feeling that we'll need both of our skills to get out of this mess," Dirk said. "Because we are in a mess. It's no secret that all of us are running from something, and the faster and farther away we get from where this started, the better it will be for everybody. And if we all work together as a crew, we will get very far, very fast, very quickly. Best for everybody, don't you agree?"

"I do, Skipper, I do. That's why I listen to you, and that's why I'm not going to do anything to the centurion until you say I can."

"Good," Dirk said.

"Then I kill him," Gavin said.

***

Ana reappeared on the ramp. He carried holsters and revolvers for everybody, and after distributing them, returned to collect his shotgun. He returned to stand guard at the ramp.

Gavin was examining the edge of the ramp with a tiny but very bright flashlight. "Dents," he said. "It'll start leaking if I don't pound them out. I'll put it on the maintenance list." He looked up at Dirk. "What do we do now?"

"Take it as it comes," Dirk said.

Their arrival had been quite noisy, and after they had grounded, groups of people had already boarded some lighters and flat-bottomed barges and were steering toward the shore. The first group was three fishermen who had been dragging lines offshore as the Heart's Desire landed. They had rowed over and beached their boat on the shore and walked up. They saw the armed men and stopped a distance away.

"Where you folks from?" the first fisherman called.

"Not here, obviously," Dirk said.

"Yep, here to trade?" the fisherman said.

"Indeed, my good man," Dirk said.

"What ye have?"

"Medical supplies, small items. What do you fellows want?"

"Doctors supplies is good. Tools, metal, or plastic. Solar panels if you have 'em."

"We've got some of that. What have you got?"

"What you need?"

"Foodstuff, of course, precious metals. What else have you got?"

The fishermen conferred with each other. As they talked, a barge-like boat propelled with poles grounded behind them. Perhaps twenty men and women swarmed off and surrounded the fishermen. A brief exchange of words preceded the group's interruption. A group of three, two men and a woman, marched toward the spacefarers. Five men stood sentry behind them, three with swords belted to their waist, two with bows and a quiver of arrows on their shoulders. They seemed alert but didn't have hands on their weapons. Their clothes showed little variation. Heavy leather pants, black leather boots, and elaborately tooled leather vests. The shirts were different colors.

The crew watched as the deputation approached. The leading local was a balding older man. His right knee didn't move correctly, and he swiveled toward them with the aid of a cane. His voice didn't match his looks. It was clear and loud.

"Welcome, strangers. I am Benjamin Bannersfield, the Alcalde of this town." He bowed once toward them, then indicated his companions. "This is Jomain Brackson, the deputy alcalde." Jomain was taller than Benjamin, with greasy black hair, a big mustache, and radiated a sense of arrogance.

"And Zelta Furchinson, the owner of one of our largest trading communes." Zelta was short and fair, with blond hair. She was middle-aged and had the look of somebody who spent a great deal of time staring at columns of figures, either on a computer screen or in books. She carried a comm unit, not a recent one, but powerful enough all the same. Jomain and Zelta bowed in their turn. "We are the trading committee. Welcome to Central Falls."

"Thank you, alcalde, I am Pilot Dirk. This is Medic Lee and Engineer Gavin," Dirk said.

"Welcome, all of you. What are your plans here, Pilot?"

"We come to trade, of course," Dirk said. "I've never heard of a trading committee before. How does that work?"

"The town empowers us to purchase things that may

be too expensive for a single individual, and we serve to regulate the trading, make sure that you get paid properly, that nobody abuses your trust, and that no prohibited items are traded, except under the council's discretion."

Gavin leaned over to whisper in Dirk's ear. "And they keep all the good stuff for themselves and resell it at huge markup to the locals."

"What type of items are prohibited?" Dirk asked.

"No recreational drugs of any sorts. No weapons, unless offered first to the trading council, of course. Other than that, we're interested in anything you have to offer."

"What about alcohol?" Gavin asked.

"We're happy to trade that," Benjamin said. "In fact—" He turned around to the crowd and gestured. Two teenage boys were standing next to a crate. One hefted the crate and brought it forward, placed it at Benjamin's feet, then pulled a bottle out. His companion carried a tray with eight glasses on it. He removed two and put them in his pocket. The first boy showed the bottle to Benjamin, who nodded. The boy pulled a wooden stopper out with a popping sound. He poured six generous shots, recapped the bottle, and put it back in the crate. The tray was offered around, and each person took a glass. The two boys bowed and withdrew without a word.

"Here is some of our pine cone schnapps, a local delicacy. Let us drink together. Free trades," Benjamin said and drank the entire shot at once.

"Free trades," echoed the other two committee members before they drank up. Dirk smiled and hefted his glass. "Free Trades," he said, then drank. The shot was sweet, tasting of plum with a pine zest aftertaste. It went down easily. Gavin and Lee drank theirs. Lee coughed a bit but only for a moment.

"Most delightful," Dirk said. "We will have to put some of that on our trading list."

"Please," Benjamin said. "Let this crate be our gift to you. Take it as a token of our esteem. We pride ourselves on our hospitality here, and we would like to encourage more traders to come."

"I don't imagine you get many ships here," Dirk said.

"We get enough," Benjamin said. "We are a small town, but many traders recognize the advantage of trading directly with the end customers."

"Stop pulling his Imperial crank, Benny," Zelta said. "He knows we're fooling him. Pilot Dirk, we get less than one ship a year on this side of the mountains. They get three, four a year on the other side, but the last one here was fourteen months ago. We'll pay more here than they will on that side, and you'll make out better here if you deal with us directly."

"Deal with you directly for what?" Gavin said. "What have you got that we could use? You don't seem to be rolling in Imperial credits here."

"We have some credits, but only a little," Zelta said. "We have lumber, anything wooden that you want. Custom carving, furniture, the works. There are trees out there that are ten feet in diameter, and we've cut tabletops and such like directly from them. The wood grain is amazing. We have cattle in the hills, so lots of leather. We'll send somebody over to measure you, and you can all have custom boots, gloves, hats, shirts, jackets, whatever you want. We've got some very soft, very supple stuff we use and some talented artisans. Handmade clothes for all of you. And a bunch of standard sizes for trade. All sorts of food, vegetables, grains, whatever you want. We have lots of different types of booze. We age a lot of it just for this reason. One of my colleagues has a cellar of brandy you wouldn't believe. Come over and taste some, and we can set you up with crates of it. We know what spacers want."

"That's fine for our personal needs, but we need things we can trade for a profit," Gavin said. "You'll have to have some sort of bulk items?"

"Copper," Zelta said.

"Copper?" Gavin said. "How? You're burning wood here."

"We've got a wood-powered smelter, believe it or not. With a bellows run by those water wheels, we can smelt copper ore and some others."

"I wouldn't have believed that," Gavin said.

"Now, what have you got? What are you trading?"

"Our big item is medical supplies. We've got a wide variety of them. And various other sundries," Gavin said.

"Those, we can use," Zelta said. "Alcalde?"

"Yes, councilwoman?" Benjamin said.

"I suggest that you and I go with the engineer and the medic here and get their list of tradeable items. I could also talk to the engineer about some specific items we need. He might have a spare, or he might be able to fabricate them. You can supervise." She turned to Dirk. "And you, Pilot, and one other of your crew could go into town and see what you see there. Perhaps something will strike your fancy one way or the other."

"I think just myself would be fine," Dirk said. A long pause accompanied the Rockhaulians' glances between each other. Ana, who had been listening without appearing to, said, "Pilot, I wouldn't mind going with you to see some of the city."

The Rockhaulians' faces cleared. "That would be fine, Pilot Dirk."

"Just give me a moment to speak with our security staff," Ana said. He sauntered into the ship. Everybody stared at each other for a moment, then they heard the hatch clang closed, and a minute later, Ana exited, followed by Scruggs. Scruggs had the shotgun slung over her shoulder.

"Ready when you are, Pilot," Ana said.

"Follow me please," Jomain said. Gavin and Lee ushered their two guests inside.

Ana and Dirk trailed behind Jomain.

"Think that they are being hospitable?" Dirk asked.

"I think we are hostages so that they make sure they get their alcalde and friend back."

"That's what I think, too," Dirk said. "They appear to have done this before."

"Unlike us," Ana whispered.

Jomain stopped at the group of people standing behind the guards. "These people are here to trade. The committee is with them right now. Today and tomorrow belongs to the committee, and tomorrow night, there will be a welcome banquet at the city hall. After that, they will be here for seven days to trade, and there will be another grand banquet at the end, before they leave. They will tour the town with me now."

The crowd muttered and dispersed. They didn't seem angry, just slightly disappointed.

"Kind of setting a schedule for us, old chap, aren't you?" Dirk said to Jomain.

Jomain was walking down a wooden gangplank to the barge that had brought him. "That is the usual way, Pilot. The council will manage the bulk of the trades, then you have some time for your crew to do personal trading and loading. Sometimes, we need a few days to collect the bulk items you purchase. And traders rarely want to waste time."

"Fine with us, alcalde," Ana said. "We're just not used to our partners being as efficient as you obviously are."

"We've had traders before. We're poor here, not unsophisticated. Our ancestors marooned us here, so we have to make the best of it." Jomain climbed down onto the barge, and Dirk and Ana followed. The guards remained behind, watching the ship.

"That's an interesting attitude," Dirk said.

Jomain shrugged. "We are here, not somewhere else. The planet is fertile enough. We have food and shelter. It's cold in the winter, colder than other places, so I am told, but we don't notice the difference. We have Imperial technology for the schools, and we have a good library.

Knowledge of how to do things is not a problem. But we are limited in what we can trade. Not much in the way of metals or manufactured goods. We have excellent quality handmade items. The suits and boots are like nothing you will ever see anywhere else. We'd like a little more advanced medical care and some more automated factory units, but those are very expensive. We can't usually afford them." Jomain turned to them and clapped Dirk on the shoulder. "And now you can see our town!"

CHAPTER 17

The town was primitive but planned. Mill wheels churned up the riverside. Each had its own attached string of warehouses and wharves. These were almost all wood construction with a smattering of brick, and the river ships were all built of wood. A two-masted sailing vessel was under construction at a yard downstream of the city. Set back from the line of mills was the town proper. A gravity-fed piped aqueduct ran down from farther up the river, and feeder lines ran off it at regular intervals. Drainage channels took street drains downriver to a chain of settling ponds before wastewater flowed back into the river. In the center of town was a central square with a fountain. Substantial buildings surrounded the square. One was Imperial construction—two-story stone with steep roofs covered with solar panels. Several one-story brick buildings lined the main square with their own solar panels. Their construction was cruder. The rest of the town was a combination of brick and wooden structures. Most had steep peaked roofs, set far apart. Almost every building had solar panels or wind generators.

"That's the library, school, and town office," Jomain said, pointing to the Imperial building. "Also, the medical suite. No central electricity," Jomain said. "Everything is solar or wind. Each house handles their own batteries, equipment, such like. We get lots of wind. Water comes from the town's system. There's a solar-powered ultraviolet water treatment plant upriver."

"Why the pointed roofs?" Ana asked.

"Snow," Jomain said. "Our winter isn't that long. Our axial tilt is too low for the seasons to last, but we get a lot of precipitation, and the snow can crush a building if it gets too deep. This way, it just slides off. Of course, that means the streets fill up, but it's only for a month. Everybody stays home that month."

"What do you manufacture with those mills?" Dirk asked.

"Anything that we can do with mechanical energy. Some are sawmills, wine presses, and presses to crush fruits and dry fruits. We export barrels of dried fruit. Grain mills. Hammer mills to beat the hides and clean them. One's a copper-stamping mill. Another runs a forge."

"Do you make guns? Revolvers?" Ana asked.

Jomain's expression darkened. "The council won't let anyone except themselves have firearms. But we can make swords. There are some wild animals in the hills—a sort of small wolf. We use the swords for protection. But no guns allowed to the commoners."

"Grain mills?" Dirk asked. "How do you trade the bulky stuff?"

"It's all water traffic," Jomain said. "That's what those schooners are for."

"What's a schooner?"

They called the two-masted sailing ships schooners. They had a useful combination of speed, seaworthiness, capacity, and could be managed with a small crew. Central Falls was the nexus of river and seaborne trade routes. Goods and people came down the steep rivers from the western side of the mountains and onto the main river, where they were met at Central Falls by schooners that exchanged the bulk goods for manufactured and trade goods. Central Falls was the center of a long, navigable ocean passage. Its river—named, of course, the Central River—was one of the largest on the west side of the continent.

"And we handle the monsoon fleet as well," Jomain said.

"Monsoon fleet? You mean like those big winds?" Ana asked.

"Yes. Twice a year, a fleet of bigger ships, four times as big as those schooners, sails from here around the southern cape, to the capital spaceport, and back the next year. At the start of the winds, we send out a convoy. At the end of the next, we get one back. Not the same ships—they have to wait a year at each destination. I've been on two of them—most of us have."

"Where are these ships right now?" Ana asked.

"Both convoys are at sea now—it's summer, the good weather," Jomain said.

"Don't you worry about storms and things like that?"

"It's not as risky as it sounds. We've got over a hundred years of records, and we still have some weather forecasting from the remaining satellites."

"Wooden ships. Good use of what resources you have, old chum," Dirk said.

"That's what we've got the infrastructure to build, so that's what we build," Jomain said. "Want some lunch?"

"Some real food would be agreeable, my good man," Dirk said. "What did you have in mind?"

Jomain led them to a group of three buildings on the west side of the square, opposite the Imperial building. Each had a sign with a name and a picture of something food-related, either a pot or a glass or a bottle. "Benta's Beer Fest," Jomain said, leading them into the smallest of the three. "Best beer in town."

He pulled open a heavy door and entered a foyer. A large man with a sword strapped to his belt leaned against the wall. He nodded at Jomain but then stood when he saw Dirk and Ana. "Strangers!" he said. Jomain leaned toward him and had a quiet word. Then the man nodded and sat.

"Let's go inside." Jomain walked into the main room. It was dark, the only windows being high up on the wall. Two large fireplaces on opposite ends of the building radiated heat. After coming in from the cold outside, Dirk began to sweat immediately. A woman bustled over to them.

"I'm Benta. Welcome, strangers. You here for lunch or entertainment?"

"Benta, we're here for lunch," Jomain said. "We'd like some food. Bring out your best."

"Let's not get too hasty," Ana said. "We're just looking around the town to start, and though we'd like a little lunch, we don't have any local money. In fact, we don't know what the local money is?"

"Hides, we denominate in terms of hides," Jomain said. "Cattle hides, believe it or not. Plenty of them around, easy to exchange, and we can store 'em."

"We have an excellent lunch," Benta said. "Soup, salad, some meat, beer for both of you. Only twenty hides each."

"Benta, these gentlemen are my guests. Bring us a lunch and put it on my account," Jomain said.

"J, shouldn't we be—"

"No, we shouldn't," Jomain said. He narrowed his eyes. "I also had a few words with Myfel at the door. He'll be handling things there. Bring us lunch and some of the good lager," Jomain said.

The three men sat and made small talk. Benta went back to the bar, marshaled her staff, and sent a waitress over.

"Here you go, strangers," the waitress said. She was shorter than them but had long black hair caught in a braid behind her head and sparkling blue eyes. She wore a tight, cropped bodice, was bare at the waist, and tight leather pants that showed off her curves. "Three lagers. Food's on the way. Anything else?" She smiled at both the newcomers. "That's quite the heavy outfit you have there, strangers," she said. Dirk and Ana were wearing coveralls over their skin suits, and the change from the cold outside to the overheated room was causing them to sweat. "Here, let me," she said. She took Dirk's arm in her hand and carefully rolled each sleeve up, taking care to let his arm brush her hip as she did. Then she leaned forward, put a

172

hand on his chest, and tugged the zipper on his coveralls down his chest. She had to lean forward to do it, making sure to brush his shoulders with her breasts. "There you go, spaceman."

"Why thank you very much, pretty lady," Dirk said. He gave her a huge smile. "My name is Dirk. What's yours?"

She smiled again. "My name is Daph. Let me know if you need anything else. Anything at all." She turned around and sauntered away. All three men's eyes followed her.

"I hope the food is as good as the view," Dirk said.

Shortly, Daph delivered two platters covered with greens and a grilled steak, then put a soup beside it. The beer was cold and tasty, but even accounting for the fact that this was the first real food they had eaten in weeks, the food wasn't very good. The soup tasted like cold water, the greens were wilted, and the steak smelled burned.

A man they hadn't met before slid in across the table from them. He nodded once at Jomain.

Jomain smiled and turned to Dirk and Ana. "This is Apsis. He's a friend of mine. I asked him to join us for lunch.

"Strangers, glad to meet you," Apsis said. "I see you have revolvers, good ones. I'll pay gold or copper for every one you can get me. Double what the committee pays. Cash on the barrel."

"I understood there was to be no personal trading 'til the committee has their go," Dirk said.

"Emperor's foreskin to the committee. I'll pay triple their going rate. I've got a place way north of town. I'll give you the coordinates, you give me a day and the amount, and we'll be ready with the gold or copper—or whatever you want—waiting at my ranch. What you say?"

"I say we'll wait 'til we deal with the committee, fellow," Dirk said.

"I think you should give this man's offer serious consideration," Jomain said. He sat back and smiled at them. "Not everybody in town agrees with the committee's monopolizing of trade."

Dirk and Ana glanced around. The room was overheated for the planet, and even in a place with this many trees, all that firewood wasn't free. The downstairs was all two- or four-person tables, with a stage at one end. An all-female staff—good-looking females at that—served guests. A second-floor balcony ran around the perimeter of the room, with many doors opening off them. Two large men with swords stood by the door, obviously guards.

"So, Jomain," Ana said. "Why did you bring us to lunch in a brothel?"

Jomain shrugged. "This isn't a brothel, it's a restaurant. I needed somewhere neutral that people wouldn't mind coming in to talk with you, and I know the owner."

"I'll bet you do," Ana said. "I was in the army. I know a brothel when I see one. And these girls are certainly attractive, but for now, I want better food than this. If this is the best you can provide, then I think we might reevaluate our trading partners," Ana said. He stood. "I think the pilot and I would like to take a walk around town, rather than finishing, this . . . this . . . whatever, Pilot?"

"I do feel the need for a walk after spending so much time in the ship," Dirk said. He stood. "Let's go for a walk, Senior Centurion."

Apsis looked startled. "Hey, wait, I paid good money—"

"Shut up," Jomain said and scrambled up after them.

Dirk and Ana walked toward the door. The two guards at the door stood from their lounging and moved to bar the exit. "Nobody leaves 'til Jomain says so."

"Are you trying to bar our egress, my good man?" Dirk said.

"Listen, space scum, your fancy ships don't smash any ice here, so unless you—uurgh."

Ana punched the first guard in the stomach, doubling him over. He hit the other in the head with a one-two punch, hooked a foot behind his leg, and shoved him to the floor. He hit the wall with his head on the way down.

"Outside. Run," Ana said. He charged through the curtain around the foyer.

They ran out of Benta's Beer Fest. A line of people stood outside the door, and as soon as Dirk and Ana sped by, they clamored for attention. Dirk and Ana charged down the road, and the crowd flowed after them.

***

"So, the only remaining items on our list are the stethoscopes, and the food and water supplies for your ship and crew while you are here," Benjamin said. The two committee members were seated in the lounge, negotiating with the crew.

"Really, it's just—the price you want to pay for the stethoscopes is too low. We won't pay for water," Gavin said. "The river is free, and if you give us any sort of issue about collecting it, we'll just maneuver to some deserted lake and pick up all we need."

"I agree about the water," Zelta said. "Suck up all you want. But I don't think the stethoscopes will fetch what you think, so how about we strike them off the list? You can offer them at the general trades the next day after the council. As far as eating, I have a tavern in town, and any of your crew can eat there every day, as my guests, no charge for food, and two glasses of alcohol per person per meal."

"That's very generous of you. Thank you," Lee said.

"She makes her money off the locals coming into her bar to see the strangers," Gavin said.

Zelta started to speak, but Scruggs interrupted her reply by coming through the door and pointing the submachine gun at the two Rockhaulers. "Hands up," she said. Both put their arms up immediately.

"Sister, what are you doing?" Lee asked.

"Centurion just called. They're being chased through the town by an armed mob, and that Jomain guy set them up with people who were trying to buy weapons. I don't have the details, but they want the committee people secured."

Gavin turned to Benjamin. "An angry mob? Buying weapons? We would have agreed to offer them to you if we had any."

Benjamin and Zelta looked at each other. "That Imperial anus, Jomain," Zelta said. "He's behind this." She turned to Gavin. "Look, this is a dispute between the first families. A local thing. Nothing to do with you. Jomain represents a faction that wants to cut us out of the trading."

"Are our people safe?" Gavin asked.

"Of course they are. If they can get to one of our family-run houses. We'll protect you. Can I use my comm?"

"Of course you can," Gavin said. He stood and gestured to Scruggs. "After, of course, you are secured, as the centurion would say."

***

"Problems up ahead, Centurion," Dirk said. They had ducked back and forth between different streets and the occasional alleyway to get away from the pursuing mob. In truth, the mob hadn't really pursued them so much as trotted after them. It became apparent that there was no violence in the offering, just very aggressive curiosity. Ana and Dirk headed toward the ship, but a gang of eight toughs blocked the road. Wearing matching dark-green shirts, headgear, and leather belts that holstered short swords, they marched side by side toward the two men. "Two bar toughs, we can take," Ana said. "Eight trained fighters will be a problem if they get within hand weapon range of us. We can kill them from here." Ana fingered his gun.

"Guns against swords. Hardly sporting, do you think?"

"You find dying sporting, Navy?"

"Not at all." Dirk said. He sighed. "But I just never saw myself, well, fighting this way. In this kind of fight."

"You mean shooting poor kids who never had a chance in life, just because they are in the way of you getting a meal?"

Dirk looked at the centurion. "Exactly. I always thought myself a better person than that."

"Me, too, Navy. Me, too." Ana said. "I guess we might find out what type of people we are, after all. Think you'll like that information?"

"Not at all, not at all," Dirk said.

"Hello, strangers," a woman's voice said. A short, fair woman with tousled blond hair stepped forward. She had a pistol in a holster on her hip. Dirk didn't recognize the model, but it was definitely Imperial-manufactured. "I'm Dena."

"We're a little confused as to what is going on," Dirk said.

"Nothing to do with you. Private dispute. We're taking care of it. Your ship wants to talk to you, then I'm supposed to take you to lunch." She turned to the guards. "Go around, give them plenty of room, but block the street." The group of guards dutifully split in two, moved to the side of the road, and filed past Ana and Dirk. Dirk and Ana had their hands on their revolvers but didn't draw them. Once past, the guards blocked the road but faced away from the two of them, toward the shambling crowd.

Dena walked toward the two men, stopped ten feet away, dropped her holster on the ground, walked up, and extended her hand.

"I'm Dena, Zelta's younger and prettier sister," Dena said. "Half sister, that is."

"You certainly are," Dirk agreed. He could see the family resemblance. Short, fair, but skinnier with an unlined face. "I'm Pilot Dirk, and this is Centurion Ana."

"Your ship has my sister, and the alcalde locked up while we sort this out. It's just a misunderstanding. Centurion, you can carry my sword belt or just leave it there, whichever you prefer." She gave Dirk a long look from top to bottom. "You're a tall one, aren't you? Where'd you get all those muscles?"

"We work out on the ship."

"Well," Dena said. She grasped Dirk's arm and led him down the road. "Let's get some lunch. You can tell me about your workout. Maybe show it to me."

"Won't your husband object?"

"Don't have one. No boyfriend either. Just lonely old me," Dena said. She looked over her shoulder. "You should call your ship, Centurion."

Ana rolled his eyes but followed.

***

Six hours later, things had quieted down considerably. Dirk and Ana were back on the ship, and Zelta and Benjamin had left. A little work on Gavin's part had managed to connect their comm systems so that they could exchange comm traffic with Zelta and Dena at their family's warehouse and offices.

"Arrival of a new group always affects the politics of a region," Dirk said. "We're just another pawn in some political game that's been going on here for years."

"I don't like being a pawn," Ana said. "But how did you know what was going on?"

"Standard stuff. Newcomers always upset any equilibrium in a static society. Ours was only a minor upset, of course, but that Jomain fellow decided to take advantage of it."

"But he didn't actually threaten you, did he?" Gavin said. "He just took you to a skanky place for a bad lunch and let other people offer you money."

"That's true," Dirk said. "We were just uncomfortable

with an unexpected situation, and we reacted."

"I'd rather a premature reaction than a premature death," Ana said.

"Regardless, we've got a deal with Dena and Benjamin's people for about half of the cargo. They're going to provide us a whole list of stuff. Nothing overwhelming, but a large variety.

"Lee, will it be enough for us to keep the ship running?" Dirk asked.

"Ask the engineer, Pilot. He did most of the talking. He seems to have a knack for this," she said.

Dirk turned to Gavin. "Engineer? You did the trading?"

"I, ah, may have served on a few free traders before, Skipper," Gavin said.

"As an engineer or as a cargo master?" Ana asked.

Gavin ignored him. "We've got as good a mix as we can get from here, Skipper. They don't produce a lot, but we've got something of everything, and we're not giving up a lot of those medical supplies, so we can try again at the next planet."

Dirk was reading a list on his comm. "Furniture. Carved walking sticks. Dried blueberries?"

"We should be able to make good money on them. Somewhere."

"Well, the somewhere is the problem, isn't it?" Dirk said.

"Not my problem, Navy," Ana said. "You promised to drop me off at a major port in the next two or three jumps."

"And I will. We'll need the maintenance that I promised the engineer here, as well. So, I can't delay that much longer."

"What happens now?" Scruggs asked. "Can I get off the ship, do some exploring?"

"It's dangerous out there. We don't know what we're up against. We might get killed," Lee said.

"Same as the last place, and everybody got off the ship there," Scruggs said. "But with less chance of drowning."

CHAPTER 18

With further negotiation, things worked out. Rather than the crew going to town, the town came to them. The city fathers, or the committee, or the local free traders' guild—if there was one— constructed benches on the far side of the clearing. They also constructed fire pits for roasting cattle and wild pigs. The crew spent the day salivating.

The council readily agreed to Ana's insistence that no weapons be worn by anybody near the ship. The swords disappeared. The trading began the next morning, with Dena in charge. Her workers brought carts of goods pulled by oxen. Most carts were from the early colonists, with aluminum frames and metal wheels. Other carts were made of wood. Dena was quite trusting, allowing the Heart's Desire's crew to load up most of what the council brought before taking anything away in the carts. By midday, the first promised collection of goods was onboard, and Dena hauled away a smaller volume of medical supplies in carts.

"You got some strange things here, Engineer," Dirk said. "Or should I say trader? Fishing rods?"

"Carved hardwood fishing rods. Extremely strong, lightweight, with geometric patterns carved on them. Could be used for a lot of things."

"And look at the two of you," Dirk said. Scruggs and Lee had come down the ramp, both wearing form-hugging leather pants, high boots, and tailored vests. "Are those the clothes they promised?"

"Yes, indeed, Pilot," Lee said. "Very stylish, don't you think?"

"When did you get the measurements done?" Dirk

asked.

"That fellow, Benjamin, used to be a tailor. He just eyeballed us up from experience, and when they sent them over this morning, it took their seamstress only a few minutes to fix up the lengths and a few other things."

"Well, you two look marvelous. I'm sure you'll be driving the local boys wild tonight," Dirk said.

Scruggs looked worried. "Local boys? You think they'll talk to us?"

"Looking like that, I think they'll arm wrestle each other for the privilege. Good hunting," Dirk said.

Scruggs tugged on Lee's arm, dragged her back to the hatch, and whispered a conversation. Dirk turned to Gavin. "I think Scruggs doesn't have much experience with boys of any sort—local or otherwise," he said. "She looks quite exotic for this town. Especially with that bright hair. I'm sure she'll get some offers. I'm surprised that we haven't got any," Dirk said. "Lots of colony worlds want to expand the gene pool, so to speak."

"Offers?" Gavin said. "I've had two. Just like you said. Both local women who wanted a little variety for the family. One brought her husband to show it was okay."

"Brought her husband?"

"He was a good sport about the whole thing. Said they had a big ranch, and needed all the strong hands they could get."

"But you didn't—I mean, how could you?"

"How could I not? They were asking for my help, and I had to help them out."

"Both of them? Both women?"

"Of course. We just went behind those crates over there—there's a pile of hides."

Dirk stared at him. "But I thought . . . you and the Medic?"

"Oh, she had her own offers. And she still needs more lovers."

"Needs more lovers?"

Gavin explained Lee's ten-lover requirement. "Apparently, the Jovians have a bit more relaxed view of things that happen onshore. They're spacers, so they have different mores. What did you do about your offers, Skipper?"

"I haven't gotten any," Dirk said. He sounded surprised.

"Some people have it, some don't," Gavin said.

***

Dinner was a rowdy, yet fun affair that went on for hours. Once the detritus of the trading was cleaned away, the clearing next to the ship transformed into an outdoor restaurant. There were about a hundred locals present, about twenty to a table. Dirk had insisted that one of the crew was always on the ship and swapped as necessary.

The planet's bright primary and dull secondary crawled across the sky so that the shadows stretched over a period of hours. As they set, the stars twinkled, the three moons glowed red, and the trees emitted a pine scent. The food steamed in the cold air.

"This meat is stupendous," Dirk said to his table as he cut into a steak. "What have I been eating?"

"The first one was beef," said the older woman next to him. "The one on the right was pork. That one is an old earth raccoon analog."

"Those cute, little, furry guys?"

"Cute? Little? Here they're about a hundred kilos each, and a small pack can swarm a person and kill it. I lost my favorite dog to them when I was a kid. We shoot them on sight."

Dirk looked at his food for a moment, then continued eating. "Tastes good, though. How do you get it so juicy?"

"Those big metal plates over the fire—we just throw the raw meat there and grill it. Add some salt to taste."

"Can't do that on a spaceship," Dirk said. "Everything is processed and dehydrated to save space and keep it from spoiling. What's this?" He held up a red vegetable.

"Radish. How do you cook on a spaceship, then?"

"We don't. Just reheat premade trays. They don't taste very good. What's in this bread?"

"That's rye. It's like wheat but different. Put some fresh butter on it."

Dirk did so. "Wow. That tastes amazing."

"I think I'd give up fresh butter if I could see another planet," the woman said.

"It would depend on the planet," Dirk said. "I've been to some places, especially mining colonies, that weren't worth seeing. You folks started as a mining colony, right?"

The crowd at the table looked at each other but didn't answer. "Try the wine," the woman said.

Dirk took a sip. "It's both sweet and tart at the same time," Dirk said. "But it must have a high acid content to pair so well with the steak."

"High acid content? That's the sweetest wine ever. You must not know much about wine."

Dirk ignored that. "What's it made out of?"

"Blueberries. You'll have some for dessert, too."

"Isn't that a little tart for dessert?" Dirk asked. He frowned for a moment. "How do you get sugar here?"

"Cold hardy sugar beets," the woman said. "You ask a lot of questions about food."

"Wanted to be a chef," Dirk said.

"How'd you end up as a starship pilot, then?" the woman asked.

Dirk smiled at her. "Can I have some more wine?"

***

Everybody was interested in the strangers—where they were from, what they did, and what they knew of news of the Empire and neighboring planets. Dena put each crewmember at a table for a half hour, replaced them with the person swapping off the ship, then moved them to the next one. That way, the townspeople could listen to the strangers' conversation and ask questions. The locals had good knowledge of the Empire, just not recent news. Perhaps a dozen had been off-world for schooling.

"We're just poor, not stupid," the local lawyer said to Scruggs. "We've got some extended family scattered on nearby planets. We use them to help us out. They can arrange things, order goods, they'll front some money if needed. The capital has an agreement with a shipping line for one dedicated ship a year, and we move the students off-world on it for a spell—usually a couple of years—then they come back and work in whatever technical field they studied. It's quite an honor. I was sent two jumps away to study law for four years."

"When was this?" Scruggs asked.

"A very long time ago. I was much younger and slimmer than I am now." He patted his prominent belly.

"What if they don't want to come back?" Scruggs asked.

"Then, their families owe the passage money. It's not cheap. A student not returning can ruin an entire family."

"So, they have no choice in the matter?"

"Not really, no. I didn't," the lawyer said.

"Would you have stayed if you could have?"

"If I could have? Yes. All those different people, all sorts of exciting things going on."

"Do you regret not staying there?" Scruggs asked.

"It would have been a great burden on my family, my brothers, my sisters. It would have ruined my parents. They would have had to sell the ranch." He looked down at the table and whispered, "But I do regret coming back, yes, just a little bit."

***

Dena collected Dirk for his rotation to the ship. She was looking especially pretty, wearing some sort of short leather dress above her knees and exposing her arms. She took his arm and walked him to the ramp.

"It must be exciting, traveling to all those faraway stars," she said.

"Quite a bit of excitement from time to time. More than a fellow can handle sometimes, I find. Were you sent off-world for training like the others?"

"No, my sister was chosen over me. She spent two years off-world, learning how to run a trading company. Accounting, finance, law, that sort of thing. She came back early."

"Came back early? Surely, that's unusual?"

"Not as much as you think. The council is very particular on who they pick. They really don't want somebody spending five years becoming, say, a civil engineer or an agronomist, at great expense, and then not coming back. Lots of the students they send get overwhelmed by all the changes, the people, the newness."

"That's too bad for her."

"Too bad for her?" Dena spat on the ground. "Emperor's anus to her. What about the rest of us, left here to rot, with no chance of seeing anything except the south end of a north-bound plow oxen? Not unless we can amass a fortune, at least a fortune by local standards, and pay our own way off. Missed the summers, my sister said. That was the reason from coming back early. Idiot. They should have sent me, I wouldn't have returned because of the weather."

"Maybe they thought you wouldn't have come back."

"Maybe they would have been right," Dena said.

"Well, the summers are beautiful here but not as beautiful as you," Dirk said.

"Very smooth line, Pilot Dirk, very smooth. But I like you, anyway." Dena leaned into Dirk, and her floral scent tickled his nose. The night was dark and beautiful, and the woman next to him was lovely. He sighed and punched the external comm unit and identified himself to Lee. A few seconds later, she walked down the ramp, buckling her holster on. "All clear, Pilot, nothing to report." She knew the drill. She walked over to the first table and sat.

"Thank you for walking me back," Dirk said.

"I'd love to see your ship. You could show me around. I could see the bridge, engineering, the holds. Just myself—there wouldn't be any problem."

"The ship?"

"Well, and whatever else you want to show me. Like your cabin."

"You know," Dirk said, "you know, that really is flattering. But that's also the first time that any of the local ladies have made the offer in the last few days. It's surprising."

"How so?"

"Well, Gavin has had several offers. The local boys can't keep their eyes off Lee and Scruggs, and even crotchety, old Ana told me he has had suggestions made to him. But me? Nothing. Am I that hideous? Or do I remind you all of some disgusting local animal somehow?"

Dena giggled and grabbed his arm.

"You are an arrogant beast, aren't you? Think all the ladies should swoon over you."

"Well, past experience would indicate—I mean, I've had some successes with the ladies in the past, but here, well, I don't understand it. Not even much in the way of flirting. Not since Jomain's girl, and that was a professional thing."

Dena giggled again. "I'm afraid that's my fault. I warned them all off. I spread the word around town. Any woman spending time with you better have the time of her life because it would be ended soon after that."

"Given a choice between letting your rivals sleep with me or killing them, you'd kill them?"

"No."

"That's good. I was worried about you for a moment."

"I'd both kill them and sleep with you if I could get away with it," Dena said.

"You're a complicated girl, aren't you?" Dirk said.

"I'm just a poor frontier woman trying to make her way in life and get some enjoyment out of it. Life is hard out here. You're seeing us on our best behavior right now. Once this ship leaves, we go back to our dreary, miserable, boring existence. I'm taking what excitement I can while I can." She pulled Dirk down to her and kissed him hard on the lips. Dirk put his arms around her, and she leaned into him.

"I can't do that," he said. His voice was hoarse. "I can't bring you on board. You might smuggle a weapon."

Dena stepped back and pulled on a belt that held her dress closed. It slid open. She shrugged her dress off her shoulders and let it fall to the ground, wearing nothing underneath.

"Why don't you search me for one, then?"

***

Dirk lazed back on his bunk, with Dena nestled beside him. Her floral scent overlaid the room. The only part of the ship Dena had really seen was the cabin's ceiling, but she didn't seem upset by that. Dirk wondered how much longer they had 'til Gavin would replace him, who was next on the ship. Dirk couldn't bring himself to care too much about it. His comm would buzz him five minutes before then.

He had just started sniffing Dena's hair again when the master fire alarm tripped. It rang out from the compartments. Dirk jumped up and looked at his comm. His comm was shut off. He didn't remember doing that. He raced, naked, to the bridge, and checked the board. All the boards showed green. No fire, but something had tripped the alarm. He paged through boards, all showing green, 'til he came to the comm screen. An urgent message had somehow set off the ship's warning systems.

"Dirk here," he said over the radio.

"Finally, Navy," Ana said. "Why is your comm off? Never mind. Unlock the ramp, so I can get some more weapons. Fire up the systems, get maneuvering and thrusters warmed up, then get ready to get us out of here. We have to pick up Scruggs and then skedaddle."

"Why, what's happening?"

"They're killing each other out here. It's a massacre."

"Why did the fire alarm ring?" Dena asked. She had followed Dirk up to the bridge.

"What do you have to do with this?" Dirk asked her.

"I have no idea what you are talking about," she said. She had taken time to dress, but her hair was mussed, and her belt was slightly askew.

"Did you turn my comm off?"

"Why would I do that?"

Dirk cursed. He slapped a button on his console to open the outer lock, then turned and ran toward his room. He ran along the connecting corridor, then used handholds to pull himself up to his stateroom.

The corridor ladder was on the roof, and in a gravity field, some of the staterooms ended up at the top or the bottom of the circular deck. They had closed the hab module lockers and shelves to account for that, and they could swivel the acceleration couches that doubled as beds to compensate for different 'downs' in planetary gravity.

Dirk pulled up to his room, punched the door button open, climbed into his couch, and groped for his revolver. Ana shuffled below him.

"Where's the girl?"

"I left her in the control room."

"Idiot," Ana said. He stormed up to the control room. "Hands up, or I kill you." He pointed his gun at Dena.

"Calm down, Centurion," Dena said. She had been standing demurely by the control board, adjusting her outfit. "This all has nothing to do with you."

"In the name of the emperor's testicles, what's going on?" Dirk asked. He had thrown on his clothes and holster. His revolver was in his hand, and he was fumbling to load it.

"We were just finishing dinner," Ana said. "They had more wine and beer out. Somebody at one of the tables got up to propose a toast, then there was a bunch of yelling going on by the road. Then a lot more noise, and people started running back. Then a group swarmed up to the tables and started killing people."

Ana yanked Dena toward the ship's locker. He produced a set of handcuffs and cuffed her.

"I didn't know we had handcuffs on the ship," Dirk said.

"They're mine. I donated them for the general good," Ana said. He pushed an unresisting Dena back toward the ramp. "Some people were armed, some weren't. There's a bunch of swordfights going on out there. I managed to make it over to Gavin, and we went to find Lee. Somebody had grabbed her. I shot them, shot some others. They lost interest in her after that. I need a bigger weapon and more ammo. They were both armed, so I sent them to find Scruggs. Hold her." Ana dashed off to his cabin.

Dirk pointed his revolver at Dena. "What's happening."

"Your people are perfectly safe. We're just having a little political adjustment is all. Myself and a few of my friends. If your people keep their heads down and don't do anything stupid, they'll be fine."

"Same could be said of you," Ana said. "Don't do anything stupid, and I won't kill you." He had returned with a submachine gun and extra ammunition. He handed a shotgun to Dirk. "Use this. Already loaded with shells. Good dispersal should hit three or four at once. You've got six shots. Make them count."

"This is a coup?" Dirk asked.

"More like a revolution," Dena said. "Overthrow the tyrants."

"Tyrants?" Ana said.

"You don't know what it's like." Dena tightened her

belt and fixed her hair. "The first families control everything. They decide where you work, what you do, whether you keep your house or not. If they don't like you, they get together with their friends and take your ranch or your house or whatever."

"But you are the first families?" Dirk said.

"I'm in one, yes, but I'm not in charge."

Ana punched the door lock again. "Bring her," he told Dirk. "But keep her under control." He turned to Dena. "You stay right next to Dirk. If you try to run, I'll shoot you in the back." He brandished his submachine gun and walked down the ramp.

***

Gavin and Lee were standing back-to-back at the bottom of the ramp, facing sideways. Both had their revolvers out, their guns pointing at a crowd just outside of easy range. A single man in a blue-green uniform lay face down about ten feet away. Another similarly uniformed man was sitting on the ground next to him, cradling a bleeding leg.

Gavin was bleeding from a sword cut to his arm.

"We went to get Scruggs, but she and the whole table had gone. They tried to rush us."

"I see you dissuaded them. Good job." Ana looked at Lee. She was trembling, her gun shaking, but she kept it pointed at the crowd.

"Wasn't me," Gavin said. "Lee did it."

"Good job, Medic Lee," Ana said. "Won't Paterfather Zeus be upset, though?"

"They've got Sister Scruggs," Lee said. "I'll shoot them all."

A cough came from the top of the ramp. "That won't be necessary," Dena said. "My people are taking over, and we've no interest in harming you. Just release me, and I'll find her and give her back, and you can be on your way."

"Not likely," Ana said. "Imperial anus, do you think

we're idiots?"

"You're businesspeople, just like me," she said. She raised her voice. "Jomain, I'm back. Give up the girl, and we can finish this up."

A long pause preceded raised voices in the distance. Ana's comm beeped. "That's Scruggs. Hang on." He shouldered his gun and hit his comm.

"Senior Centurion." Scruggs's voice was high, but she seemed under control.

"Are you okay, Recruit?" Ana said.

"Yes, sir. I'm sorry, there were too many of them. As soon as the stabbing started, a bunch of them piled on me. I couldn't handle them all."

"Nobody expected you to."

"I think I broke one of their arms, through," Scruggs said. "And I shot one of them."

"Great job. I'm proud of you. What's your status?"

"We're over by the river, in the woods."

"Who's 'we,' Recruit?"

"Zelta's people and me. When the shouting started, they piled on me and dragged me away with them. They haven't hurt me or anything. They say they just want to protect me."

"Don't believe them."

"I don't."

"How many are there?"

"There's about ten people here. They have a few firearms, and some of them took swords from the other group."

"Other group?"

"We're surrounded by about twenty people with swords. They're saying that I won't come to any harm if I surrender to them."

"No, you won't. We'll see to that. Tell them we have Dena."

"Her sister is here, Zelta."

"Put her on," Ana said.

Another voice came on after a pause. "This is Zelta. The girl is safe, and she won't be harmed."

"She better not be. We have our own hostage. Hurt Scruggs, and I'll shoot her."

"Her? I thought you had Benjamin there?"

"Benjamin? No we've got your sister, Dena. Walk Scruggs toward the ship, and we'll trade her for Dena."

"That witch? Not a chance. Shoot my sister. Kill her. Or we shoot your crewmate."

CHAPTER 19

"Just so we're clear," Ana said over the comm. "I have no problem shooting your sister or anyone else for that matter, but if anything happens to Scruggs, I'll come after you personally."

"Good luck with that," Zelta said. "You'll never find me, and the others will have rescued me by then."

"Maybe I can't find you," Ana said. "But by the emperor's rosy anus, I can surely find your town, and a starship's main drive makes a nice, hot flame for all those wooden buildings."

"You do that, and we'll kill the girl," Zelta said. "But I don't want to do that. Just kill my sister, and you can come get her. Let us know your decision. You have five minutes."

"We need longer—"

The comm clicked off.

Dirk turned to Dena. "Why does your sister want you dead?"

"Because she's a grasping, cowardly bureaucrat, and she's always hated me."

"That's nice," Dirk said. "Sisters who don't get along. I've never heard that before. I didn't get along with my sister, but I've never asked strangers to kill her."

"She's mismanaged the family fortune for years. She's paid too much attention to Benjamin. She botched her time off-planet, and she's screwed up the trading. She needs to go."

"Still doesn't explain why she wants you dead," Gavin said.

"Jomain and I had arranged to take over things. We just wanted to remove the men loyal to her and replace them with ours. It worked reasonably well. Most of the first families are gone now, and the rest will be scared of me and my men. She was in the way before, but won't be now. I won't hurt her, I'll just send her out to one of the ranches. She can crunch numbers there forever if she wants, the dried-up old hag."

"And we can believe as much of that as we want," Dirk said.

"Look," Dena said, "killing me won't get you anything. They'll still have your crewmate, and if you try to kill me, my men will rush the ship. More of you will get killed. We'll deal with Zelta, eventually. Just let me go. I'll negotiate with the others, show them that a new person is in charge, and they better listen."

"What makes you think they'll listen to you?" Dirk asked.

"They either listen to me, or they're in trouble. It'll work out."

Ana stepped forward, adjusting something. "Everybody get ready to get inside." He turned to Dena. "I don't think you understand the gravity of your situation here."

"You don't dare hurt me," Dena said.

Ana smacked her on the side of the head with the butt of his submachine gun. She moaned and collapsed in a heap.

"All evidence to the contrary," Ana said.

***

They had all returned to the lounge. Lee had bandaged Gavin's arm, saying she'd do the permanent workup later. Dena was handcuffed next to the medcomp in the hold. Lee had confirmed she wouldn't die, but she was still woozy, claiming to be in a lot of pain, but Dirk had stopped Lee from giving her a sedative. "She needs to be able to move under her own power, if necessary, and talk." He turned to the others. "Let's discuss our options," Dirk said.

"We shoot sleeping beauty here," Gavin said, "dump her out the air lock, go over and collect Scruggs."

"If they follow their agreement and don't just shoot her."

"True," Gavin nodded. "Senior Centurion, I'm surprised you didn't suggest just leaving Scruggs here. You were ready to throw her out an air lock earlier."

"If she needs to be thrown out an air lock, I'll do it myself. But I'm not leaving some locals to do the job for me." He made locals sound like a curse. He took a deep breath, then another. He appeared to be having some trouble getting his wind back.

"Are you okay, Centurion?" Lee asked.

"Fine, fine. I just need some basic." He stepped up to the tap and pulled a glass. Dirk watched him out of the corner of his eye and saw him slip something from a pocket and into his mouth. A pill, it looked like. He didn't drink from the glass but came back and sat at the table, the full glass in front of him.

"We're not leaving anybody behind," Dirk said. "I'm not leaving anybody behind. Not again."

"Again?" Ana asked.

Dirk ignored him. "Gavin, can we fly?"

"Full tanks, Skipper," Gavin said.

"For the moment," Dirk said. "Let's assume that if we did that trade, that ends up with us having Scruggs and Dena here dead. Dena's crew isn't going to be happy. What's going to happen to Zelta and her friends after that, and are they going to like it?"

They all thought about that for a moment. "I don't think it will be good for them," Lee said.

"I wonder if we can trade for that?" Dirk said.

***

A half hour later, Dirk was sitting in the pilot's seat, drinking alcohol. Lee was sitting next to him, running scans. Ana and Gavin walked back to the ramp.

"Skipper is drinking a lot," Gavin said.

"He's done that every deorbit, and we're still here. He needs it to get in the right frame of mind for his piloting, I think."

"What frame of mind is that?"

"Suicidal insanity."

"It seems like he could do it differently," Gavin said.

"Feel free to volunteer to drive the ship yourself if you want," Ana said. "I don't think you'd do a very good job, though, especially compared to the pilot. He's uniquely skilled in my experience."

Gavin stopped and looked at Ana. "That's almost a compliment, Centurion."

"It is a compliment. I can't do his job, but I recognize expertise when I see it. By the way." He turned to Gavin.

"Yes, Centurion?"

"Thank you for trying to go back to get Scruggs. That was well done."

"I wouldn't leave her."

"I'm glad to hear it. Now, let's do this thing." He tapped his commo. "Scruggs, you ready on that end?"

"Yes, Centurion. They've all agreed. There's a barge or something that we can use."

"Right, the pilot will start in a moment. As soon as we fire off, do your thing."

"Understood, Centurion," Scruggs said.

Ana made it to the ramp. "Ready here," he said over the intercom.

No responses followed, but the thrusters whined and the ship lifted. "Showtime."

***

Lee was watching her board. "Due west, Pilot, that will take us over the river."

"Understood," Dirk said. He was sweating pure alcohol. The ship lifted with a ting. At least one person out there had a firearm and had decided to waste a round against a steel-hulled ship. Dirk swung the ship up on a standard takeoff. The surrounding countryside came into view—flat, with the rivers gleaming in the glow of three moons. This side of the town showed a few lights. Over near the river, where Scruggs's group was, bright lights of firearms flashed, but they were already too far away to hear.

"They need twenty minutes, they said." Lee touched her panel. "We can circle around for that long over here, turn north, then east, then south to pick up the river."

"Got it."

"Scruggs should contact us when they're on the river," Lee said.

Dirk banked the ship, following the river for a short distance. He took a shortcut over a small group of hills and moved out to sea. He headed straight out to sea for five minutes 'til he was over the horizon, then took a long detour north. Small islands flashed by underneath, but the main shore was not visible.

"Turning east," Dirk said and swung the ship.

Lee keyed her comm. "Scruggs, we've turned back. ETA is ten minutes."

"Understood," Scruggs said. "What should I do?"

"Go with them to the river, help them escape, like we discussed."

"I don't trust these people. They said they'd kill me if I tried to run away."

"Sister, we don't trust them, either. But they have to keep you alive to get our help, and they need our help badly. Remind them of that."

***

"Our ship is on the way." Scruggs turned to Zelta. They were in the middle of a small collection of woods that offered no cover, but in the dark, they could hide in the bushes. They had revolvers and two rifles. Zelta had a shotgun. They shot down the first group to rush them.

Their opponents were just shadows in the distance by then.

"You sure they can do this?" Zelta asked.

"Our pilot is excellent. Centurion says he used to pilot Imperial drop shuttles."

"Wouldn't know it by looking at him," Zelta said. "Seemed like a regular Imperial navy twit to me." She turned to the men. "We can't stay here."

"Why not?" one of the men asked. "Just wait here 'til my family hears of this. They'll be in town in a few hours, more than enough to take care of this mob."

"First," Zelta said, "when the sun comes up, they'll see us. We've only got so much ammunition for the firearms, but they can loft arrows down on us all day long. Second, your family is a bunch of cowards. We'll be lucky if they send somebody to look around. Counting on them for a rescue, we might as well shoot ourselves now."

"You can't talk about my family like that," the man said.

"Boberin," a woman's voice said from the darkness, "you know damn well your uncle is a worthless bastard who never liked you. He'll stall 'til you get carved up, then come in after we're all dead, demand the blood price, and spend it on a new pair of shoes. Just shut up and listen to Zelta."

Boberin sighed. "What do we do now, boss lady?"

"Get ready," Zelta said. "We're going to rush the boat. Sampson, Merek, Chantilly, and Garcia. On the signal, run as fast as you can 'til you get on board. Cut the lines, man the poles, get it moving. The rest of you follow just behind them. If anybody tries to cut them off, stop and shoot them. Keep the girl in the middle with you. Derholm, stay with me. We're rearguard. Once everybody is on board, push off, take us out into the middle of the current, and paddle downstream for all we're worth. Got it?"

A chorus of yeses followed Zelta's orders. Zelta turned to Scruggs. "Here, girl."

She extended a holster with Scruggs's revolver in it.

"I'm not helping you shoot people," Scruggs said. "You kidnapped me."

"Those are Dena's people out there. They're going to try to kill us."

"This isn't my fight," Scruggs said. "And they don't want to kill me. They want to keep me alive to trade for Dena."

"It wasn't your fight at the start, but it is now," Zelta said. "You are with us now. Take the gun."

"If I don't?"

"Don't you want to be able to shoot back?" Zelta said. "They might shoot you by accident in the dark and the noise."

"Wearing a gun won't stop that. Helping you won't stop that." You might shoot me yourself.

"Nope, it won't," Zelta said. "But if you don't help us get to that boat, I'll shoot you myself. And if I can't, Derholm will."

"If that's your plan, why not just shoot me now? I'm not a coward. I'm not afraid of you." Scruggs said.

"Young lady, I don't care if you are a coward. What I care about is that, if you aren't there to talk to your ship on the comm, it might just buzz us with its main drive, and we won't survive that."

"Pilot Dirk would never do that," Scruggs retorted.

"What about that centurion fellow on the radio? What do you think he'd do if we didn't bring his people back?" Zelta asked.

Scruggs shrugged and belted on the revolver.

"Zelta, this is not a good idea," Derholm said.

"If she shoots me, shoot her in the head," Zelta said. "Everybody ready?" A pause hung in the air. "Go, go, go."

The group ran out of the brush and into the field. The first four men were the youngest and the fastest. Unencumbered, they outpaced the main group. The armed group ran in a tight circle surrounding Scruggs. A shadowy figure zoomed in from the side, a glint of steel shining in the moonlight. One man on Scruggs's right stopped, took careful aim, and fired.

He missed, but it must have gone close enough to startle his opponent, who dove to the ground, invisible in the dark. The group raced on.

In the back, behind Scruggs, the man who had fallen reached for a comm. "They're heading for the river."

Another figure rose in the darkness in front of the four runners. Before anyone could react, she speared the first running man. He shrieked and collapsed. Before the woman could retrieve her sword, three revolvers riddled her with shots. She didn't even gasp as she fell.

Zelta stopped at her fallen man. Fecal odor erupted as he voided himself. "Leave him," she said to two men with her.

"No, no, no, no, no. Bring him," Scruggs said. "We don't leave anybody behind." She leaned over, grabbed him, and dragged him forward. The two men helped. The wounded man screamed the whole time they dragged him.

Scruggs stumbled as the ground softened. They had hit a dirt field. Shadows flowed behind them. Zelta turned and fired the shotgun in their pursuers' general direction. The shadows shrank into the ground. The group ran on.

The man Scruggs dragged stopped screaming and slumped. Scruggs stumbled. Zelta came up to them and checked the man's pulse. "Emperor's testicles. Leave him."

"Is he dead?" Scruggs asked.

"He's got a foot of steel through his intestines. What do you think?" Zelta said. "Keep moving."

Then a different voice asked, "What am I going to tell his wife?"

Something swished through the air. "Arrows!" warned a voice.

Scruggs yelped. A line of fire slashed her shoulder.

"Are you hurt?" Zelta asked. Scruggs twisted. Everything worked—just hurt. "I'm fine." They started to run again. Arrows swished in the air again, but they blended in with the twilight.

The three in front had reached the flat boat. The first ran to a tree and sawed at a rope with a knife. The other two leaped, caught up the bow, and clambered over. Once on board, they grabbed large poles, plopped them over the side, and shoved the boat forward. The boat moved about two inches and then got stuck.

Arrows hissed again. One clattered on the boat. The next group clambered over the bow. It was too tall for Scruggs. She had to stop and jump up and just managed to grasp the gunwales. She pulled herself up, but she wasn't going to make it.

"Everybody on board, we're untied. Get up. Get up." Scruggs recognized the voice of the man who had cut the lines with his knife.

A hand pushed her foot up from below, and she was propelled up enough to scramble on board. The wooden deck scraped her face as she rolled over. Pine scent filled her nose.

She stood and turned. Shadowy figures ran in the dark. Another swishing sound followed, and the man next to her yelled and fell back.

Scruggs yanked her revolver out of her holster and pointed it at the shore. Her hand was shaky, and her blood was pounding in her ears. The centurion's voice whispered in her brain. Both hands. Point. Breathe. Hold. Fire. She pulled the trigger. A shadow dropped. Had she hit it? Maybe.

Zelta was boosted up beside her and sprawled next to her. The night flashed as the shotgun discharged into the boat. Curses filled the air.

Then the last man clambered up and rolled over the gunwales. More arrows swished, then Zelta's barking shotgun. Scruggs emptied her revolver at the shore, the way she was trained. Two rifles joined her. The men on the poles heaved, then heaved again. The boat made way into the middle of the river. Scruggs reloaded her revolver. The rifles on either side snapped at a target. Hissing arrows ripped the air again but only harmless splashes behind them. Lights blossomed on the riverside, and Scruggs could see other boats pushing off from the shore.

"Who's hurt?" Zelta asked. "Scruggs, I heard you yell."

"It's a scratch, I think," Scruggs said. "It doesn't hurt right now."

"I'll look at it while you get on the radio," Zelta said.

"Okay," Scruggs said. She holstered her revolver and flipped her comm open.

"And tell them to hurry. We don't have much time," Zelta said.

"Why not?" Scruggs asked.

"I blew a hole in the bottom of the boat by accident. We're sinking."

***

Lee looked at the screens. The ship flew as steadily as if it was on rails. They were flying nape-of-the-earth courses, shooting around trees and hills, across streams, flashing past the occasional farmhouse. Lee would have been more impressed with the flying if the cockpit didn't reek of alcohol and sweat, and if Dirk's arms hadn't been shaking so much.

Dirk jerked, causing a sharp embankment of the ship, and something tall flew by below.

Ana's voice squawked over the intercom. "What was that?"

"Windmill, I think," Lee said. Dirk righted the ship and flew on. They crossed a large river, and Dirk centered them. Lee checked her screens. "Thirty seconds to cut-off. Ana, they say they are sinking fast. You'll have to drag the whole thing into the ship."

"Understood. The ramp's down. Gavin and I are on it," Ana said.

"Ready, Pilot?" Lee asked.

Dirk was silent.

"Ready, Pilot?" Lee repeated.

Dirk was still quiet. Lee slapped his shoulder hard. "Power down in ten seconds," she yelled.

"Ten, yes," Dirk said. Lee counted down and then snapped a switch. The thrusters went silent, and the ship ghosted. They weren't an airplane, but the hull was streamlined, and it generated lift. The ship sped along above the river, slowing down and losing altitude rapidly. A light blossomed in front of them as somebody waved a flashlight. Dirk gently tipped the controls to the right, then back, and they were centered on the light. Ever so gently, he descended the ship. The water whooshed as it splashed up the sides of the ship as the ramp contacted the river.

Dirk slipped the ship sideways a touch, and the flat-bottomed boat emerged before them. He pushed the controls down, and the ramp dug into the water. Lee slapped the exterior lights on.

***

Scruggs stared upriver. Their barge was slowing as it took on water, and the poling wasn't helping much anymore. They were in the river current now, but so were their pursuers. The boats pulling after them were gaining. One was larger than their barge, with a steam-powered wheel. Pot shots from their rifles dug into the heavy wooden sides. A single arrow flew out and dropped behind them.

"Why just one arrow?" she asked Zelta.

"Ranging shots. Saving ammunition. Once they have the range, they'll just fire from behind that bulkhead. Enough arrows, and eventually, they'll get lucky," Zelta said. "When do your friends get here?"

"Soon," Scruggs said. Another arrow wafted up and dropped down. It thudded into the barge next to her.

"Take cover," Zelta said.

"What cover?" somebody said. Scruggs looked around.

The barge was a flat piece of wood, with three-foot sidewalls and an angled bow. Nothing offered a safe hiding space.

Another swoosh sounded, and a flight of arrows dropped onto the boat. One of the two men poling yelled and dropped into the boat, an arrow sticking out of his shoulder. Zelta went to him. Derholm ran, grabbed the pole, and pushed. One of the riflemen shouted as an arrow pinned him to the bulwark. The other rifleman stopped firing and came to his aid. Counting the two wounded and Scruggs, only seven people remained. In the confusion, Scruggs had missed some being left behind.

Zelta stood back up. Her hands were covered with blood. "He's done." She looked down at her bloody hands, pensive, then up at Scruggs.

A growl came from upriver. "Here they come," Scruggs said.

Zelta stepped up to Scruggs and smeared her bloody hands across Scruggs's face.

"Imperial testicles. What's that for?" Scruggs said. But then bright lights flashed on as the Heart's Desire came swirling down the river. Down blast as the thrusters reignited spat giant rooster tails of water behind it. All the exterior lights came on, and the ramp was down, touching the water.

"Hang on," Scruggs yelled. "This will be rough." Zelta picked up her shotgun and fired at the pursuers.

"There's nothing to hang onto, either!" the remaining rifleman stated. He looked up as the Heart's Desire centered on the barge. The ramp dropped more, then aimed under the bottom of the barge. The rifleman dropped onto his stomach and put his hands over his head.

The Heart's Desire bracketed the barge and slammed it up the ramp, knocking the barge crew off their feet. One of the poling men went over the side.

The ramp scooped the barge and sucked it upward and

into the ship. The remaining crew dove to the bottom of the barge as it slid up the ramp toward the hatch, where it stuck.

"Everybody out!" Zelta ordered. They scrambled out of the barge and up the ramp. The Heart's Desire wobbled from side to side, then pushed as the thrusters fired harder. Ana and Gavin grabbed anybody coming up the ramp and threw them inside. Zelta and Scruggs hopped over the gunwales. Zelta had dropped her shotgun. Scruggs made it over just as the barge tipped and slid down. She reached up and teetered on the edge before Gavin grabbed her and yanked her in. Ana slapped a release valve, the ramp flopped down, the barge fell away, and they blasted up into the night sky.

CHAPTER 20

"Help Scruggs," Zelta said as the Heart's Desire angled upward. "She's been hurt—bad."

"I'm fine," Scruggs said as Gavin and Ana rushed toward her. She was slumped against the hull, breathing hard, next to the ramp.

"You're covered with blood," Ana said. He and Gavin cradled her head as they inspected it. They turned her head from side to side but couldn't find a wound.

"It's not mine. She put it on me."

"Put it on you," Ana said. "Why would she do that?" He looked at Gavin, then his eyes narrowed, and he stood and turned around. One of Zelta's crew had stepped behind them and was pointing a revolver at Ana. He swung it to face Gavin, then swung back to Ana.

Zelta spoke up. "Easy up, spaceman. We're taking the ship. Tell the pilot to put us down right away, and nobody gets hurt."

"A whole bunch of people have already gotten hurt," Ana pointed out.

"Not our doing," Zelta said. "If my stupid sister hadn't started her little war, everything would have been fine.

"It seemed to us," Ana said, "that maybe it wasn't just your little sister. She seemed to have a lot of friends who were in agreement with her. That was a pretty big fight down there."

"Wasn't your fight, though, was it, spacer?" Zelta said.

"Still isn't," Ana said.

"So, no need for you to take sides, then," Zelta said.

"But taking our crew hostage—that suggested we should take sides. Pointing a gun at us here—that kind of makes side-taking a requirement."

"Tell your pilot to land, or it will go badly for you."

"We were planning on landing, putting all of you down somewhere away from town. That's the deal. No need for guns."

"We'll still be doing that, just that you'll be staying with us. Tell your pilot to land."

"We were planning on landing you out at some ranch."

"Land next to town."

"Why would we do that?"

"I need to get in contact with my friends."

"What did you mean by us staying with you?" Gavin asked.

"Well," Zelta said, "there will have to be some sort of inquiry about what Dena did—the fighting, and all that."

"We had nothing to do with that," Gavin said.

"Says you," Zelta said. "Call the pilot and tell him to head back to the town. There's a ranch one mile north of the falls on the west side. Land there."

"Or what?" Gavin asked.

"Merek," Zelta said to the man with the gun. "Shoot the girl there if they don't call the pilot. Oh, and, boys, don't mention that we have a gun on you. Your captain is kind of simpleminded—it would just confuse him."

Ana and Gavin exchanged glances. Ana nodded. Gavin leaned over to the intercom and pushed a button. "Captain Dirk, Engineer Two here."

There was a long pause, then Lee said, "Engineer Two, this is Medic Two. Captain is busy, piloting."

"We have an issue, a drive issue," Gavin said. "We need to land to see to it." He released the button.

"Tell him about the ranch," Zelta hissed.

Gavin punched the button again. "Medic, please tell the captain we need some parts as well. We've talked to the locals, and they indicate there will be a source for them at a ranch a mile north of the city on the west side of the river."

"Understood, Engineer. Will you need my assistance

with the repairs?" Lee asked.

"That's a negative, Medic," Gavin said. "I think you helped quite enough last time. No, I'll make do with the centurion's skilled assistance."

***

Lee stared at the intercom, then turned to Dirk. "Pilot, did you hear that? The centurion's skilled assistance."

"I did. Something's not right," Dirk said. He was still sweating, but the shaking had gone away.

"What should we do?"

"Is there a shotgun in the arms locker?"

"Yes."

"Get back there and load up. Once you're ready, I'll tell them we're going in for a landing. Give you five seconds to get set, then hang on for the next thirty seconds. I'll bounce us around the sky. After thirty seconds, get down there and sort them out with the shotgun. You think you can do that?"

"I can try. If I can't, I can give the shotgun to the centurion, or the engineer."

"That will work. Get back there," Dirk said. She got up and went hand over hand out of the cabin. Less than a minute later, she intercommed back. "In position, Pilot," Lee said.

He punched the intercom on his board for the hold. "We're turning now. Should be on the ground very shortly. There's a bit of weather ahead I'll have to go through. It will be rougher than our last landing," Dirk said. "Just not as long." He counted to five, then violently threw the stick over.

***

Dena rubbed her wrists. The handcuffs had hurt. She was surprised she could pick them. She'd seen an example on a school video and practiced on an old pair at the ranch when she was younger. The technique had worked on the different pairs she had found around the ranch, but she wasn't sure if it would work on off-world models. The crew seemed to have forgotten that she was there. She'd gotten bruised as they banged around, but nothing major. She slowly slid forward. Banging and crashing had started a few minutes prior but then it quieted. The ship turned, so she edged up to peer into the forward hold to see what was going on.

The ramp was still down in front of her, and large splinters of wood and what looked like a wooden plank blocked it from closing. Gavin and Ana stood next to a seated Scruggs. Blood covered Scruggs's face. Dena recognized her sister standing with her back to her, and one of her men, Merek, pointing a gun at the two spacers. Two more of Zelta's men she didn't recognize bent over a third man. He appeared to have an arrow sticking out of him. She caught the tail-end of Dirk's voice over the intercom. "Our last landing," he said.

If we're landing, I don't have much time, she thought. She took two running leaps and threw herself in a tackle at Merek.

Then the ship spun around her.

***

Given how bad Dirk's landings were, normally, Gavin, Ana, and Scruggs braced themselves and gripped what they could as they waited for Dirk to maneuver. A figure flew out of the gloom from the back of the hold toward Merek, then Dirk threw the ship into a hard left.

Merek fell sideways, and Dena missed him completely. But as she pinwheeled across the hold, she slammed into a sliding Zelta and knocked her over. Dena grabbed her sister tight with her left hand and beat her sister with her right as they slid over to the far corner.

Merek dropped his gun and slid into a wall. The three others went flying as the ship spun, banging into various poles, boxes, or walls. They yelled—first in surprise, then later, in pain as their arms and legs hit metal.

Ana hung onto the intercom and ramp controls. Scruggs had her hand on a grab bar, all of them swaying. Gavin managed to hold on for a moment, then lost his grip. He cursed, then launched himself toward a fenced cage and hit it spread-eagle. He held tight there.

The ship reached the end of its turn, then suddenly pitched up, then back down. Everyone not holding onto something also flipped up, then slammed down. The three cursing sliders cursed more. The revolver bounced onto the ramp and got stuck in one of the hydraulic arms. Merek slammed into the wall. The Zelta/Dena mass bounced. Dena was on top, and she drove all the air out of her sister's chest. Zelta gasped for breath.

Dena continued hitting her as they slid.

The ship swung left this time, and everybody except the spacers banged over to the other side. Dena had managed to position herself better, using Zelta to take the worst of the bangs. The ship held the turn for a moment, then came back to an even keel.

Lee flipped out of the main hatch and landed on her feet, shotgun held forward. "Nobody move."

Ana, Scruggs, and Gavin loosened their grip. The cursing trio kept cursing and showed no desire to move. Dena smacked her sister once more, then leaned back.

Merek stood and spread his hands. "Listen, lady—"

Scruggs scooted behind him, kicked his legs out from under him, and kicked him twice in the ribs. She straddled him, put a knee in his back, and pulled his arm back, immobilizing him.

Ana skated by her. "Well done, recruit," he said. He scrambled over to Lee's side and held out his hands for the shotgun. Lee handed it to him without a pause. Ana racked it to load and stepped forward to where one of the cursing forms sat up. He pointed it next to his head and pulled the trigger.

BOOM.

"Next one is in your head. She said stay down," Ana said. "Lee, tell the captain to land us—safely land us. ASAP. We'll kick these folks out and be on our way."

"Got it, Ana," she said and clambered up the ladder.

"You three, and you," Ana said, pointing to the men with the shotgun barrel, "in that cage there. Gavin, can we lock it?"

"No problem," Gavin said. He slid over to a fenced compartment, keyed in a code, and held it open. Ana gestured with his shotgun. "In. Gavin, anything in there that can cause us trouble?"

"Just furniture," Gavin said. The four men scrambled into the cage, and Gavin swung it shut.

Ana turned his attention back to the two sisters. "Now, you two. Captain probably wants to talk with both of you."

Zelta and Dena had managed to stumble to their feet, just inside of the ramp. Zelta was grasping one of the hydraulic arms to stay upright.

"And I want to talk to him," Zelta said. She looked down for a moment, stooped, and came up with the rogue revolver in her hand. "But first, I think I have a few other points to make."

Before Ana could even threaten anything, Dena swung around and kicked her sister's knee. Zelta dropped, fell onto the ramp, screamed, and dropped out into the darkness. Dena spun around the support and peered out to the ground. Then she turned back to the group.

"Oops," she said.

***

"I don't care if you don't know where you are," Dirk said to the four men in underwear at the ramp. Lee had found a flat clearing, and Dirk had dropped them. "Sun's coming up soon, and the river is west of here. Go west and figure it out yourself. This is your planet, not mine."

"But we could be hundreds of miles from anything,"

Merek said.

"In that case," Ana said, brandishing the shotgun. "Nobody to hear me shoot the four of you, and nobody to see me bury you, either. I vote for that. Won't take long."

"River's maybe twenty miles away," Lee said. "There's bound to be traffic there. You can walk there in a day or two at the most, and somebody will pick you up."

"I'm firing up as soon as you're all off the ship," Dirk said, "and I'll be using the main drive right away. Anybody too close gets fried."

"How close is too close?" Merek asked.

"Start running at the bottom, and don't stop," Ana said. "That should be far enough. Maybe."

The four trooped down the ramp, two of them holding one of their fellows. Dirk turned to Dena, who was lounging against a wall, guarded by an angry-looking Scruggs.

"Want me to strip as well?" she said. "I'll bet I do a better job of it than they did."

"Out you go," Dirk said.

"Take me with you," Dena said. "I've got no future here."

"Your sister's dead, aren't you in charge now?" Dirk asked.

"It's not that simple. I was supposed to capture her and send her to a ranch up in the hills. We're actually civilized here. We're okay with political exile, but we frown on fratricide," Dena said.

"Not really our problem," Dirk said. "Shouldn't have killed your sister."

"Half-sister. And that was an accident, I didn't think she'd fall. You could have closed the hatch."

"Jammed," Ana said. "But still, not our problem. Get out."

"I won't last an hour. Those are Zelta's guys out there. Merek fancied himself in love with her. He'll chase me down and beat me to death."

"Should have thought of that before you shot at us," Ana said.

"But I didn't—shoot at you I mean," Dena said. "In fact, I've never raised a hand at you. I was on the ship when the fighting started, remember? And my people didn't do anything to you. After the initial confusion, we left you alone. I was even on the ship to explain things to you."

"Is that what it's called, explaining?" Gavin asked.

Dena shrugged. "We're a backwater planet, I take my fun where I find it. Dirk was fun. But the main reason I did it was to make sure I was on the ship while things went down."

"That was the main reason you were on the ship?" Dirk asked.

"Don't flatter yourself. I've had better," Dena said.

"I'll have you know, missy, that any number of women—"

"None of whom are here right now. But to the item under discussion, I've never hurt any of you, shot at any of you, threatened any of you, or anything else. Have I?" Dena stared at each one of them in turn.

"She's telling the truth, Skipper," Gavin said. "And she did try to capture Zelta."

"I made sure that you were well taken care of when you were here," Dena said. "Fed you—fed you very well, clothed you, traded with you. Honestly traded with you. Wanted you to come back. If my stupid sister hadn't acted the way she did, things would have worked out."

"You started things," Gavin said.

"Are you sure about that? Yeah, I had some of my people there. But why did she have so many well-armed troops around her at that dinner. Could it be she was trying to get her own spaceship? She sure jumped right to that as soon as she got on here, and that's after you saved her from getting killed."

Everyone took a quiet moment to reflect on that.

"And there are other reasons to take me along with you," Dena said.

"Oh, do tell," Gavin said. "What other reasons could there be?"

"How about money?" Dena asked.

***

"You sure this is the place?" Lee asked. The Heart's Desire was powering over the river, downstream of the falls.

"Yes, I came back from a trip with the capital fleet. We overnighted here, and I took a long walk and stashed half of my profits down here," Dena said. "Some Imperial credits, some gold, a revolver, and two bags of gemstones."

"Seems a long way from anything," Dirk said, looking at the cameras.

"It's on the direct route the fleet takes every year, and I wasn't the only one going onshore. There were thirty boats. Probably fifty of us took a break while we waited for the tide to change. I hiked up to the top of that hill there. You see that big tree at the top? There's a pile of rocks next to it. Look for the black rock. It's about two layers under that.

"And you did this because you thought you might need escape money to get off-planet?" Lee asked.

"There was some talk of marrying me off on my return. Older guy. Nice enough but lazy, and his ranch was the back of beyond. I did well enough with the traveling fleet that my uncle decided to put me into the trading side of the family. If he hadn't, if I'd been sent to the hills, I'd have caught a schooner down, picked up my loot, and taken my chances on one of the late monsoon schooners. Tried my luck in the capital."

"And the banking codes?" Dirk asked.

"On the chip. Like I said."

"You realize that if we get to a civilized planet, and

those codes don't work, there will be problems."

"There won't be problems," Dena said.

Dirk and Lee exchanged glances, but then began the landing sequence.

***

Ten minutes later, everybody was assembled at the ramp.

"No, I'm not going," Dena said. "Second I step off that ramp, you'll lift and leave me here."

"You can trust us," Dirk said.

"No," Dena said. "I'm fine right here. I've given excellent directions. One of you go find it."

"What if we get there, and there's no money?" Ana asked.

"That would be pretty unfortunate for me, then, wouldn't it," Dena said.

"Who's going?" Gavin asked.

"I'll go," Ana said. "Pilot has to stay with the ship. Same with you, Engineer, and you're banged up from that little incident. It's at least two miles, and it's uphill. That will just mess you up. I'd like somebody to go with me, though. Maybe the medic, here?"

"Why her?" Gavin asked.

"If I get hurt, she can help me. If she gets hurt, I can just carry her back. And that leaves Scruggs here to watch this one." Ana pointed at Dena.

"You don't trust the two of us alone with Ms. Sexy Pants here?" Gavin asked.

"She worked her way on board the ship before. She'd probably try again. Won't work with Scruggs, though."

"She doesn't go that way?" Gavin asked. "How do you know?"

"I don't know if she goes that way or not, and I don't care in the least. But I'm pretty sure Scruggs blames her for the kidnapping and wants a chance to shoot her, isn't that so, recruit?" Ana said.

Scruggs dropped her hand to the revolver at her belt. "Anytime, please, Senior Centurion."

"There you go," Ana said. "Let me get a shovel. Medic, if you can bring your pack, and some water, we'll head out. Probably four hours round trip. Scruggs, lock Ms. Sexy Pants here in the cage, and don't let her out 'til I'm back." He walked back to the ship's locker. Lee went to get her medical kit.

Gavin turned to Dirk. "Centurion's right, Skipper. I could do with taking some pills and laying down for a while."

"Go ahead," Dirk said. "I'll go up to the bridge and stand watch. After we secure the prisoner."

Dena didn't wait to be asked, but she walked inside the cage and pulled the door shut. The lock clicked closed. Ana and Lee came down and conferred. Ana checked the cage lock, had a quiet word with Scruggs, then stepped out. Scruggs was left alone with Dena in the hold. Scruggs went and sat on a pile of clothes loosely baled together.

"You going to sit and watch me all four hours 'til the centurion comes back?" Dena asked.

"Yes," Scruggs said.

"Well, I won't be any trouble. I want off this planet as much as you."

"Kind of an odd way of showing it," Scruggs said.

"How old are you, kid?"

"I'm not a kid. I'm eighteen standard. Not much younger than you."

"Not much younger in years, but experience, we're a world apart," Dena paused. "Why are you here, kid?"

"What do you mean?"

"This ship. Why are you on it? Things aren't quite right here. Not sure what, exactly, but this isn't exactly a regular trader. I've been on a few, and you five are a bit . . . unconventional."

"Is that why you picked us?"

"I saw a chance and took it. What about you? What

made you get on this ship?"

Scruggs was silent for a while, then she said, "I wanted to see the galaxy."

Dena laughed. "Me too, I just had to do a lot more than you to get my chance."

It was Scruggs's turn to laugh. "You think so? You have no idea what I actually had to do to get on board here."

"You going to tell me?"

"Not right now. Maybe someday." Scruggs stretched back on the pile of clothes and took the sword out of her sheath. She dragged a stone along it.

"You saw a chance and took it?"

"Something like that. I wanted to join the Marines, but that didn't work out."

"The Imperial Marines?"

"Yes."

"You don't seem like a heartless killer oppressor."

"Oppressor?" Scruggs stopped running the stone along the sword. "The Imperial Marines are a force for good. They protect the Empire."

"They protect the emperor—and the corrupt Imperial families—and profit off our misery."

"Misery? What are you talking about?"

"You're not doing that right, you know." Dena gestured at the stone. "Is this the first time you used a whetstone?"

"Yes. I need to get the centurion to show me."

"Give me your sword. I'll do it." Dena extended her hand.

Scruggs shook her head. "Nice try. What did you mean by misery?"

"How do you think we got on this fool planet? We're all descendants of a group of exiles from two hundred years ago. Our ancestors were fine 'til the Empire came along, attacked our planet, killed half us, enslaved the rest and then sent them out to work in the mines here. And when the mines closed, they left us here to die."

"That's not possible," Scruggs said. "The Empire doesn't do things like that."

"You don't know much about the real world, do you, girl? Or about history."

"That can't be right."

"It can be. My sister always worked with the traders. I would rather have shot them."

"Not going to get that chance now, are you?"

"Don't need it. You folks are doing exactly what I want. Getting me away from Rockhaul and out to see the galaxy."

"The Empire part of the galaxy."

"That's good enough for now," Dena said. She looked around. "For now."

CHAPTER 21

"Captain, you are a pirate," Devin said. He was in full Imperial uniform since his valet hadn't replaced his senators' robes. He was seated on the Pollux's bridge. The man he was addressing was dressed in a freighter captain's standard working gear. Skin suit, coveralls, ship slippers. His nametag said Volvina. Two Marines in combat armor stood behind him.

"Am not. Just a merchant trying to make a living," Captain Volvina said. "Got no cause stopping me like you did. All our papers are in order."

"You're armed. You have two laser batteries installed."

"Nothing wrong. Need to defend ourselves out here. You Imperials won't do it."

"Imperial regulations prohibit armed merchant ships within Imperial borders."

"Need them for defense."

"Armed merchant ships have attacked traffic from Ekaterinburg."

"Wasn't me. Lots of ships look like mine. Standard design. You can't go making wild accusations. We're citizens of New Kharkov. We've got rights."

"You're colonials, not citizens, and you only have the rights I give you. Do not task me, sir, or I'll have you spaced this instant."

"Can't do that. Even colonists have rights."

Devin stood and gestured. The Marines stood and lifted the captain up 'til he was dangling.

"Out the air lock with this insolent dog," Devin said. The Marines hastened to obey and pulled him toward the air lock behind the bridge.

"You can't do this, you bloodthirsty maggot," the

captain yelled. One of the Marines slugged him in the stomach, and he fell silent as he tried to suck in enough air.

The subprefect coughed. Lyon turned to him. The subprefect raised an eyebrow. Devin grimaced. "You, subprefect, were going to tell me that, as he is a citizen of New Kharkov, I can't just space him. I need a trial, a judge, evidence, and proof."

"I was just going to ask what you wanted for lunch, sir." The subprefect smiled. "Soup or salad. And perhaps during lunch, inquire about any recent changes in Imperial judiciary proceedings. Things are different than I remember."

Devin hung his head and rubbed his temples, then sighed and pushed his comm. "Belay that order. Don't space that captain. Put him in the brig with the rest of the people." He turned to the subprefect. "Thank you for stopping me from making a mistake. Again."

"I live to serve, sir."

"Impudent, aren't you?"

"Did I actually hear you call him 'insolent dog?'"

"I heard that in a vid. He called me a bloodthirsty maggot."

"Indeed. But he does have a point. We're the first warship here in over a year. If they don't protect themselves, who is going to do it?"

"They are under the Empire's protection."

"One day a year? They can have a holiday, then call it protection day."

"The Empire has need of its ships elsewhere at this time."

"So, we won't protect them against pirates, and we won't let them protect themselves against pirates."

"If we let them arm ships, they'll become pirates themselves."

"Well, at least they have a choice now. Be captured by pirates or become a pirate."

"We serve the emperor. The edicts are clear."

"You should have killed them all."

"What?" Devin sat up straight. "You just stopped me from killing one of them, and now you want me to kill the lot?"

"The edicts are clear, yes. We are supposed to send the ship in under guard to the nearest base, have them charged. We'll have to escort it. That will take forever. The trials will take forever. We'll have to hang around. They'll hang eventually, quickly if they get the wrong judge. If they get a merciful judge, he'll just exile them to some hard labor planet. Meanwhile, the only ship in this sector that is actively suppressing pirates—us—won't be doing it while we do this canine copulation trial. The remaining pirates will capture so many ships, they'll be plating their solid gold ships iron to hide the wealth."

"Now you're saying that we need to kill all of them?"

"Either we kill the people who aren't following the laws, or we let the people following the laws get killed. A lot of them. And if we keep letting people who follow the laws get killed, pretty soon, people will stop following them. Dead if they do, dead if they don't."

"They're stupid laws—you said so yourself, and now you want me to enforce them?"

The subprefect looked around. "I didn't hear the bell ring."

"What?"

"The one that tells us to switch sides on the debate. I argue your part, you argue mine. Keep talking. I like where you're going with this. Tell me more about stupid laws."

Devin hung his head in his hands again. "How many pirate attacks here?"

"We can prove at least nine in the last year. Could be more. Probably a lot more."

"As long as we're here, there won't be any more."

"But we won't be here long, will we?"

Devin grimaced. Lionel stepped forward 'til he could speak softly. "Let them go. Put them back on the ship.

Don't even bust up the laser. They need it. They're just poor people trying to make their way."

"I can't. There are records."

"Bridge crew and I will take care of it. We never found them. There never was a boarding. The Marines will never talk. Engineering will call it a maneuvering test. We can do this."

"I swore an oath. I serve the Empire."

"The Empire as it was, not as it is now."

They both turned as a console beeped. The technician tapped his screen. "Courier ship in-system, sir. It's looking for us and has message traffic. One with high priority from our detached group. It's labeled 'Dirk Friedel.'"

"Acknowledge," Devin said. "Send it to my queue. I'll review it shortly."

"Sir, there's another message here. It's a personal message to you, but its title is also 'Dirk Friedel.'"

"Acknowledge that one, too," Devin said.

"Sir, there's an Imperial signature on it."

Devin looked at the subprefect, who shrugged. "I'm going to my cabin. Send both." He exited the bridge into his day cabin.

The subprefect looked at the bridge crew. The bridge crew looked back at the subprefect. The helm officer turned to his board and paged through screens until he came to the maneuvering controls. He typed in a course, then held his finger over the Execute button and waited. The comm officer held up his hands and counted with his fingers. He got to seventeen before the comm beeped and Devin's voice boomed through. "Helm. Maximum speed for the jump limit. Have engineering stand by for a combat refueling on the other side and follow full speed to our destination." The comm clicked off.

The helmsman looked at the subprefect, who nodded. He mashed his finger down, and the Pollux raced away. The comm opened again. "And, subprefect, target that merchant ship and destroy it with a missile. No

223

communications to me for the next six hours."

The subprefect looked startled. He turned to the weapons tech, who was already setting up the shot. "Execute." The weapons tech pushed a button, and they all turned to watch the freighter on the main display screen until it exploded. "This part is new."

The comm beeped again. It was the tribune again, but he said nothing for a moment.

"Sir?" the subprefect asked.

"Send the padre down to the cells. Get their religions on file and track down somebody from each one of them."

"The padre, sir?"

"Yes. And send the cook down to speak with them and ask them what they want for dinner."

"Dinner?" the subprefect looked around. "What are their choices?"

"Whatever they want that the galley can provide. Fresh vegetables. Alcohol. If the galley doesn't have it, break into my private stores."

"Feed them from your private stock. Understood, sir. Will this be a regular thing, Tribune?"

"For these people? No. Not a regular thing. Just this once."

CHAPTER 22

The odd humming that signified jump space permeated the lounge. The five crew members had squeezed around the lounge table. Gavin had welded an extra chair to the floor, providing everyone a seat. Scruggs slurped her food as the others watched.

"I don't know how you can eat that," Gavin said. "It's so bitter." They were eating some sort of jelly from Rockhaul.

"It's delicious," Scruggs said. "I love that cranberry paste. If you don't want yours, I'll take it."

Gavin slid his tray across the table. "Have at it, kiddo." Scruggs took it and began to spoon the paste into her mouth.

"I miss the grilled meat from Rockhaul already," Gavin said.

"Do you miss getting stabbed in the arm?" Ana said. "Because if you enjoyed that, I can arrange for that to happen again. I'm sure that Navy's bimbo girlfriend would do it, free of charge."

"She's not my girlfriend," Dirk said.

"Notice he's not disputing the bimbo characterization," Ana said.

"Nobody is stabbing anybody," Dirk said. "Not today. By the way, what was in that pile of things of Dena's?"

"Some Imperial gold credits, a half dozen credit chips, an info chip—all encrypted," Ana said, ticking things off on his fingers. "A handful of tiny rocks—raw gold nuggets, I think, some tiny gems, some personal keepsakes. An old book, a carved piece of rock, that sort of thing."

"And a treasure map," Lee said.

"A treasure map?" Gavin asked "Really?"

"No, not really. Just some sort of map fell out of the book. Printed on hard plastic paper, a planetary orbit display, with coordinates and directions. Could be a map to a ranch back on Rockhaul."

"Give her back the credits and the data chips," Dirk said. "If there's nothing that can be used as a weapon, give her the book and the carvings. Take the nuggets and gems, and we'll have them valued first chance that we get. We'll deduct them from the cost of her transportation."

"Not that many nuggets, and they're pretty small," Ana said.

"The bulk of the money is supposed to come from her off-world credit," Dirk said. "But a down payment would be good."

"Why give her back the gold credits?" Gavin asked.

"Everybody should have a bit of money in their pocket," Ana said. "Even prisoners. Makes them feel they have something to lose, makes them easier to handle."

"What about recruits?" Lee asked. "Do you pay Scruggs something?"

"I should. Actually, we should. Actually, you should." Ana gestured at Dirk. "You're the captain, after all. Captain pays the crew." Ana looked thoughtful. "We're all kind of crew now."

"That's an idea. I'll think about that," Dirk said. "Anybody have any updates from their watches to share? Gavin, is Dena causing us any issues with life support?"

"No, Skipper," Gavin said. "We've got plenty of spare air and water, and we're stuffed to the bulkheads with food, so we're good 'til we reach Reik Colony."

"Reik Colony?" Ana asked.

"Our next stop," Lee said. "Four more days in jump, and we'll be there."

"Any ships?"

"Some free traders call there, according to the sailing instructions. No passenger lines."

"So, nowhere I want to leave the ship, then," Ana said.

"I wouldn't advise it, no," Dirk said "Lee, how's our passenger?"

"No trouble at all," Lee said. "Scruggs and I take her for meals and bathroom breaks three times a day, and she's caused no problems at all. She does say she's bored."

"I thought you gave her a comm unit?" Gavin asked.

"She's hooked into every database we'll let her use, and she's reading them all. She and I had a long talk about a ship's medic job yesterday. She asked all sorts of questions about how to do things on ships and what different wounds and things."

"Like she'll be any use as a medic," Gavin said.

"She'll be an excellent medic," Lee said. "She sort of is already. Better than me at some things. I've never had to saw a leg off or deal with sepsis and gangrene."

"Gangrene?" Gavin asked. "What's that?"

"Bacteria infecting your flesh and rotting it off after a bad wound."

Gavin looked queasy. "Yuck. How do you get that?"

"They have all these small ranches and backwoods settlements that are too far away from town to have real medical care. There's bacteria in the air and in the soil. If you get hurt, you can get infected, and because you're not in a hospital, it can get serious quickly. She said one rancher was out by himself and cut his leg with an ax. He just laid out there for days 'til somebody found him. By then, he had gangrene. He didn't make it. Another was hit by a falling tree. They couldn't shift the tree, so they had to cut his arm off. He survived."

"Wow," Gavin said. "Can't they fix that?"

"Yes, they've got a medical robot in town, but just a basic one. And just in town. They don't have a lot of comms or transport outside of the main settlements," Lee said. "If you get into trouble, and you're not in town, better hope your buddies can fix you."

"It is a subsistence economy," Ana said. "I looked at some of those ranches—they're pretty big, mostly self-sufficient. They produce food, clothing. And they build things like furniture and houses themselves. There's no shortage of wood.

"What about machine tools and suchlike?" Gavin asked.

"Use old ones, I think, from the founding. Population is declining," Ana said. "I talked trading with some people at that dinner. They said there were fewer ships every year. Twenty years ago, there was two or three a month at the capital and several a year at Central Falls. Now it's only three or four a year at the capital, and we were the first in over a year out there."

"So, you just grow up, live, and die in the same farm?"

"They call them ranches, Engineer," Ana said.

"I call them somewhere I'd not want to be. No wonder Dena was scheming to get away," Gavin said.

"She should have stayed on the farm, should have listened to her old man," Ana said. "Look at all the trouble she caused."

Scruggs had been quiet 'til then, but she stood. Her face was flushed. "Why? Just because somebody tells you that you have to stay somewhere, you should do it? Not try to go anywhere, not try to better yourself? Stay home and do as you're told?" She rounded on Lee and Gavin. "If I'd stayed home and not tried to get off-planet, you two would be dead in that flood. And you, Centurion, they would have spaced you first chance they got if I wasn't in the lock with you. And you, Pilot Dirk, you, you . . ." She glared at Dirk for a moment. "You'd have to clean your own bathroom." Scruggs pushed her way out the chair and fled the room.

Everybody was quiet for a moment. "That was unexpected," Dirk said.

"And overdue as well," Ana said. "She's coming along nicely. A good trooper. She did well down there." He turned to Gavin. "And I mentioned this earlier, but I want to say it in front of everybody. Engineer Two, Medic Two,

I appreciate you trying to rescue Scruggs. I owe you a favor for that."

"You don't like either of us. Now you owe us a favor?" Lee asked.

"What's liking you have to do with anything?" Ana asked.

Lee looked at Ana. "I would have tried to save my sister, regardless."

"Still doesn't matter. I asked you to do something for me, and you did," Ana said.

Gavin watched him for a moment. "Senior Centurion, you helped haul us into that raft from the river. If going after her was a favor for you, then I would like to think that we're even, and you don't owe us anything."

"Suit yourself," Ana said.

Dirk looked around at the three of them. "That's the second unexpected thing that's happened in ten minutes. Must be a special day. Jump is coming up. What's our status? Engineer, how are things?"

"Plenty of fuel, Skipper," Gavin said. "We cracked as much as we needed and more. But I'm starting to see wear on filters, nozzles, and some other components. We're not in the red zone yet, but a lot of things have moved into yellow. We can only go a few more jumps before we need maintenance. After that little barge incident, the hatch is leaking—I need new seals, and I need to hammer out some struts. Plus, we're short on light bulbs. I'm going to go around to everyone's cabin and pull some bulbs. We need them in engineering."

"Do that. What about our trading situation?"

"Your guess is as good as mine. We've got lots of, well, 'general cargo' is the term. Food, toys, trinkets, leather stuff, furniture, and the medical supplies, of course. We have things to trade."

"Medic? How is everybody?"

"Scruggs was beaten up a bit, but it's mostly just bruises. She was creased by an arrow, but that's just a flesh wound. Gavin's arm is healing. Centurion has a fractured arm that he didn't mention until I checked him on the med comp, but that will heal with some supplements, which we have."

Dirk turned to Ana. "You didn't mention that you were wounded?"

"I was breaking heads, and some of them broke back. It wasn't relevant at the time. I'm fine."

"We have plenty of food," Lee said. "And of different variety. The foods from Rockhaul are mostly dried and preserved. We'll be able to skip eating trays for weeks. Longer if Scruggs just eats jam for the next month."

"We've all expended ammunition, Pilot," Ana said. "That needs to be replaced. But we picked up some of those swords. Good weapons on the right planet."

"I didn't ask you for a report, Centurion," Dirk said.

"You're getting one. I'm the closest we have to a security officer now."

"What are we going to do with swords?" Lee asked.

"I can use a sword. Not very well, but well enough," Ana said. "Some places don't allow firearms. But they will allow 'primitive weapons.' Some scanners don't even notice them—think they're just crowbars or something like that." Ana turned to Gavin. "Can you use a sword?"

"I'm better with knives," Gavin said.

"Maybe if I ground it down to be a cutlass?" Ana asked. Gavin shrugged and began to eat the remainder of his food that Scruggs had left.

"What's a cutlass?" Lee asked.

"It's a type of sword. Usually issued to Marines, or ship's security. Shipborne troops don't like to use weapons that can shoot holes in the hull. Swords do the trick. Are you trained in swords, Pilot?"

"I know the basics."

"Maybe you can teach Scruggs a bit?" Ana asked.

"Is that all you want to teach the girl, weapons?" Lee asked.

Ana looked at her. "You're teaching her Zero-G maneuvers. Why not add some emergency medical training as well?"

Lee nodded. "That's not a bad idea. Pilot, what do you know about our next stop?"

"System is called Reik. No idea why. Two planets with plenty of water—well, ice, but cold, and can't breathe the atmosphere. Too much methane, not enough oxygen. Mildly acidic, so nobody lives there. All the action is in the asteroid belt. Local Belters and a couple of corporate stations. We're hitting the biggest one, orbiting the local gas giant. Free fuel, and we can try to sell some of the freshest food and maybe some exotic stuff. They do light manufacturing and repairs for the local ships, so we might be able to get some of the engineer's repairs done."

"How long 'til I can get off?" Ana asked.

"This is the second last stop for you, Centurion. One more after this, and we're back on a space lane, and you can leave. That planet is called Papillon, which means butterfly in Francais. It's got at least two regular passenger lines calling there, it's on a trade route, moderate population on the surface."

"I'm looking forward to it," Ana said.

"And," Dirk said. "A bank that will accept Dena's credit chip, she said."

"Even better," Ana said.

***

Reik was a difficult system to deal with. All the major ore bodies were inside the jump limit, rendering the gas giant's orbital station the only place to meet up with anything. They hadn't bothered to check the sailing almanac to see where it would be, and they came out of jump almost in opposition to it. They had to trundle along a strange orbit to catch up.

"We'll have to cut across the system and use a gravity assist to swing around the fourth planet, then stabilize our orbit to meet the station," Lee said.

"What's the planet called?" Dirk asked.

"No name. Just Reik IV. Station is called Reik Station."

"Very imaginative," Dirk said. "How long to get there?"

"Four days," Lee said.

"Four days? We could almost jump to another system in that time."

"Can't fight spatial geometry, Pilot," Lee said.

"Well, we'll keep the same watches 'til we're there. Any weird landing instructions we should know about?"

"They have a beacon, that's all. They want a standard package sent. Ship information, crew IDs, including Imperial ID numbers, cargo to trade, cargo to buy, and a list of prohibited items that we'll keep on board and not import."

"What's prohibited?" Dirk asked.

"Not much. A bunch of drugs that I don't recognize. Grenades, explosives, rocket launchers. Non-frangible bullets. Personal sidearms are okay, but if they catch you with armored bullets that can harm station equipment, that's an immediate death sentence. Sentence is to be carried out 'immediately by a vote of five or more station residents'—it says in the briefing."

"Standard station rules, then," Dirk said. "Bring us in, please navigator."

"I'm the medic, Pilot Dirk."

"Of course you are. You just happen to be temporarily filling the navigator's position. Set a course, please."

"Understood, Pilot. Will you take care of the commo package?" she said.

"Of course, I, uh, Emperor's balls," Dirk said.

"What?" Lee asked.

"Who do I tell them we are?"

The all-crew meeting took place in the lounge. Everybody crowded in, except for Dena.

"Shouldn't she be here as well?" Scruggs asked.

"First, she's not crew. She just kind of snuck her way on board under false pretenses," Dirk said.

"But didn't we agree that we all had done that?" Scruggs said. "That we're all here under false pretenses—none of us is who we say we are, and we're all running away from something."

The silence stretched.

"We can't trust her. She tried to steal the ship," Lee said. "We can't trust somebody who tries to steal ships."

"She didn't do anything violent," Scruggs said. "And in terms of stealing ships, didn't we agree that we stole this ship? We're certainly not taking it where the owners wanted it, are we, Pilot Dirk?"

"Well, not exactly," Dirk said. "But calling it stealing is harsh. I mean, they gave me considerable leeway as to when I had to get where they wanted me to go."

"I thought we were traveling far away from where they wanted us to go, and we are now going in more or less the opposite direction," Scruggs said.

"Well, that's just details. We haven't actually stolen the ship until we don't arrive at Parsifal on time," Dirk said.

"So, we haven't stolen the ship yet, but we're just waiting for a timer to expire, then, Pilot Dirk?"

"Right."

"So, since we're intending to steal the ship at a future date, and we've formed a plan and taken action on at least one aspect of the plan, doesn't that make us a criminal conspiracy? And us all guilty of conspiracy to commit piracy?" Scruggs asked.

Dirk looked nonplussed. "Where did you learn that?"

"Centurion gave me some reading to do. Isn't the penalty for conspiracy to commit piracy immediate death by hanging?"

"Whoa, whoa," Gavin said. "Nobody is going to get hung here. There are lots of extenuating circumstances that a court will have to consider—level and amount of violence, cargo value, commercial confusions, that sort of thing. And besides, only a senior noble can have you hung with immediate effect. Otherwise, you have to be referred to the sector courts, and the duke has to make a ruling, and if there are Imperial security concerns, he or she has to call back to the capital," Gavin said.

Another long pause interrupted, then Ana said, "You seem to know a lot of detailed information about Imperial procedures regarding handing of piracy, Engineer."

"Did you have to give her that reading assignment?" Gavin asked. "Couldn't you have stuck to having her learn how to tear a man's intestines out with a hook or something?"

"Centurion has already taught me that," Scruggs said. "But I haven't been able to practice it. And I don't really have a good hook."

"Nor do we currently have a man whose intestines need to be dragged out," Dirk said. "But keep up your practice. You never know when that skill might be handy."

"We're all pirates now," Lee said. "I didn't think of that."

"I think it's kind of cool," Scruggs said. "I ran away and became a space pirate. Centurion, shouldn't we have some sort of flag or badge for our uniforms or something?"

"What do you want, recruit? Should I get you an eyepatch?"

"Oh, yes, please, Centurion. Could we have one? I'd like one in blue, match my eyes." She gave a disarmingly wide smile.

"Recruit," Ana said, "if you think that any self-respecting trooper will wear a blue eyepatch—" Ana cocked his head and regarded Scruggs. "Recruit, are you messing with me?"

"Oh, no, sir, Senior Centurion," Scruggs said. She gave him an innocent look. Ana regarded her warily.

Dirk broke in. "Be that as it may, we have to tell these

people who we are, and why we are here, and we need to tell them something."

"Can't use our real names," Gavin said.

"Is Gavin really your name?" Lee asked. "Lee is my real name, but I just assumed . . ."

"Dena can use her real name. Nobody here knows her. She's never been off-planet before," Scruggs said.

"Not . . . yet she hasn't," Dirk said. "But somebody will be looking for her, and eventually, questions will catch up. Better if nobody knows that she's been here. Or at least here with us."

"It's not exactly going to be a secret that we left with her, Skipper," Gavin said.

"We're all from the same mercenary family from Pallas," Ana said. "We all have the same last name. I'll give you a horribly long Greek-sounding name that nobody can pronounce, so we'll tell them just to use our first names. That's very common."

"All having the same last name?" Lee asked.

"Yes. Big families there. Pallas is poor, backward, dirty, and mean."

"Kind of describes you, Centurion," Gavin said.

Ana ignored him. "Pallas is always exporting people—technicians, mercenaries, that type of thing. They have decent schools, and everybody learns standard, so they can talk to the Imperials. The story is, we all worked for different companies, had different contacts and different skills, and randomly came back together on Pallas station when we were discharged from our contracts at the same time. We were all drinking together and agreed we didn't want to go Downport and back to our crappy hometowns. Since we were all distantly related, we agreed to crew a ship and work together to see what could happen. It's very common."

"It is common," Dirk said. "I've actually heard of it before, just not in this sector."

"Which is why it will work here, no other Pallas ships

to dispute us. A bit strange, but family ships, especially family free traders, are pretty normal."

"We'll all need some sort of Pallas ID—or know what one looks like at least—to show the station," Gavin said. "How do we make that work?"

"I can do that. I have some codes that will register as Pallas codes—basic ones, and they can authenticate basic ID issued from Pallas."

Everybody looked at the centurion.

Finally, Dirk spoke. "You have codes that will authenticate us as Pallas citizens?" Dirk asked.

"Very low-level codes, but basic IDs? Yes."

"How did you come up with those?" Dirk asked.

"Who's looking for you, Navy, and how much is the reward?" Ana asked. "Are we sharing now?"

"My mistake, Senior Centurion," Dirk said. "I apologize. Pallas codes would be wonderful. Tell us who we are, and we'll follow your lead."

"I'll get on that right away. Everybody, send me your standard code info, and I'll sign it as being from Pallas," Ana said.

"But what about the ship?" Lee said. "We need documents for that."

Gavin huffed a long breath. "I may be able to help with that."

CHAPTER 23

"Heavyweight Items, Reik Station here," station ops said over the radio.

"That's a stupid name for a ship," Ana said. He was sitting behind Dirk at the weapons console, even though they had no weapons.

"It's the name of the ship on the ID documents I had," Gavin said. "Better than nothing."

"And it's a close enough match to our size and cargo capacity that it would take a serious onboard inspection to prove it wrong," Dirk said.

"Best we not let anybody get on board to make a serious inspection, then," Gavin said.

"Forged ship IDs. Were you a pirate, Engineer?" Ana asked.

"Fake personal IDs. Did you do illegal mercenary recruiting, Centurion?" Gavin asked.

"Please, keep quiet, you two," Lee said. "I don't want to think what Paterfather Zeus would say about consorting with pirates and mercenaries."

"How about Imperial deserters?" Gavin said. "Our pilot buddy there used to be in the navy, but I don't think he was honorably discharged."

"My discharge status—or lack thereof—is not up for discussion. I thought we agreed not to talk about these things."

"God, save me, Paterfather Zeus," Lee said.

"And aren't you wanted for stealing all that medical equipment?" Gavin said.

"I didn't steal it," Lee said.

"Right, you just pretended to sell it, then didn't. I think that's called fraud."

"And we have a failed revolutionary locked up in the hold," Scruggs said from her post, hovering behind the control room.

Everybody considered this for a moment. "So, what's your story, then, youngster?" Dirk asked. "Since we're all pointing out each other's flaws. What do we call you?"

"I'm just a girl trying to make her way," Scruggs said.

Dirk surveyed her for a moment. "Pirates, mercenaries, deserters, fraudsters, revolutionaries, and runaways—this is who we are," Dirk said.

"Sounds like the title of a bad old earth country music song, Skipper," Gavin said.

"What's country music?" Lee said.

"I'll play you some," Gavin said.

"Not where the rest of us have to listen to it, please," Ana said. "I've heard that type of music before."

"What's wrong with country music?" Gavin asked.

"What's wrong with abusing a cat with a fork? They sound about the same," Ana said.

The station repeated their call, interrupting them. "Heavyweight Items, Reik Station here. Do you copy?"

"Sorry, station," Gavin said. "We were just discussing our favorite music. We're on course to dock. Do you have a berth for us?"

"Roger, Heavyweight Items. Correct answer to your question is old earth synthotech. And about the documents you transferred . . ."

All five of them tensed during the pause.

"Ops says everything is fine. All of your documents are in order. You are cleared for seven days at regular docking rates for space and utilities. Payment due on arrival at dockside. Everything else, you negotiate directly with the merchants in question."

They let out breaths with a whoosh.

Dirk closed his eyes and exhaled again. He keyed the mic. "Thank you, station. Where are we docking, please? How do we find it?"

"Ring C, like Charlie, spot seven. Easy to see. You are right after that Imperial courier boat that is latched. You'll be next to them, sharing an air lock."

Dead silence hung in the cabin.

"The empress's hairy vagina," Scruggs said.

***

The crew went back to the lounge to argue. They had put one of the external cameras on the screen, and they could see the courier boat at the next bay. A repair crew swarmed the top of the hull.

"We should leave right away," Lee said. "That Imperial courier is a problem. The longer we stay here, the longer they have to learn about us. We don't want any Imperial notice. They could come over and arrest us at any time."

"You mean," Ana said, "you don't want Imperial notice because you think they might be looking for you for fraud."

"Or they might arrest her for being in company with a forger. Should we ask them?" Gavin asked.

"Which forger?" Dirk asked. "You or the centurion?"

That silenced Ana and Gavin.

"Look, that isn't a warship. It's a courier. They carry important people from base to base and broadcast messages. They're not interested in local fraud or customs issues or faked identifications or anything like that. Even if they are interested in us, they won't arrest us."

"Why not?" Gavin asked. "They're Imperials, aren't they?"

"There will be two crew—three at most—on the ship. Pilot, navigator, maybe an engineer, and space for two passengers. They can't arrest us. They don't have any space."

"They can shoot us down when we leave," Lee said.

"No, they can't," Dirk said. "That model courier has two missiles for self-defense, that's it. The regulations require them to run, not fight. They're faster than anything except a purpose-built warship, and they're faster than most of those."

"Know a lot about courier ships there, Navy. Ever been stationed on one?"

Dirk ignored him. "They can jump farther and quicker than any merchant ship, have better computers and sensors. They'll see any threat before it sees them, and they just route around it. They'll jump into a different system rather than fire those missiles."

"So, what are they doing here?" Ana asked. "This system isn't on a courier route, is it?"

"No, it's not," Dirk said. "Far from it."

"So, why are they here?" Gavin asked.

"Look here," Dirk pointed to the screen. "And here. That's a fueling crew. They're topping up on fuel, and those boats are probably eighty percent fuel. That's a sensor package being swapped there. Best guess, they're on a direct route to somewhere, least time travel, and needed to be fueled up."

"You don't have to come to a station to do that," Ana said. "They could have radioed in for a fuel barge to meet them."

"Probably, there wasn't one available," Dirk said. "Those things have to be in place ahead of time, and if this was a special mission, they'll be ahead of any communications. And I think they blew some sensors. They go so fast, their sensors need to be in tip-top shape. That repair crew is swapping a sensor mounting out— they're almost done. Even on these direct routes, things happen. I'll bet they hit this system and bust a scanner or had it bust elsewhere, and the captain calculated the time for a fuel tanker to meet them, and it was just as fast to get to the station, refuel, and have the repair done at the same time."

"Surely, there aren't spare Imperial level sensors on a mining station like this?" Lee asked

"Doesn't need to be," Dirk said. "They have their own

spares, triple redundancy. And everything is designed to be swapped by a minimal crew. Getting here on a station would just speed things up."

"So, they're not here for us?" Lee asked.

"The pilot makes sense," Ana said. "They're not here for us. It's just a coincidence. They'll not be interested in system-level crimes. Only Imperial crimes. We can ignore them, I think." Ana smiled for the first time in a long time. "Unless any of you have Imperial crimes that you've committed."

"Can we all go on-station, then?" Scruggs asked.

Ana smiled a disarming grin at her and then pointed a finger at Dirk. "Not all of us. I think some of us might have to stay on board."

***

After the discussion, they agreed to ship supplies and consumables first, trading second, and crew leave third. Lee hadn't wanted any crew leave, but Gavin and Ana had insisted.

"If nobody leaves the ship, that's strange," Gavin said. "Station ops will remember. The chandler will remember. Emperor's balls, the bars and restaurants will remember. A friend in ops will have called them already that a new ship's docked, and they'll expect to see crew coming out and spending money."

"Much as I normally hate to agree with the engineer," Ana said, "he's correct. After we get our resupply business done, we need to be seen, but just enough to blend in the background. A ship that puts four crew members into the bar and restaurants won't be noticed. A ship where nobody leaves is an oddity."

"So, who goes and when?" Gavin asked.

"You and the medic go to the chandler and look at parts," Ana said. "You're an engineer. That makes sense. And Jovians aren't unusual on stations, and most of them have some engineering trade."

"You mean freaks, not Jovians, don't you, Centurion?" Gavin said.

Lee stiffened.

Ana paused for a moment, looked at Lee, then back at Gavin. "Jovians," he said, enunciating the word slowly, "are not unusual on stations, as I said. We'll need to do some trading to get money, and we'll need a bit of cargo-handling to deal with that—and some security, of course. Scruggs and I can handle that."

"You mean the recruit and you can handle that," Gavin said.

"There's a point to this correction, Engineer," Ana asked.

"Nope, just strange to see you using people's names is all."

"I promised the captain here that I would be polite until he arranged a private meeting for you and me, Engineer. I keep my promises." Ana rounded on Dirk. "And I assume the captain keeps his promises. Going to arrange a meeting here for us, Captain? Should the engineer and I be discussing personal weapons?"

Dirk looked away from the screen. He had been staring at the courier ship. "Not here. Not now. I said I'd arrange it on a planet—not enough privacy on a station."

"Well, we'll be at a planet eventually," Ana said. "And I'm prepared to wait. What about you, Engineer?"

"I'm as patient as you are, Centurion."

***

Lee and Gavin toured the station after clearing the air lock. Both were dressed in skin suits but with station slippers and emergency air packs rather than the bulkier, working ones. They had coveralls on, looking like the crews of a half dozen other ships that were docked. Reik station was almost identical to a dozen stations they'd each seen over the years. Bulk-refining operations, shipping platforms, and offices from a couple big corps took up eighty percent of the space, and the remaining twenty percent was entertainment for bored miners or the odd prospector that hunted around the belt.

Prices were high. Gavin couldn't get a price for spares over the net, so he had to go directly to the single chandler.

"This," Gavin said, after reviewing the prices, "is robbery. We're not paying this."

"Well, actually, you are," the clerk said. "This is the only place on-station that sells ship supplies. If you don't buy it from us, you're not buying it."

"You just jacked up the prices 'cause we're not locals," Gavin said.

"Yup. No law against it neither."

"Imperial turd," Gavin said.

"You buying anything, friend?" the clerk asked. "Because if you're not, then why don't you move along?"

Gavin made a rude gesture, then turned toward the door. "Come on, Lee, we'll figure something out," Gavin said.

"Is this wise?" Lee asked. "Don't we need these parts?"

"We do, but we're not going to pay this much."

"You'll negotiate them down."

"Not us. Don't worry, we just need to see the skipper," Gavin said. They returned to the ship and punched the Air Lock button. Soon, Dirk's head appeared back at the door and let them in. They walked to the lounge.

"How's your girlfriend?" Gavin asked.

"Sleeping. She's still locked in her cage."

"You'll have to let her out eventually, Pilot," Lee said.

Dirk sighed. "A problem for later. What do you two need?"

"This," Gavin said, producing his list.

"I thought you went to buy these. Huh, these prices seem very high."

"These prices are very high, Skipper. Have you sold anything yet?"

"I put the foods, spices, jams, and suchlike up on the station trading board. I've had a lot of interest—lots of bids," he said.

"Here's my plan," Gavin said. "Add an addendum to your prices. Take these prices for the spares, cut them in half, and say you'll accept them as credit on the bids at that rate."

"How will that work?" Lee asked.

"See here," Gavin said, pointing, "class three water pump. Chandler wants two hundred credits for it. The locals can probably buy it for eighty or less. Tell anybody who bids that you'll take a water pump at a credit of one hundred credits. They'll either take one of their spares and trade it to us or just buy one from the chandler and resell it to us. We're here for parts—remember, that's what we need."

"But we need more than just parts, we need some other stuff. What if people offer us just equipment and no cash?"

"Just tell them part of the bid has to be cash," Lee said.

Gavin and Dirk looked at her. "What? It's pretty sensible."

"It is sensible. Good job there, Medic Two. I think we'll put you in charge of our trading from now on."

They posted the changes, and in a short time, they had a variety of bids that matched their criteria. Half ship parts, half credits. Gavin listed them in order of importance and asked for immediate delivery. He and Lee stayed at the air lock as a stream of visitors showed up to swap fuses, valves, control lines, filters, sensors, tools for spices, dried fruits, seeds, jams, and different kinds of alcohols. Either Ana or Scruggs was always near the air lock with a revolver in a holster. Scruggs had taken to wearing a sword she had picked up on Rockhaul, as had Ana. In less than a half shift, they had filled eighty percent of their needs. Even their wooden products had hit pay dirt.

"I'll take both those table and chair sets off your

hands," one store owner said. "No credits, but I'll swap you the chain, flanges, pipes and nozzles, and all the other parts on this list here."

"We want half in credits," Gavin insisted.

"I don't have enough credits," the man replied. "But I do have a back room full of ship parts I've took in trade over the years. It's worth considerably more than what you're asking by your prices, and I'll give it all to you for those table sets."

"We don't need all this stuff," Gavin said. "Nine hundred feet of docking chain? We barely need forty."

"I'll never use it. I furnish cubes. But to you, it's worth a lot, and you'll always find some use for it. Trade it to some prospector you meet out in the dark. And getting rid of furniture is harder than you think."

Gavin put him on hold and talked to Dirk and Lee. "A third of what he's offering is stuff on my list, a third is stuff we might need, maybe, and a third is duplicates of stuff we already have. And he's right—we can always trade it."

"We got credits from everybody else," Lee said.

"Let's do it," Dirk said.

Gavin got back on the comm and worked out the arrangements. "Bring it by, and we'll swap."

"It's too much for one pallet. We'll need to do two or maybe even three," the store owner said.

"So, give me what you can on the first one, and I'll give you one table set, then I'll give you the second set after the second swap. But we have to do it today."

"Can't," the store owner said. "It's too heavy. I can get one pallet there in about an hour, but the second won't be ready 'til first shift tomorrow.

"Fine, we'll shift one today. The other tomorrow. But right at the start of first shift."

"See you in an hour," the voice said.

***

Ana and Scruggs appeared at the bridge. "How we doing, Navy? Got what we need?"

"Almost all of it," Dirk said. "Gavin and Lee did a good job negotiating. Things squared away down below?"

"Yes. We got that table set out you wanted. Should we put it out for people to look at it?"

"Got a buyer, sight unseen. Put it outside the air lock. Somebody will be by shortly. One of you two stay with it, though."

"It's been a long shift. How about the shore leave after that?" Ana asked.

"That's true, Skipper. Me and Lee, we'd like a non-ship meal for a while," Gavin said.

"Will it be as good as what we ate on Rockhaul?" Scruggs asked.

"Absolutely not," Lee said. "Station food isn't good. It's just different."

"And somebody else cooks it and cleans up," Gavin said.

"How's that different from here?" Scruggs asked. "You just put it in the microwave, and I do the cleanup, not you."

"It's just . . . different . . . somehow," Gavin said. "We need somebody to watch the ship."

"I'll do it," Dirk said. "I've seen plenty of stations. I don't need to see this one."

"It doesn't seem fair that the pilot stays on board, and we get to go off," Scruggs said.

"The pilot doesn't want to go on-station, recruit," Ana said.

"Why not?"

"He's worried about his identification," Ana said.

"But why, Centurion? His ID's the same as ours. If he's worried about his ID, shouldn't we be worried about our IDs?"

"Our IDs are fine," Ana said. "Because we've never been here before. People ask who we are, we'll show them our IDs. They check 'em, they check out. They have no reason to believe we're not who we say we are. But the problem with Navy here . . ." Ana smiled at Dirk.

"What problem, Centurion?" Dirk asked.

"The problem with you, Navy, is that some of the people on that courier may know you under a different name, so they might be surprised to see an ID that says you're from Pallas, when they remember you from before. Or they might have seen your picture somewhere."

"Where would they see his picture, Centurion?" Scruggs asked.

"On a wanted poster, probably."

CHAPTER 24

"But where does the fuel go, sir?" midshipman Calroy said. He was seated at the far end of the table from Devin, the Lord Lyon, Subprefect Lionel, and most of the officers of the ISS Pollux. Lord Lyon insisted his officers dine with him once a week.

"Depends on which item you're talking about," Devin said. He ignored the slight amusement that swept the table and stirred his soup. Normally, junior officers were expected to keep quiet at table, but Devin was known to be approachable. "The fusion plant fuses the hydrogen and converts it into electricity. That gives us power shields, weapons, and environmental items. And the thrusters use it, of course. The main engines combine it with oxygen and dump it out the nozzles. And the jump drive makes it into negative energy. The negative energy warps space in front of us, so we accelerate past light speed. That uses the most fuel, of course."

"But why so much, sir?"

"I don't really know. I learned in school, but the explanation made no sense to me. The chief engineer could explain it to you better than me. Chief?"

"It makes sense to me, sir," the chief engineer said after swallowing his soup. "Just need to follow the math, youngster," she said.

"Math," Calroy said. "Surely, that's not something for officers to concern themselves with?"

Every head at the table turned to regard Calroy. He raised a languid eyebrow. "That's the type of thing the crew sees to, is it not?"

Devin took another spoonful of soup as he regarded Calroy and swallowed it, then turned to his steward.

"Steward Imin, this is excellent. Thank you so much."

"Old family recipe, sir," Imin said. "We use cumin. Serve it to the crew once a month, I do. Plenty more, sir, if you'd like a second bowl."

"That would be marvelous, please. Anyone else?" Several of the other officers lifted their bowls and nodded. Imin stepped through a connecting hatch behind Calroy.

"Sir," Calroy said, "you let the crew share your rations?"

"Eh?" Devin said. "Share? What do you mean?"

"Well, eat the same food as you. As the officers."

"Food is food, youngster," Lionel said. "Officers digest the same as everyone else."

"But cumin is an expensive spice," Calroy said. "Should it not be reserved for officers? For nobles?"

Devin and Lionel exchanged glances. "Subprefect, do you understand what the lad is talking about?" Devin asked.

"I'm a bit confused, Captain," Lionel admitted. "Explain yourself, son."

"Sir," Calroy said. "But this sharing with the men, the lower orders, isn't that, well, kind of democratic?"

The two senior officers looked at each other. "Are you sure he's actually in the navy?" Devin asked.

"His orders were correct," Lionel said. "But I didn't really pay much attention."

Devin turned to Calroy. "Who are you again? How did you get on my ship?"

"I arrived on the courier, sir. My mother specified that I was to attend on your ship and only your ship, and the emperor was most gracious in assigning me here."

"Your mother?" Devin asked. "I'm not sure I know her. Who is she again?"

"The Lady Gwendolin, Countess of Perth-Major," Calroy said. "Eighty-seventh in line to the throne."

"Lady Gwendolin," Devin said. He shook his head. "Doesn't ring a bell."

Subprefect Lionel snapped his fingers. "Wendy," he said.

"Wendy?" Devin asked, looking at him.

"Wendy. Warp-speed Wendy. From Rigel."

Devin laughed. "Of course, Warp-speed Wendy. I haven't talked to her in years." He turned to Calroy. "And how is your mother?"

"Well, thank you, milord. She sends her affections," Calroy said.

"Best make sure her husband doesn't hear about that," Lionel whispered.

Devin ignored him. "And did she ever marry that fop—the artsy fellow?" Devin turned to Lionel. "What was his name, Subprefect?"

"Conroy, Calvin, something like that. No, Calroy, that was it." They both raised their eyebrows in unison, then turned back to Midshipman Calroy.

"My father, sir. Lord Calroy."

"Well, my greetings to him, then," Devin said.

At that moment, Imin returned. He stopped at the bottom of the table and served the soup to the officers.

"So, you are not fond of math, then," Devin asked, "Mr. Midshipman Lord Calroy, Eighty-eighth in line to the throne, that you are?"

"No, sir," Calroy said. "It's not a proper study for gentlemen." Imin hovered at his side, and Calroy shoved his soup plate at him. He banged his arm into the ladle, and a gob of soup splashed on it.

"You clumsy idiot," Calroy yelled. He smacked Imin's shoulder hard enough that the man dropped the soup tureen, which crashed to the floor with a spray of soup.

"Fool! Peasant. Look what you've done now," Calroy raved. He stood and smacked him again. "Lowbred imbecile. I'll teach you to spill soup on your betters."

He slapped Imin. Imin put up his hands to ward off the blows. For a frozen instant, nobody moved. Then, as Calroy raised his hands again, the two officers grabbed him by the shoulders and slammed him back into his chair. They held him there while he raved at them. Lionel ran down the table, stepped in front of him, slapped him once, then reached forward and used his fingers to hold Calroy's lip closed. "Be silent if you don't want to make this worse." He turned to help Imin up.

Devin stood. "Imin, are you all right?"

"Little surprised, sir," Imin said from the floor. "But no harm done. I've had worse on a boarding. Just surprised. The soup, though." He surveyed the orange slop on the floor.

"Leave the soup. We'll take care of it," Devin said. He leaned over to the wall and pushed an intercom. "Bosun, report to my dining cabin immediately," he said. "Everyone, resume your seats. Except you, Lionel." Devin stood and walked down to the foot of the table. "Well, now I know why your mother sent you to me for instruction." He helped Imin brush off his jacket. "Ruined, I'm afraid. Well, the youngster here will buy you a new one. Take one from stores and see that it's charged to him. Ah, Bosun."

"Bosun McSanchez reporting as ordered, sir." The bosun stepped into the dining room and regarded the bemused looking officers and the stained floor. "Am I too late for the food fight, sir?"

"A touch, yes," Devin said. "Bosun, are you familiar with cumin?"

"A spice, sir. Imin and the cook make an excellent soup out of it. Looks a lot like this one here, for sure."

"You enjoy it?"

"Very much, sir. Expensive, though. Purser doesn't have the budget for it. That's why we only have the soup once a month."

"Well, we're going to serve it once a week now to anybody who wants it. Tell the purser to order more. Lots more. I'll authorize it."

"How much more, sir?"

"However much he needs. I don't care if he fills shuttle bay three to the brim with crates of the stuff."

"Might use it for more than soup, sir. Lots of other good meals you can make with it."

"Outstanding. Bosun, are you also familiar with math?"

"Math, sir? Two plus two and all that, sir?"

"That's right."

"Very familiar, sir."

"And what's your opinion of it?"

"Oh, I'm much in favor of it, sir."

"Much in favor, are you?"

"Much, sir. Very useful. Think everyone should use it."

"Even officers?"

"Oh, officers especially, sir. Lots of good uses for math. But no idea why you're asking me. Why, Mr. Imin there, he has advanced degrees in math from several core universities."

"I didn't know that," Devin said. He turned to Imin. "Advanced degrees?"

"Several, sir," Imin said. "It's a hobby with me."

"And do you use this 'math' in your job on the ship, steward?"

"Oh, yes, sir. Calculating the amount of cumin to put in soup, counting how much money I'll need to spend on a new uniform."

"Use it for anything else?"

"Yes, sir. I used it off Rigel, that battle. Lost the main computer, we did. Our fusion gun was in local control. We had no sensors, but we had a voice link to one of the radars. They were cut off as well. I got the vectors from them, calculated the angles, and used that to target the rebel ship and blow a hole in it."

"Blew a hole in it? What for?" Devin asked.

"So the Marines could go in and storm the rebel's bridge, sir."

"And did they—storm the bridge, I mean?"

"They did, sir. Captured the rebel commanders."

"How do you know this?"

"Well, I was with them, sir. Helped out a little."

"And your help, did it use this math thing that we're talking about?"

"Yes, sir. Used it to angle the lasers to burn through the bridge door and to bounce the grenade thing around."

"Outstanding." Devin said. He smiled down at Calroy. "I remember your mother now—quite well. She and I are old, old friends. She sent you here for a reason. And now, I know what that reason was."

"You do, sir?" Calroy asked. He looked frightened.

"I do. Bosun, Mr. Calroy here, is to learn this math thing that Mr. Imin is so fond of. Learn it well."

"Of course, sir. How much learning does he need?" the bosun asked.

"I think that's up to Mr. Imin. Mr. Imin, how long does it take to learn 'math?'"

"Could take a lifetime, sir—to master it, but I think I could do a basic 'shipboard math for morons' in a few months. Perhaps a year."

"Outstanding. Mr. Imin, you will assign Mr. Calroy here some math to learn every single day. Exercises or some such. Until you are satisfied."

"Sir."

"Bosun, Mr. Calroy here will report to you at the start of each day's shift with his answers to the previous day's math questions. If they are not complete or not correct, you will beat him. Once for each wrong answer. At least."

"Yes, sir. With a stick, sir?"

"A stick would be excellent. Do you have such a thing?"

"I can lay my hands on one, sir."

"Excellent. Mr. Calroy?"

"Sir?" Calroy said. He was now aware that something had gone very, very badly wrong.

"Tomorrow, the bosun will show you a stick. Assume it's a cylinder. He'll give you the length and diameter of

253

said stick and also what material it's composed of. You will calculate the mass of the stick. If you are incorrect, he will beat you. He will continue to beat you until you get the mass right."

"Sir, but what if I can't get it right?" Calroy said.

"Then, it will be a very, very unpleasant day for you. Oh, and Mr. Calroy—"

"Sir?"

"Mr. Imin received the Imperial starburst for his actions at Rigel. For using math. That normally means that every crew member, enlisted or otherwise, salutes him first, and he returns it. We don't salute each other inside the ship, normally, but I'll make an exception for you. You'll salute him every time you see him. Bosun, I think Mr. Calroy is finished with his dinner. Take him to his room."

"Sir," the boson said. He grabbed Calroy's arm and hauled him out of the chair and through the hatch.

Devin turned to the assembled officers. "Gentlemen, this dinner is not to be wasted. One of you, call the cook and have it sent here and have a plate sent to my cabin. Two plates. I need to have a short discussion with the subprefect. Carry on eating."

The officers stood as Devin and Lionel walked into the tribune's cabin. Once the door closed behind him, Devin walked over to his wine cabinet, removed a bottle, then poured two generous helpings. He handed a glass to Lionel. "The emperor."

"The emperor," Lionel agreed. He drank. "Um. The good stuff. You must be very worried."

"What in the name of the emperor's hairy testicles was that about?"

"I've been trying to tell you, but you haven't listened. When was the last time you were at court?"

"Ten years?"

"Try again. Wasn't it before you and Wendy at Rigel were—"

"We're not going to talk about Wendy. But it was before that, yes. Imperial anus, was it that long?"

"I don't think you've been at court for nearly thirty years. Not a full court, anyway."

"When father died, I was there."

"Long enough to bury him, see to your family, then back on the ship. I doubt you were on the capital a week."

"Four days. What's going on?"

"This is a message from Wendy. Showing us how bad things have gotten."

"She used her son to send us a message?"

"She and Calroy have been split since a few years after the boy was born. Almost twenty years ago. Calroy raised him at court while Wendy stayed on active service. She's like you. She barely gets back."

"They split up twenty years ago? How do you know this?"

"Well, I still keep in contact with her cousin."

"Wendy's cousin, that girl who—"

"You said we weren't going to talk about Wendy, and I think that includes her cousin." Lionel downed his glass. "Some more of this would go well."

"The Empire is going to hell, and we're out here chasing pirates."

"We're out here chasing pirates because the Empire is going to hell. Do you know, I think we're the only Imperial ship in this sector? And we might be the first one here for two years?"

"That's ridiculous."

"Check the records. Remember what those merchant Skippers said—they were arming themselves because there were no Imperial ships to suppress piracy."

"Suppressing piracy isn't our only job."

"We're not doing the other ones, either. Look at that fiasco they put Dirk in jail for."

"Disobeying Imperial directives is a hanging offense."

"What about disobeying the local duke's orders—

claiming to act in the emperor's name—when those orders have been obtained by the confederation bribing him to look the other way?"

"The duke is the emperor's regent."

"Even when the duke is a corrupt idiot who's only trying to enhance his own power, at the expense of the rest of the Empire?"

"You don't know that's the way it was?"

"There's the better part of a battalion of Imperial Marines who disagree, disagree enough to assist in breaking Dirk out of an Imperial prison."

"That was nicely done." Devin took another drink. "With that sort of loyalty, I'd like to have troops like that under my command."

"You probably already did. I checked. Some of them were on the Antares with you."

"Really?"

"Top notch troops. Loyal. Fearless. Just like Dirk."

"I'm not happy about this situation," Devin said.

"You once said he was like a son to you."

"The son I never had. That's what makes this harder."

"How are we going to catch him? He could be anywhere."

"One system at a time, Lionel. We'll check one system at a time."

CHAPTER 25

Marko watched the group of four spacers enter his bar. Well, it wasn't his bar—the corporation owned it, but he felt proprietary about it, since he spent most of his time here. A neatly dressed, gray-haired, older man looked like he had a bit of a paunch, and a dark-haired, younger man walked like a dancer. He'd be dangerous. He spotted an exotic-looking girl—who he thought was a Jovian—and a fresh-faced, young woman. The young woman was a looker. So was the Jovian, for that matter, if you liked tall, willowy, and muscular. They all entered together, and the young man scanned the room for threats. The younger girl did as well, a beat later. It was more a deliberate action with her than an instinct, like with the young man. She had to think about it. The old man looked asleep, and Marko couldn't read the Jovian.

Just a typical group of spacers crew out for some excitement. They had revolvers—which wasn't unusual—and long knives on their belt. Was that a sword?

Marko watched the waitress take drink orders and waited 'til a round of beer showed up. He strode up to their table, collected a chair en route, and sat at the head of it.

"Greetings, strangers," he said. "I am Marko of this station. I am a finder of things. Whatever you need on-station, I can locate for you. Parts. Food. Companionship. Other things. Marko knows all. Marko can find all."

"For a suitable fee, of course," Gavin said.

"Marko does not take payment from you, he simply brings you to the best merchants on the station. They reward him for his actions."

"Meaning we overpay for everything, and you split the

257

difference with them. No thanks, we'll use the directories."

"You will not find everything you need in the directories. And certainly not at the prices Marko can find for you," Marko said.

"Since what I need is food and beer, and this is a bar, I think I can find everything I need there without your help, Marko," Gavin said.

"Marko is sad at your decision but not unsurprised. Many visitors first try to make their own arrangements until they realize the value of Marko's help." Marko stood. "Farewell, strangers. I am to be found here most days, in the corner. Speak to me of anything you need, and it will be found."

"Tell me, Marko," Ana said. "Have you ever heard of something called poker?"

Marko smiled inwardly but didn't let the grin crease his face. "I have heard of this. It is some sort of game, is it not?"

"Indeed," Ana said. "Perhaps you could find somebody who knows how to play."

"I understand there is sometimes money at risk in these games," Marko said.

Ana flashed an Imperial credit tab to the table. "Sometimes, Mr. Marko."

Marko sat again. "Marko can find these people. What is your name, friend, and when would you like to meet them?"

***

Scruggs hadn't even wanted to learn poker.

"You're with me, recruit," Ana said.

"Senior Centurion? I don't know how to play poker," she said.

"Necessary skill for a soldier. You'll have to learn. No time like the present. Let's go."

Marko led, and Scruggs and Ana followed him to another bar through a gaming section. Scruggs recognized roulette wheels—she had seen them and a card game called Blackjack on the vids. They passed through the gaming area into a back room. The room had a table at the center with a green cloth on it and five chairs around it. Three were full. A woman stood behind a counter at the back. Two very large, very armed men greeted them on the way in.

"Weapons go with us," the first one said. "Pistols, knives, whatever. Buy chips at the counter there, and we take five percent of your buy for the house. Drink prices are on the wall."

"Five percent, and we have to pay for our own booze?" Ana said. He handed over his weapons, stomped over to the lady, and laid down a modest credit amount. "Robbery. And we haven't even started yet." The men at the table watched in interest as the lady deposited a pile of chips in front of him.

"Centurion," Scruggs whispered. "I don't have that much money."

"Relax, recruit," Ana said. "Half of these are for you. Just play as best you can, take advice from those men, and do what you think is right."

"I don't know how to play. I'll lose everything."

"Just do your best. Don't worry, you don't owe me anything, even if you lose all of these."

"I don't?"

"No, this is a training exercise, and I'm your training officer. I'm expected to supply equipment for you to train on, and this is for you. Use your best judgment. With one exception."

"What's that, Senior Centurion?" Scruggs asked.

"When I touch my chin like so," Ana demonstrated, "and cough, you need to bet every single chip you have on your hand. Every single chip, all at once, and say 'all in.' Understood?"

Scruggs nodded. "Chin and cough. Bet everything. All in. Understood, Senior Centurion."

He slapped her shoulder. "Let's go have some fun." They walked over to the table.

"Friend," one of the men said, "what is your name?"

"I'm Ana, and this is Scruggs."

"Friend Ana, I am Sepp, and this is Gio and Cola."

They were so alike, Scruggs almost couldn't tell them apart. "Is this your first visit to our fine station?"

"My first time here," Ana agreed. "Scruggs?"

"I've never been here," Scruggs said. "I've never even been off-planet before or in a casino."

Sepp raised his eyebrows. "Never been to a casino? But where did you learn to play poker?"

"I don't know how to play poker," Scruggs said. "I never learned. This is my first game."

"Of course it is," Sepp said. He scrutinized Scruggs. "Might I ask your age, young friend?"

"Eighteen standard. Is that a problem?" Scruggs asked.

Sepp, Gio, and Cola's eyes flicked to Scruggs, then to the pile of chips in front of her, then up to Ana.

Ana shrugged. "She wanted to learn. Everybody has a first time," he said.

All three men smiled, and Sepp waved the waitress over. "Friend Scruggs, since this is your first time in a casino and your first time playing poker, as a gesture of hospitality, I will pay for your drinks. Please order what you like."

"Oh," Scruggs said. "That's very generous, thank you." She smiled and thought carefully. "May I have some peach juice? I used to get that back home on high festivals.

The men looked nonplussed, but the waitress smiled. "One ultra-expensive, non-alcoholic drink coming up."

***

"Because they are all the same color, then I win," Scruggs said. She was seated at the poker table with Ana and "the three stooges," as she privately called them. They had played poker for several hours. She squirmed and rose from her chair. She pushed herself down—the lower station gravity had taken some getting used to.

"Not quite," Sepp said. "It's because they are all the same suit. All diamonds. Remember the four suits we showed you?"

"Right, I do," Scruggs said. "And this is called a flush, then?"

"Yes, do you remember the order of the hands we taught you?"

Scruggs did—sort of, but then messed it up when she tried to say it out loud, so she had to go back and look at the list they had given her. The table was a narrow oval. She and Ana barely fit on the same side, even though they were crammed together. Ana was to her right, then Sepp, Gio, and Cola spread out 'til Cola was just to her left.

Things were confusing, and Scruggs knew there was a great deal of money on the table. Ana had purchased her initial stake, as he called it. They had played for hours, and Scruggs had come out a winner. She wasn't sure how, but she had three times as many chips in front of her as before. Ana had slightly more, but the three men were losing badly. Scruggs had no idea why she was doing so well.

"You win again," Gio said to Scruggs. "You seem to have a knack for it." He leaned back and lit a cigarette. Scruggs stared at it.

Scruggs shrugged and raked the chips into her pile. She wasn't sure what was happening. The centurion was smiling, affable and pleasant, so she knew something was badly wrong. But he didn't seem to be in a hurry to leave, and whatever her part was in this, she wasn't going to let him down.

"I seem to be somewhat embarrassed here, Friend Ana," Cola said. His pile of chips was very low. "Friend Scruggs has the advantage of me."

"Bad luck for you, my friend," Ana said. "The cards are not running your way."

"I will replenish—if that is acceptable to you," Cola said and gestured the casino lady over. "Add more money to the table, that is."

"Of course, friend Cola," Ana said. "We must give you the opportunity to win some of your money back, shouldn't we, Scruggs?" he said.

"Yes, Ana," Scruggs said. Centurion had told her to use his first name, which she found very hard to do, but he had insisted.

"Excellent," Cola said. He flipped a credit chip in his hand. "But the hour grows late. Perhaps we could speed things up and make them more interesting. We are but a crude mining station here, and we often deal with more primitive means of payment. Are you familiar with these?" He produced a small case that fit in the palm of his hand and flicked it open. In the case were four rows of small, thin, gold coins, perhaps eighty or a hundred per row. They gleamed in the overhead light.

"I have seen those before, friend Cola." Ana reached into his coveralls and produced a case of his own before snapping it open one-handed. His was much smaller but still gleamed gold. "I have used them before, and I love to make things interesting."

A delay followed while the casino lady called for another person, who fed the coins into a machine that counted and shone a laser on them. A quick display of weight and volume, and examination of the light reflected, and everyone seemed satisfied. The chips were returned to the casino, who calculated and accepted a credit chip back, involving a fee Scruggs didn't understand.

Everyone had their drinks refreshed and settled down to play again. Ana pushed half of his gold coins in front of Scruggs. A waitress arrived with a drink and leaned down to Scruggs's ear.

"Honey, you can't possibly be as young and stupid as you look," she said.

"What do you mean?"

"You're in for a world of hurt if you keep playing."

"I trust Centurion—I mean, I trust Ana. He knows what's going on."

The waitress looked at Ana for a moment, then back at Scruggs and smiled. "Centurion, huh? That explains it. I'll stay late to see how this works for you."

Common consent appointed Scruggs as the first dealer. She hated dealing. The game was called Five-Card Stud, and she was supposed to call out the order of betting.

She dealt one card facedown and one card faceup for everybody. "Jack bets," Scruggs said. She pointed at Gio. The bets came round, and she called. She almost always called. She didn't understand the odds but dealt the next round of cards.

"Jack bets again," Scruggs said. Cola coughed, and the centurion pointed. "Sorry, pair bets," Scruggs said. Her face reddened. She always messed up when she was dealing.

The deal passed several times to her. She won more than she lost. The centurion was betting heavily and losing heavily. Several times, he coughed but didn't touch his face, so she continued. She had several more miserable rounds as a dealer, but she won more often than not.

"I think I'm out for a few rounds," Ana said. He pushed his cards back into the pile. "I've only got this left." He pointed at the six coins in front of him.

"Bad luck for you, friend. Do you wish to quit for the evening?" Cola said.

"It's almost morning, really, or almost first shift, at least. No, not at all. Friend Scruggs here is doing well. Let's let her play the three of you for a while, and I'll watch."

"Fair enough. She is the big winner here tonight," Cola said. "Let us continue."

Scruggs won the next two hands, not a big winner, then the deal passed to Sepp. He dealt them each one card down and one card up. Her hole card was a jack, but she showed an ace. She had learned enough by then to know that was a good start. The others had low-value cards showing, so they bet after her. The bet with raises came to her, but she called, as normal. She got another ace.

"Pair of aces showing for the lady," Sepp said. "Possible flush for Gio. Possible straight for Cola. Dealer shows a pair of twos. The lady bets."

Scruggs made the smallest bet possible, just one of the coins, as she always did. The others bet higher, as they always did, but more aggressively this time. She called as per usual, but it was a very large amount.

"Another ace for the lady. Three of a kind showing. Gio still shows a flush. Possible straight for Cola. Dealer gets another two, so three of a kind showing. Lady bets."

Scruggs swallowed. She peered at her hole card. It was still a jack. She looked around.

"Young friend, your bet," Sepp said.

Scruggs struggled. She looked at the others, then the centurion. "I'm not sure."

"Let me help." Gio smiled at Scruggs. "You are in the lead with three aces. I may have a flush at best—with the cards I show—even though all spades, I cannot make a straight flush. If I make a flush, I will beat Cola here." He pointed to the man next to him. "He has a possible straight showing. It cannot be a flush because of the mismatched suits. If he has a straight, and I have nothing, he beats me. If I have a flush, I beat him. It all depends on our hole cards. Of course, we could have neither. You." He paused and took a drink from the glass in front of him. "Your three of a kind will not beat either a straight or a flush. But you may have a fourth ace in the hole card there, or if not, you may still improve to a full house, three aces, and a pair. It is difficult, is it not?"

"Ana?" Scruggs said.

"He's telling the truth. It all depends on what the next cards are," Ana said. He looked at the three men. "She's my friend. If she lets me, may I look at her hole card?"

"Of course," Sepp said. "She is still learning, after all."

Ana raised his eyebrows at Scruggs. She nodded, and he leaned over and used his hand to flip up the edge of her card. It still showed a jack. He nodded once and looked at Scruggs. "It all depends on the next card. If I were you, I would call."

Scruggs nodded once and then counted coins in. "Call." She wasn't sure, but the three men opposite her seemed to relax a bit. She wasn't even aware that they were tense.

Sepp dealt the final card. For her, a jack. "No improvement for Friend Lady showing," Sepp said. "Seven of spades for Friend Gio. Still possible flush. Six of diamonds for friend Cola. Possible straight there. A five for the dealer. Dealer has three twos showing. Lady bets."

Scruggs had no idea what to do. "What's it called when you have a pair and three of a kind again?"

"That is a full house, Friend Scruggs," Sepp said. "With your aces showing, you will beat all other hands except for a straight flush and four of a kind."

"Got it." Scruggs looked around. She looked at the centurion. He coughed and touched his chin. She looked at Sepp's cards. She looked at Cola's cards. She looked at her cards.

Wait, he touched his chin. She nodded and pushed all her chips forward. "All in."

There was a gasp from behind her. Scruggs looked up. She had been so busy concentrating on the table, she hadn't noticed that all the waitresses and casino staff had gathered to watch.

Sepp, Cola, and Gio couldn't hide grins. "Are you sure, Friend Scruggs? That is a daring move."

Scruggs wanted to look at the centurion but didn't. "Nope. I'm going to win. I'm all in. All my money is there." She looked down. "Uh, what happens now?"

Sepp, Cola, and Gio smiled at each other. Sepp spoke for the group.

"Well, strictly speaking, we should count how much

you pushed in and match the bid. But we are all down a bit from you, and it is late. Perhaps if we all agree to simply push all our money in, the winner takes the entire pot?" He smiled at her. "It is a bit irregular, but in the spirit of the evening, why not?" He didn't wait for an answer but pushed all of his coins in. The other two followed suit.

The crowd stirred, but Scruggs didn't wait. "Good idea. It's late. Let's finish this." Centurion had told her to use her judgment.

Gio flipped his hole card up. It was another spade. "I have a flush, as you see. I may beat the others."

"Emperor's balls to you, Friend Gio," Cola said, good-naturedly. He flipped his card to complete his straight. "I had hoped you were not so well set. Well, my bad luck."

"Unusual to see both a straight and a flush appear in the same hand," Ana said. "But it explains all your high bets, doesn't it?"

"Indeed," Sepp smiled. "That was good luck for you, Gio, but I have done better." He flipped his hole card. It was another two. "The two is the least valued of the cards, but enough of anything makes a win. I have four of a kind. The pot is to me." The crowd whooshed as he leaned forward to grab the chips.

Ana's hand lashed out and caught Sepp's. "Friend Sepp, the lady may yet beat you." He bared his teeth at Sepp. Only a stupid person would call that toothy expression a smile.

"Of course, of course," Sepp said. He leaned back, and Ana released his hand. "Please show us your hole card, friend Scruggs."

Scruggs reached for her card.

"As you see, a jack," Sepp said, "so a full house, a powerful hand, but not enough to beat—"

Scruggs had flipped her hole card over. It was no longer a jack. It was another ace.

"Four aces," Ana said. "Scruggs wins. Collect your money, Scruggs. Into your pockets."

Scruggs gaped at him.

"Now, recruit," Ana said.

Scruggs responded to his command voice.

Ana stood. "Good game, gentlemen." He extended his hand and shook the others. They seemed dazed. "Barkeep." Ana pulled a handful of the gold coins off the table and handed them to a hovering bartender. "A round of drinks for everybody, and the rest is for you and the staff." The staff cheered.

Scruggs had used both hands to pull piles of the coins off the table and dump them in her pockets. She filled both of her coveralls' front pockets, but there was still more. She grabbed a double handful and pushed them into her leg pockets, and Ana snagged the remainder into one fist and propelled her toward the door with the other.

"That was supposed to be a jack, you Imperial turd—" Cola said from behind her.

"That's what I dealt, that's what I gave her," Sepp said.

Ana and Scruggs made it to the door. The two security men blocked it. "Might be a bit of a problem, friends," one said.

"You know exactly what happened here," Ana said.

"Some sort of cheating. You might have been dealing off the bottom of the deck," one said.

"Friend, neither of us was the dealer. That was friend Sepp."

The two men looked at each other. One pursed his lips.

"Give us our weapons, and we'll be on our way," Ana said.

The two men looked at each other, their pursed lips turning into a frown. Ana pushed Scruggs gently behind him, then laid a fistful of coins on the counter. "That's for you two. Give us our guns and knives, and we'll be on our way."

"Might not be that easy, friend," one of the guards said.

Ana stepped into a stance that Scruggs recognized from their fighting class. He looked different. Younger. More dangerous.

The two guards reacted to the stance by moving a bit farther apart. "Think you can take us both, crazy old man?"

"Not a chance," Ana said. "Not before you get reinforcements. But I can hurt both of you bad. Probably maim both of you for life before your friends get here, and my friend will be out the door and on our ship. And I haven't had a good fight in a long time. If I go down, I'm taking at least one of you with me permanently." He stared at the two steadily. "Or you can hand us our weapons, make those coins disappear, and say you never had any instructions otherwise. And besides, isn't it kind of poetic justice?"

The two men looked at each other, then grinned. One went to the coins and swept them up. The other went back behind a counter and produced their holsters, swords, and revolvers. "Ammunition is locked up in the back room. You want to wait while I call for that?"

"Nope. Free trades," Ana said. "Let's go, recruit." He grabbed Scruggs and pulled her out.

"Come back soon, friends," the other guard said.

CHAPTER 26

"Are you going to leave me in here forever, Dirk?" Dena asked. She was lounging in the cage Dirk had locked her in.

"I should," Dirk said. "We don't trust you. You should know that."

"Why? I've never hurt any of you. Helped you when I could, and I haven't caused any problems on this passage. And frankly, I'm a paying customer, so I should at least have a room to myself."

"You might jump ship on this station."

"And do what? Take up a career as a cargo loader? If I'd wanted a dead-end manual labor job with no hope for advancement, I could have found that back on Rockhaul."

"Good point," Dirk said.

"And," Dena said, sticking her chest out, "we could at least do other things together."

"I don't have time for that," Dirk said.

"You're a pilot on a ship docked at a station. You've got nothing but time. And unless you're saving yourself for someone somewhere else—which your recent activities don't really indicate—you're not getting anything here. The Jovian is half interested in the engineer, and the kid would have you in a heartbeat, but you're too priggish to take advantage of that."

"Priggish?"

"Yes. It means—"

"I know what it means. Are you talking about Scruggs? She's just a child."

"That centurion is teaching her to kill people with spare carpentry equipment, and from what I heard, she shot several of Zelta's gang with expanding lead bullets. That's hardly the action of a child."

"They're a gang now, are they?"

"A cabal then?"

"She's just a kid," Dirk said.

"Not much younger than me, really," Dena said. "And you didn't inquire too closely on my age when you showed me your cabin."

"But you were older, sophisticated. A lady, a trader."

"I was a single girl on a backwoods planet who'd never been away from home. Schoolgirl Scruggs had been to more planets than I have. And you were just a smooth-talking space pilot, spinning a line to a poor little girl."

"Didn't this poor little girl try to kill her sister and start a war?"

"Everybody needs a day job," Dena said.

Dirk's comm beeped. He flipped it up. "Yes?"

"Navy, we got problems," Ana said.

***

The bar was noisy, so Lee leaned closer to Gavin. "It's simple. The Praetorians are the emperor's or the empress's personal household unit. Guards and retainers. All Praetorians are Jovians. Not all Jovians become Praetorians, but most do. We serve the emperor, not the Empire. We support him in all things."

"Because of some war two hundred years ago?"

"Even today, there are people who think we are less than human, devils, animals who should be destroyed. The emperor protected us when the naturalist faction was hunting and killing all the genetically altereds. Emperor Arjan, Jove bless his name, enlisted us on his side. He treated us like his own family."

"But you're a medic."

"You don't have to be a soldier. There are many other jobs. Administration. Medicine. There are even veterinarians. We train in what we want as students, at the emperor's cost. We have our own lives, but if we are called to serve, then we must go. And why would we not? Without the emperor's protection, there are people who would kill my family, my parents, my nieces, and nephews. The emperor protects us, and we protect him."

"So, the emperor gets a fearless, fanatical, personally loyal corps of supporters who will do what he says with no questions."

"And in return, we get our lives."

"Sounds a bit naive to me. What about all the evil things the Empire has done? The rebellions? The massacres?"

"I know of no such," Lee said. She took another drink.

"You don't know of any? Boy, let me tell you, I—" He closed his mouth.

"You what?" Lee asked.

"Nothing. Look, doesn't hanging around with all these criminals kind of . . . taint . . . your allegiance?"

"Minor crimes do not count the same with us, as long as we protect the emperor. Only disloyalty is an issue."

Gavin pointed at her. "You don't think, say, that Dirk or Ana are disloyal?"

"Criminals now, perhaps. But Dirk was in the navy. Ana has admitted to being in a colonial army unit. Those are loyal formations. I don't have to like them, but I don't have to do anything, as long as I think they are loyal to the emperor. Scruggs is too young, and she saved my life. But I do have one concern."

"What's that?" Gavin asked.

"You." Lee pointed. "Are you a loyal servant of the Empire?"

Gavin smiled. "I'm just a small planet boy trying to make his way."

"But are you a patriot? Do you support the Empire?"

Gavin stared at her for a moment. "I am a Patriot. Yes, indeed."

"Good," she smiled at him. "Because I am beginning to like you." She began to eat the food on the tray in front of her. "This tray is not bad."

Lee continued talking as Gavin's comm beeped. He couldn't hear, so he brought it to his ear. Empty beer glasses and the remains of a meal sat in front of them.

"It's true that it's pretty much the same as ship food, but it is a change," she said, spooning white mush into her mouth.

Gavin looked back at her. "Skipper says Ana got into a fight." He kept his comm to his ear.

Lee looked at him for a moment, then scooped more mush. "This looks exactly the same as those super-potatoes." She chewed. "But tastes better somehow."

"Standby, Skipper," Lee said to his comm. He looked at Lee. "Skipper says he's in trouble, might get hurt," Gavin said.

Lee stared at him levelly. "And that is our problem now? He hates both of us. Would he help us in a fight?"

"He already has, kind of, back at Rockhaul," Gavin said. "He shot at everything."

"That's because he likes to shoot things, not because he's on our side." She examined her spoon. "You know, I don't think this is super-potatoes. I think it's that other vegetable. Cauliflower? The consistency is different."

"Lee, we should help him out. He helped rescue us from that flood. He takes his turn on the boards. He stood with us on Rockhaul and faced down those guys of Zelta's. He's crew, really."

Lee glared at him. "He still thinks I'm a freak."

"Yeah, but he doesn't say it anymore, does he? He's trying to be polite."

Lee continued glaring, then gave up. "Let's go." She left money on the table, and they stood. Gavin went back to his comm. "Leaving for the ship now, Skipper. We'll meet you there." He put the comm down. "Ana's trying to get back to the ship, has some people chasing him. Scruggs is with him."

"Scruggs? We better run, then," Lee said. She jogged

along the corridor outside the restaurant. "Why didn't you tell me that to start?"

"Wanted to see how you reacted," Gavin said. "I didn't think you'd help the old guy."

"Surprised?" Lee asked.

"Yes. Yes I am," Gavin said.

***

"Right, I'll wait for you here, Centurion," Dirk said. "I'll be at the air lock. Lee and Gavin are on the way. If everybody gets here with no problems, we'll seal up and drop. Otherwise, I'll come looking for you." He punched his comm off. "Centurion's in trouble. He and Scruggs are running from some thugs. Something to do with a poker game. He said Scruggs won a big pile of money, playing cards with some cheats."

"You believe Scruggs won a pile of money?" Dena asked. She stepped up and clawed the wire cage.

"He also says these cheats are after him with guns and crowbars, and there's going to be violence."

"You believe all of that?" Dena asked.

"Scruggs winning money? Not likely. The centurion getting into a fight? Very likely. We have to help him."

"Why?"

"What?"

"Why do we have to help him? I certainly don't owe him anything. He smacked me on the side of the head, remember?"

"Well, you were threatening. I mean, you were—"

"I was standing next to him, unarmed, telling him I'd get his girlfriend back, and he decided to knock me out."

"He's pretty protective of Scruggs. She's more like his daughter, really. Or granddaughter, if I read the ages right."

"Whatever. And he's polite to you, but there's something odd there. He doesn't really think you're in charge. More like he figures as long as he agrees with you, he'll do what you suggested, but as soon as he disagrees, he'll put you out an air lock or shoot you in the head."

"It's not like that," Dirk said.

"It's exactly like that. Why are you helping him?"

"Well, I . . ." Why was he helping him?

"So, no good reason, then."

Dirk didn't say anything but went over to the locker on the wall, keyed in his code, and selected a revolver.

"Why not just leave him here to his problems? He'd do the same to you, just leave you alone."

Dirk selected frangible bullets and loaded them. A brawl in the corridors was one thing. Payments for damages and injuries would clear that. Shooting a hole in a station would lead to a death bounty and very few questions as to who from his crew deserved it.

"Crew," Dirk said. "He's crew. I help my crew. Not leaving any behind."

"That washed-up old man is crew?" Dena asked. "Really?"

"Yes he is," Dirk said. He checked the loads in his revolver and spun it once. "I help my crew. And I certainly don't run and leave them when they're in a fight. Not this time."

"What does 'not this time' mean?"

Dirk selected a holster belt from the locker.

Dena shook her head. "Have it your way. Want help?"

"Help?" Dirk said.

"Yes, help. I can shoot, probably better than you, given where I grew up, and you already know I don't lose my mind during a fight."

Dirk pulled his holster belt on. "That's actually a good idea," he said. He nodded at Dena. "That is a very good idea."

Dena curtsied. "Then let me out of here."

"You'll need a weapon," Dirk said.

"I've got something in my bag. Get this door open, and I'll show you."

Dirk fumbled with the code on the door. It didn't work the first time. He tried again with no luck.

"Um . . ."

"You don't remember the code?" Dena said.

"No, normally, it's Scruggs . . ."

"Who lets me out—I know. And you've already tried it twice, so you don't want to try a third time because you'll lock it for ten minutes or something?"

"Fifteen minutes," Dirk said in a low voice.

Dena blew out a blegh, then slid her fingers through the mesh above and below the lock. By carefully positioning her fingers, she was able to reach each of the code buttons. She typed a five-key pattern in, and the door clicked open.

"Oh," Dirk said. "You know the code."

"Since the first day I was here," Dena said, stepping out. "And I didn't use it. Now do you trust me?"

"A bit more," Dirk said.

"Enough to let me get something out of my bag?" she said.

"Yes."

"Enough for me to come with you?"

"Yes."

"Good," Dena said. She walked past Dirk and rooted through the bag they had confiscated from her. "I knew that knowing that code would help."

"Oh, it's not that. Or not just that," Dirk said. "With all this fighting after this, no chance of you running off on this station. They'll shoot you. You'll have to stay with us."

***

Ana slapped his comm onto his belt. He and Scruggs were running down a corridor, trying to find the stairs to the rim. "Should have paid for the wireless comm options," he said. "Turn left here, I think." He and Scruggs turned and jogged. Scruggs was making a hard go of it. They ran down a corridor, turned again, and met a blank wall. He cursed, pulled out his comm, and played with the mapping software again.

"Centurion, I need a break," Scruggs said, breathing hard. "These are pretty heavy."

"Too much of a wimp, recruit? Can't carry a little weight."

"My pockets are ripping, I think."

"Should take better care of your clothes, then, recruit— if as little as . . . Emperor's anus." Ana calculated in his head. "Can't carry maybe sixty kilos of metal in your pockets. And a metal sword, ammunition, and everything else. Sorry, recruit, that was my mistake. Let's reposition that load."

He took double handfuls of coins from her, piled them into rows, and set them into his own pockets. They loaded up their belts, empty holster, leg and thigh pockets, and anywhere else they could jam them. Ana took each revolver out of its holster and spun the cylinder. Scruggs did the same.

"I didn't realize gold is so heavy," Scruggs said.

"Yes, if you have to steal things, don't bother stealing silver. Gold or platinum at the minimum. Diamonds if you can."

"I've never seen a diamond," Scruggs said.

"A girl who's never seen a diamond?" Ana said. "Didn't your mother or your sister have one?"

Scruggs looked at him, then back down the corridor. "I think if we go spinward rather than anti-spin, we'll find the stairs, Centurion."

Ana nodded. "Sorry. Not my business. Understood, recruit."

***

Dirk removed his revolver from his holster as he and Dena ran toward the banging at the air lock. He looked at what she had in her hand. "A piece of wood? A funny-shaped, small piece of wood with a string on it. You're going to hit them with that? They won't feel a thing."

"It's not just a piece of wood, and I don't hit them with it. I have these." She showed him a handful of rocks.

"Oh boy, you're going to throw rocks at them?"

The banging continued.

"Come on, we need to let the centurion in."

"Are you sure it's him?"

"No, and before you ask, that camera doesn't work. Gavin got some as spares, but he hasn't put them in."

"Right, you swing the lock open, and I'll take a shot at them," Dena said.

"With your rocks? No. You swing the lock open," Dirk spun the cylinder on his revolver. "I'll take care of them. If it's not the centurion, I'm going to go hard. Get on top of them right away. Locking levers there, pull it, then spin the wheel."

Dena didn't argue anymore. She pulled the lever, put her hands on the wheel, then looked at Dirk.

"Go," he said.

She spun the wheel and pulled the air lock in. Dirk stepped around the door, brandishing the handgun. A large, uniformed man with a long object in his hand faced him. Dirk pointed the revolver at him. "Drop it! Drop it! Down, down on your knees!"

The uniformed man registered surprise, then fear, as the revolver inched closer to his face. He dropped the box on the floor, and it split open. The smell of alcohol filled the air lock. He dropped to his knees. "Don't shoot, don't shoot." Another man in coveralls hovered behind him.

Dirk pointed his revolver at the second man. "Hands on your head, both of you. Now, now, now." Dirk waved the revolver like a lunatic. The big, burly men dropped to their knees and put their hands on their head.

"What are you? Station security? Imperial police? Who sent you? Why are you here? What do you want?"

The man in front worked his mouth for a moment, but no sound came out. "Well? What do you want?" Dirk yelled.

"Table," the second man said.

"What?" Dirk said.

The first man looked up at him, hands still on his head. "Table and chairs. We're from Chen's Supply Emporium. You're supposed to have a table and chairs, friend. For us."

Dirk looked at the two men. Their coveralls said Chen's on their breasts. They didn't have any weapons.

"We're supposed to give you that ship stuff." The first man gestured over his shoulder with his chin. Dirk looked out the air lock toward boxes of shipping equipment stacked on a pallet.

"We trade 'em for a wooden table and four chairs," he said.

Dirk looked at the two in silence, then pocketed his revolver.

Dena slid around from behind Dirk and sniffed the air. "What's that smell?"

The man looked down at the pool of alcohol and glass on the air lock floor. "Expensive whiskey, friend, a gift from the boss."

***

Gavin and Lee stopped at the bottom of the stairs and collected themselves. "Docking ring," Lee said. "Spin or anti?"

Gavin looked at the numbers painted on the far wall. "Spin. Two berths. Walk briskly but don't run. Don't want to attract notice if nobody wants us."

"Got it." Lee said. She turned and moved down the hall. Gavin reached down and unsnapped his holster. "We see these guys, we shoot first. You going to have a problem with that?"

"Yes," Lee said.

Gavin stopped. "Yes?"

"I can only shoot in self-defense," she said.

"You pushed a shotgun in the skipper's face an hour after you met him, and you swung a sword back at Rockhaul."

"That was different. I was being attacked already. They must act first. I can only respond."

"Lee," Gavin said, "if they act first, we'll be dead. You'll be dead. I'll be dead."

"Nevertheless, that is what Paterfather Zeus and my honor requires."

"Coming through!" A voice yelled from in front of them. They flattened their back against the wall as two big men sprinted by, pushing a wheeled cart with a table and two chairs on it.

"Those men were barefoot," Lee said.

"That's odd. Where would they lose their shoes? But not our problem. Lee, you have to fire first."

"No."

Gavin shook his head. "Centurion was right about Jovians," he said softly.

Lee glared at him. "If you don't like Jovians, I was fine before I met you, and I'll be fine after you leave. Especially if that is sooner than later." She stopped, put her hands on her hips, and glared at him.

"Lee, we don't have time for this now," Gavin said.

"When will we have time for it?

"Scruggs needs us," Gavin said.

Lee's face went slack. "Of course. We will help her. This can wait. Let's go. We have to beat them to the ship."

They cleared the arc of the corridor, and their berth came into view.

"Looks like we're a bit late already," Gavin said. Four men in greasy coveralls had arrived at the loading dock in front of the ship.

* * *

"Well, those guys aren't here to pick up furniture," Dirk said. The air lock was open—both doors—and he and Dena were standing in it. Four men had just rounded the corner and had stopped to confer. Two carried boarding shotguns. Dirk had his revolver in his hand. Dena had her hands by her sides, gripping the odd piece of wood. "Are you going to throw more of your rocks at them?"

Dena hissed at him. One of the men turned and marched over to the air lock. "Ahoy, the ship," he said, holding his shotgun loosely, pointing it at the deck.

"Sorry, not taking passengers today," Dirk said. "Ship's closed to outsiders."

"Wasn't going to be asking, friend," the man said. "Names Mathin. I'm looking for an older man and a young girl. Name of Ana and Scruggs. Want to talk to them."

"Never heard of them," Dirk said.

"Funny, station ops shows them as crew members of your ship."

"Must be an error, Mr. Mathin. We don't have anybody by that name," Dirk said.

"And you would be?" Mathin said.

"You can call me Pilot."

"Well, no problems, then, friend Pilot," Mathin said. "We'll just wait here a spell, see if anybody like them comes by."

"You try to get on my ship. I'm authorized to shoot you."

"Authorized, allowed, and encouraged, friend," Mathin said. "Can't be havin' people breaking station rules about boarding ships uninvited. Station staff would shoot me themselves for breaking the rules regarding ship security. Of course," Mathin smiled, "cargo bays are public places. My friends and I will just stay here, see who comes by."

"You might be waiting a while then, friend Mathin," Dirk said. "Big station, plenty of places for people to go instead of here."

"Plenty of places we have friends waiting, not just here," Mathin said. "Everybody has to be somewhere.

We're here. Our friends are everywhere else."

***

Scruggs watched as the centurion lowered himself to his knees and pushed a rod with a mirror on the end around the corner. "Remember, recruit, only fight on your terms. Determine the enemy's strength first. I see, two— no, there's three there now, talking to each other. One has a slung shotgun. The other two have shock sticks. No cover in the corridor." Ana slid back and leaned against the wall, breathing hard. "They'll see us coming. Get on the comm, ask the captain to set up a diversion, then we'll rush 'em. Should be able to get you at least onto the ship. I'll take two, you take one. If the captain gives us even a little support, we can do it." He slid backward and took a deep breath.

"Understood, Centurion," Scruggs said, leaning against the wall, panting. Gold was heavy. She pulled out her comm. "Calling the captain now."

"Wait, wait. Something's going on. They're pulling out weapons. Now they're facing down the corridor, away from us." He pulled the mirror rod back and stuck it in a pocket. Scruggs had to help pull him to his feet. His face was red, he was sweating, and the wheezing had gotten worse. "Next time, we steal diamonds. Let's go." He lumbered around the corner and began to run.

***

Lee and Gavin marched down the corridor toward their air lock. Three men in greasy brown coveralls had been waiting. Two had shock sticks, and one had a boarding shotgun. All three turned to watch them approach. The two with shock sticks stepped forward and blocked the hall, sticks swinging in front of them.

"Mathin, strangers," the shotgun man called down to the cargo bay.

"Is it them, friend Beevan?" a voice asked.

"Two. A man and a woman. One's Jovian."

"Jovian?" Mathin said. "Not them then." CRACK. CLATTER. "The emperor's holy testicles—that hurt."

The shotgun man called Beevan turned and brought his gun around to point at the docking bay. Something snapped through the air and hit his shoulder. He yelled and fell backward, dropping the shotgun. A boom of a weapon from the cargo bay followed, accompanied by another yell.

One of the stun stick men surged toward Gavin. The other turned around and spied Ana and Scruggs lumbering toward them from the other corridor. "They come," he yelled.

Gavin jumped forward at the man facing him. The shock stick swung by him. He grabbed the proffered arm and banged it against the wall once, twice, and the man dropped the stick.

Gavin yelled in triumph and then screamed. The second shock stick man had reversed, turned, and stepped behind his compatriot. He slammed his stick into Gavin's back. Gavin howled as the current pulsed through him, then dropped to the floor. He couldn't move his body as he lay there and stared down the corridor's floor. Grunts and thwacks came from Lee's direction behind him, but he couldn't see what was going on.

The first man he had disarmed shook himself and scuttled back to retrieve his dropped weapon.

"Hey, you!" Ana was running down the hall. He seemed to be stumbling as he ran. His sweating face was red. He launched himself forward into a tackle. The first man held his stick up, the stick sizzling as it fired, but the two of them collided in front of him. The current jolted them, and they went still.

Gavin raised his gaze to Beevan, who rolled over, scrambling for his shotgun. Trying to bring it up one-handed proved difficult. Another thwack and a ping bounced off Beevan's shoulder. He yelled and dropped the shotgun again. Scruggs came by and kicked his legs from under him, and he dropped and lay still.

A second later, the stick hissed before a body slumped onto Gavin.

A row of bodies in the corridor lay still in front of him, shock man one, Ana, and a groaning Beevan. Then Lee's face dipped into his vision. "Are you okay?"

***

"Get them on the ship now," Dena said. "Drag 'em. They're still knocked out. Dirk, help the kid." She stepped past Lee and grabbed Gavin's coveralls. "Grab his collar and pull, like this." Lee and Dena pulled Gavin by main force around the corner to the cargo bay. Gavin twitched. "What happened to him?" she asked.

"Just shocked—get him over the coaming here. Lift on three. One, two, lift." Lee and Dena pulled Gavin up and over the hatch's edge and into the air lock.

Scruggs and Dirk were dragging Ana around the corner.

"He weighs a ton," Dirk said. "Are you okay, Scruggs?"

"Just tired. He's got an extra twenty or so kilos on his belt."

"Just dump his belt, then," Dena said from the air lock. "What's in it, anyways?"

"Twenty kilos of gold," Scruggs said.

"Make sure his belt gets on the ship, I meant to say," Dena said, running over to help them pull him on board.

"Lee, get set up to drop," Dirk said.

"Right away, Pilot," Lee said. She scrambled up to the bridge.

"What happened to him?" Scruggs pointed to Mathin, who was slumped against the wall. "Is he dead?"

"Broken arm, sprained ankle, and a big bump on the head. Get their shotguns. We can use those," Dena said.

"And those ship parts. Scruggs, help me toss them on

board." Dirk and Scruggs ran to the pallet and threw boxes into the air lock. Dena went for the shotguns.

"You shot them?" Scruggs said to Dirk.

"She shot them." Dirk pointed at Dena. "With that wooden shot thing."

"Slingshot," Dena said. "Threw rocks at them, right, Dirk?" She bent over and scooped up the boarding shotgun before tossing it in the air lock.

"Threw rocks at them," Dirk agreed.

Gavin stopped twitching and moaned.

Ana burped and whispered. "Scruggs?"

"Here, Centurion," she said, running over to him. "You're on the ship. We're dropping now."

"Belt?" he said, scrabbling at his waist.

"Inside, Centurion, you were too heavy to move with it."

"Pills," he said.

"What pills, Centurion?"

"Left outer pocket. Yellow pills. Put one in my mouth," Ana said. Scruggs scrabbled into his pocket and pulled out an unlabeled container. She took out a pill and fed it to the centurion. He lay back, sweating, his breath whooshing.

Gavin sat up. "That hurts, hurts a lot. What's that smell?"

"Move over," Dena said, shoving him to the side. The air lock was filling fast with boxes, belts, and shocked crew. "Nothing but the finest station whiskey that Dirk smashed here in the air lock," Dena said, tossing more boxes into the lock.

"Why'd he do that? What's that in aid of?"

"That's a good question," Dena said. She turned to Scruggs. "What's all this in aid of, kid?"

Scruggs plunged a hand into her pocket and pulled out a fistful of gold coins and rained them down onto the deck.

"Gold," she said.

Imperial Deserter

CHAPTER 27

THWACK. The metal nut slammed into the target on the wall, leaving a dent before it fell. It was high and right of the bullseye but right next to a half dozen similar dents.

"Excellent grouping, Ms. Sexy Pants," Ana said. He was at the lounge table, piling gold coins. "Great control. You're not adjusting for the ship's accel, but that's not surprising, given how little time you've spent in space."

"I just need more practice for that," Dena said.

"Why bother? It's not much of a weapon. Not against prepared troops."

"Knocked down those shotgun men."

"Unprepared troops."

"Ever been hit by a fast-moving rock?"

"I've been hit by fast-moving bullets," Ana said. "Good combat armor stops them dead, and it will do the same for your little rocks, Ms. Sexy Pants."

"Keep calling me Ms. Sexy Pants, and I'll try my shots at your head," Dena said.

"You're welcome to try," Ana said. "I'm game. But if you shoot at me, I'm going to shoot back. Things might not turn out the way you expect." Ana stopped counting for a moment to take a drink of basic. "But I'm afraid Navy here has some strange rules about us shooting or stabbing each other. I'd say that would extend to this—what do you call it again?"

"Slingshot," Dena said. She turned to Dirk. The crew had returned to the lounge after the hurried drop from Reik. "Can I break the old man's fool head?" she asked Dirk.

Dirk sighed. "No, you can't kill him. Or hurt him. And you have to be respectful in address. No old man. Call him

Centurion. He can call you . . . friend Dena."

"You've got to be kidding," she said.

"Nope," Gavin said. "We all agreed. Well, really, the skipper agreed, but we all said we'd follow his lead. Politeness is the order of the day. Why, I call him Senior Centurion, and he calls me Engineer."

"That's true, friend Dena, I do," Ana said.

"But why friend?" Scruggs asked.

"Why not? Everyone on the station used it," Ana said. "If she has a different title she wants, I'm happy to use it." Ana turned to Dena. "What did they call you on Rockhaul?"

"'Annoying little sister,' 'stupid girl,' 'impoverished,' 'poor,' and variations of the word loser. You know what?" Dena looked around. "I guess I'm friend Dena from now on. For all of you."

"Welcome aboard, friend Dena," Gavin said. "Welcome to the crew." He extended his hand and shook hers, as did everybody else—even Scruggs, although begrudgingly.

"So, she's part of the crew now?" Dirk asked. "Don't I get a say in this?"

"As much as any of us do," Gavin said. "And she saved us with that slangshirt thing. So, as far as I'm concerned, she's in this with us."

"What is the 'this' that we're all in together? Aren't you all just regular free traders?" Dena asked.

Nobody would meet her eyes.

"I thought so," Dena said. "I knew something wasn't right." She shrugged. "But too late to be picky for me, though, isn't it?"

"Way too late." Ana said. "But to more important matters." He gestured to the coins in front of him. "One thousand six hundred forty-four gold coins. I get my stake back. That was two hundred. You'll have to trust me on that. That leaves one thousand four hundred forty-four. Captain, that's you, Navy, gets three shares. Engineer and navigator are officers, so they get two shares. That's you two." He pointed at Lee and Gavin.

"I'm not the navigator," Lee said.

"Yet, you seem to do all the navigating, but it doesn't matter because you're definitely the medic. That counts for two, so two it is. I've decided I'm the master-at-arms. That's two shares. Crew normally gets one each, but the recruit here did such an outstanding job during that poker game, I think she should get an extra share. Agreed?"

Everybody looked puzzled, except Gavin, who flashed a big smile. "I agree. All in favor?" He and the centurion raised their hand. "All opposed?" Nobody raised their hand.

"What are we talking about?" Dena asked.

"Yes, what's going on?" Lee asked.

"No opposition, motion carried and noted, Centurion," Gavin said, still grinning.

"So, two shares for Scruggs. I just heard Dena called into the crew, so that's a share for her. Total twelve shares. That's—let's see, if one hundred each, one forty-four left—one hundred twelve per share." Ana counted out a pile of coins. "In reverse order of rank, then. Friend Dena, one hundred twelve for you." He pushed a pile of gold coins toward her.

"You're giving these to me? Why?" Dena asked.

"He's not giving them to you. That's your share," Gavin said. "Crew is entitled to their share. We split all the money. Wait, what about ship costs?"

"Weren't any on this run," Ana said. "It was a private venture of sorts. But we'll calculate it in next time. Recruit, here's your two shares." He pushed two large piles and one small pile toward her. "Two hundred twenty-four."

"Centurion?" Scruggs asked.

"That's how it's done in mercenary companies," Gavin said. "Shares for all. The centurion has decided that we should share, like in a mercenary company."

"And you agree with him?" Lee asked Gavin.

"Oh, I knew he would agree with me, Medic," Ana said.

"How did you know that?" Lee asked.

"Because that's what he's used to. It's done the same way where he used to work."

"Where did he used to work?" Lee asked.

"In a pirate ship, of course," Ana said.

***

The argument dragged on, so Gavin went down to the stores to break out some booze. He took Dena with him, and she showed him how to match the wine to the provisions.

"We are not pirates," Lee declared.

"That's true," Ana agreed. "To be pirates, we'd have to attack national ships, like system Militia ships or Imperial ships. We're more like armed scavengers." He took a sip from the glass in front of him. "This wine is outstanding with this cheese. What is it?"

"You take last year's cheap, sweet wine," Dena said, "and distill it to make it stronger, then mix in some of this year's wine to give it flavor."

"It's excellent . . . but there is no way I'm trading shots with an Imperial ship, not even a destroyer or a corvette. They'll blast us out of space and not even have to slow down for it."

"You seem to know a lot about fighting Imperial warships, Centurion," Gavin said. He chewed the last of a cracker. "Can I have more of that cheese?"

"Maybe Navy here told me," Ana said. "He's always a font of knowledge about things Imperial. Should we fight Imperial warships, Navy?"

Dirk pushed his glass out in front of Dena, who refilled it again. "What's the wine called?" Dirk asked.

"On old earth, it would have been called Port," Dena said. "We found a recipe for it and adapted it. The cold weather kept killing our grapes, so we modified things a bit. We couldn't do the delicate tasting wines, but now this is a specialty. I wanted to brand it as 'Colonial Port' and sell it for ten times the price, but the olds called me down on it, said it was just another wine. Idiots."

"That's a great idea. Colonial Port it is. I think we can get ten times as much for it," Gavin said. "It's all about the presentation. We should set a standard price list for these wines. A very high, standard price."

"But what's this blue stuff in the cheese?" Scruggs said.

"You sure you want to know?" Dena asked.

"Of course," Scruggs said.

"It's mold," Dena said. "Greasy cheese mold. We stored the cheese up in caves in the mountains. The mold spores drop on it and start to spread in the cheese. When It's good and moldy, we take it down and box it and sell it."

Scruggs looked appalled. Dena smiled at her. "You're eating rotten cheese."

Scruggs spat out the cheese and stared at it. She looked around the table. "We're all eating rotten food?"

"You are," Dena said.

Scruggs glared at her. "You're giving us rotten food." She looked at everyone else. "But you're all eating it as well. I don't think you should be eating rotten food. Are you all making fun of me?"

"We're not making fun of you, Scruggs," Gavin said.

"I may not understand what's going on all the time," Scruggs said, "but I do my part. If you ask me to do something, I do it, even if I don't understand it. And you all take advantage of me. I don't know what happened with that poker game. I'd never played poker before. I can tell it wasn't my skill that won that money. I'm still not sure what happened. But Centurion said play poker, so I played." Scruggs stood. "He said bet, and I bet." She wiped her mouth and put down the napkin. "Then we ran away after I was willing to fight those men. I stabbed somebody back at Rockhaul. And when Centurion tells me to fight somebody, I fight. Just because I don't understand some stupid game is no reason to make fun of me or to give me rotten food." She turned around and stomped toward her quarters.

"Scruggs, wait." Dirk said.

"I don't want to eat with you."

"Recruit Scruggs," Ana said. "This is not Dirk asking. This is the captain ordering. Return to your seat."

Scruggs glared at everyone but stomped back to her seat and sat quietly. Everyone was silent for a moment. Then Lee spoke up. "Sister Scruggs, you know I hold you in high esteem, and I hold myself in your debt."

"Well, yes," Scruggs said.

"First, I am eating this, and I am enjoying it. The mold gives it flavor."

"I thought mold was bad? That it meant rotten food?" Scruggs asked.

"Some mold tastes bad. Some has no taste but will kill you. Humans and Jovians have been eating this mold in cheese since old earth. It adds to the taste and is quite harmless."

Scruggs looked down at her cheese. "It did taste good 'til I knew what it was."

Lee nodded. "It still tastes good to me, and I knew what it was. If you don't want your share, I will take it. I enjoy the taste. But to your second point."

"I think you are making fun of me."

"I ask this. Do you truly, truly not know how you won that poker game?"

"No, I don't understand what happened. I know it was very strange that I kept winning. I didn't know what I was doing."

"Those men were cheating you," Lee said. "Centurion told us about it."

"Cheating?"

"Yes, they kept dealing you winning hands, over and over again, so you would keep betting. Did you notice you kept winning, and they kept losing?"

"Yes."

"Does that seem normal?"

"Not now, no. At the time, it was kind of exciting."

"Once you were overconfident, they dealt you a last hand that looked very possible of winning all. Remember the last set of cards?"

"Yes, it was confusing. There seemed to be no way the others could win against me, but they kept betting."

"Except for someone in the corner, who had something nondescript but turned out to have a winning hand."

Scruggs remembered the four twos that Sepp had. "Yes, they showed me the other hands, and they gave me a high-value hand I'd never had before. I thought I would beat everybody."

"They were taking advantage of you because you were a new player and did not understand how rare such an event was. The chances of your full house being in the same hand as a four of a kind is very, very low."

Scruggs thought about this. "They were cheating by giving me better cards?"

"Yes. They controlled the deals that were sent to you, so you would always win. They dealt falsely."

"But how did I win?"

"The centurion," Gavin said.

"What did the centurion do?" Scruggs asked.

"He cheated the cheaters," Gavin said. "He figured out that they would cheat you, so he made sure they thought they had you, and at the last minute, he swapped cards."

Scruggs looked at a smiling Ana. "Do you remember when I checked your hole card, that last hand?" Ana asked.

"Yes, sir."

"I swapped your jack for an ace I had palmed. I was watching them. They liked to give you aces to make you feel important. So, when I got one in the deal, I just kept it and waited to see if they would set you up. When they did,

I just made sure you got the last ace you needed."

"You cheated!" Scruggs said.

"I cheated the cheaters, yes," Ana said. "But what do we care? They were trying to steal your money, and I stopped them."

"But, how did you know I would do what you needed?"

"You're very reliable, recruit. You always do as you are told. I knew I could count on you."

Dirk stirred. "Do you understand, Scruggs? We knew you were naive, and we used that to help all of us, including you. They would never have tried something on the centurion, but you were believable. We all got some of that money you won. You did, too."

Scruggs looked down at the pile of coins in front of her. "I got this for being stupid?"

"You got that for doing your job, your job on the ship," Dirk said. "In fact, speaking of jobs, there is something else to take care of. Centurion?"

"What do you want, Navy?" Ana asked.

Dirk frowned. "You said you are the master-at-arms, correct? Is that how the master-at-arms talks to the captain?"

Ana straightened and threw him an innocent salute. "Yes, sir, I am. My pardon for the form of address, sir. What can I do for you, Captain?"

"Scruggs has been reporting to you for how long now?"

"Nearly six weeks, Captain."

"Please summarize her training."

Ana narrowed his eyes. "Sir. As much as possible, she has received basic level-one ship Marine training, excluding combat armor, energy weapons, and drop-ship experience, but including shipboard combat, hand-to-hand, basic rifleman, basic handgun, and basic edged weapon experience."

"Edged weapon?"

"Knife and sword. She could handle a cutlass."

"Firearms?"

"Shotgun, revolver, and such rifle and submachine gun training as I could provide."

"Does she have a ship side specialty?" Dirk asked.

"Sir," Ana said, "training facilities are limited, but I think with more exposure, she would make a decent backup sensor technician."

"I see. And has her efforts been satisfactory?"

"Very much so, sir. Training should never stop, of course, but I have no complaints."

"So, would you say that her basic training is done?"

"Yes."

"So, she should graduate, then?"

Ana looked at Dirk and smiled. It was such a big smile, so unexpected, that everybody recoiled. "Wait here," Ana said. He got up, scooted around the table, then walked back to his room.

"What's going on?" Dena asked.

"Shush," Gavin said. But he was smiling, too.

Ana returned and stood next to the table. "Come over here, recruit," he said.

Scruggs looked at Dirk, who nodded. She went to stand in front of Ana.

"We don't wear uniforms on this ship," Ana said. "But uniforms do not the soldier make." He leaned down and pinned two sets of bars on her ship suit. "Congratulations on your promotion, Private Scruggs," he said. He stepped back and saluted his fist to his heart.

Everybody clapped, except Dena, who looked nonplussed. Then Gavin elbowed her and she clapped.

Scruggs blinked for a moment. "I'm a private."

"A soldier," Ana said.

Scruggs thought for a moment. "A soldier," she said, smiling.

"In a pirate army," Lee said.

CHAPTER 28

"I don't want to be a pirate," Lee said as they sat around the lounge, waiting for the jump to start.

"Should have thought of that before you joined the criminal fraternity by stealing those med supplies," Ana said.

"Again, that's fraud," Gavin said. "Not theft."

"Much difference in the penalties, then, Engineer?" Ana asked.

"If you stole this ship, then doesn't that make you pirates?" Dena asked.

"We did not steal the ship," Dirk said. "It will just not be where the owners want it to be in . . . about a month. It will be somewhere else."

"The captain is correct," Scruggs said. "We are not guilty of piracy. We're guilty of a conspiracy to commit piracy. It's different."

"Do they hang pirate conspirators the same as pirates?" Dena asked.

"Conspirators get a slightly better view as they are hung," Gavin said. "Hang 'em from higher up, they can see more."

"That's a horrible thought," Lee said.

"But why are you all here, then?" Dena said. "I mean, how did you get together before you all came to Rockhaul?"

Everyone became silent and looked at each other for a moment. Dena turned to Dirk. "They said you were in the navy. You never said no, but you never said yes. What's the truth? Were you in the navy? What did you do?"

Dirk shifted. "I'll tell you when the time is right."

"I've got a feeling," Dena said, "that whatever you're

hiding, the time isn't really ever going to be absolutely right, so why not now?"

Dirk took another drink. "Don't want to talk about it."

Dena rounded on the others. "Was he really in the navy?"

"Yes, he was," Ana said. "He's so Navy, he probably has a picture of the emperor on his socks. He doesn't give any real details about it, but he was a mid-level officer—shuttle pilot for sure. And I was in the army—an army—I can't hide that from anybody. Which army doesn't matter, but you can tell I was in charge of recruits for a while, and I've been in a few fights. The engineer here," Ana pointed at Gavin, "was an engineer on a trading ship of some sort. But a bit more than an engineer. He's not as good with the drives as some I've seen, but he knows a lot about general systems. He's pretty handy with hand weapons and knows his way around a brawl."

Ana took a drink from his glass. "The medic is definitely a medic—a very good one, from what I've seen. Of course, she's Jovian, so what's she doing out on her own? Nobody ever asked that question."

Lee suddenly looked worried. Gavin and Dirk looked at each other. "What do you mean, Centurion?" Dirk asked.

"You two didn't catch it because you've been in big organizations, navies and such, and seeing a single Jovian there isn't unusual. But other than that, they always move in family groups. A family running a ship, three couples with their kids, owning a bar on a station. Four brothers as prospectors. Always some sort of family group. But she's on her own. Why is that?"

All eyes turned to Lee. She looked even guiltier than before.

"And," Ana said, "why was she stuck on that ship by herself? She should have just hopped to the next Jovian-crewed ship that came by."

"Maybe there weren't any Jovian ships on-station?" Lee

said.

"For six months?" Gavin said. "That doesn't seem reasonable."

"And who were you running from?" Lee said. "You—and the captain and the centurion, for that matter—don't want to be anywhere near Imperial ships."

"True," Gavin said. "You weren't too fond of running into Imperials, either. So, you see, friend Dena, of all of us so far, we only agree that we want to avoid Imperial notice. Or any official notice, really. And we've agreed to work together 'til we get to a big port where we can sell what we have and move along."

"What do you mean?"

"Our not-navigator over there," Gavin said, pointing to Lee, "has done a bang-up job. We can jump a bit farther than other ships—at least, when everything is working correctly. So, she's plotted a course that takes us away from regular trade routes. We've avoided all Imperial notice, excepting that courier, which wasn't for us anyways. We're only two jumps from Papillon, which is our destination.

"What's at Papillon?" Dena asked.

"From your point of view," Gavin said, "a bank where you can pay us what you owe us. Ana's leaving us. He's trying to find a port with regular passenger connections, so he can go somewhere. Somewhere not us."

"And also," Ana said, "Gavin and I have a discussion to finish, don't we Engineer?"

"That we do, Centurion," Gavin said. "That we do. Seems like Papillon will be the first place we can finish it."

Dena looked back and forth between them. "What type of discussion?"

"One that might leave only one of them alive," Dirk said. "And I promised to arrange it."

"You should come and watch. It will be entertaining," Gavin said.

Dena shook her head. "And the rest of you?"

"I'm going with the centurion, if he'll have me," Scruggs said.

That surprised everyone.

"Recruit, that would not be wise," Ana said. "I'm not going anywhere you need to be."

Scruggs looked at Ana. "Isn't it supposed to be private now, not recruit?"

Ana blinked. "Yes, sorry private."

Scruggs watched him for a moment. "I dragged you back on board, you know. The others helped, but if it had been up to them, you might still be there."

"There was the gold," Dirk said. "That helped."

"Could have just pulled his belt back on," Gavin said. "That would have worked. I voted for that."

Scruggs continued. "Centurion, you're training me and paying me like I'm a mercenary in your mercenary company. The way I understand it, that means you're responsible for me. And you can't just dump me at the first port we arrive at."

"It's hardly the first port," Ana said.

"Sounds dishonorable to me. Kind of unethical, don't you think, Medic?" Dirk asked.

"Indeed. Very dishonorable," Lee said.

"And if a Jovian think's you're being dishonorable, well, that really takes the cake, doesn't it, Centurion?"

Ana glared at everyone. "I don't care what a freak thinks," he said.

"Freak?" Gavin said. "I thought we had rules about that."

"We do," Dirk said. "Centurion?"

"Sorry, my apologies. I don't care what you think of me, Medic. And as for you here, Engineer, your time will come, at least if Navy here keeps his promises."

"I keep my promises," Dirk said. His voice was mild, but his glare hardened.

"What do you want, Private?" Ana asked.

"I need more experience, Centurion," Scruggs said.

"After Papillon, I need to travel for another few months, away from Bishop's world. That means, I'll have been . . . away . . . for a long time. That's far enough. I can go on my own then. Besides, I might have not been much use before, but I seem to be helping out now. Maybe you can find another poker game," Scruggs said.

"Maybe I can," Ana nodded. "That's fair. Private, you're welcome to come with me for the next ninety days, my choice of destinations, and I'll even pay your way."

"Pay her way? You going to take luxury cruises?" Dena asked.

"I'm a useful fellow to have around in a fight," Ana said. "Haven't been able to show it here, but I'm not bad with some ship weapons. Lots of big freighters will take on a gunner who also acts as a guard if they're heading out to backwater planets on the verge. As long as I'm not too picky on wages, they'll take an apprentice as well."

"Two of the crew leaving at Papillon then," Dena said. "What about the rest of you?"

"I think the medic and I might move on as well," Gavin said. "We've discussed maybe finding a berth together."

"Somewhere that gets along better with freaks," Lee said.

"A Jovian ship?" Dena asked.

"Lots of ships will take an engineer and navigator combination," Gavin said.

"Especially since you have IDs, now that say you're an engineer and navigator," Ana said.

Lee and Gavin looked at each other. Lee dug out her comm, typed something, and nodded.

"Didn't pay close attention to that, did you?" Ana asked. "I gave you the goods. You, Engineer, are now an engineer level 2 from Pallas, and she's both a medic two and a navigator level 1. Pallas certs, of course, but they're an Imperial colony, so should get you on anywhere."

Dirk nodded. "That was well done, Centurion."

"Surprised you, didn't I?" Ana asked.

"Yes," Dirk said.

"I said I'd do it, and I did. And if I'm going to do something, I do it right. And don't worry, those IDs are permanent. They're going to be valid unless somebody calls back to Pallas and checks them. So, you'll be in good shape unless you give somebody a reason to query Pallas directly. And 'cause of the way they're authenticated, I can't take them back, even if I want to. They're yours forever."

"So, I never have to be Dena from Rockhaul again?" Dena asked.

"Nope, you are forever after Dena from Pallas. Just don't try to go back to Pallas—or talk to anybody from there—unless you learn Greek first."

"That just leaves you, Pilot," Dena said.

Dirk was quiet. "I'm staying with the ship to Papillon. The rest of you do what you need to." The jump alarm bonged. "Stations for jump," Dirk said.

"One question," Dena said.

"About the jump?"

"About whether I can stay out of my cage?"

***

The jump was uneventful, and the next system didn't even have a name, just a catalog number. It also didn't have people, vegetation, mountains, or rivers.

"It's a scum world," Lee said. "Flat rock mixed with swamps. Atmosphere, plenty of pressure, but almost no oxygen. Carbon dioxide. You don't need sealed skin suits—or any skin suits, really. Just an oxygen bottle to breathe. Warm and wet, with plenty of water. Algae in the seas."

Dirk drank an entire bottle of Dena's port before the landing. They spiraled down, screaming, and hit with their usual slam and thud.

"Good landing, as always," Ana said, unclipping his

harness.

"The emperor's hairy anus," Dena said, her face white. "Is this normal?"

"With Pilot Dirk," Lee said. "Always."

"Do you ever get used to it?" Dena asked.

"Eventually. Navigator," Ana said to Lee, "any threats we should know about?"

"Nothing listed. No animals, no people, no rivers to wash us away. This place is visited by ships every couple of years, so there is actually good information in the sailing directions."

"Regardless. The private and I will go outside. One of us on the ventral hatch with rifle and binoculars. The other will deploy the hose for the fuel processing plant. I'll take the first shift dragging the hose. Private, you're up top."

"I can help drag a hose," Dirk said. "It's within my competency while we're on the ground."

"Maybe a short nap after your beverage might be best, Skipper," Gavin said. "Or perhaps just stay in and watch the board. Best not to be moving heavy equipment."

"If there are no threats," Dena asked. "Why the guard?"

Gavin laughed, "We've been a number of places, your home among them, where we thought everything would be fine. Turns out we were wrong. The guard is a good idea. Somebody whose job it is to just look around sees things the rest of us don't." There were nods all around. "Fuel-pumping and processing will take at least three shifts. I want to stay six, if it's okay. We got a number of parts at Reik that will be easier to put on in gravity. A new hatch seal to replace the cracked one. New chains and a new magnet on one of the docking chains. Easy to do here, and the navigator and I can do it while we're here."

"Then here's the plan," Dirk said. "Fueling first. Once it's pumping, Gavin and Lee do maintenance. Scruggs, Ana, and I will rotate half shifts, watching the boards and guard duty. Tomorrow, we'll see where we are.

"You trust me to watch a board?" Scruggs said.

"You've had enough practice. You know to wake somebody if there is a problem. Besides, you're sharing with Navy here," Ana said. "Even drunk, he knows what a green board looks like."

"If everyone is leaving the ship in a week or two, why are we doing maintenance?" Dena asked.

"Because things can break at any time, and you never know what can kill you," Ana said. "I don't agree with the engineer on much, but maintenance happens every day. Otherwise, things will break at the worse possible time."

"What's she going to do?" Scruggs pointed at Dena.

"She can help Gavin and Lee," Dirk said.

"What if I don't want to?" Dena said.

"Can always go back in your cage," Scruggs said.

"Who's going to put me in there?" Dena said. "You?"

Scruggs stood and faced Dena. "If that's what the captain wants."

Dirk coughed. "Look, it's not hard, and it's not like there is anything else to do on this swamp. The engineer and medic will need parts and tools and things held. You can help with that, can't you?"

"If you say so," Dena said. She glared at Scruggs.

Gavin got up. "He does. He's the skipper. Fuel first, repairs second, sleep third, let's see where we get tomorrow."

It was a long day for everybody.

***

"Skipper," Gavin said the next day. "We're chock full of fuel, we've cracked as much H and O as we need, and the water tanks are full. I even purged the containers and the cargo hold and pumped this carbon dioxide stuff in for an hour. Won't hurt anything, but it will kill bugs, mold, anything we might have picked up."

"Outstanding. What about maintenance?"

"I've bolted on or swapped just about everything that

we could do. We have two new nozzles from that trade, but we'd need a shipyard with a crane to do them, or no gravity."

"We're ready to lift, then?"

"Can I have an hour to reorganize the hold? Move a few things around to make unloading easier?"

"Yep. What after that?"

"Then we lift, and it's full speed for Papillon."

CHAPTER 29

"Tribune, we are never going to find them at this rate," Subprefect Lionel said.

Devin, the Lord Lyon, slumped into his acceleration couch and glared at the screen. "Scan, why haven't you reported?" he asked.

The scan technician turned slightly and glanced at the subprefect. The subprefect spoke. "Deguals was doing something for me, Tribune. Carry on, Deguals," Lionel said.

"Sir," Deguals said, "system is uninhabited according to records. No radio traffic present. No beacons. Blink analysis shows no drive signatures moving. Detailed examination of planetary orbits shows nothing in unpowered orbit visible to our sensors."

"What's your confidence level?"

"Very high on the outer gas giants, sir. Not as much on the inner planets."

"Close the inner planets 'til your confidence level is very high there as well," Devin ordered.

The navigator tapped his screen. "Yes, Tribune. There are four planets inside the jump limit. We'll burn a lot of fuel getting there and examining them."

"Do it anyways," Devin said.

"Scan," Lionel asked, "what's the composition of those inner planets? Any water? Atmosphere?"

"No water on any of them, sir," Deguals said. "Minimal atmosphere on one. Very heavy on the carbon dioxide. And this is a very active star—there have been two coronal mass ejections since we've been here. We'll have to keep strong magnetic shields up as we survey."

"Well, that would kill any life," Lionel said. "Scan,

what's there for a ship? Any kind of resources?"

"No atmo, no water, no fuel. Nothing really."

"If you were passing through this system, what would you do?"

Deguals looked back. He took in his brooding captain and the inquisitive subprefect. "Stay outside of the jump limit. If I needed fuel, I might try to get some from one of the gas giants. But the composition is not quite right. I might try to catch some ice chunks, but we haven't seen any."

"What if you needed repairs?"

"Sir, there's nowhere with an atmosphere worth mentioning, so it's just as easy—easier, really, to do any repairs out here."

A long silence ensued, broken by the navigator. "Heading for the inner system, Captain. First flyby in thirty-seven hours. Others after that, depending on what we find."

Lionel looked blandly at Devin.

"Five years," Devin said. "You were wrong. Five years."

"I'm wrong about a lot of things," Lionel said. "So, I'll need some context to find out exactly what I'm wrong about by five years, Tribune."

"You said there hadn't been an Imperial ship in some of these systems in two years. You were wrong. Most of them, it's longer. Five years for some. And you were correct about us being the only ship in the subsector right now."

"Five years? As bad as that?" Lionel asked.

"Oh, the couriers pass through, fleet units transit to the border with the confederation and the union but none stay. And they always take the fastest route. The main trade routes see ships every year, but once you are off the main routes some places, there's nothing for years and years."

"No wonder those ship captains felt the need to arm

themselves."

"Even if we don't find Dirk, at least we're showing the flag."

"This is an uninhabited system," Lionel said. "Who are we showing the flag to?"

Devin glared at him. "I hate it when you're right."

"Condescending superiority, it's one of my finer qualities," Lionel said. He turned to the front of the control room. "Scan, how long 'til the standard blink test is finished."

"Thirty-seven minutes if it produces a clean sweep, sir. Longer if it finds something unusual."

Devin grunted. "Navigation, cancel our course. Deploy to first, finish that scan. Second, if it's negative, make sure we can jump right away."

"Understood, sir. Course computed, standing by, to execute."

"Already computed?" Devin asked. "How so fast?"

"Sir, I've been running that calculation since we arrived and updating it constantly," Deguals said.

"Obviously, this crew has a better idea of how to do this than me," Devin muttered. "What am I doing here, then?"

"Tribune, we need you to say 'execute' from time to time," Lionel said.

Devin shook his head. "Execute," he said.

"Tribune, could we have a jump destination if the scan is negative?" Deguals asked.

"Do you have a suggestion, scan?" Devin said.

"Tribune, we could assume a regular freighter left Bishop's world approximately six weeks ago and proceeded outward from there. Assuming regular jumps and some time for basic maintenance, we can construct an expanding sphere of worlds it could have reached. After, say, twelve weeks, they're probably going to need a shipyard or major trading station of some sort. We're faster than them, so we could jump to the larger stations that it could be headed for and either arrive ahead of it and issue warnings or arrive after it and inquire of local authorities of any issues. Given our current position, the next place we should jump for," Deguals consulted a list, "is Legatos-IV. Long jump, sir, but puts us ahead of them, and we can post rewards."

"Post rewards for who?" Devin asked.

"Why, for whoever the Tribune wishes to, sir." Deguals said.

Devin regarded him suspiciously. "That was a very detailed and precise suggestion, Deguals," he said.

"Thank you very much, sir."

"It wasn't really meant as a compliment. I know you were with me back in Antares, but how long have you served with me?"

Deguals looked at the subprefect, then back to the tribune. "Two years on Pollux, sir, but thirteen in your sphere."

"My sphere? What in the name of the emperor's hairy testicles is my sphere?"

Deguals, again, looked to the subprefect, who cleared his throat. "Many of your former crew, sir," Lionel said, "they find they are more . . . comfortable serving with either you or some of your former officers. Officers you have trained. They call it your sphere. Captain Ramis, for example, is a popular transfer location for many people from Pollux when they run out an assignment. They find that he is much like you, and they do well on his ship. Eighty or ninety percent of your former crew transfer to a command under one of your former officers."

"Ninety percent? How is that possible," Devin asked.

"We bribe the personnel people, sir," Deguals said. "If we have to. But given your reputation, normally a simple request is all that is necessary."

"What? What do you mean?" Devin said. He turned to Lionel. "What does he mean?"

"You're a hardship posting," Lionel said. "You're

always out in the back of beyond. Never in the core. Never with the regal fleets, always with a small task force or small ship actions. You fight other ships. Or opposed boardings. Or ground combat. Most officers and most crew don't want that. They want to be in the core where they get easy shore leave and access to the Imperial court. You're a bit of a punishment posting."

"I'm a punishment posting? Me?" Devin asked. "Imperial anus. I should space the lot of you for talking like that."

"There it is, see, Tribune? Spacing people. Fighting. That sort of thing."

"I . . ." Devin pointed at Lionel. "My quarters." He got up and walked to the back of the bridge.

"The next jump, Tribune?" the navigator asked.

Devin stopped and looked around his bridge. "You and Deguals figure it out. Your discretion." He stomped off the bridge and into his quarters. He had just cleared the door when he stopped suddenly, turned around, and shouldered his way back past the subprefect.

"Scan, Navigation," he said.

"Sir?" they both responded in unison.

"Execute. Execute. Execute. Execute. That's four executes. Next four things for jumps, courses, scans, whatever you figure out. Execute. Call me when you run out of executes."

"The Empire," Deguals said, giving the crossed chest salute.

"The Empire." Devin agreed and went back into his office.

***

Devin drank an entire glass of wine before he said anything. Lionel sat up and sipped his.

"Subprefect," Devin said. "Are you building a secret army for me out here?"

"Oh, no, sir," Lionel said. "No such thing. Perish the

thought."

"Good," Devin said. He put his glass down. "I was worried for a moment."

"You've got no need of an army. Now, a navy, that we do have. Or at least a squadron."

Devin looked horrified. "What do you mean a squadron?"

"You and three other ships commanded by former officers of yours. Destroyer, a frigate, and two corvettes."

"But a squadron?"

"Small one for now. But you're due a promotion. A destroyer or a light cruiser, probably. Then all the other captains will move up. None of the regular nobles want to command some pirate-hunting commerce destroying escort ship out in the outer rim. So, with a few bribes, you get another colonial command, and all your former ships will have loyalists on them."

"Loyalists? What in the name of the emperor's hairy anus are those?"

"We'd need Marines, of course. You haven't had a lot of those. Now, when we catch up to Dirk, you should talk to him. I'll bet he can scare up a battalion of Marines who will listen to him."

"Catch up to Dirk? I'm supposed to arrest him or kill him."

"That would be unfortunate. You should talk to him first."

"This is a revolt. This is rebellion. This is treason."

"Treason to who, Devin?" Lionel asked. "We've always followed your orders and always will. And you are certainly loyal to the Empire. Loyal to the emperor. And certainly loyal to the empress. We just see farther than you. Someday soon, you'll be given orders that you'll find hard to follow. Or impossible. You'll refuse. Then things will get interesting."

"What orders could I get from the emperor that I would possibly even think of refusing?"

"Orders to kill Dirk Friedel for one. I think you've got those already, and you're moving heaven and earth to not fulfill those."

"What do you mean?"

"If there is a more effective way of not finding a fleeing Imperial officer than visiting every uninhabited rock system in the sector, I don't know what it is. What are your orders regarding Dirk? You've been pretty cagy, and you've received an awful lot of messages recently."

Devin got up and poured another glass of wine. "Lots of messages?"

"Courier ships a few weeks ago. What do they say?" Lionel asked. "There's a betting pool."

"The crew has a betting pool on secret messages from the Imperial Navy?"

"Not those ones. The one from the empress. I've got 'Come home and see your godson, get confirmed.' 'We're making you Imperial chancellor' is pretty popular as well, and 'I'm leaving the emperor for a Varrien rug merchant' has a few adherents."

"The empress hates Varrien rugs," Devin said. "Isn't this betting prejudicial to order and good discipline?"

"You have the best disciplined crew in the Empire. People fight each other with knives to work for you. You handed the bosun a death sentence, and he smiled when you did."

"What are you talking about? What death sentence?"

"He's beating some sort of education into that midshipman. If it doesn't take, if he ever gets posted on a ship run by that one's friends, or even somebody who wants influence with that kid's family, he's a dead man."

"I don't believe this," Devin said. "This is treason."

"I haven't said a word against the Empire or the emperor. Just certain particular nobles, and a way of . . . governing that has become popular over recent years."

Devin regarded him for a moment, then walked to his desk and pushed a button. "Have Bosun McSanchez contact me immediately," he said.

A pause preceded the bong of his comm.

"Tribune, Bosun McSanchez here."

"Bosun, what is my sphere?"

"Tribune?"

"The subprefect is here. He referred to my sphere. What is it?"

"It's ships commanded by your former officers, sir. Ships where the crew can expect to serve the Empire honorably. Ships that go out and do enforcement, or patrols. Ships that do their duty, sir, not that just sit at a core world and go on parades."

Devin stared at the comm. "Bosun, is that Caldor midshipmen learning any math?"

"Not much, sir, but I'm hopeful. He doesn't like the rod, but he's finally learned how to calculate the mass of it by trial and error."

"Will he learn, do you think?"

"Probably not, sir. Dumb as a bag of rocks, that one."

"He has a cousin. I'm thinking of posting you to his ship. What do you think will happen to you there?"

"Won't last a week, sir. I'll be dead."

"Dead? That's not possible. Imperial officers don't kill their crew."

"Beggin' the Tribune's pardon, but the navy has changed since last you were at the capital, sir. Soon as that kid gets a message out, I'll suffer some sort of accident."

Devin stood, silent. Finally, the bosun broke back in. "Tribune, sir, it's my sleep shift, and I'm on duty in a few hours."

"Of course, sorry to wake you, Bosun," the tribune said. He paused for a moment. "What is your bet in the pool? On my secret messages from the empress. What did you bet?"

"Imperial chancellor, sir. You'd do an excellent job. I hope the empress sees clear to do that."

"Thank you for your confidence. Good night, Bosun."

"Good night, sir."

Devin sat and sipped his wine.

"He's a fool," Lionel said.

"You don't think he should be like us, chastising that midshipman?"

"What? No, that doesn't matter. I meant the bet. Rug merchant is much more likely."

"How long has this been going on?"

"Nobles killing people they don't like? Since the start of the Empire for some, I guess, but it's definitely picked up in the last ten years."

"I meant you setting up this sphere thing."

"You set it up."

"How did I do that?"

"Just by being you, Devin. Just by being you." Lionel said. "What are your orders regarding Dirk?"

"Well, I have the original order from the sector governor to recover an escaped fugitive. It's the usual dead or alive, but it's my choice."

"Sector governor is a civilian."

"But a civilian appointed by the emperor."

"And then?"

"Then I received an update from naval headquarters on that courier, changing it to shoot on sight."

"Pretty straightforward." Lionel said.

"But the same courier delivered a message from the empress. Personal. Said not to kill him but to catch him and deliver a message."

"Complicated. Who ranks who? Emperor's sector governor, naval admiral, or high-ranking noble's personal command. What was the message?"

"It was encrypted. No idea what it said."

"What do we do now?"

Devin stared at his wine. He sighed, walked to his desk, and punched a button.

"Bridge. Navigator here."

"Navigator, when do we jump?"

"Twelve minutes, sir."

"And after that?"

"We have some scans and some options mapped out. What are your orders, sir?"

"My orders?" Devin looked at his wine again. "Execute. Execute. Execute. Then get back to me."

CHAPTER 30

"Nice-looking planet," Ana said. Their screen cast Papillon's features. Blue water. Brown continents. White clouds.

"Standard atmosphere," Lee said. "Can grow human standard vegetation, so grows its own food. Some mining. Plenty of water. Some trade routes. An actual shipyard, a small one, can fix drives."

Dirk, Ana, Gavin, and Lee were at their usual seats at the control panels. Scruggs was sitting in the lounge, listening on the intercom.

"What's the downside?" Ana asked.

"A long way from the central worlds," Lee said. "Very active star. Big solar flares make any space industry expensive and hard to shield, so there is only minimal orbital infrastructure. Kind of hot and damp." She examined her star map again. "This is sort of the last outpost of civilization. Big group of unaligned planets out past this, none with much in the way of population or resources. Imperial traders come out here, but they turn around."

"Also, not an Imperial colony." Gavin said. "It's an unaligned world. The Empire, the confederation, and the National Associations all touch here. They play them off against each other to keep their independence."

Dirk looked back at Lee. "Is there a confeds base here?"

"Not here, a few systems away. They patrol out to here."

"I can't meet any confeds," Dirk said. "None."

"Why?"

Dirk ignored her. "Give me the course."

"Empire runs the starport though," Gavin said. "Well, sort of. An Imperial company has management, and it's extraterritorial, but there aren't any Imperial troops here."

"How do you know that?" Dirk asked.

"I read, Skipper. I read."

"Well, we'll be in scanning range soon," Lee said.

Scruggs looked up from her comm as Dena wandered into the lounge. She'd been spending a lot of time in Dirk's cabin, and he hadn't objected. Quite the opposite. Her hair was disheveled, and she was wearing one of Dirk's shirts.

"Friend Dena," Scruggs said.

Dena regarded her lazily for a moment. "Why do I feel from you that the 'friend' is an insult, recruit?"

"That's private, not recruit. And maybe it's because you're more perceptive than I give you credit for."

"Could be. You know," Dena said, pulling a meal tray out. "Your captain is quite a man. Very athletic when he puts his mind to it."

"I wouldn't know," Scruggs said.

"No, you wouldn't, would you? But I'll bet you want to," Dena said.

Scruggs reddened. "He's the captain. That wouldn't be proper."

"Proper? We're with a bunch of wanted criminals. Emperess's vagina we're not only with wanted criminals. We are wanted criminals. Why does proper bother you?"

Scruggs glared at her, started to say something, then stopped. "You kind of do have a point."

"Yep. How come you didn't go for him?"

Scruggs dipped her spoon into the mush on her tray, then looked up at Dena. "How come you did go for him?"

Dena shrugged. "I was the fourth daughter of the fourth daughter of a big extended family. The overall family was rich. My part wasn't. My parents worked themselves to death. Every time they got something worthwhile going, somebody else in the family took it from them. Everything worthwhile that I got, I got by jumping on it when it was offered and fighting for it. Dirk was there, so I jumped on it and fought for it." Dena poured herself a cup of basic and drank it down. "This is vile."

"It's good for you," Scruggs said.

"I believe it. Most of the things that are good for you are either boring or disgusting."

"Do you love him?" Scruggs asked.

"Love him? I don't know anything about love." Dena shrugged. "It doesn't matter. Like I said, you see something you want, you better jump on it, or somebody might take it away from you before you even get a chance. I wasn't sure that I wanted Dirk, but best take it while it was on offer."

Scruggs looked at her for a moment. "You're very brave, coming out into space by yourself. It must be hard for you, leave everything you knew behind and go among strangers."

Dena nodded at her. "Brave. Foolhardy. Whatever. A life unlived isn't worth living, I don't think. What about you?"

"What?"

"You don't exactly have your family with you on this trip."

"I took this trip, as you call it, to get away from my family," Scruggs said.

"Who are your family?"

"Nobody I want to talk about."

"So, you're out here all alone, just like me."

"I have the crew."

"They're not a crew. Or they won't be after this stop. They're all splitting up. You're splitting up."

"That's . . . I don't know what to say," Scruggs said.

"Say that life is what happens to you while you're making other plans."

The screen above them flickered to a different display as Lee focused on something. The intercom cracked.

"Pilot, check out these ship beacons," Lee said.

A pause accompanied Dirk as he paged through a number of screens. The two women watched.

"Pilot?"

"I see them," Dirk said. "There's two national traders of some sort here. One in orbit—looks like a passenger liner—and one on the ground. And some confederation ships. A confederation freighter at the ground port. And two others."

"I've never seen ships like those," Lee said. "They look kind of like big bulk freighters, but that's an odd shape."

"They're Confederation Armed Auxiliary cruisers," Dirk said. "I've seen them before. Take an Imperial bulk freighter, double the size of the drives so that they're faster, and give 'em a big weapons suite and military grade sensors. They can trade anywhere and fight anything except a purpose-built warship."

"How do they make any money? I assume that the drive and weapon space takes away from their holds?" Gavin asked.

"Confederation government subsidizes construction, so they can use them if there's a war."

"You said you've seen them before," Ana said. "Where?"

"Not important," Dirk said. "But we're going to give them plenty of room. And I'd as soon as that national trader in orbit not get too close to us, either."

"It's streamlined. How come it's not on the ground?" Gavin asked.

"Probably has something onboard it doesn't want any authorities to see."

"Like what?"

"Like a company of their naval landing specialists, two drop shuttles, and heavy weapons. That's a camouflaged assault ship," Dirk said. He pulled a bottle out of the leg pocket of his skin suit. "I'll land us as soon as we're in orbit."

Everyone rushed to strap in.

***

"We'll send Scruggs and Dena off first," Dirk said. Everyone was standing at the bottom of the loading ramp, looking more or less green-faced. Dena was dry heaving a few meters away from the bottom of the ramp. "They can find a bank. Friend Dena, are you okay?"

"That was the worst landing I've ever been in," Dena said. She heaved again.

"That's only your second ever landing, as far as I know," Ana said.

Dena wiped her lips. "How many landings have you been in?"

"Hundreds of combat landings, probably thousands with all the others added in," Ana said.

"What do you think, then?"

"It was truly, truly horrible. But as long as landings equals takeoffs, I'm happy. Hey, Navy, how are we going to get them to the bank? That's a long walk."

"It is," Dirk said. Papillon's spaceport took advantage of the fact that land was cheap here. The spaceport occupied a massive tract outside the only city on the planet. Each landing pad was a hundred-meter-wide circle of fused dirt that had a ten-meter earth berm bulldozed around it. The berm had an opening on one side, wide enough for a dirt road to run in. The roads connected to run back to a warehouse complex several kilometers to the north. "They said there's a shuttle bus that runs every hour during the day, or we can pay for taxis."

"Best order up a taxi, then," Ana said. "Less people see us, the better."

"Aren't you worried I'll dump Scruggs and run away with your money?" Dena asked.

"Nah, Private Scruggs will be armed, and she doesn't like you," Ana said.

"How do you know that?"

"Because I don't like you, either, and I recognize the signs."

"Do you like anyone, Centurion?" Lee asked.

"Not as a general rule, no. But particularly in friend Dena's case. But even if it wasn't the case, I'm not worried about her running off," Ana said.

"You don't think I'll run off?" Dena asked.

"I don't care if you run off or try to run off. One thing I do know, you've never been off that stinking mud hole you call the planet of your birth before, so you don't know how things work in civilized places. Or semi-civilized in this case." Ana swept his hands around. "You don't know the rules here, how to get on a ship, who to bribe, how to do anything. You try to cheat us, you won't know where to hide, we can hunt you down, no problem. Or if you try to get on another ship, you won't know the rules there, either, and they'll end up cheating you of all your cash." Ana smiled. "Best thing for you is to stay with us and learn how things go from people who you know won't kill you for sport." Ana smiled some more. "Not that I wouldn't do that if the occasion warranted, but I don't have a reason right now."

"No killing for sport," Dirk said. "Not without a reason."

"Speaking of reasons, Navy," Ana said, "this is kind of a deserted place out here."

"A deserted place with lots of people passing through and lots of official notice. Also, theoretically, Imperial jurisdiction. Not near the ship."

"But you will find a place nearby, Navy?" Ana asked.

Dirk looked grim. "As promised."

***

A tanker truck and a supply truck were first to arrive. Negotiation on the radio had resulted in a flat fee for fuel, water, and a standard pack of food trays. They didn't really need them, but buying a standard pack made them fit in, lessening the chance of locals recalling anything suspicious. The truck driver took Imperial credit chips and commenced pumping the fuel. They weren't down much, and by the time they stowed the food and paid for everything, the taxi pulled up as the fuel truck decoupled.

The taxi had an enclosed cab, with only benches in the back. It was covered in rock dust and smelled like rotting fruit.

"You take out the benches and move garbage in this?" Gavin asked.

"No," the taxi driver said.

"Smells like garbage," Gavin said.

"Oh, we do move garbage," the driver said. "But we don't bother to remove the seats. You can't bring those."

"Bring what?" Gavin said.

"Those." He pointed. "Revolvers. Shotguns. Any weapons. No knives, firearms, lasers, energy weapons, no explosives. Nothing. You're going to be searched at customs, and anything they find, they keep."

"They have to find it first," Gavin said.

"Up to you. But they always find it. Don't bring anything you want to keep, is all."

"So, no fighting? How do we defend ourselves against the local criminal element?" Dirk asked.

"Captain, no offense, but you kind of look like you are going to be part of the local criminal element, like maybe they are your cousins or something."

"I resent that remark."

"Resent all you want. We're the only shuttle company in the port. You don't like it? I can go home."

"Fine." Dirk looked around. "I saw some oceans and rivers on the way in. How does customs feel about fishing?"

"Fishing?" the driver asked.

***

The ride to customs had taken about ten minutes at

speed. For such a massive starport by area, there wasn't much road traffic. A dozen ships occupied the field, shuttling cargo. The driver had dropped them off at the customs desk.

"Enjoy your fishing," he said.

The customs clerks were thorough. They'd been forced to disrobe down to underwear, and they even had checked that closely.

"I feel like, after this, you should be buying me dinner, or at least a drink," Dirk said.

"I'll buy the ladies several if they're interested," the male clerk said. "Tell them I'll be in the Starburst Lounge mid-second shift if they want to chat. All quite attractive looking."

"I'll pass that along," Dirk said.

The clerk examined their IDs. "You are all from Pallas?" he asked.

"That's right," Dirk said. He was listed as the captain, so he answered for all the crew.

"You don't look like any Palladians I've ever seen," the clerk said.

"Well, we are," Dirk said. The clerk looked at him for a long time. "Do I know you from somewhere?"

"Not possible," Dirk said. "My first time on Papillon."

"You remind me of somebody."

"I have that type of face," Dirk said.

The clerk frowned at him, then picked up the fishing rods. "Now, what are you going to fish for with this?" the clerk asked. He hefted Dirk's six-foot-long, thin but stiff fishing pole. A reel was attached at one end, and a line ran from the reel through carved holes to the tip.

"Whatever we can. We've been cooped up so long, we need some time with nature. I saw a river running through town. I assume there are fish in it."

"There are fish in it, and you don't even need a license. Take all the fish you want."

"That's mighty generous of you Papillonians," Dirk

said.

"Not really. They're poisonous. Good luck, though."

"Thanks," Dirk said. The group proceeded through the gate. The clerk waited 'til they walked away, then picked up his comm and punched in a number. When it answered, he said, "That list you gave me? One of those guys just cleared the gate."

***

The group reconnected past the customs gate and stepped into the town. Dirk, Gavin, Ana, and Scruggs carried fishing poles. Dena had disassembled her slingshot, and the pieces hadn't invited comment. Lee had a medical kit with her. Dirk had visited a currency changer inside, and a few gold coins resulted in a startling pile of currency.

"Exchange rate is in our favor. Some for everybody. Scruggs, you and Dena visit the bank, conclude our business, then head back here. Shouldn't take you more than an hour."

"What if I don't want to come back here?" Dena said.

"Then, don't," Dirk said. "We promised to bring you here. You're here. You can go away if you want. Or go to the Starburst Lounge— the customs clerk said he wanted to buy you two a drink. After we get our money. Scruggs, when you get back, we'll do some banking. One way or another, Centurion is leaving us here, but he gets his share first."

"I'll be walking away. Gavin will probably be taking a different mode of transportation, though."

"Shouldn't we have some food together or something?" Lee asked. "A final crew dinner or something?"

A long pause followed. "We're not really a crew," Dirk said. "Just people running in the same direction. We all meet back here in an hour for the final money div up, and then we're all on our separate ways. Let's go." He strode off into the town, and Gavin, Ana, and Lee followed.

Scruggs stared after them 'til they disappeared. She sighed and turned back. Dena was standing quietly, looking around. "What, friend Dena? No sarcastic comment about me pining after Dirk?"

"It's real, isn't it?"

"What's real?"

"I'm on another planet. I made it. I got away from them all."

"Don't know whether you got away, but this is definitely another planet," Scruggs said.

Dena looked around again. "I thought it would be different."

"Different how?"

"Don't know. Just different. You know what?"

"What?"

"I'll never see my family again. Or my friends. I just realized I can never go back. I'm alone out here, all by myself."

"We all are. Are there people you'll miss?"

"No. Yes. Yes—some. I didn't think about them, but yeah, I'll miss them. Maybe I can send them a message or something."

"Why bother?" Scruggs asked. "You wanted to get away."

"This isn't what I expected."

"Life rarely is," Scruggs said. "Let's go to the bank." She turned and walked away. Neither of them had noticed a nondescript local sauntering along the road after the other group.

CHAPTER 31

The bank proved to be anticlimactic. A sweaty walk down to the main street brought them to an office complex. Only two staff were in the office, and when Dena presented a credit chip and a code chip, they readily transferred a balance from a local account to her chip. Dena handed the chip to Scruggs, who checked the amount, then pocketed the chip. Dena closed the account and took the rest in Imperial credits. They left the bank and waked back to the street.

"Back to the customs dock?" Dena asked. "What's that smell?"

"Algae or fungus. Every planet smells different." Scruggs said.

"This one smells like rotting vegetables."

"You'll get used to it. Once you've been on enough planets, you don't even notice it after the first days," Scruggs said.

"Planet-hopper, that's me." Dena looked up and down the street. "How about having something to eat?"

"Why not," Scruggs said. They walked down the road and stopped at the first place they saw, a bar that advertised lunch in the window. They went in and sat down.

"Do you know what vegetables are in that salad?" Scruggs said. She pointed to a picture on the menu.

"I've heard of them all in books, but I don't think I've eaten any, except carrots," Dena said.

The waiter arrived with their salad as they puzzled out the offerings on the board. "You ladies spacers?"

"Yes."

"Looks like you just arrived."

"Why are you asking?"

"Because we're busy, and if you sit there, trying to figure out what to eat when you don't know what anything is, you'll be here forever. Take two of the specials. Fresh vegetables in the salad, freshly made soup, and the meat is a cow analog. Not steak but still tasty. Comes with two glasses of white wine. Not amazing but local and cheap."

"Why not?" Dena said. They ordered the special and crunched through the salads.

"These are tomatoes," Dena said. "I've heard of them. Didn't have them at home. Too cold."

"And I think this is cucumber," Scruggs said. "It's tasty."

The soup was made of some sort of vegetable. Dena didn't care for it, but Scruggs ate both bowls. The main course was spicy meat with potatoes.

"Not as good as Rockhaul meat but a nice change from ship food."

"Everybody thought that the food at Rockhaul was great," Scruggs said. "Even the captain, and the centurion, and they've been everywhere."

"I guess I'll never know that again, really. Aren't you worried about the centurion and Gavin fighting?"

"No, Centurion will win. He always does. It's a shame, though. Gavin was nice enough. A little scatterbrained is all."

"You're not worried, even a little bit?"

"Nope. Centurion can take care of himself. I'm not worried about that." A group of men walked by the restaurant toward the customs dock. "Huh," Scruggs said. "Now that is something to worry about."

"Who are they? Do you know them?"

"Never seen them before, but I recognize those uniforms. Centurion and the captain both told me to look out for them."

"Who are they?"

"Those are confederation uniforms. They're off those

warships in orbit. I better call the captain."

"Captain's scared of the confederation troops?"

"He said he'd met them before, somewhere."

***

"This seems as good a place as any," Dirk said. Just west of the customs gate was a road lined with disreputable-looking warehouses and storage yards. He led the way between a fenced storage yard full of metal beams and a two-story warehouse with a dented metal door facing the street. A small stream in the distance had eroded the surrounding wasteland, creating a sunken riverbed that was shielded from view in all directions. "I scoped this out as we were landing."

"I'm surprised you notice anything at all when you're landing, Skipper," Gavin said.

"I always have a backup place to land if it's available. Riverbeds are good—the water slows us down, and there are rarely buildings or people to hit."

"Good place, Navy," Ana agreed. "Nobody can see us. We can go about our business in privacy. And plenty of places to bury a body if need be. Nobody will find it here for years."

"And if anybody asks, we're fishing," Gavin said.

***

Gavin and Ana stripped the reels off their fishing poles and threw away the line and sinkers, which left them with two-meter-long wooden poles.

Ana swung his experimentally left to right. "A little light, but it will work."

Gavin spun his pole with one hand, twirling it between his fingers, then passed it off to his other hand. "Not bad, not bad at all."

Lee looked unhappy. "Pilot, are we just going to watch them beat on each other with sticks?"

"That's kind of the point," Dirk said. "We came here so that they can beat on each other with sticks."

"It's barbaric. Dishonorable."

"I thought that you didn't like the centurion," Dirk said. "What do you care if he gets beaten to death with a stick?"

"I don't like him," Lee said, "but, well, he's been a sufficiently useful crew member."

"Sufficiently useful? That's great praise," Ana said. "And anyways, it's not me who is going to get beaten to death. It's your boyfriend here."

"I don't think so," Gavin said. "I've been holding myself back for weeks now. I'm ready."

"Not yet," Dirk commanded, stepping between them. "Here's how we're going to do this. Both of you, back away six feet." Dirk waited 'til they both moved. "Right. First, can we possibly skip this? You've been in the same crew for weeks now, and you've worked well together. Centurion?"

"What is it, Navy?"

"Do you have any objections to the way the engineer has handled his duties? His engineering duties?"

Ana shook his head. "I do not. I have to say, under other circumstances, I'd be happy to ship with him. He's good at his job, does good work, and he's not afraid of getting dirty."

"And he's good in a fight," Dirk said. "Not so?"

"True."

"He helped drag you back on the ship after you got shocked. He had a chance to leave you behind but didn't."

Ana nodded. "I know that, Navy. I don't see how it matters. This is a personal thing."

Dirk turned to Gavin. "Engineer, you have any complaints about how Ana has handled his duties? Standing watch, standing guard duty on planets. Teaching the recruit-private."

Gavin laughed. "Skipper, I will say he's the most useful

ground pounder I've seen in a while. He knows his job, and he does his job. Willing to do fetch and carry for engineering work, and he never hangs back in a fight. I like that."

"Has he helped you when asked? With your duties?"

"Skipper, he's a better scan tech than you are. And he taught that kid a lot."

"You realize he helped drag you back into the ship when you and the navigator here nearly drowned."

"I'm not the navigator, I'm the medic," Lee said.

"According to your ID, you are both now," Dirk said. "Engineer? Did he or did he not save your life?"

"Did. He did."

"Right." Dirk paused. "So, the two of you both agree that the other is competent, professional, brave, and hardworking." He looked at each in turn, and they nodded.

"And both of you agree that the other is a good crew member, one that I should keep on board."

"You'll never find an engineer as good as him out here, Navy. Keep him," Ana said.

"Centurion knows his trade, Skipper. He does good work. Keep him."

"Given all this," Dirk said. "Why are we having this fight?"

Ana lowered his stick and stepped backward. He regarded Gavin, then Dirk. "Navy, I just hate this kid, and I want to kill him. Can we get going?"

Gavin nodded. "Same here. I've been dreaming of kicking this old man around for weeks. Can we get started?"

Dirk put his head in his hands, then straightened and stepped back. "Go."

***

"There are four of them," Senior Sergeant Vlasov said into the comm unit. "Three male, one female. The female is tall and skinny. She may be a Jovian. One matches the description, and he looks like the picture." His three men watched him as the voice on the other end asked a question. His comm was bulkier than normal and had a foot-long antenna extended. A thin metal attaché case sat on the ground below him.

"Well, how will I know if they are Imperials?" he said. "I can hardly walk up and ask them." He looked at his men. One of them raised his hand. "Wait one," Vlasov said. "Bandanovitch?"

"Citizen Sergeant," Bandanovitch said. "The older man is wearing a skin suit that looks like the ones I have seen Palladian trained mercenaries wear. It has the extra reinforcement pads for their light body armor sewn on. And the one in charge is wearing a surplus Imperial Navy skin suit."

"They said they were from Pallas, so that proves nothing," Vlasov said. "Why do you think the other skin suit is Imperial?"

"Cuff and collars. I have seen one close up, and I recognize the locking ring."

Vlasov keyed his comm again. "Visual observation, Lieutenant— Citizen Lieutenant—shows them wearing Imperial or at least Palladian clothes. Yes. He did? Now, sir? How are we to get them back on the ship?" Vlasov paused and listened some more. "Right away." Vlasov put down his comm and stared at it, then shook his head. He pushed the collapsing antenna down and handed the comm to the shortest of the four men, who slid it into a custom holster on his belt.

"Right, follow them down this alley. Bandanovitch, Greigov, hit him with the stun stick and bring him back."

"Just stun the target, sir," Bandanovitch asked. He pulled a stun stick from a long pocket sewn into his coat. His partner, Greigov, did the same.

"The target must come back onto the ship alive."

"What about the others, then, sir?"

"I will deal with them." Vlasov reached down and

opened the attaché case. He removed a small machine gun from it, loaded it, and racked the slide. Then he closed the case and handed it to the radioman.

"Pretty lonely place," Greigov said. "We can just bury them here."

"No killing," Vlasov said, leading the way down the alley. "Not until we know we have the right person." The group of four men reached the end of the alley, and Vlasov held up his hand to make them wait. He crouched down on his knees, then peeked around the corner of the building. He watched for a moment, then got up from his knees and leaned his whole head around the corner.

"How did he get the submachine gun down here?" Greigov asked Bandanovitch.

"A truly massive bribe to the customs agent who searched us. The same agent who told us that this Imperial crew was here."

"Is that why we're here?"

"I heard the citizen lieutenant talking. Every ship in the Navy is looking for this guy. We just happen to be the lucky one who was in the right place at the right time."

Vlasov stepped forward 'til he was completely exposed, then walked forward. He turned and waved the other three toward him. Bandanovitch and Greigov jogged up to him, shock sticks held ready. The radio man brought up the rear.

The four of them had moved far enough that the shallow stream bed came into view. One man and the Jovian woman stood with their backs to them. The man had his hand on his hips, and the woman was fumbling with a medical kit. In front of them, two men—one older and one much younger—had stripped to skin suits and were whirling fishing poles around, rapidly thrusting and striking each other. Both had manic grins on their faces, tossing insults at each other.

The four confederation troops stared at the scene. "Citizen Sergeant?" Bandanovitch asked. "What is going on?"

"I have no idea," Vlasov said. "They are hitting each other with sticks. Have you ever seen anything like this?"

"Never."

"Imperials are strange," Vlasov said. "Right, down there and take them."

***

"Have you ever seen anything like this?" Lee said.

"Never," Dirk said. "These two must be specialists in sticks."

"They're so fast," Lee said. Ana and Gavin whirled their sticks like they had no weight at all. They thrusted, feinted, stepped forward and back. Dirk and Lee stood and watched.

"Take this, old man," Gavin yelled. He pointed his stick at Ana's stomach and charged forward. Ana struck it down hard and stepped forward, swinging his stick up in an arc.

Gavin ducked, recovered his stick, and swung at Ana's ankles. Ana jumped and let it pass under him, pulled back, and slammed a hit toward Gavin's unprotected head. Gavin thrust and jumped forward before rolling over his stick. He jumped to his feet as Ana's stick hit the ground behind him, roiling dust.

"That the best you got, kid? I teach that first day to all my newbies," Ana said. He feinted high with his left hand, then rocketed his right forward. Gavin caught it on his own stick and pushed back. Ana stepped forward, and Gavin slid his hands back and swung at Ana's thigh. Ana screamed at the solid hit but smacked his own down on Gavin's exposed hand. A bone cracked. Gavin screamed and dropped his right hand.

The two separated. Ana was limping—badly. Gavin's right hand hung loosely by his side, holding his stick with his left.

"Having problems standing, old man?" Gavin said.

"Come closer and see," Ana said, his boast ringing hollow as he collapsed.

Gavin sauntered up and spun his stick with one hand. "Time for a beating you'll remember, old man," he said. He showed off by spinning the stick again. Quick as lightning, Ana struck at it with his own. Instead of trying to get past it or hit his hand, he hit the end of it hard.

Gavin's stick spun away behind him. Ana rolled over and swept his leg under Gavin's feet, who was too startled to react. He tripped over Ana's stick and fell forward. Ana rolled over and reached for him, managing to grab his neck. He put all his effort into it and squeezed. Gavin reached up and grabbed Ana's nose to peel his nostrils back.

Both strained for a moment, then a pup-pup-pup-pup accompanied a blast of dirt and small rocks toward them. They both released simultaneously and rolled away.

Dirk and Lee turned and stared at the bank.

A group of four men stood there. Three in front and one behind them, all dressed in confederation ship suits.

"Durriken Friedel," the lead man said in a strong confederation accent. He held the submachine gun he had just used to shoot at Ana and Gavin. "On behalf of the confederation, you are under arrest for crimes against humanity, war crimes, execution of prisoners, and bombarding defenseless cities."

A long silence brewed. Lee's jaw dropped. Dirk stood frozen. Ana and Gavin had rolled apart and stared at the tableaux.

"Wow, Navy," Ana gasped. "I'll finally admit it. You are way more bad ass than me."

CHAPTER 32

"Centurion, Centurion, come in. Centurion, there are four confederation troops in town, and I think they're following you," Scruggs said. She and Dena had paid their bill and followed the confed troops. The troops moved steadily through the town without looking back and shortly arrived on a deserted street with warehouses on either side. They stopped to check something on a comm, then disappeared between a building and a fenced yard.

Scruggs stared at her comm. "No answer."

"They must have started their fight," Dena said. "And those confed guys just went down that alley up there."

"Follow them. Come on." Scruggs said. She and Dena ran down the street to the alley. They peeked around the corner and looked down the bare alley, then cautiously advanced. A clack-clack and yelling sprung from around a corner. Dena snuck up and peered around the edge for a moment, then stepped back. She waved Scruggs down. The four men approached the edge as Scruggs looked. The leader voiced his speech clearly.

"Crimes against humanity? What does that even mean?" Dena asked.

"He's that Durriken Friedel," Scruggs said. "I never knew."

"Which Durriken Friedel would that be?" Dena said.

"We've got to help them," Scruggs said.

"And I should help a planet killing war criminal why?"

"He helped you escape whatever it was that thing you wanted to escape. He brought you here."

"As I recall, I had to pay for this escape. And the bringing."

"Aren't you two lovers?" Scruggs asked.

Dena shrugged. "I've had better."

Scruggs looked appalled.

"Oh, I don't tell him that," Dena said. "I mean, he's reasonably skilled, but nothing special."

Scruggs continued to look appalled.

"You really don't have much experience with men, do you?" Dena asked.

Scruggs continued to stare. Dena ignored the stare. "We should walk back quietly, let these folks conduct their business."

"You won't help the captain?"

"It's four against four. They've got a good chance."

"The centurion and Gavin could be hurt."

"That's their fault. They hurt each other. They can take their chances. Besides, they still have their sticks."

They peered around the corner again. The two men with shock sticks dropped from view as they climbed down to the streambed.

Scruggs looked at Dena. "If you don't help Dirk, you've got no way off this planet. The confeds will take him away, and the Imperials will take the ship. You'll be stuck here."

Dena closed her eyes and sighed. "Well, it wasn't my planet he bombed. What's your plan here?"

"Get your slingshot ready. I'm going to charge the one with the SMG while he's distracted. You keep hitting that radio guy until he's down, so he can't call reinforcements."

"Then what?" Dena asked. She pulled the slingshot from a pocket and loaded it up with a rock.

"As the centurion says, we'll assess the tactical situation and improvise our response."

"What does that mean?"

"It means I have no idea," Scruggs said as she sprinted toward the group.

***

The two men with shock sticks scrambled down the

bank. Gavin had rolled away and stood. Dirk and Lee stood, frozen.

Ana tried to get up, but as soon as he put weight on his foot, he collapsed. "Hey, confed guy," Ana yelled, "what's going on?"

"Surrender, and you won't be harmed," Vlasov said. He pointed the submachine gun. "Choose now. Do you surrender?"

"Well," Ana said. He looked at Gavin. "To quote the man, the situation has developed not necessarily to our advantage, while the general trends of the world have all turned against our interest."

Gavin giggled, then broke into laughter. "I didn't know you read history, Centurion," Gavin said. "All we need now is a joint declaration."

"I didn't know you read history, either."

"One of my hobbies," Gavin said.

Bandanovitch and Greigov had reached Lee and Dirk, where they were menacing them with the shock sticks. The earth exploded as Vlasov fired another round of shots at Gavin and Ana. "Hands on your heads. Now."

Gavin looked at Ana. "Truce while we get this other thing sorted out."

"Agreed, but we can restart again any time, as long as we arrange it properly."

"Agreed."

"Quiet," Vlasov said. "Do you surrender or not?" He cocked the machine gun, then turned as a running Scruggs tackled him.

Vlasov and Scruggs flipped over the bank's edge and rolled down the steep bank. Vlasov lost his grip on his SMG, and it went spiraling up into the air. He and Scruggs continued to flip over and down the hill.

Bandanovitch and Greigov turned to watch.

"Dirk," Lee yelled. She swung her med kit at Bandanovitch's head, then dove at him. Bandanovitch raised his arm, shocking her as he went down. Her momentum propelled them to the ground. Lee's twitching body pinned his arm. Dirk scampered forward, stomped a foot on Bandanovitch's arm, and pulled the shock stick free. He jumped back as Greigov swung at him and missed.

Vlasov's roll ended with a thud as his head contacted the ground. He lay there, unmoving. Scruggs crumpled to a stop next to him. She had hit a rock. Her eyes rolled around, and her breath came in gasps.

A yell and a crack resounded from above. Gavin ran over and dove for the SMG. He caught it with one hand but couldn't do anything with it.

"Ana!" Gavin yelled and threw the SMG at Ana.

Ana rolled to a sitting position, grunting as his leg hit the ground. He caught the SMG, pivoted a bit, aimed, and fired. Greigov yelled as his shock stick was flung out of his hands.

Dirk thrust the shock stick forward, and Greigov writhed, then dropped to the ground, twitching.

Ana swung the SMG to point to Bandanovitch. "Hands on head."

"No trouble," Bandanovitch said, raising his hands. "I just want—"

Dirk shocked him, and he fell.

Dena appeared at the top of the ravine, her slingshot in her hands. "What's going on?"

"We got them all," Dirk said. He looked at the uniforms for a moment. "Confeds?"

"Yes, Scruggs said they came off the cargo ship at the port. There was a fourth. He ran off."

"He's calling for reinforcements now, then," Dirk said.

"Nope." Dena stepped away for a moment, then came back into view, carrying a metal box riddled with dents. "I hit his radio, and he dropped it. I don't think it's working now."

"We need to get back on the ship and out of here before he calls in," Dirk said.

"He'll need big comms to talk to those ships in far orbit," Ana said. "He'll need a spare set somewhere."

"Probably one on his ship."

"So, we need to get back to our ship first," Dirk said. He fiddled with his shock stick for a second, then located a knob on the side. He twisted the power up to full, stepped forward, and systematically jabbed each of the confed troopers on the ground. Vlasov had been groaning but fell silent when Dirk stabbed him.

Dena looked worried. "Is he dead?"

"Just very, very stunned for a long time," Dirk said. "Plenty of time for us to get out of here."

"I would have just shot 'em," Ana said.

"I know that," Dirk said. "That's why I stunned them. Gavin, get those rods. Centurion, can you stand?"

"For a little while, but I can't walk."

"Right." Dirk bent down and rolled Lee over to check her. "She's breathing. Dena, check Scruggs." Dena hopped down and fussed over Scruggs. Dirk dug through Lee's kit for a syringe, then approached Ana.

Ana looked at the syringe. "That's what I'm talking about. Give it here, Navy." Dirk bent down, jabbed it into Ana's leg, and injected him with it.

"What is it?" Gavin asked.

"Local painkiller," Dirk said. "We need to get moving. Can you help Ana up the hill? Use the fishing rods."

"Better if you did it, I think," Gavin said. "My hand is messed up."

"No, Scruggs and Lee have to be carried, at least for the first fifteen minutes 'til they come to."

"Give me a shot for my hand." Gavin said. Dirk found another syringe and dosed him. Then he dug around in the box for a shock recovery drug and hit Lee with it. Scruggs got a shot of stimulant.

The crew stumbled up the hill and toward the road. With the aid of a stick and leaning on Gavin, Ana hobbled along. "Just sprained or a minor fracture, not bad," he said through gritted teeth. Dena lifted Lee into a fireman's carry and moved toward the road. Dirk followed with Scruggs, all leaving the confed troops by the stream. Dirk threw the SMG and the shock sticks over a fence into the metal storage yard behind some steel beams.

Ana moved faster and faster as the drugs kicked in, and by the time they were on the street the customs gate was on, he was able to walk with just his stick.

Scruggs and Lee had woken halfway there. Both had vomited—a side effect of coming out of the shock—splattering Dirk, Dena, and themselves. Dirk sat Scruggs down and encouraged her to stumble along, and Dena did the same with Lee.

They arrived at the customs desk. Vomit soaked Dirk's left side. Lee was still drooling on herself. Scruggs's clothes were torn and covered with dirt from her wild roll down the hill. Gavin's hand had begun to bleed, and he had covered it with a bloody bandage. Ana was still leaning on his stick.

The customs clerk surveyed the group in front of him as Dirk pushed their IDs through for departure.

"Purpose of your visit?" the clerk asked.

"Fishing," Dirk said. "We all went fishing."

***

After a ride in another smelly taxi, they all strapped into their chairs, four in the control room, Dena and Scruggs on couches in the lounge. "Heavyweight Items, you are clear to lift," the radio said.

"Thank you, port control," Dirk said. "Lifting now."

Everyone was quiet as they cleared the planet. Dena punched the comm. "Crimes against humanity?" she said to Dirk.

"Don't want to talk about it. Won't talk about it."

"You don't seem the type," Dena said.

"I'm not," Dirk said. "It's a put-up. There's more to it than it looks."

"So, are you—"

"No, no I am not," Dirk said. "Navigator, are you up to putting a course in?"

"Sure," Lee said. "Where to?"

"Just get us out of this system to somewhere we can refuel. Wait, Engineer, what's our status?"

"Better than it should be. We'll hold together for a few more jumps."

Dirk looked over his shoulder. Ana was paging through screens on his console. "Centurion, Engineer, I'm sorry that your little tête-à-tête got spoiled. I'll arrange another one when I have the leisure."

Ana looked over at Gavin. "Actually, Navy. The kid and I had a good talk. I think we settled a few things. Still some things to adjust, but I think you can put that in abeyance for a while. What say you, kiddo?"

Gavin smiled. "I'm with you, old man. We're not completely done, but no need to force the issue right now. Though I would like your opinions on the joint declaration."

"An unnecessary prolongation of suffering, I would think," Ana said. "Don't you agree?"

"Nope," Gavin said. "But we can discuss it later."

"What are you talking about?" Lee asked.

"History stuff." Ana said.

"Right, so I'll just hold on to this death duel thing for now, agreed?" Dirk said. Ana and Gavin both assented. "As soon as Lee gives us a course, we'll get out of here."

Ana tapped his screen. "Navy, I've been looking at screens. Those two confed ships are moving."

"Where are they moving to?"

Lee tapped her screen and typed. "Moving to intercept us."

CHAPTER 33

"Tribune, those confederation ships are moving," Deguals, the comm officer said. He was sitting at the sensor station on the Pollux.

Devin, Lord Lyon, looked up from his discussion with the subprefect. "Ships move, comm," he said. "Can you be more precise?"

"They are moving in concert to intercept a Pallas registered freighter that has just lifted from the base."

"Intercept? What type of intercept?"

Deguals tapped his screen. "Close enough to do a zero-zero boarding in about an hour if everybody stays on the same course."

"Has the Pallas freighter asked for assistance?"

"No, Tribune, it just lifted and is barreling out of the system. Highest possible speed to the jump limit."

"That can't be much for a freighter."

"About twice as fast as a standard freighter. In fact," Deguals continued tapping his screen, "by the acceleration profile, and what scans we have at this distance, it's the same model as a freighter that escaped customs ships at Bishop's world weeks ago."

"What do you mean, weeks ago?" Devin asked.

"We initially arrived during that... unpleasantness with the prison people, sir. While we were discussing things, a ship was being chased by customs out of the system."

"The same ship?" Devin asked.

"Same type of ship, Tribune. Different registration."

Devin looked at Subprefect Lionel. Lionel smiled. Devin turned. "Deguals, you've found him."

"I haven't found anybody yet, sir. I've just located a colony ship that might be in trouble."

"It's him. I know it. It was your plan, your search that brought us here. I should have let the crew organize things from the start. Subprefect?"

"Sir?"

"Can we take those two auxiliary cruisers?" Devin asked.

Lionel cast a set of schematics on the screen. He loaded a simulation. The rest of the bridge crew sat up and performed calculations.

"Big. Very big," one officer said. "Compared to us."

"But not military shields or armor," another said.

"We can't even see their drives as we pass."

"We can shoot for drives first before we get close," another said.

Devin sat quietly while his offers argued. He waited 'til Lionel turned to him. "Well?"

"Absolutely. Slowly converging course. We're faster. Our long-range sensors and control are nebulas better. We can shoot them to pieces from a distance before their weapons can even range."

"Downside?"

"They can either board or destroy that freighter before we get anywhere near. We have to jink around all over the place and slow down to keep out of their range."

"Unacceptable."

"Thought so. Second plan. Full speed in, and we can get between those two groups for a very short window. We fire everything at close range. We'll hurt them very badly."

"Will we disable both of them?"

"With a very high probability, yes."

"And the downside?"

"They'll get excellent shots at us. If they hold their nerve, they'll be able to hit us with everything as we whizz by. If they focus on one spot and get very lucky, they could pierce the shields and drill through some armor. If they hit anything vital, we'll be a long time getting things fixed up."

"Recommendation?"

"Charge 'em like a herd of tabbos. Drive right in."

Devin nodded. "Helm. Set course to hit that lead ship. Maximum speed."

"Right away, Tribune."

Devin looked at the screen. "March to the sound of the guns."

***

"Can we get away from those confed ships?" Gavin asked. He was at the engineering console next to Ana. Dirk and Lee sat at the main consoles below.

"We're a freighter. They're a warship. What do you think?" Ana asked.

Gavin thought about that. "An auxiliary warship, but I guess you're right. We're not going to outrun anything, are we?"

"Not starting from the same planet, we're not," Lee said. "If we were at one of the outer planets—"

"We're not," Dirk said. "We're dropping as fast as we can. Navigator, how long till the jump limit?"

"Have to figure it out exactly, but I can tell you that those confed ships are going to be right up to us long before that."

"Call coming in," Ana said. "From an Imperial ship."

"What Imperial ship? Where's this Imperial ship?" Dirk asked. "Lee, what's going on?"

"Call is personal for a Durriken Friedel," Ana said. "That you, Navy?"

"I can't see it," Lee said. "Don't know where he is. Centurion? You're the scan tech."

"Scan tech? We have a telescope, a radar, and the cheapest infrared scope on the market. We rely on beacons to find stations, never mind ships."

"Any idea who it is?" Dirk asked.

"Beacon just came up," Ana said. "ISS Pollux. You

know anybody on that ship?"

"Devin's ship," Dirk said. He stared at his screen.

"You on first-name terms with a lot of Imperial captains?" Ana asked. "Should we put him through?"

"I don't want to talk to him," Dirk said.

"Another beacon just lit up," Ana said. "No, two beacons. Iron Trader and Star of Canopus. Those confed ships. Saying they are 'auxiliary patrol vessels' messages from them, too." Ana read it. "Text only. 'Cut acceleration and stand by to be boarded. Any attempt at resistance will result in your immediate destruction.' Well, pithy lot, I'll give them that."

"How long till we're in range of their weapons?" Gavin asked.

"Don't know," Ana said.

"You don't know. Why not, old man?"

"Well, kiddo, there are three reasons." Ana began to tick things off on his fingers. "First, we don't have good-enough sensors to tell what—if any—weapons they have. Second, even if we knew what weapons were on board those ships, we don't have any idea of the capabilities or ranges or whatever. It's not like we have a database of weapon hit probabilities at ranges or something like that."

"Right, sorry," Gavin said.

"You seem to be used to ships with better sensors than merchant ships. Is that so?" Ana asked.

"Like you, I have a past," Gavin said. "What was the third thing?"

"Most important. Let's say we did get all that information. What would we do about it? We have no weapons. All we could do is throw rocks at them."

Dena's voice came through the comm. "I can use my slingshot."

"There you go," Ana said. "At least somebody wants to fight back. That will double our chances from completely suicidal to almost completely suicidal. Good news all around."

Lee spoke up. "I can see all the beacons now. That Imperial ship just accelerated and is heading right for us."

The cabin group exchanged glances. Dirk sighed. "Let me talk to him."

"Your wish is my command, Navy," Ana said. He switched the channel on. "I'll turn your camera on, too." He also played the audio on the speaker and the microphone.

A figure came up on Dirk's console. Ana had also echoed it to the others so that they could all see.

Devin, Lord Lyon's, face came up. He was silent for a moment. "Lord Duke Friedel," he said.

The three in the cabin looked at each other. "Duke?" Gavin whispered.

"Lord Duke?" Lee whispered back.

Dirk ignored them. "Tribune, you're looking well."

"As are you," Devin said. "Or better than I expected, given the circumstances."

"What do you want, Tribune?"

"You're under arrest."

"For what this time?" Dirk raised an eyebrow.

"You know, I have absolutely no idea," Devin admitted. "There must be a list somewhere. Why don't you pick your favorite?"

"Saving the lives of Imperial citizens, ending an unjust war, doing the right thing?"

"Heinous crimes," Devin said. "Any acts of mercy are inappropriate in the absence of a direct order from the emperor."

Dirk glared. "So, serving the emperor means turning your back on justice and fairness, Devin?"

"It does seem so, yes, Dirk." Devin grimaced. "My sister says hello."

"How is she, Devin?"

"She's well. Has her own fleet now. A small one but still a fleet. He gave her a new battleship to go with it."

"I always said she was a better tactician than you," Dirk

said.

"In this, as in many things, you are correct. She gave me a message for you. I'll send it over." Devin looked over his head and nodded at somebody.

"What's in it?" Dirk asked.

"Don't know. Very long. Encrypted. Very high encryption. We can't read it. Or break it for that matter."

It was Dirk's turn to be silent. "Have you seen her recently?"

"No. I haven't been back to the capital in ages, and she's too busy empress-ing. Knitting. Setting up high tea. Bombing rebel planets into submission."

"He knows the empress," Lee hissed at Gavin.

Dirk continued to ignore them. "She still knits?"

"I have gloves from her," Devin said. "Dirk, what are you going to do?"

"I'm running away."

"You can't run away from me. I have to stop you."

"I'm not the only one on board. You can't just blow up the entire ship."

"I could. I won't. We're much faster than you. I'll just get close enough to take out your drives and board."

"What are your orders about me?"

"I've got one that says to execute you on the spot."

"Any other orders?"

"None that I'll talk about on this channel."

Ana broke in. "Excuse me, your glorified imperialnesses, but the senior captain of that confed ship is getting antsy."

"Who are you?" Devin asked.

"For the sake of argument, let's say I'm the comm officer. I have a confed captain about to blow her top on another channel."

"Let her," Devin said. "I have no quarrel with her."

"She seems to think she has one with us," Ana said. "And with you. So, in the interests of a full and frank dialogue," Ana manipulated some of his controls, "Confed

Captain, you're on with Durriken Friedel."

Someone new appeared on the screen, wearing a confed uniform with a bridge in the background.

"I am Corvette Captain Kutchow of the confederation of independent states," she said. "Durriken Friedel, I have a warrant for your arrest. Cut your acceleration and stand by to be boarded. If you do not do so, I will fire on you." She frowned as Devin appeared on her screen. "Who are you? What do you want?"

"My name is Devin. My title is Imperial Tribune. My job is to blow you out of space if you fire on Imperial freighters. And I love doing my job," Devin said.

"That ship contains the notorious criminal, Durriken Friedel," she said.

"I agree. I have a warrant for his arrest as well," Devin said.

"I also have a warrant for his execution," Kutchow said.

"Me too," Devin said. "Those are pretty popular these days."

"You've been ordered to kill him, too?" Kutchow asked. Devin nodded on the screen. "Well, then, let me fire on them and blow them up."

"There are Imperial citizens onboard that vessel."

"They will not be harmed when we board."

"I'm not slowing down, and I'm not letting anybody on board," Dirk said. "We'll resist a boarding."

"With what?" Kutchow asked. "You have no weapons. You can't stop us intercepting you. We'll shoot out your drive and send troops across, opposed boarding or not."

"You can't fire on an Imperial-registered ship," Devin said. "And you certainly can't do an opposed boarding. We'll resist any of those attempts."

"Why bother? He's a dead man either way. We are going to board and get him."

"Hey there, Mr. Imperial Tribune," Ana said. "Is that any way for a foreigner to speak to you, telling an Imperial officer, an Imperial noble, what to do?"

"Shut up," Devin said.

"And you, Ms. Confed Captain. You have your orders. You going to let some jumped-up Imperial tell you what to do?"

"Shut up," Kutchow said.

Lee paged through her board 'til she found the proper control, then cut Ana's microphone. "Centurion, are you crazy? They'll blow us up."

Ana pointed at the screen. The confed captain had cut her mic while she spoke to someone. A moment later, she came back. "Durriken Friedel, cut your acceleration and prepare to be boarded. You have two minutes. If you do not do so, we will fire on your drive."

"That's an Imperial-registered ship," Devin said.

"With criminals on it."

"Imperial criminals. You shoot at him, we'll shoot back," Devin said. "Once we start, we won't stop till you're destroyed."

"We eagerly await your attempt," Kutchow said. She looked at her screen. "Ninety seconds," she said before cutting the channel.

Devin looked at Dirk over the channel. "How do you do it? Every time—every single time I get near you, I end up having to do something stupid."

"It's a skill," Dirk agreed.

Devin put his head in his hands for a moment, then looked up at Dirk. "The Empire," he said, saluting.

"The Empire," Dirk agreed, returning the salute.

Devin turned on his bridge and spoke to somebody. "Battle stations." He cut the channel.

CHAPTER 34

"Crew meeting," Ana said. "Scruggs, Dena, up here. Everybody, listen up. We need to decide this together."

"Why?" Lee said. "They're going to kill us all."

"Maybe not," Ana said. "Depends on how we play this."

"You're a duke?" Scruggs looked at Dirk.

"Yes," Dirk said.

"You know the empress?" Dena said. "What does she look like?"

"She's beautiful, wonderful," Dirk said.

"Oh," Dena said. "Is she prettier than me?"

Scruggs looked at her. "What?"

"I wanted to know before I die," Dena said.

"Don't buy into this dying thing," Ana said. "Lee, we need a serious number on how long it will take us to get to the jump limit."

"Moment," Lee said. She turned to her screens.

"Can't we just stand by and wait to be boarded? Let those other two ships sort it out," Gavin asked.

"No, for three reasons," Ana said. "First, whoever wins, they're going to shoot our beloved captain, Navy, over there." He jerked his finger at Dirk. "Second, if they do board us, we'll probably all be shot for resisting arrest or shot while escaping or something. Third, even if they don't kill the captain right away and don't shoot us all right away, they will certainly check all our identities very, very thoroughly. Then they'll have to shoot us."

There was a long period of silence while everyone considered this. "You know," Gavin said, "you use this one-two-three reason style a lot."

"I learned it at command college. It's very effective.

Keeps the options manageable, gives people the illusion that they are part of the decision, and moves things along quickly.

"So, you've already decided what to do?"

"Of course. He's the pilot. She's the navigator. You're the engineer. I don't bother you when the issue is within your competence. I'm the master-at-arms, this is a tactical situation, and I'm in charge of tactics."

"Weren't you in an army somewhere?" Dena said.

"We've established that," Ana said. "Why?"

"You know we're on a spaceship, and this is going to be a space battle, don't you? Not some sort of fight in the woods?"

"This isn't about space or ground. It's about leaders and command and loyalty. Look, if those confed guys get onboard, we're all dead sooner or later. They won't leave witnesses. If the Imperials get onboard, Dirk's dead for sure, and the rest of us . . . who knows. I don't know what's in everybody's past, but it will not end well for us if the Empire boards. And that Devin guy sounds like he was Navy's best friend here. Is he?" Ana rounded on a silent Dirk.

"He was my first commander," Dirk said. "Best one I ever had."

"See? He doesn't want to kill Dirk. He just needs an excuse not to. One that he can live with."

"How do we stop him from killing Dirk and killing us?" Dena asked.

"We just convince him to kill other people," Ana said.

"And how do we do that?"

"Let me explain. First, we commit suicide," Ana said.

***

After Ana had explained his plan, everybody tried to talk at once.

"I don't think it will work," Dena said. "I vote no."

"You don't get a vote," Lee said.

"I carried you back to the ship while you puked on me. I get a vote. I should get two. One for being here and one for being puked on."

"You almost got Scruggs killed in a war."

"It wasn't a war, it was a revolution. And besides, it was an adventure for her. She had fun. Didn't you, Scruggs?" Dena turned to Scruggs.

"It was kind of exhilarating," Scruggs said. "I vote for the centurion's idea. He's never let us down yet."

"You're voting for a lunatic who wants us to ram those confed ships?" Gavin asked.

"Well, I wanted adventure," Scruggs said. "I think smashing headfirst into another ship is pretty adventurous."

"We should do it," Lee said.

Everybody turned to her.

"This is unexpected," Ana said. "I thought you'd vote no. Why yes?"

"I didn't like the way that confed captain spoke to you."

"You're going to commit suicide because somebody's speech patterns offended you?" Gavin asked.

"We're an Imperial ship," Lee said. "They shouldn't speak to us that way. They should respect the Empire. The confed captain was rude."

"You two are crazy. We'll die," Gavin said.

"My family have been Praetorians for dozens of years. We serve the Empire. I'm not afraid to die in the emperor's name."

"I don't think you can equate rudeness with high treason," Gavin said.

"You know, freak," Ana said. "I've changed my mind. You're okay. You can go on a doomed, death-defying suicide run with me anytime." He put his hand to his heart and gave the crossed chest salute.

"Currunt ad bellum," Lee said.

"I've heard that before," Dena said. "What does it

mean?"

"It's the motto of the Imperial Marines," Gavin said. "It comes from old earth. It means 'run to the guns.'"

"'March to the sound of distant guns,' more correctly, Engineer," Ana said.

"I'm going to die, and I have to take language lessons first?" Dena said.

"Adventure awaits," Gavin said. He turned to Ana. "What do I need to do, Centurion?"

"Just keep the thrust up," Ana said. "Navy, now's your chance to weigh in here if you want." He waited for Dirk's reply. Dirk didn't look up from his screen. "As I thought. Lee, can we program a converging course in?"

"No," Lee said.

"What do you mean, no?"

"We're a merchant ship, remember?"

"Even merchant ships can plot intercept courses."

"We can't. Remember the problems with the software? And even if it was up to date, we have avoidance software. We don't have convergence software."

"So, we can't do this electronically?"

"Not exactly, but there is a way."

"What?" Ana asked.

Lee turned to look at Dirk. Ana followed her glance, nodded, and smiled. "Private?"

"Centurion?"

"Go to my cabin, there's a bottle of Francais Brandy there. Bring it up. Have a swig first." Scruggs left.

"Navy," Ana said. Dirk didn't move. Ana leaned forward and slapped his shoulder. Dirk rocked forward and looked up.

"What?"

"Showtime, Navy. Warm up the thrusters. Lee will guide us as close in to those confed ships as she can, then you take over and try to ram them, but pull us off at the last second."

"Why would I do that?" Dirk asked.

"Because they'll shoot something at us, something short-range, probably a warning shot. And as soon as they do that, your good friend, the tribune there, will blast them out of the galaxy for shooting at an Imperial ship."

"I won't do it. I don't care."

"You owe us."

"No. I won't kill everyone again."

"Kill everyone again? What did you do?"

"Doesn't matter. They're all dead, and I killed them."

"You owe all those friends of yours that you got killed on that planet."

Dirk sat up straight. "You don't know what happened there."

"According to the records Scruggs showed me, you started a war."

Dirk nodded. "I did. You know how I started it?"

"By accident?"

"Incompetence. I'm a horrible pilot. And I'm a coward." Scruggs arrived, and Dirk seized the brandy. He took a big swallow. "I was scared to death. My hands were shaking. We were all loading up. I was next to the two other shuttles. They were loading as well. As soon as they filled, they were supposed to lift. I was going to be last. They were slow, but they finally filled up."

Dirk swigged another gulp. "I was stupid. I didn't wait. They were lifting, and I popped up right behind them. I didn't give them enough separation. I banged the engine of the cutter in front of me. It cut out and started to go down. Crystal, the pilot—she was amazing. She got it up and stabilized the shuttle. She kept lifting slowly but began to pull away."

Dirk took another sip. "But I was too scared. I just pushed the throttle. I hit her again. This time, she went down. She crashed into the town. There was confusion. The Pride of Nairobi was watching. She thought the confeds had fired on us. They blasted every confed battery they could find, then the confeds fired back. It was a madhouse."

Dirk drank again. "When things calmed down, all the shuttles and their crews—except for me—were dead. Crashed or shot down. The city had been pummeled by both sides. One of the confed ships had been destroyed, and the other was so damaged, we had to board it to save the crew. It was a disaster. And it was my fault."

Dirk sat still, staring at the screen. Nobody spoke for a long time.

"Cool story, Navy," Ana said. "But we have a situation here, right now, and we need a pilot."

"I can't do it," Dirk said. "I killed them all."

"That was in another country, and besides, the wench is dead now," Ana said. "It doesn't matter."

Gavin looked startled. "You keep surprising me, Centurion."

"One of my favorite playwrights," Ana said. "Well, it's up to you, Navy. We can't do it. So, if you're just going to roll over and die, maybe get on with it. The rest of us just keep going, you know."

"I can't," Dirk said.

"Think of it as penance for your guilt," Ana said. "Besides, if you change your mind, you can still kill yourself."

Dirk looked at them for a moment, then turned to the controls.

***

"Closest approach in sixty seconds, Tribune." Lionel said.

"Stand by."

"Firing solutions locked in," Lionel said.

"Very well."

Lionel stared at him. "Weapons targeted on both confed ships, as requested," he said.

"Thank you."

"Optimal range in forty-five seconds."

"Understood."

Lionel waited. And waited. Around the bridge, fingers were poised over screens. The entire bridge watch focused on the tribune. Then glanced at Lionel. One started to speak, but Lionel shook his head. He turned to Devin. "Do we have permission to fire, Tribune?"

Devin was silent. Lionel got up from his station and walked over to the captain's console. He leaned over and spoke quietly. "We need to fire first for this to work," he said.

"We can't fire first. You know that."

"We can. You've got that recording from the confeds."

"No."

"They'll destroy Dirk's ship, his Imperial-registered ship and those Imperial citizens in it."

"Not yet."

"Status change," the scan tech said. "Pallas freighter has cut accel."

Lionel and Devin looked at each other. "I didn't expect that," Devin said.

"Another status change," the scan tech said. "Pallas freighter has reoriented and is under accel."

"Course?" Lionel asked.

"Right at the nearest pursuing confed ship, sir. Collision course."

"Didn't expect that, either," Devin said.

"Nor me. But that will surely irritate the confed captain."

"What will she do?"

"What would you do?"

"Laser bloom!" the scan officer said. "Confeds have fired on the freighter. Warning shot."

Devin and Lionel looked at each other and smiled. "Another status change on the freighter—" the scan tech said.

"Never mind," Devin said. "All stations. Weapons free. Fire at will on the confed ships as we pass. Long live the

Empire!"

***

Two hours later, Dirk sat in the control room, watching his board. He took great gulps of air. He always hated being on suit air, and it would be several hours before all the holes were patched, and they could re-air the ship. Lee was next to him, talking on the intercom. She turned to Dirk. "Engineer says he, Ana, and Scruggs have the truss banged back into shape. He's going to reroute a control run, and we'll be up to full power."

"Good work. Him, Ana, and Scruggs? Any problems between the two of them—or the three of them?"

"They seem to work well together. Ana and Scruggs both take orders, and all Gavin needed was somebody to swing a hammer, really."

"Why not Dena?"

"Absolutely no experience on the hull of a ship. She can learn, I guess, but now is not the time."

"Not really. Have you got a destination picked out?"

"The farthest away we can jump to and refuel, and right after that, the farthest away we can jump to and refuel, then we'll talk."

"Can they track us?

"Maybe. It will be hard. And unless they follow us right away, they can't watch us leave for the next jump."

"Good enough."

"Captain, uhh, I mean Duke, or what do I say?"

"How about just Pilot on this ship? That work for you?"

"It does, Pilot. Those things they said."

"Don't want to talk about it," Dirk said. A comm light flashed on his screen. "They keep trying to talk to me, too," he said. A second light flashed.

"Pilot, that's the narrow beam indicator."

"They found us," Dirk said. "If they know where we are, might as well talk." He punched the button and looked at his screen. "Hello, Devin."

"Dirk."

"How's the confeds?"

"One won't fly again. They've evacuated to the other. That one has no weapons left but drive capacity. I've given them three days to depart to confed space."

"Good battle, what we saw of it. Going in the textbooks."

"They didn't expect us to come so close. Their targeting was off. We got in some great shots before they corrected."

"Still, a magnificent job."

"Even my sister will be pleased. How about you?"

"Something hit us. Not a missile, or we'd be dead. We think a chunk blasted loose from something. Some holes. Bent a truss, knocked some thrusters offline, and broke some control conduits. We're just about finished repairing them."

"You're lucky you weren't killed."

"I agree.

"And you are well beyond the jump limit now. Have enough fuel to jump somewhere?"

"Somewhere."

"Away from the Empire?"

"Far away."

"You sure you want to do that? Leave the Empire?"

"It's not my Empire anymore."

"You say that. Do you believe that's true?"

Dirk looked at his board. "You going to come out and chase me?"

"I'm in a high-parking orbit right now, so I can keep an eye on those confeds."

"I see."

"And also, you're not the only one with control conduit problems. I've got all my weapons, but I have a great deal of difficulty controlling my drives."

"How long to fix that, Devin?"

"Since all my officers know who you are now, and they think they know what my orders regarding you are, I expect it will be fixed exactly one hour after you have jumped out of the system. That way, I won't be exposed to the choice of not doing my duty or killing one of my oldest friends."

"Good crew you have there."

"The best. What are you going to do now?

"Now? Run some more for a while. Jump somewhere, run some more."

"You can't run forever, Dirk," Devin said.

Dirk shrugged. "You've been wrong before. Maybe you're wrong now." Dirk turned. Lee was waving at him— he had set the call to private mode. "What?"

"Everybody is back inside, and Engineer says we're ready. My board is green. What should I do?"

"Goodbye, Devin," Dirk said and closed the channel. He looked at his own board for a moment, then looked out at a view port.

"Jump," he said.

GET A FREE EBOOK

Thanks for reading. I hope you enjoyed it. Word-of-mouth reviews are critical to independent authors. Please consider leaving a review on Amazon or Goodreads or wherever you purchased this book.

If you'd like to be notified of future releases, please join my mailing list. I send a few updates a year, and if you subscribe you get a free ebook copy of Sigma Draconis IV, a short novella in the Jake Stewart universe. You can also follow me on Amazon, or follow me on BookBub.

Andrew Moriarty

ABOUT THE AUTHOR

Andrew Moriarty has been reading science fiction his whole life, and he always wondered about the stories he read. How did they ever pay the mortgage for that spaceship? Why doesn't it ever need to be refueled? What would happen if it broke, but the parts were backordered for weeks? And why doesn't anybody ever have to charge sales tax? Despairing on finding the answers to these questions, he decided to write a book about how spaceships would function in the real world. Ships need fuel, fuel costs money, and the accountants run everything.

He was born in Canada, and has lived in Toronto, Vancouver, Los Angeles, Germany, Park City, and Maastricht. Previously he worked as a telephone newspaper subscriptions salesman, a pizza delivery driver, a wedding disc jockey, and a technology trainer. Unfortunately, he also spent a great deal of time in the IT industry, designing networks and configuring routers and switches. Along the way, he picked up an ex-spy with a predilection for French Champagne, and a whippet with a murderous possessiveness for tennis balls. They live together in Brooklyn.

Please buy his books. Tennis balls are expensive.

BOOKS BY ANDREW MORIARTY

Adventures of a Jump Space Accountant

1. Trans Galactic Insurance

2. Orbital Claims Adjustor

3. Third Moon Chemicals

4. A Corporate Coup

5. The Jump Ship.

6   The Military Advisors

Decline and Fall of the Galactic Empire

1. Imperial Deserter

2. Imperial Smuggler

3. Imperial Mercenary

4. Imperial Hijacker

Made in United States
Orlando, FL
19 March 2024

44969181R00217